CW00881074

Also, by Richard Theodor Kusiolek,
"Angels in the Silicon," "Star Traveling," and
"Cyber Security versus Privacy - Mobility in a Global World."

MAN OF SEVEN SHADOWS

THE SEARCH FOR TRUTH

RICHARD THEODOR KUSIOLEK

MAN OF SEVEN SHADOWS
THE SEARCH FOR TRUTH

iUniverse books may be ordered through booksellers or by contacting:

iUniverse
1663 Liberty Drive
Bloomington, IN 47403
www.iuniverse.com
1-800-Authors (1-800-288-4677)

Because of the dynamic nature of the Internet, any web addresses or links contained in this book may have changed since publication and may no longer be valid. The views expressed in this work are solely those of the author and do not necessarily reflect the views of the publisher, and the publisher hereby disclaims any responsibility for them.

Any people depicted in stock imagery provided by Getty Images are models, and such images are being used for illustrative purposes only. Certain stock imagery © Getty Images.

ISBN: 978-1-6632-0470-7 (sc)
ISBN: 978-1-6632-0472-1 (hc)
ISBN: 978-1-6632-0471-4 (e)

Library of Congress Control Number: 2020912240

Print information available on the last page.

iUniverse rev. date: 08/06/2020

ACKNOWLEDGMENTS

National Academy of Science of Ukraine,
Professor- Leonid V. Hubersky

Publisher staff - Melissa Bauer and Earl Thomas

DEDICATION

I am dedicating this book to my daughter, Melissa Rose Sanders, who was always cheerful and encouraging. I wish to thank Dr. Vlad Genin, University Dean, for his mentorship and inspiration. My nephew Jim Warwick gave me the positive mindset that I needed to complete the manuscript. I want to thank Oleksiy Mykolayovich Illyashov, who extended insights into the culture of Ukraine. I acknowledge Galina Wells, who gave me a historical insight into the Russian Orthodox Church and Fr. George Kurtow and Fr. James Guirguis.

CONTENTS

INTRODUCTION

Man of Seven Shadows
"Those who cannot remember the past are condemned to repeat it" - George Santayana.

Includes Bibliography sources, and Endnotes

According to the DNA test, the author's ancestors go back beyond 1500. Ancestral biological records show that from the years (1670-1790), German, French, and Scandinavian ancestry, plus 72% (1800 – 1918) Eastern Europe Russian and Balkan. Richard Theodor Kusiolek's family roots connect him to Ashkenazic Jews, who flourished during the Holy Roman Empire (800 -1806). Remarkably Richard Theodor Kusiolek's ancestry was traced to a single woman who lived 6,500yrs ago.

"A man who does not remember his family's history has no right to have a future." – Anonymous

PROLOGUE

"There have been individuals since the dawn of history. Espionage is the second oldest occupation, have conducted spying and espionage operations, and there have been people who have turned against their side and worked for competitors and worked for those opposing the country or the group that they're working with. It's been a problem from the beginning, and it continues to be a problem ..." stated Gary Berntsen, former CIA official, on the July 2017 Sophie Shevardnadze TV interview.

In very early prehistoric times, the Korka Clan found a way to live as a bonded family that could gather great resources by only spying, collecting intelligence, and selling what information they picked. They believed that they descended from the Stars and worshiped the glowing green stone that fell from the sky at that time. They had no fears of any forces in their environments that would stop them from just using their tradecraft to send in their family agents to spy on other tribes or global sovereign states. With this actionable knowledge, they could win every battle, overcome any enemy, become an elite governing entity, or become a shadow. Korka organized clandestine activities by his sons, who become defector intelligence agents to facilitate the gathering of intelligence information by other humans. They also specialized in lightning strike assassinations by whoever had the gold, silver, and paper money to pay them. Before and during the First World War, they planted family members in the crucial organization to listen and report. This methodology was followed very strictly by

Korka Clan Chiefs. As technology improved, they could still plant a "bug" in the same embassy or defense department where a Korka family member was employed.

The Novel, Man of Seven Shadows, is an espionage spy thriller rich in "black comic" storm of incompetence, immorality, family rivalry, imperial ambition, lurid glamour, sexual excess, depraved sadism, and moments of gloom, and doom. The European relevance has always consisted of ancient times of blood and death. The novel focuses on the conditions of war, the occupation of spying, and how it affects people through the prism of seven historical European-related Eras. The book is rich in history and spycraft centered around lands located in Eastern/Central Europe, and the second-largest territory on the continent after Russia. The historical capital situated on the Dnieper River in north-central Ukraine. Man of Seven Shadows is not a story of Ukraine as we know it today, but at a time in which families stood together as one unit for daily survival and economic, political power. However, at times, family members attack other family members for control and kingships.

The Novel, "Man of Seven Shadows," traces the Korak ancestral family roots beginning with their historical journey through the seven portals of time as generational members of the Stone Age tribal ancestors start from Neolithic times (5300-2600 BC). The Korka tribe continues to the 2013 third Revolution that attempts reforming the existing social order and refers to the Ukraine Maidan anti-Russian Revolution. The reform movement subsequently evolves into the Eastern Ukraine Civil War from 2014 to 2020 from the 2013 third Revolution against the existing social order. Finally, the war is referred to as the Ukraine Maidan anti-Russian Revolution and, subsequently, the Eastern Ukraine Civil War from 2014 to 2020, achieved their warrior credentials by fighting the Mongols in 1237, as they watched their village burned and destroyed by the Mongol hordes. Their war cry; namely, crush the tyrants. We are all bound together by Motherland, Spartans, real men who are strong-willed, physically strong, brave, and bold.

We are courageous people who protect the Slavic peoples and our leader. Over the seven centuries, the Korak Clan experiences forced migration and slave labor to work communal agricultural lands, but they eventually resist and become foundational pillars of kingship. With the brutality of their historical roots, the family threaded with acts of rebellions against economic and religious exploitation. After that, a family tradition emerges to engage in corruption military espionage to gain financial and political power for their family. The reader will see slices of the reality of how the family's intelligence activities influenced the outcome of critical historical events, namely, the Mongol Conquest, Napoleonic Wars, the Argonne battlefield of trenches, and in December 1941 the Nazi invasion of the Korka's family homesteads.

In the winter of 1941, the Germans had conquered Western Europe and held most of the Mediterranean. They had attacked Russia, and at this point in history, it was clear that Adolph Hitler was going to capture all of Kyiv, Leningrad, and Moscow, and it looked like the war in Russia would be over in a few months. Kolya and Borya Korka resist pressures to join the Schutzstaffel S.S. as prison camp guards. Instead, they enter the British Intelligence Service to spy on German troop movements and battle plans. The Russian winter and Red Army reinforcements arrived in December 1942, but the German blitzkrieg campaign's supply lines disastrously stretched. German troops had no winter clothing, ammunition, and food. The road turned from mud to icy death traps for German transport and soldiers. As the Germans retreat with the few forces left, Kolya organizes the family to destroy any food sources and plant explosives under any troop trains. Many of Hitler's best troops froze to death on the battlefield. During his battle to crush Moscow during a similar winter campaign, Hitler's generals failed to learn from Napoleon's 1812 defeat.

The 2014 Minsk Agreements did not last very long as counter-intelligence agents from members of the Korka family infiltrated the E.U. and NATO peace process. The Organization for Security and Co-operation in Europe (OSCE) hires Bogdan Korka as a monitor along the boundaries of the Kyiv Army and volunteers of the Donetsk Peoples Republic (DPR) and the Lugansk Peoples Republic (LPR) in the Donbas Region.[1] In 2015, "the leaders of Ukraine, Russia, France, and Germany agreed to a package of measures to alleviate the ongoing war in the Donbas region of Eastern Ukraine. The talks that led to the deal, overseen by the Organization for Security and Co-operation in Europe (OSCE), were organized in response to the collapse of the Minsk Protocol ceasefire in January–February 2015. The new package of measures intended to revive." Kyiv's Oligarch President Petro Poroshenko orders armed Special Forces agents to gain entry into Crimea to bolster his political stature. However, several Russian troops killed in a firefight with Ukraine intelligence officers trained by Germany. On August 12, 2016, the President of Russia Vladimir Putin declared that a new peace talks with Ukraine in parallel with the G-20 meeting in China in September 2016. Two years before the Kyiv government's Ministry of Internal Affairs and Defense ordering firefights along with the DPR/LPR that demonstrated that diplomacy was a meaningless charade.[2]

The "dark aspects" of the intrigue by the powers of the U.S., E.U., NATO, and Russia drop a sizeable dark cloud on any peaceful resolution. Korka ancestors' intelligence strategy to stir up the flames of war and economic discord for their profit and power continue to this day in this former Soviet Russia territory. At the July 2017th G20 Summit sponsored by Germany, new peace talks initiated by the American President Donald J. Trump, but the Europeans refuse to engage in the negotiations. The killing of the population of the Donbas Region by the Ukraine Army, trained by the German, Swedish, and American armies, then is to continue for two more years and ends upon the assassination of a President. The novel, "The Man of Seven Shadows," concludes with a present-day spy craft intrigue between Sergey Korak and the Interior Minister, Mykhailo Kliayav, and triggers the 2013-2014 city riots in Odesa and Kharkiv Ukraine. The consequences of Sergey Korka's spycraft results in the Russian annexation of Crimea, arming of the

Donetsk and Lugansk militia population, and the Kyiv's random artillery military battles, which led to over 13,000 killed in the eastern "Donbas Region."[3-4] On December 19, 2019, "Any move related to the status of the rebellious eastern Ukrainian regions should be coordinated with those regions, (Vladimir)Putin said, adding that Kyiv should not unilaterally take decisions on any "decentralization" issues that go beyond the framework of the Minsk Agreements that remain the only plausible way to resolve the Ukrainian crisis." Some positive steps were made the President of the Russian Federation admitted, such as troop withdrawal from several areas in eastern Ukraine, and the extension of the law on Donbas's special status. Some new areas along the line of contact designated for troop withdrawal in 2020, during the latest Normandy Four meeting.

CHAPTER ONE

FIRST DAWNING
OF LIGHT

FROM THE LOWER PALEOLITHIC, approximately 1.8 million years ago, until 40,000 years ago, Europe was populated by Homo-erectus and Homo Nanderthalensis. In the Upper Paleolithic and Mesolithic, from about 45,000 to 6,000 years ago, Europe had Homo sapiens hunter-gatherer populations. During the last glacial maximum, much of Europe de-populated and re-settled, about 15,000 years ago. The European Neolithic began about 9,000 years ago in southeastern Europe and reached northern Europe by about 5,000 years ago.[1]

Map-Kazakhstan – Courtesy of Vladimir Okhotin-AboutKazakhstan.com

FIRST DAWNING OF LIGHT

Levak and Korka sat by the fire and raised their eyes to the marbled sky swirling above them, the clouds shifting in pulsing gusts coming over the ridgeline. They strained to see through the darkened grey mass. Last night, the entire night sky had been lit up with a fireball that was half a mile across, a bright light from a large stream of cosmic energy moving across the skies at 70 million miles per hour, emitting a loud sound, crashing less than a mile from their mountain caves, and waking the members of the village. A large fiery explosion then could be seen, like a sunrise trapped within the canopy of trees. Soon after, the forest below the ridge began to burn. Levak lowered his gaze and spoke with power, shuttering all who listened with the knowledge that powerful forces would direct their destiny.

"This is a clear sign from the Gods that we of the tribe, Tiger Claw, will rule the Earth throughout time."

As Levak raised his muscular body, all the assembled villagers could see the one-inch square glowing green stone tied with woven horsehair and hanging from Levak's chest. Prince Levak, the son of Lord Korka and leader of their tribe, spoke again,

"my father has decided that we must go to the site in the morning and create a tower of the stones brought from the upper world that opens and closes. If we are true to this sign and we worship the star rocks, our power as a people will grow, and many will fear our ability to be strong warriors, and we shall take slaves from other tribes."

At that moment, the night skies opened and a blanket of dazzling stars appeared, and although the night was cold, the fire in his eyes burned brightly, and the Korka clan knew that their destiny changed as a people.

The ancestral roots of Levak and Korka's Tiger Claw clan began 1.77 million years ago in a historical era of extreme survivability and geographic challenges for them. It was a world of Etruscan wolves, deer, saber-toothed tigers, and other assorted animals; the area is centered on modern-day Moldova and covering substantial parts of western Ukraine and northeastern Romania. The Tiger Claw tribe started over 210,000 years ago and increased their awareness of territoriality and the power that came from spreading with other villages.

ICE age European-courtesy of the Kirsten Ukraine Museum

Levak was the firstborn of Lord Korka and Tiaka, born during meteorite shower on the warmest day of the year. As a child, Levak was irritable and depressed. Rarely would he smile, and when he did, it was the result of another child in the village bitten by poison snakes. Tiaka loved her baby son, and at the age of nine, he appeared to show signs of wisdom and spiritual quality that was recognized by his father, Korka, the leader of the Tiger Claw. Both his father and mother noticed that his skin wounds would take longer to heal and that he was often fatigued.

At night, Levak would dream of the day that he and his clan would not struggle against the beast, the weather, and the lack of food for all family members. At the age of 11, Korka took his son under his wing and discussed the importance of being a leader, and learning to gain power over other tribes by entering their villages to spy on their food locations and how many warriors that they had. One day, Levak was approached by Tiaka's sister's son, who pushed Levak into the muddy swamp. As he stood up, covered with mud and with the entire village laughing at him, Levak rushed the 15-year-old boy and struck him with his right fist, breaking his enlarged jaw and nose. Levak screamed at the crying boy, "Don't you dare treat members of our family in that manner. We are one family that fights as one tree and takes from others. We have much work to do today. Now take my hand and stand with me." The members of the Clan, upon hearing this, rose in a great cheer.

"Korka's son will be a great warrior leader someday," they agreed.

Levak was as muscular as his father, but slightly smaller in stature. As he and his brothers were barefooted, their soles harden into a thick layer of skin. Levak had black hair that ran down his back and was held with an animal bone. By 13, Levak had already learned to use the wooden bow and snake poison-tipped stone arrows. He learned from his father how to sharpen the edges of the Flintstones to make part of the point of a good throwing spear.

At age 16, Levak saved his parents life. It had snowed in the early morning, and the snow was high, but both Korka and Tiaka were wrapped in animal fur to protect them from the cold. They were silently approached by a massive snow bear who immediately slashed into the back and stomach of both with its giant paws. The blood oozed out of their wounds, but they were alive. The Lord Korka and Tiaka lay in the cold snow tundra waiting for the enormous fifteen-foot polar bear to move away. Korka used his hand signals to alert Tiaka to remain motionless and calm. They looked into each other's blue eyes and held back their breaths, so the giant white bear could not see that they were still alive. They laid in the snow bleeding from the great bear's random mouthfuls from their back, buttocks, legs, and shoulders, but this time for some reason, the bear's bites were not deep enough to go in through the stomach and on to their life-sustaining organs. Korka and Tiaka knew that screaming would not help their survivability. They lost track of how long they laid motionless. They just trusted Lord Kishka to save them. At that moment, the great white bear stood over them and let out a roar, and fell backward into the high snowdrift. A spear had sunk into the bear's head. Korka gasping for breath saw his son Levak and faintly whispered, "my son, you have saved us" The blood from the bear's fatal head wound squirted on the snow into an endless trail of blood.

Levak stood over his parents, "Father and Mother, I saw the bear attacking you. I ran back to where I stored my flintstone spear. I ran as fast as I could without the bear seeing me. I am a mighty warrior with the power of Kishka, making me sail across the snow."

Korka and Tiaka tried to stand up to thank their son, but the wounds from the bear had made them both weak. Levak knelt over them and kissed their foreheads.

"I will come back to help you. Move towards the high rocks and hide there until I come back with clan members to help you."

Soon as the sun was setting, twelve strong warriors of the

Korka village, ran with Levak in the lead. They were the best and would lay down their lives for their Lord Korka and his wife. Levak was with them, and he spoke when the small warrior party reached the forest's rock base.

"You must now carry them on your backs, or we can make a wooden stretcher to carry them back to the village cave. We will then have them both rest by the fire. Quickly move as the darkness of the night will come soon."

Lord Korka's firstborn son showed leadership and resourcefulness, but also behavior that was troubling for his father to observe. Levak was callous and showed a lack of empathy for the enemies and members of the tribe. He was not good at detecting fear in the faces of members of the tribe and tribal slaves, and many members of the tribe kept away from Levak. He appeared not to feel the emotion of revenge, but many still wanted to engage with him and to express disapproval of his many unethical actions. He would smash the faces of his enemies and let their bodies grow rotting in front of his lodge. Levak felt no disgust looking or smelling the bodies of his enemies. Prince Levak showed a lack of emotion, especially the social emotions, such as shame, guilt, and embarrassment. The future moved through the shadows of the past as the Tiger Claw tribe grow to 2,600 men, women, and children. Every tribe conquered, a Tiger Claw warrior would be given to the defeated villages to spy and provide a monthly consul to the Lord Korka and Prince Levak.

Levak was an expert in using his spear and arrows to kill the numerous grass-feeding mammal monsters that would run but could turn quickly and attack their pursuers. The mammoth was the tribe's primary meat source and had tusks were well over 36 stones in length. Mammoths had long, three feet long, dense hair and underfur, very long curved tusks, and lived in the flatlands that surrounded Korka's Tiger Claw cave village. The tusks were used in mating rituals, for digging in the winter snow for food, and for protection. Once during a hunt, one of these great beasts charged a tree that Levak and his ten-year-old younger brother Zak were crouched behind. The mammoth broke the tree in half without any noticeable pain to its head. Levak and Zak struggled with their spears and large rocks to stop the movement of this beast that the villagers called Thunder God. Levak pushed a large stone from the cliff and struck the head of the mammoth, and momentarily the animal slowly fell upon the eight-foot-thick grass. The two boys slowly approached the mammoth, but knew that they must immediately act.

"Keep stabbing its belly," yelled their father, Lord Korka, who was observing from a distance.

With each twelve-inch thrust, the blood of the mammoth flowed like a small stream on the grass until the lush, thick green, turned a bright red. Korka ran to the site where the beast made sounds as if the sky opened up and thundered as Korka and his two sons pierced its stomach and threw massive stones upon its head. Soon, the mammoth laid exhausted and slowly dying as if it accepted its fate to die on this day at the hands of these hairy-like animals who stalked them.

"Look Levak, we are the mighty warriors, and no beast can stand up against us when we work together with stone, spear, and arrow," said Zak. "Hurry, we must cut this beast in sections and drag the meat to our caves. Blow into the tusk horns and announce to the entire village to come to help. Set up sentries as the saber-tooth tigers will soon come to challenge us for this meat," yelled Korka.

Young Zak grabbed his sizeable hollowed-out horn that was strapped to his shoulder and blew the alarm loudly. The time for work had come for the entire village. Korka looked forward to the evening around the cave fires. It would be time to eat and celebrate their hunt. The Woolly Mammoths would normally have required the entire Korka family clan, all tribal warriors, and the most reliable elders to hunt and kill this beast, as it was not an easy feat. Their killing and butchering efforts took over six hours from the time when the hunt began at the rise of the bright starlight to the period of dark shadows. Korka and all of his seven sons plus twelve village warriors joined the struggle as this would result in a vast bounty of meat and hides for their entire village. After the long summer series of hunting foraging, for they were dependent upon the acquisition of food by such means, the village had food and hides for the entire winter months. The village could also trade the meat and hides with other communities.

The relationships of the Tiger Claw clan with other tribes were not always peaceful, and occasionally led to raids and conflict. In particular, the Medved tribe from the east was especially troublesome due to their proclivity for theft and deception. Due to ongoing and continued inter-communal struggles, Levak organized a plan of attack for warfare with various tribes from the North. In the first battle, his brother Josak was killed by an arrow that pierced his head. As Josak laid on the battlefield with the tribe, Lord Korka came to Josak's side and cried with great anguish saying,

"my son, you have fought bravely and showed our tribe what a mighty warrior you were. I will carry you to our encampment and place you upon the green glowing star rocks. Josak, your spirit can then enter the sky and follow us."

Korka picked up the limp body of Josak and placed his body on the cart, he then pushed it back to the main encampment located 3 miles from the battle scene. Once the ceremony for Josak was completed and his body buried by the star stones, Korka ordered the people to assemble, and when they did, he spoke, "today, we achieved a great war victory. Unfortunately, my son Josak was taken by our god in the sky. He will now protect us as a God and protect our future generations. He was a good boy, and before the battle, he told me of his plan to build a wall around our village and to organize tree sentinels to watch for any tribe approach."

The Tiger Claw clan prospered, building ten-foot wooden fences to keep out other tribes that were a danger to their women and children. Korka awoke from a deep sleep and began to think of the last five years. Earlier, he had an outburst of anger and hostility that resulted in some families leaving the clan. Korka would merely disassociate himself from his friends and family members. Lord Korka believed that this was only a sign that he must be more aggressive and punish those who decided on leaving the tribe, a practice thought of as dishonest, deceitful, and at times, dangerous. Why should he care because they did not like his actions of routinely tying tribal member's upside-down at the nearest tree branch? Korka climbed the highest point of the village and screamed,

"I am the Lord Korka, and no one shall come to be greater than I am!"

He had a belief that he could outwit those who pursued him to kill him for his actions. He knew that he could always win in battle, or find some way to escape death. One morning while the tribe was camped near the Kemijoki river, Korka turned around on his bed of horse skin and leaves. He stood up and stretched his massive arms. Something appeared to be wrong. It was too quiet, and he felt a broad sense of lurking danger. Soon, he began to hear screams and saw men covered with mud and feathers moving along the village wigwams and cave entrances. Korka grabbed his mammoth bone ax and rushed out into the cold, foggy morning air. The first intruder that he saw he struck, and the headless body just fell to the ground. Soon, he was covered with blood as he rushed five more of his enemies.

Korka yelled, "alarm, alarm, alarm zbrati svoje orožje!"

Soon, all of the Tiger Claw warriors joined the battle to protect the horses, women, children, and the elderly of the tribe. For over two hours, the carnage continued until one hundred and twenty blood-soaked bodies lay silently on the cold ground. An eerie silence came back to the village site, and Korka walked among his people. They had won the battle, and it was over, but two more of his children were dead: Karok and Jakok. Unfortunately, they both had their skulls crushed with a throwing spear.

Neolithic star circle -Ancient History
Encyclopedia -Adamson drawing 4/26/2012

Korka turned his eyes from the tribe up to the sky.

"Oh, great Star God, lead us into the future so that we can honor you with our battles and the slaying of those who stood against us in treachery! Take my remaining children and give them the power to grow into warriors. Now, I will protect our tribe by giving one member of our tribe to the alien tribes that we encounter. Now and in the future, we will always have spies in each tribal camp that might attack us. I have spoken as a messenger of the Star God. Beware of those who attack us in word or deed!"

Korka declared with an anguished voice. "Over time, they will be ceremonially allowed into our army and tribe. Slowly and with daily pain, torture, and beatings, we will make them into loyal warriors of the Tiger Claw people! We will become strong and take over many lands."

He knew then that a spy must live a life of lies. Spying has its rewards; information could be more valuable than a dozen Mammoth hides. So, the first root of the clan of Korka's spying tradition began on the plains overlooking the river Kemijoki. Korka knew that to be a great leader, he must rely on the intelligence of family spies that he had selected. Like tradecraft, each generational curtain lifted so that a member of Korka's Tiger Claw warriors class trained and prepared for the creation of a Global Spy Ring, superior deception tactics, and the silent mental gymnastics required of a spy. Lord Korka set up a skills requirement that each warrior selected must-have. Korka wrote these skills and rules of joining the Tiger Claws' secret inner group on scrolls made from the soft leather of dead horses. First, the intelligence of the warrior must be high, and his ability to observe, survey, and research targeted tribes and villages is a crucial requirement. Second, the warrior must learn the language by infiltrating and learning the culture and creating disguises. It is essential to fit into the environment and not to attract attention. If the plan of attack from the Tiger Claw was known by opposing tribal spies, then it would be imperative to leave the zone of operations quickly. Third and above all, the warrior must be loyal to Lord Korka and members of his family, past, present, and future. In a special ceremony, the candidate spy warrior and a Korka family member share the heart of a tiger. Each will bite and eat a small portion throwing the remains in the circle of the green star stones. If the rocks continue to glow, the warrior is accepted. If the boulders stop their ethereal burning, the warrior was rejected and stoned to death.

After the battle near the Kemijoki, Levak walked over and held his mother's hand, and witnessed as his father Korka went to his remaining younger children and had them stand inside the circle. He looked into their eyes as he spoke, "You will be the foundations of our conquest of all the tribes from now and for all eternity. You will be strong and honorable. Go into the present and future life and gain for my conquest and wealth so that your mother and I will be happy in the Star God's kingdom of light and fires in the night skies." He then turned, walked away, and stayed in the forest for ten days to fast and mourn his losses.

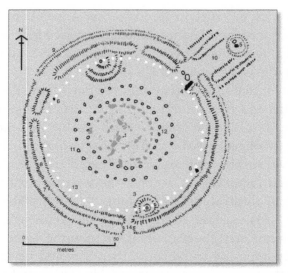

Neolithic megalithic- Ancient.Eu -Brian Haughton 12/14/2010

Years later, Korka had reached the old age of forty-two and the entire village was celebrating their great king when he was suddenly killed with a poison arrow shot by an assassin from the Medved Tribe, near the present city of Vyborg, Finland. Members of the Tiger Claw tribe grabbed the killer of their Lord Korka and broke his arms and legs bones with stones. Once he was dead, his body was fed to the dogs and the bears. The tribe members made an eight-foot-deep pit and placed the Star Stones into a circle around the hole. The fallen Lord was lifted and placed near the star stones on a bed of sweet-smelling plants. Each member of the tribe walked by Korka's body and spoke,

"Oh, Great Lord, we dedicate ourselves to the Star God. Travel peacefully into the stars and give us your power into the centuries."

As the village celebrated the death of Korka, Levak spoke of his father, mother, and siblings. He asked all village members to sit around a massive fire and talk of their memories of Lord Korka. "I loved my father," Levak said.

"Korka, the Lord of both Light and Darkness, entered the high forest lands as a twelve-year-old young warrior from the top mountain home of his ancestral clan. As he grew to manhood, he developed his personality throughout his life by mimicking those around them. At sixteen years of age, my father was an adult member of the tribe. He became a giant of a young man, rising ten feet and four inches from his feet to the top of his head and at three hundred and sixty pounds with legs like giant redwoods logs. His face consisted of a sharp elongated jaw, an aquiline nose, flat cheeks, a large rounded brain backbone, and a smooth forehead. He could run from the cave entrance at high speed with his long muscular legs. With his spear, he could kill a wild boar or a tiger with one throw and then, with his strength, lift the spear and run after another wild animal that came too close to their village."

Levak could feel warm tears on his face, and he turned to see similar moisture patterns on the faces of his mother and siblings.

THE REIGN OF LORD LEVAK

After the prescribed fourteen days of grieving, the tribal leadership went to Levak, Korka's eldest son, and declared him as leader of the Tiger Claw clan. Over the years of survival and conquest, Levak had grown into a robust and charismatic figure. He stood six-feet four inches in height, weighing 203 pounds. Levak soon began plans to move his tribal people further southeast and find lands of vast animal herds and grass containing grains. Levak knew that the only reasons that people kill are for shiny stones, being with or without women, and stealing from other members of his tribe. Levak always wondered how Korka and Tiaka could survive in the cold days and nights of Northern Europe and provide survival to their nine children?

It was not until five days later and after Levak had studied the stars, that he summoned those in the village.

"I want to speak more about those early days. Hunting and killing the wild animals were the primary job of the men in the tribe. Lord Korka's great-grandparents and their parents hunted a variety of mammals, but they did not farm the land or gather bounty from the trees."

Levak slowly moved his muscular body and stood on a large rock overlooking the assembled villagers, "We will herd these horses to our village and tame them to follow our commands. We will no longer hunt them as we did. Also, our village will have a yearly supply of food, hides for our tents, and to keep us warm." His younger brother, Sunak, who at twelve years old, was already six feet tall and smaller in stature, but he had an attitude of a conqueror, spoke up,

"My Father Lord Korka also had a dream that we can use the horses you seek to help us carry all of our leather tents, poles, and children to the next location."

The Shaman of the Tiger Claw Clan once recalled how Lord Korka called the villagers together to share his dream from the night before. Lord Korka stood within the circle of the Green Star Stones and spoke,

"I have dreamed that we do not need to stalk and run after the horse for food. If we could find these horses and breed them, for food and war, we will be a powerful force to unite all the tribes. We will send warriors to the lands further southwest."

Herd of Przewalski's tarpan-like horses. -
Courtesy of blogspot.com

Levak spent many nights at the evening fires, remembering what his father told him of the early days of the Tiger Claw Clan's beginning. Levak sat cross-legged, staring into the burning fire pit. He spoke emotionally,

"these small horses graze south of the Tiger Claw encampment. Our Lord Korka observed them and witnessed their ability to move fast and far; the horses could gallop out of harm's way and make the most of scarce grazing grass. Korka, soon learned that the horse could be an advantage of the tribal warriors. The body of the man and horse could become a unified fighting force and allow the Tiger Claw tribe to attack other villages for slaves and warriors."

Levak spent the months and years after his father's return to Kishka's embrace talking over the fires of the night to all would listen of the wonderment of this father. Without the horse, the survival of our Lord Korka and members of the Tiger Claw Clan would never have built a Dynasty to rule nations by integrating their intelligence-gathering craft with the speed of the horses.

Soon, Levak allowed Sunak to begin organizing a semi-nomadic life for the tribe. With his remaining brothers Josk and Zak, they set up a network of campsites and lived in different locations according to how the food sources responded to seasons. At the campgrounds that Josk developed, the surrounding area became the tribe's basecamp.

Neolithic megalithic Stonehenge - Ancient.
Eu -Brian Haughton 12/14/2010

Their Neolithic village was near the river Kemijoki (Swedish: Kemi älv, Northern Sami: Giemajohka), with its 550 km (340 mi) length, is the longest river in Finland. It runs through Kemijärvi and Rovaniemi. The tribe would spend the majority of the time there during the year exploiting local resources, such as wild plants, the small beginnings of agriculture and foraging were compatible with their semi-nomadic ways of life. Josk sat on a large flat stone and spoke,

"Lord Levak, I will organize a portion of our tribe to perform hunter-gatherer functions for part of the year and some raising seed plants, gathering them and storing them for those months in the warmer seasons. Women, children, and older men dedicated to starting on a small scale. Those who are cultivating land, raising crops, and feeding our village animals would be protected night and day by twelve of our best warriors."

Levak listened intently and stood up, towering over his seventeen-year-old brother. "Yes, brother, indeed, this is a good plan for maintaining the safety and food sources of our people. Begin to separate those who will farm and those who will seek meat sources. It continues to snow heavily, and during the summer, the water flows into our encampment each Spring. I will begin to move them further South to find warmer days and nights. Now, we have stolen six horses from the peoples in the Southwest and East, and we can begin to breed these small animals for meat, milk, and transport." The winter periods were long, and the Tiger Claw spent the majority of their time not farming the wild seed plants.

The tribe still lived in the cold northern regions and the densely-forested areas. Levak, with the help of his brothers, founded southwestern campsites that were experiencing shorter winters and warmer summers for farming. The sons of Korka began to organize forest clearance, root crops, and seed cereal cultivation. Zak spent time in those encampments and reported to his Lord,

"Levak, we are learning how to store these seeds that can stay stored for six to eight months. We need more animal bones to make wedges in the soil and drop the seeds into those wedges. Next, we cover them and use hides to carry water from the streams to allow these plants to grow. If we could use the horses that you will soon have to help us move through the plots, we could produce more seeds to create a sizeable abundant supply for our village and encampments. Perhaps, we could use any surplus to trade with other tribes."

As Levak remembered Lord Korka, he ruled his tribe along with a hierarchical social structure. His immediate family managed the allocation of food resources, and they became to be extremely important. The village members respected them and gave them gifts and slaves. Levak and his remaining brothers, Sunak, Josh, and Zak managed cultivation, harvest, and storage so that the people could prepare the food at any time. Large pits over one hundred feet deep were dug out of the solid rock for storing the grain so that they could be used as a public storage source all year round. The storage location was in the center of the village, so that all could have access to the grain. Soon, religious rituals performed around the storage site. The site soon became a holy site, whereby the people could kneel and bow their heads to their God, Kishka.

Levak had always viewed his father as an oracle who was ordained by Kishka and became divine by the green star stones. Levak would speak nightly that "the Tiger Claw clan, led by Lord Korka, moved frequently as a tribe. Their life centered on horses that roamed along the vast steppes. Korka was a powerful lord who was raised by his early nomadic family one hundred miles north of Lake Baikal in the frozen land, only known, to us, as RUZA. In the summer, the vast forest sheltered our family from the rains and the fierce summer mosquitos that attacked any living man and beast for blood to lay their eggs in the marshlands."

Levak spoke often during each night's massive fire in the ten years since his father, Korka, was assassinated. "We must learn from the past so that we do not make mistakes in the present. So, let me start with the beginning…" He would continue on most nights, not noticing if he had the attention of an audience.

"My father was the first leader of the Tiger Claw tribe who was incapable of feeling guilt, remorse, or empathy for his actions. I admired my father, for he ruled the tribe with cunningness and manipulation. He knew the difference between right and wrong but dismissed it when he was in battle or when he ruled on tribal issues. He rejected silly emotions, such as love. I saw how Lord Korka reacted, without considering the consequences of his actions, and he was incredibly egocentric. He wanted to be praised by his people and entertained by the women of the tribe when he grew bored with my mother, Tiaka. I always admired him, for he could conceal his real personality. To be clear, my father had no real emotions. He taught his sons to have the same method of ruling and a rejection of right and wrong. Only one of the seven sons would decree, but all seven of us would need to learn to show no emotions and react based on the absolute truth to power. Victory is the truth. The God of Wind blew down from the high skies. It was our Lord God, Kishka, who gave us the wind to cool the village during the summers and to brush away the flies that bit into the villager's bodies. The glowing green star rocks taken from the exploding star when it crashed into the forest lay in a circle around a wooden carving of a horse. I have ruled as he taught me and why I must also teach others the same leadership qualities. You may find this being disloyal, but my mother, Tiaka, needed the moral and life guidance of my father, Korka. Without it, my mother would listen to the poisonous serpents that surrounded their mountain cave entrance. Tiaka worshiped the serpents to determine if Kishka was lying to her. The snake would speak to her by licking the air with its tongue and hissing. Tiaka was born to be stubborn and self-centered; therefore, she never believed the words of her Lord Korka."

At thirty-one years of age, Levak was growing tired again. He stopped hunting daily, and now often moved closer to the fire to remove the aches and chills in his body. "Pass me more horse drink and meat, and I will continue the story of our beginning," he said to one of the children near the wood pile. "Yes, I remember our uncle Luchka and my father were attacked by the saber-toothed tigers when on the animal hunt for the village's families. The tiger had two sharp canine teeth, among other sharp teeth in powerful jaws. Their strong jaw and neck muscles made it easy to stab prey with their large sharp teeth. The tigers ate mammoths, rhinoceros, and other thick-skinned animals. Many times, the tiger had swiftly attacked younger children who played too close to the rock caves and dragged them away to be eaten and shared with their cubs. Over five children had been attacked and eaten by the tiger as the children's mothers watched and frantically tried to rescue them, but without a large force of male warriors with stones, spears, and arrows, nothing could kill the beast. The children died, and the tribal mothers went on with life and to become pregnant again. It was their Star God's will that the children served the tigers. It was the will of the Star God that these children selected for the future good of the village. We were saddened by this and remained in pain for very long," he continued on deep into the night, and even deeper into his memories.

Over generations, their population grew; and new weapons for warfare were made out of copper and tin, referred to as Bronze. They also made bronze tools so that they could use for cultivation and harvesting. The stone tools abandoned for Bronze tools. The Tiger Claw population prospered, and many children were born to help with the protection of the village and to wage war upon other communities. Korka's sons and their sons ordered the town to build megalithic structures that had the power to please Kisha their God and to remember those who died in battle. As the tribe grew into a war-like settlement, each new chieftain ordered that selected tribal members who had the skills of spying and assassinating to move further west and South. As they chose, they moved with their families, and they maintained their cultural roots and the tradition of building megaliths to honor Kishka. Their culture of spying, assassinations for gold or silver, attacking other villages for ransom, and implanting their family members into the societies that they conquered, was maintained and passed to their sons and their sons. Their town was independent and consisted of a hierarchical male who set the social rules.

Penkovka Cultures Map -Courtesy of Florin Curta, Phd. Sofia 5/11/2015

The Tiger Claw clan grew into an ethnic group of people who shared a long-term cultural continuity and who spoke a set of related languages known as the Slavic languages. Soon in the "Byzantine era of the 6th Century CE, they were known as Sclaveni people, or "Sklavenoi" and were early Slavic tribes that raided, invaded, and settled the Balkans in the Early Middle Ages. Eventually, they became known as the ethnogenesis of the South Slavs." The tribe had grown and become a force to be feared, and they were traveling further south with a vision to set up village outposts in Thrace (known today as Greece). They became the first kingdom on the Greek mainland. The "Tiger Claw" tribe continued to flourish and expand in wealth and territory. They began to build a culture of art, architecture, language, philosophy, literature, religion, and democracy. The descendants of Korka and Levak were now a powerful tribe, which stretched from western Poland to the Dnieper River in Belarus. The historical inhabitants of the tribe had a common shared cultural trait of spycraft, murder for hire, and conquest. Lord Levak's children and grandchildren promoted many sub-Slavic tribal extensions, but had to use brute force to ensure the standard culture and family traits of loyalty and self-sacrifice. Slowly as the Tiger Claw clan traveled south, their Gods changed, and they had not one god, as they did with the Star God, but now many Gods to explain their fears.

CHAPTER TWO
DEATH AND CONQUEST
(THE BARBARIANS AND ROMANS)

TRIBAL GROWTH INTO A POWERFUL CLAN

AS SLAVS, THE TIGER Claw Peoples grew in numbers and viewed by other tribes as fierce warriors with a firm belief in Kingship. Their military strategy was to sack and loot the town they attacked. Everyone killed except boys who could grow into warriors. Their destruction was senseless, and they defaced any work which was not depicting their God Perun.

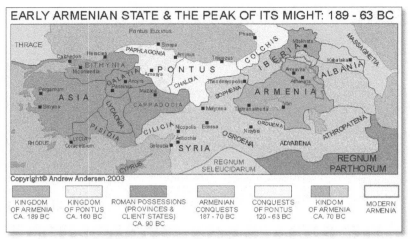

EARLY ARMENIAN STATE & THE PEAK OF ITS MIGHT: 189 - 63 BC

Copyright© Andrew Andersen.2003

| KINGDOM OF ARMENIA CA. 189 BC | KINGDOM OF PONTUS CA. 160 BC | ROMAN POSSESSIONS (PROVINCES & CLIENT STATES) CA. 90 BC | ARMENIAN CONQUESTS 187 - 70 BC | CONQUESTS OF PONTUS 120 - 63 BC | KINDOM OF ARMENIA CA. 70 BC | MODERN ARMENIA |

Map of Kingdom of Armenia arm-Tehran – Courtesy of armeniapedia.org

BEGINNING OF RED DAWN

In Armenia, the descendants of Korka become part of the Roman Legion engage in battle in which the warrior Vachir, the son of Nasan Chieftain of the Red Dawn, fights bravely and with great courage, but is struck on the head by a Persian flat bronze sword and bleeds to death on the battlefield. Also, over 25 warriors and one hundred ninety thousand village people, men, women, and children hung upside down and their throats cut to bleed upon their village soil. Red-dawn's Warlord Nasan cries openly and lifts his son's lifeless body with the blood still warm and streaming from Vachir's head wound. "We will mount a great war and kill all of them, men, women, and children." Still, in great sorrow, Lord Nasan lays the body in a separate rock-walled grave. Vachir's weapons placed to his left and jewelry to the right. His daggers and sword were made of bronze and gold and set to the left of his head. Based on Vachir's warrior status, a bronze spouted basin, bronze battle knife designed with a wide, square blade carefully lowered near Vachir skull. Also, four gold rings with a bull's head placed on his lower stomach, chest, throat, and forehead. The one-hundred ninety-two Red Dawn tribal members killed in battle placed with their heads facing the North Star within a deep sizeable common grave. Each body before wrapped in tree leaves, one gold ring and necklace placed on the forehead and mouth of each frame.

Other warrior family groups also demand a separate grave for their fallen warrior and are about to be placed in the communal burial pit. The family members are angered, and they draw the daggers to kill the burial slaves. Just when they are about to attack, a loud voice echoes from the circle, "I the Lord Nasan orders the remaining members of Red Dawn to go to the western shore and sacrifice bulls to the God Poseidon. I will bathe with the young daughter of the Persian General Artaphernes.[1] Those who do not hear my command will hang upside down and truck with the children of our village with olive branches. So now go to western shore!" [2] Footnote: (Emperor Carus launched a successful invasion of Persia in 283, sacking the Sassanid capital Ctesiphon for the third time. The Romans probably would have extended their conquests had Carus not died in December of that year. Over 25 bulls then sacrificed for each fallen warrior. The waves turn a crimson red as the throat of each beast is cut, allowing blood to flow freely. After five hours, the ceremony ends, and the villagers return to their mud-brick houses. [3]

ARMENIA

After a brief peace early in Diocletian's reign, the Persians renewed hostilities when they invaded Armenia and defeated the Romans outside Carrhae in either 296 or 297. "However, Galerius crushed the Persians in the Battle of Satala in 298. The resulting peace settlement gave the Romans control of the area between the Tigris and the Greater Zab. The Battle of Satala was the most decisive Roman victory for many decades; all the territories lost, all the debatable lands, and control of Armenia lay in Roman hands." [4]

Roman-Persian Frontier, _5th_century- "A History
of Later Roman"- Stephen Mitchell

ARMENIA BORN AGAIN

After the Armenia division in 384, the Roman–Persian frontier
is stable throughout the 5th century according to Frank Viviano's
book, "The Rebirth of Armenia was key power a thousand years
before Christ's birth." During the epoch of Julius Caesar's Rome
and the First Century before Christ, Armenia was a kingdom
under Tigranes the Great. Armenia stretched from the Caspian
Sea to the Holy Land. Turn it forward again, to the ninth century,
and the giant Armenia of Caesar's day has been carved up into
provincial satrapies of Byzantium and the Arab caliphate.[5]
Historically, the caliphates were polities based in Islam, which
developed into multi-ethnic trans-national empires. During the

medieval period, three significant caliphates existed: the Rashidun Caliphate (632–661), the Umayyad Caliphate (661–750), and the Abbasid Caliphate (750–1258). The fourth major caliphate, the Ottoman Caliphate, established by the Ottoman Empire in 1517, was a manifestation whereby the Ottoman rulers claimed caliphal authority. During the history of Islam, several other Muslim states, almost all of them hereditary monarchies, have claimed to be caliphates."[6]

Turkic invasions destroyed the Byzantine rule of Armenia. Instead of rebuilding on their kingdom, the population left in the 12th century. All families traveled hundreds of miles west to the region of Cilicia along the Mediterranean coast. The Ancient city of Ani reported in chronicles that Armenia was on the eastern border of Turkey, across the Akhurian River from Armenia. Ani was a city of thousand and one Orthodox Christian Churches. Ani was built on several trade routes and grew to become a walled city of more than 100,000 residents by the 11th century. In the centuries that followed, Ani and the surrounding region attacked and reconquered by Byzantine emperors, Ottoman Turks, Armenians, nomadic Kurds, Georgians, and Russians claimed and reclaimed the area. The residents were always subjected to attacks and many slowly left the city for other safer locations. By the thirteenth century, the community fell in decay and by the 17th century abandoned except for wild animals. In the 19th Century, Ani came alive and was mentioned in utopian literature. Ani came alive but with the outbreak of World War I it was economic and physically isolated. It's short rebirth soon turned to dust.[7]

ROME'S ENEMIES LEVAK SLAVIC CLAN (14 TO 68 A.D.)

Later, as the legions of Rome expanded their territory and marched against Slavic tribes (in the Roman Era (753 BC to 554 AD) they were called "barbarian" enemies of Rome during late antiquity.[8] A succession of family barbarian Slavic lords with the name Levak kept the Korka family tradition of employing clan members as a professional class of spies, extortionist, and informers. As was the process, rewards resulted in a share of the gold, silver, and precious stones found in the Roman and Goth villages that they sacked and pillaged. As a bonus, they could take any woman of the defeated tribe as either slave to torture or make into wives. Some ancestral members of the Tiger Claw lived in ancient Sparta and became some well-organized secret police that controlled the helots and ruthlessly suppressed any sign of rebellion.[9] In Rome, particularly under the Julian emperors, a professional class of Tiger Claw informers received a share of their victims' confiscated fortunes, was employed by the state ..."[10] Tanaki had married an Asian Mongol Yaba from the East near a lake called by the people, Boykol or Baikal. Yaba migrated west to escape the treatment he received from his Goth tribal members. Yaba was branded on his forehead the symbol of a "traitor." As the Tiger Claw tribe continued their migration, they had three children named Nasan, Altan, and Subotai. Nasan was born in a small cave. After two years Tanaki gave birth to another boy that she named Altan. Altan was born in a small village in Penkovka by the river Pripet. Twelve months later a beautiful green-eyed boy was born on the open plain of Eurasian Steppes. Yaba named the boy Subotai. Levak IV (Korka) great-grandson of the marriage of Tanaki and the slave Yaba where graced with three sons who would become Nasan, the warlord of a new Mongol tribe named by the Red Dawn villagers from the blood that flowed from their kills of warriors that they met in war. The second son Altan would be the beginning career seed that grew into the practiced art of spycraft. The third child, Subotai, would be viewed by all members of the Red Dawn as a spiritual Shaman who could control the heavens and create cures that would heal those wounded in battle. The Lord Nasan led his people to live a life as a nomadic tribe that was primitive, uncivilized, and to embrace a culture of death and barbarianism. After ten years Levak IV decided that his Slavic tribe would now live in permanent settlements located in forests, near lakes and swamps. Levak IV had the old star power to rule them as their Lord or King. When the members of the tribe saw the Star Stones in their temple, all members of the tribe knew that they were the only chosen people in the star world.

"All not chosen shall die by our swords and battle-axes. We are the new powers of this world," spoke Levak IV as the mass migration of men, women, and children assembled with their carts and animals. As time progressed, the territory of the Tiger Claws expanded. Three of the sons born from the marriage of Nasan and Khutulan; namely, Dalan, Vachir, Temunder would set up settlements in Germania's forests. Others soon reached into the western region of Russia and the southern Russian steppes, where they came in contact with people who did not speak as they spoke, but spoke many different languages. The two daughters, Taban and Dasoh, soon called these warlike tribal people who spoke this strange language, Iranians. Iran is the oldest civilization which began with the formation of the Proto-Elamite and Elamite kingdoms in 3200–2800 BC. Iranians are with the Slavic tribe of Tiger Claws by marriage and patronage.[11]

PERSIANS (IRANIANS)

According to Iranian researchers, Iran had three historical eras, namely, (A) the prehistoric period beginning with the earliest evidence of man on the Iranian Plateau (c. 100,000 BCE) and ending roughly at the start of the 1st millennium B.C.E.; (B) the proto-historic period covering approximately the first half of the 1st millennium B.C.; and (C) the period of the Achaemenid dynasty (6th to 4th century B.C.).[12]

The First Persian Empire and at times referred to as the Achaemenid Empire and created by Cyrus the Great in 550BC and located in Western Asia, was open to many cultures. For example, the civilization of Elam, was on the Plateau in lowland Khuzestan. By approximately 6,000 BC village farming had extended over the entire Iranian Plateau and in lowland Khuzestan. Tepe Sabz in Khuzestan, Hajji Firuz in Azerbaijan, Godin Tepe VII in northeastern Luristan, Tepe Sialk I on the rim of the central salt desert, and Tepe Yahya in the southeast have all yielded evidence of extremely sophisticated patterns of agricultural life. Settled village farming had the same cultural connections in Afghanistan, Baluchistan, Soviet Central Asia, and Mesopotamia. In 625 BC, all the regions became one under the Iranian Medes in 625 BC, who ruled by cultural and military power in the region. Iran expansion from parts of Eastern Europe in the West to the Indus Valley in the East, making it the largest empire in the world at the time.[13]

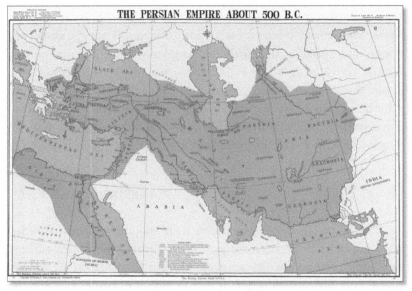

Achaemenid Empire- Courtesy of i.imgur.com

The Achaemenid Empire collapsed in 330 BC, following Alexander the Great conquests but reemerged shortly after as the Parthian Empire. Under the Sassanid Dynasty, Iran again became one of the leading powers in the world for the next four centuries.[14] Historical artifacts hidden and uncovered in 1924, demonstrated later that this is based "on Slavic languages, sharing a striking number of words with the Iranian languages, which can only be explained through diffusion from Iranian into Slavic."[15] Later on, as all the Tiger Claw Slavs moved westward, they came into contact with German tribes. Historian, Józef Rostafiński, noticed that in all "Slavic languages the words for trees such as the Beech, Larch, and Yew are borrowed from foreign languages. More than likely implies that during early times these types of trees were unknown to the Slavs, a suggestion that could be used as a clue to determine where the Slavic culture originated from."[16] Slavic mythological evidentiary materials were very sparse as writing not introduced into Slavic culture until the 9th and 10th centuries C.E.[17]

THE BARBARIANS

"Historically speaking ... a barbarian is someone not belonging to an empire ..."[18]

According to Friedrich Engels in his book The Origin of the Family, Private Property and the State (first published in 1884), Germania covered an area of 500,000 km2 or 190,000 sq. Mi and had a population of 5,000,000 in the 1st century B.C. The areas west of the Rhine were mainly Celtic (specifically Gaul's) and became part of the Roman Empire in the first century BC.[19]

Imperium Romanum Germania- Map Courtesy of Raquel Hermoso

"Greater Germania (Magna Germania); it is also referred to by names referring to its being outside Roman control: (Germania Libera), "free Germania" formed the larger territory east of the Rhine. Germania in its eastern parts was likely also inhabited by early Baltic and, centuries later, Germania Slavica in modern historiography."[20]

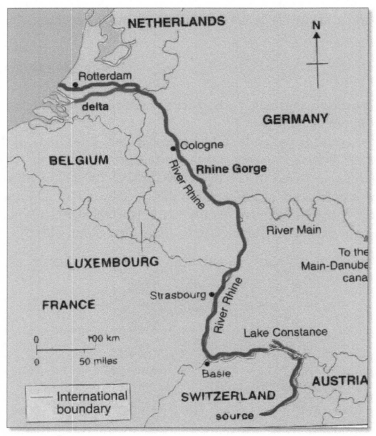

Rhine River boundary – Map Courtesy Homework by Mandy Barrow

Germania not homogeneous but inhabited by different tribes, most of them Germanic but also some Celtic, proto-Slavic, Baltic and Scythian peoples. The tribal and ethnic makeup changed over the centuries as a result of assimilation and, most importantly, migrations. The Germanic people spoke several different dialects. The occupied Lesser Germania divided into two provinces: Germania Inferior (Lower Germania) (approximately corresponding to the southern part of the present-day Netherlands) and Germania Superior (Upper Germania) (roughly corresponding to present-day Switzerland, southwest Germany, and Alsace).[21] In Europe, there were five major barbarian tribes: the Huns, Franks, Vandals, Saxons, and Visigoths (Goths). Each of them despised Rome. The primitive tribes did not want to be ruled by the Roman Empire. The barbarian tribes only wanted to steal the riches and destroy Rome. The barbarians were on a consistent basis destroying Roman towns and cities in the outer edges of the empire.[22]

The Red Dawn clan originated when the Warlord Nasan discarded his wife Khutulan for the blue-eyed Nordic slave Nataliya. Soon they had twin boys that they named Yasher and Irek. Both of the twins would turn to the religion of Allah and the book of the Muslim faith. Their third son Luarka became the next Shaman of the Tatarik Hun Tribe. Germanic or Celtic barbarian, but Hunnish. - Believed to be of distant Mongol stock, Attila ravaged much of the European continent during the 5th Century C.E. Apparently, Attila was as great a menace to the Teutonic tribespeople as he was to the Romans; he and his forces finally defeated by both Germans and Romans working together. In 451 C.E. (Common Era), Huns were defeated 451AD by the Goths and the Romans. "Attila supposedly died soon after. The rumors of his cannibalistic practices are not unfounded; he is supposed to have eaten two of his sons, even.) He does make an appearance in the Volsung Saga, as Gutrune's second husband after Sigurd's death."[23]

Altan turns 26 years old and works at Radik's Tatarik Hun tent and because of his skills of seeking out crucial military information on the actions of the Hun Generals Dengizich and Octar. Altan is granted the tribes' jade round stone for his reputation as a secret security operative. Soon Altan would become a trusted council member of the Penkovka region.

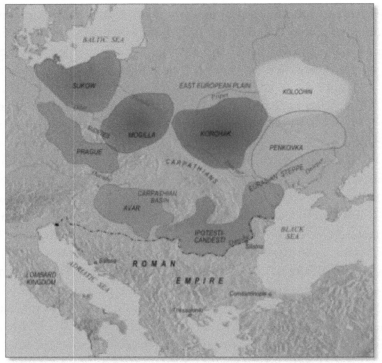

Slavic archaeological cultures – Courtesy of Florin
Curta, PhD. Sofia Lecture 5/11/2015

XIONGNU - HUNS' ANCESTORS

Since Joseph de Guignes in the 18th century, modern historians have associated the Huns, who appeared on the borders of Europe in the 4th century A.D., with the Xiongnu ("howling slaves"). They had invaded China from the territory of present-day Mongolia between the 3rd century B.C. and the 2nd century A.D. Due to the devastating defeat by the Chinese Han dynasty, the northern branch of the Xiongnu retreated north-westward. Their descendants may have migrated through Eurasia, and consequently, they may have some degree of cultural and genetic continuity with the Huns. "In the 18th century, the French scholar Joseph de Guignes became the first to propose a link between the Huns and the Xiongnu people, who were northern neighbors of China in the 3rd century B.C."[24] Archaeologist Otto J. Maenchen-Helfen believed that written accounts were not reliable. Still, actual archaeological research was a better gage of revealing the truth of ancient peoples. Scholars then began to use Helfen's approach that the Xiongnu were the Huns' ancestors. The similarity of their ethnonyms is one of the most important links between the two peoples. Looking at the translations by the Buddhist monk Dharmarakṣa of Indian religious texts in the 3rd century A.D., the monk first used the word "Xiongnu" when translating the references to the Huna people into Chinese. A Sogdian merchant described the invasion of northern China by the "Xwn" people in a letter, written in 313 AD. The Frenchman historian Étienne de la Vaissière claimed that both documents prove that Huna or Xwn was the accurate transcriptions of the Chinese "Xiongnu" name. His contention was that nomadic clans kept their Xiongnu identify many generations after the fall of their empires. However, Christopher P. Atwood, did not favor that identification because of the "abysmal phonological match" between the three word. For instance, Xiongnu begins with a voiceless velar fricative, Huna with a voiceless glottal fricative; Xiongnu is a two-syllable word, but Xwn only has one syllable. Zhengzhang Shangfang, a Chinese scholar believed Xiongnu was pronounced (i.e. hoŋ.na) and that corresponded Huna in Late Old Chinese. Further, Chinese sources such as the Chinese Book of Wei contain references to "the remains of the descendants of the Xiongnu" who lived in the Altai Mountain region in the early 5th century A.D.

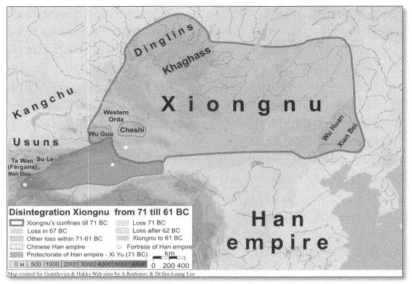

Xiongnu Map – Courtesy of A. Rodionov & Dr. Siu-Leung Lee

Most ancient texts in Europe and Asia, including Chinese, Indian and Islamic studies, read that Huns originally came from north of China. According to Edwin G. Pulleyblank, a Canadian Sinologist and professor emeritus at the University of British Columbia, European Huns comprised two groups of tribes with different ethnic affinities and the ruling group that bore the name "Hun" directly connected with the Xiongnu.

HISTORICAL MARKERS

Both the Xiongnu and Huns used bronze cauldrons or a large metal pot (kettle) for cooking and boiling over a fire, similarly to all peoples of the Eurasian steppes. Archaeologist Toshio Hayashi concluded that expansion of the cauldrons could indicate the route of migration of the Hunnic tribes from Mongolia to the northern region of Central Asia in the 2nd or 3rd century A.D., and from Central Asia towards Europe in the second half of the 4th century, implies the Huns' association with the Xiongnu.

Powerful Xiongnu - Courtesy of ancientorigins.net

As in Egypt, the Huns practiced artificial cranial deformation, but there is no evidence of such practice among the Xiongnu. This custom had already been practiced in the Eurasian Steppes in the Bronze Age (2300 BC to 1200 BC) in Europe and the early Iron Age (1200–1000 BC), but it disappeared around 500 BC. In the 1st century B.C., cranial deformation again started to spread among the local inhabitants of the Talas River region and in the Pamir Mountains. In addition to the Huns, the custom evidenced among the Yuezhi and Alans. The long pony-tail, which was a characteristic of the Xiongnu, was not recorded among the Huns. Historian Hyun Jin Kim had concluded that to refer to Hun-Xiongnu links regarding old racial theories or even ethnic affiliations simply makes a mockery of the actual historical reality of these extensive, multiethnic, polyglot steppe empires. Kim stated that the ancestors of the Hunnic core tribes were part of the Xiongnu Empire and possessed a strong Xiongnu element. The ruling elite of the Huns claimed to belong to the political tradition of this imperial entity. There still seems to be a historical gap between the Chinese reports of the Xiongnu and the European records of the Huns and 300 years to many historical changes that made the various theories disputable.[25]

HUNNIC EMPIRE COLLAPSES -SOUTH OF THE DANUBE DIES

As the 5th century C.E. was coming to an end a vertex of political instability that affected the entire region of the Balkans as a result of the fall of the Hunnic Empire. Attila's Hun campaigns left large areas south of the Danube unsuitable for living and therefore empty. The borders of the Roman Empire bordering the Balkans were kept with difficulty, as new groups like the Slavs, were moving within the devastated region.[26]

CNM12-AreaofActs – Map Courtesy of ccel.org Bible of St. Phillip

Between 531 and 534 CE Roman forces engaged in a series of military campaigns against the Slavs and other barbaric groups. "During the 550s C.E., the Slavs advanced towards Thessalonica, entering the region of the Hebrus River and the Thracian coast, destroying several fortified settlements and (according to Roman sources) turning women and children into slaves and killing the adult males. However, they could not reach their target: Thessalonica saved from disaster due to the presence of a Roman army under the command of Germanus. Later during the early 580s C.E. or A.D., the Slavs combined with the Avars (Rouran

Khaganate of Mongolia, north of China.) to overwhelm Greece, Thrace, and Thessaly."²⁷

Thessaly ancient regions central - mapsofworld.com/Greece/regions/

The Romans made a "pact with the Avars, who received an annual payment of 100,000 gold solidi in return for leaving the Roman borders untouched. The Slavs, on the other hand, did not take part in the agreement, and they marched on to Constantinople in 585 CE but were driven off by the Roman defenses."²⁸ The Slavs continued attacking other settlements, and they finally established the first Slavic permanent settlements in Greece. Archeologists believe that they were the Mycenaeans who settled on the Greek Mainland in 1600 BC.²⁹ Early in the 600s CE, Rome organized a campaign against the Slavs with no positive results. The Slavs and the Avars joined together once again, forming a massive force in

626 CE and, aided by the Bulgars, laid siege to Constantinople. The barbarian coalition almost accomplished its goal, but the Romans managed to repel the attack. After this event, the Avar-Slav alliance came to an end. The Slav occupation of Greece lasted until the 9th century C.E. when the Byzantines finally expelled them. By that time, the Slavs had a solid presence in the Balkans and other regions in Central and Eastern Europe.

SLAVIC CULTURE

Archeologists were able to learn that the Slavs occupied a vast region early in the Middle Age, which encouraged the emergence of several independent Slavic states. From the 10th century C.E. & A.D. onwards, the Slavs underwent a process of gradual cultural divergence that produced a set of closely related but mutually unintelligible languages classified as part of the Slavic branch of the Indo-European language family.[30] From pre-history to 2018, the Slavic languages are still spoken, including Bulgarian, Czech, Croatian, Polish, Serbian, Slovak, Russian, and many others, stretching from central and eastern Europe down into Russia.[31]

ROMAN DEFENSES FALTER

The Roman Empire and Europe in the early fifth century, allowed its defenses against the barbarians to disintegrate. The historian Niall Ferguson wrote on November 15, 2015, "As its (Europe and Rome) wealth has grown, so its military prowess has shrunk, along with its self-belief. It has grown decadent in its shopping malls and sports stadiums. At the same time, it has opened its gates to outsiders who have coveted its wealth without renouncing their ancestral faith."[32] In the fifth century, acts of barbarism reached new heights of brutality. As Rome was falling, Roman Senators and Generals made public speeches of unity. Still, they sought revenge against those who created the decay of the Roman Republic.[33] Historian Bryan Ward-Perkins wrote, "Romans before the fall were as certain as we are today that their world would continue forever substantially unchanged. They were wrong."[34]

ST. URSULA AND 11,000 VIRGINS

King Dionotus of Dumnonia in southwest Britain, told his daughter princess Ursula to break a sale on the readiest ship to join Etherius, Ursula's fiancé her future husband, the pagan Governor Conan Meriadoc of Armorica. To show great piety and virtue, she requested 11,000 virginal handmaidens also to take the journey. After a miraculous wind storm brought them to cross the English Channel in a single day to a Gaulish port, upon arrival, Princess Ursula spoke that before her marriage, she would undertake a pan-European pilgrimage. She headed for Rome with her followers and persuaded the Pope Siricius, and Sulpicius Bishop of Ravenna, to join them. According to historical research, they moved on to Rome, and Pope Siricius asked to join St. Ursula's group. They set out to return to Cologne. Back in Britain, Etherius, Ursula's fiancé, also decided that he would join them. When they finally arrived at Cologne where they surrounded by the aggressive Huns who were interested in women for pleasure only. Ursula and her young girls resisted this violation. Julius, the Huns leader, instructed his Army to kill them all, including Etherius and the ex-pope Siricius. Julius decided not to kill Ursula as he thought she was so beautiful he wanted to marry her. Ursula firmly refused his proposal because she wanted to keep the promise; she had made to God to remain a virgin. Julius went into a bad rage. He threw an arrow towards her, which pierced her heart and killed her.[35] According to stories, Ursula and her companions were martyred by the Huns' beheading them in Cologne.[36]

Martyrdom of Saint Ursula by Caravaggio Courtesy of Met Museum

Most portrayals of Ursula's martyrdom are landscapes with a multitude of massacred virgins. Mr. Christiansen, citing a ship's prow behind the king and three diagonal oars behind Ursula, believes that Caravaggio's "Ursula" is set at the docks.[37]

SPIRITUAL WORLD

The Three Branches of Human Spiritual Yearnings that shaped the cultures of the "region." Without religion, all societies begin to crumble. Thinking outside of ourselves into the realm of the outer spirit gives the majority of a society hope and stability. The pillars of the three great religions were founded and affected by the Korka clan's ancestral lineage.

CHRISTIANITY

First, "Christianity developed out of Judaism in the 1st century C.E. Founded on the life, teachings, death, and resurrection of

Jesus Christ, and those who follow him are called 'Christians.' Christianity has many different branches and forms with accompanying a variety of beliefs and practices. The three major branches of Christianity are Roman Catholicism, Eastern Orthodoxy, and Protestantism, with numerous subcategories within each of these branches."[38] Christianity thrived in the West. Today it is the largest religion in the world.

BUDDHISM

The second great religion, Buddhism, founded in the late 6th century B.C.E. by Siddhartha Gautama (the "Buddha"), is critical in most of the countries of Asia and near Asia. Built-in the 6th century, when Bamiyan was a holy Buddhist site, two giant Buddha's carved. In 2011, the demolition by the Taliban Muslims of the two giant Buddha's, cut from a cliff in central Afghanistan 1,400 years ago and considered one of the world's artistic treasures, was tragic. However, indicative of the destruction of non-believers by Islam written in the Koran) "Built in the 6th Century before Islam had traveled to the central Afghanistan region, the two Buddha's of Bamiyan were famous for their beauty, craftsmanship and of course, size. The taller of the two Buddha's stood at more than 170 feet high, and the second statue was nearly 115 feet high. They were once the world's most giant standing Bamiyan Buddha's.

ISLAM

Islam, the third high religion, is traced to its origin in 570AD. Muhammad forced to flee to Mecca, Saudi Arabia. However, his teachings tended to inspire the poor social classes to revolt against the Saudi Arabian royalty. The religion was forced to flee Saudi Arabia but spread in 1297 to Southeast and West Asia by the 10th and 11th Centuries. The fact proves that Islamic terrorism promoted by the House of Al Saud. The ancestral home of the

House of Al Saud was Diriya that was burned to the ground by the Ottoman Empire. Diriya was the town where the Al Sauds allied in the 18ᵗʰ century with a radical Muslim preacher, Muhammad Ibn Abdel-Wahhab. In the 21ˢᵗ century, the Al Sauds promoted the Muslim preacher's brand of religion-terrorist; namely, Wahhabi Islam. Wahhabi Islam is the religious foundation for ISIS Sunnis to create a caliphate in the Middle East (i.e., Iraq, Afghanistan, Pakistan, Libya, Somalia, Syria, Yemen, and Egypt). The Al Sauds were granted absolute rule as long as they did not interfere with Wahhabi Islam and protected the holy places of Mecca and Medina. Before the 21ˢᵗ century, there were never mass executions and beheadings, as seen from 2000 to 2018, with the spread of "Islamic Terrorism." Islam highlighted by the following, namely, "There is no God, but one God. Muhammad is the messenger of God." From a pure perspective, that is the fundamental Islamic creed. The sword of the Islamic religion symbolizes the brutality of this creed amongst its believers. Islam's main text is the Koran having prophetic elements stolen from Judaism and Christianity, but its tradition is monotheistic. Further, the religion borrowed from the Old Testament, the last judgment doctrine, and that of a mighty vengeful God. In Islam to be worthy, one must be giving, do good works, and have an honest prayer to achieve divine redemption. The seven essential elements of Islam Theology are as follows

Only One God,

Angels (Gabriel is right & Jinor is the evil angel),

Koran,

Last Judgement,

Prayer five times daily,

Almsgiving,

Fasting- the month of Ramadan, and

Pilgrimage to the Mosque at Mecca.

As Islam spread to Asia from the 13ᵗʰ to the 17ᵗʰ Centuries, it did not seek mass conversion or a replacement of native religious beliefs, but merely as an addition.

21ˢᵀ CENTURY REALITIES

The Afghanistan Taliban was an Islamic fundamentalist political movement. The Koran teaches that a war with the infidels is a jihad. If a Taliban Mujahideen dies in Jihad, he is a martyr. If another Muslim dies, then all Muslims who fight with a member of the Mujahideen become martyred. Terror based Taliban spread throughout Afghanistan and formed a government, ruling as the Islamic Emirate of Afghanistan from September 1996 until December 2001, with Kandahar as the capital. Suicide bombers volunteer to die in the name of Allah. The entire majority of Afghanistan embrace Mujahideen. Taliban in Pakistan was not as active as the Taliban in Afghanistan. Their leader was Mullah Omar.[39] The southern part of Afghanistan was 70% Pakistan and 30% Afghans. Their base of operations was in many villages, and each had a military duty. In the 21ˢᵗ Century, Islamic Taliban and ISIS militants destroyed priceless statues in Iraq, Pakistan, and Syria. They also stole priceless antiquities from museums to sell to private collectors (such as U.S.A. Christian collectors) to finance their military destruction of the Shia and Roman Christian societies in the Middle East. ISIS was fueled by the United States of America, which replaced the former colonial powers of the French and British Empires in the Middle East, namely, Libya, Egypt, Palestine, Saudi Arabia, Iran, Afghanistan, Turkey, and Syria.[40]

EVOLUTION OF A TERRORIST DESCENDANT

The second illegitimate son of the slave Nataliya and Nasan, Irek, travels to the Eastern territories held by those who practice the Islamic religion. Irek soon related as an ethnic Pashtun of the Ghilzay branch and living near Kandahār, Afghanistan. Irek only receives minimal 5ᵗʰ-grade education but excels in madrasah studies. He soon becomes a Jihad warrior for Allah and dreams of the kingdom that awaits him. Irek has a bright smile and makes boyhood friends quickly. His friends all meet to play a game of hitting a round stone with a large flat stick. The stone pitched at the player. Upon hitting it, the player runs in an inverted pyramid track. One hot day as they played the game, Irek boast,

"try to throw the stone as hard and fast as you can! I will take the stone outside of the pyramid track. I am a descendant of the star stone God Korka and thus a God as well."

They all laughed. The smallest boy looks at Irek and laughingly utters what all the other young boys were thinking, "You stand six feet eight and how can such a big man hit a small stone," they asked. "You will see, just pitch the stone as fast as you can."

A round stone was selected and thrown as fast as the thrower could. The rock traveled towards Irek, but it was too high and struck Irek's right eye. Immediately he screamed, and blood began to pour from the stone embedded in Irek's eye socket. His friends ran towards Irek, but they knew that they could do nothing except removing the stone. After the stone removed, they dragged him to a small stream to wash the eye wound. Irek realized he had no vision of his right eye.

Then the boys made a bed out of wood and placed him on the top. They marched over a mile to bring him to his mud hut. His newly pregnant girlfriend, Aadabbulla, screamed when she saw the blood and the shattered eye socket.

"Come, bring him to the bed in the corner, and I will find herbs to heal his wound. The four boys aging from sixteen to nineteen carried Irek to the bed and carefully laid him on the goatskin. "My love, I will be gone for a short time; please try to rest," Aadabbulla softly spoke. Three hours had gone by, and she had not returned. As Irek lay in bed, he awoke by a vision to restore peace from the tribal and ethnic violence in the many Afghan villages and cities. He awoke, he sat up and reached for sizeable ceramic basin filled with water. He washed his face and body, placed mud on the wound to heal the injury, and returned to his students at Hia village Madrasah. He opened the door of the mud and stone school building. Twenty-five men and boys who were students bowed their heads to show admiration and respect for Mullah Irek. He entered and stood in front of them and spoke,

"I had a vision instructing me to restore peace. Now, my madrasah students, I order you to take over cities that do not follow the Prophet, Mohammad. Once that is accomplished, I will establish an Islamic Emirate. I will take the cloak of the Prophet Muhammad from the mosque in Kandahār that will symbolize that I am Muhammad's successor. Now rush into all cities, killing the infidels and non-believers, gathering slaves for selling, and seizing their properties in the name of Allah."

Irek, after all, was influential in what he said to them. Irek left the classroom, whispering to himself,

"I will become the Jihad commander of the faithful. I and those who follow me will create a caliphate free of wars and friction between those in my caliphate."

Two years later, education and employment for women all but ceased; capital punishment enacted for transgressions such as adultery and conversion away from Islam. Singing, dancing, and other forms of popular entertainment were prohibited. Mullah Irek, a proud Sunni warrior, took up the sword Jihad to fight the infidels. During prayer, a spear sailed into his compound, and it struck Mullah Irek's chest. He died instantly. The Muslim warriors he was leading entered the compound only to find that he was set on fire by the ISIS terrorist, just the burned bones of Mullah Irek remained. They collected the bones that they found among the ashes and carried them to their temple dedicated to Muslim Jihadist martyrs who died in the fight against the infidels. Later, they carved a stone altar and placed the bones inside a wooden box. Small spoons of his ashes would only give to the families of a warrior of Allah who showed courage in battle and suicide martyrdom. In other locations, the Korka Clan continued to gain land and wealth by marriage and the merger of tribes that they conquered. The Eurasian Steppe was to hear the thundering sounds of thousands of mounted Mongols who owed their allegiance to the Great Hun Attila.

HUNS ATTILA (ATLI)

The Huns were a nomadic murderous people. Between the 1st century A.D. and 7th century A.D., Huns lived in Eastern Europe, Caucasus, and Central Asia. Within European cultural traditions, the Huns lived East of the Volga River or part of Scythia, The Huns' arrival paralleled with the migration westward of Scythian people or Alans.[41]

SCYTHIAN PEOPLE -THE ALANS.

"In early times, the main mass of the Alans was settled north of the Caspian and Black seas. Later they also occupied Crimea and many territories in the northern Caucasus. The history of the Alans divided into three periods:[42]

(1) From the beginning of the Christian era to the great migration of peoples; (2) From that period to the Mongol invasion; and (3) After the Mongol invasion

During the first period, the Alans appear as a nomadic, warlike, pastoral people who were professional warriors and took service, at various times, with the Romans, Parthians, and Sasanians. Their cavalry was particularly renowned. They participated in Mithridates' wars with Rome (chronicled by Lucan), as well as in Roman campaigns in Armenia, Media, and Parthia in the 1st and 2nd centuries A.D."[43] The Huns split the Alans into two parts, the European and the Caucasian. Some of the European Alans drawn into the migration of peoples from eastern into western Europe. They passed into Gaul and Spain with the Germanic tribes of Visigoths and Vandals, some even reaching North Africa. The Alans fought on the side of the Romans in the battle of the Catalaunian Fields (A.D. 451), when

Aetius defeated Attila, chief of the Huns. In 461 and 464, they made incursions into Italy. After Attila's death, Alans struggled, together with the Germanic tribes, to free themselves from Hun domination.[44]

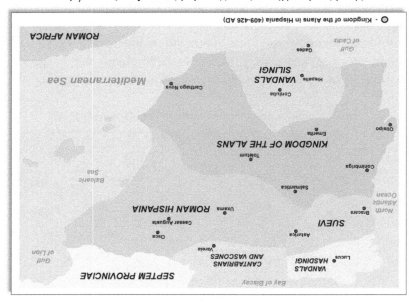

Alan Kingdom Hispania – Map thehistoryofspain.com/alans

Within the Alans scholarly research," "Large Alan hordes settled along the middle course of the Loire in Gaul under King Sangiban and on the lower Danube with King Candac (the historian Jordanes sprang from the latter group). Another settlement is indicated by the name of the Spanish province Catalonia, which is but a slight deformation of Goth-Alania,' province of the Goths and Alans,' The proper French name "Alain" and English "Alan" are an inheritance from the tribe. The Alans left an imprint on Celtic folk-poetry, e.g., the cycle of legends concerning King Arthur and his knights of the Round Table.[45]

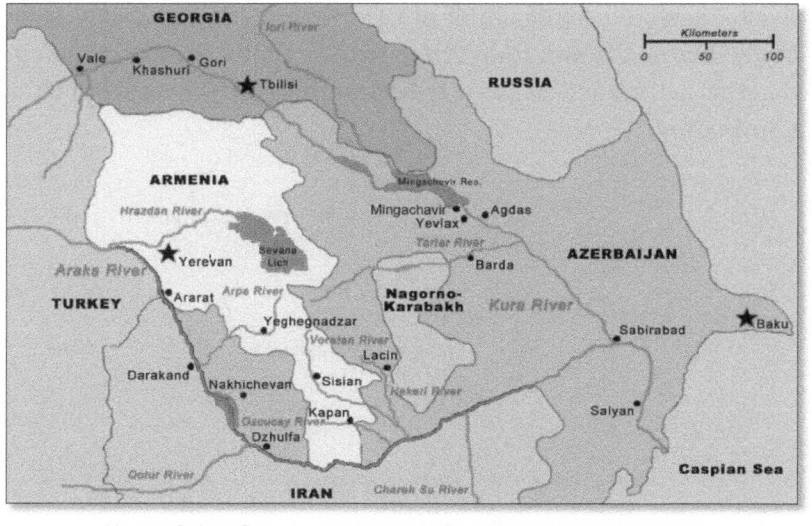

Map-of-the-Caucasus-region – Courtesy of edmaps.com

Part of the European Alans remained in the lands bordering the Black Sea, including the Crimea. "Caucasian Alans occupied part of the Caucasian plains and foothills of the main mountain chain from the headwaters of Kuban river and its tributary, the Zelenchuk (in the West), to the Daryal gorge (in the East). They became sedentary and took to cattle-breeding and agriculture. Towns developed, elements of state organization appeared, and political and cultural ties established with Byzantium, Georgia, Abkhazia [see Abḵāz], the Khazars, and Russia. Dynastic marriages concluded with these countries. From the 5th century on, Christian propaganda first conducted by Byzantine, later also by Georgian missionaries. The Alans adopted Christianity in the 10th century, and an Alan episcopal see was created."[46] In 91AD, the Huns were said to be living near the Caspian Sea and by about 150AD had migrated southeast into the Caucasus. By 370AD, the Huns had established a vast, if short-lived, dominion in Europe. By 440AD, the Huns had used hit and run tactics to take large portions of Europe and arrived at the Danube which was controlled by Rome. The bloodthirsty notorious barbarian of all time was Attila[47]. The

Huns consisted of a confederation of warrior bands and eager to integrate other groups. Also, to increase their military power, in the Eurasian Steppe of the 4th to 6th centuries A.D. Most aspects of their ethnogenesis (including their language and their links to other peoples of the steppes) are uncertain. Walter Pohl explicitly states: "All we can say safely is that the name Hun, in late antiquity, described prestigious ruling groups of steppe warriors. The Roman historian Ammianus Marcellinus, who completed his work of the history of the Roman Empire in the early 390s, recorded that the "people of the Huns lived beyond the Sea of Azov near the frozen ocean."[48] The Sea of Azov, a northern extension of the Black Sea, is located on the southern coastlines of Russia and Ukraine. The sea has an estimated surface area of approximately 14,500 sq. Miles (37,600 sq. km). Its maximum depth of only 46 feet (14m) makes it the shallowest sea on the planet.

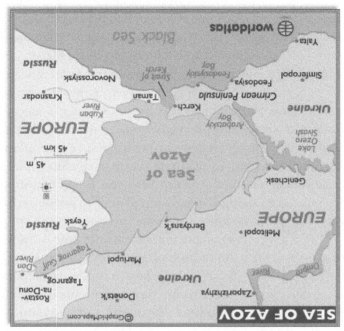

Azov Sea – Map courtesy of Worldatlas Quebec Canada

Researchers associated them with the Scythians in a letter, written four years after the Huns invaded the Roman Empire's eastern provinces. The "equation of the Huns with the Scythians, together with a general fear of the coming of the Antichrist in the late 4th century, gave rise to their identification with Gog and Magog (whom Alexander the Great had shut off behind inaccessible mountains, according to a popular legend." This demonization of the Huns reflected in Jordanes's *Getica*, a 6th-century Roman bureaucrat, written in the 6th century, which portrayed them as a people descending from "unclean spirits" and expelled Gothic witches.

Altan the son of Tanaki Korka and the slave Yaba, would take a drawing of battle plans in heavily guarded restricted areas of parchment with details about sensitive Hun surveillance techniques and send them via a particular carrier to the Roman battle commander, Maxsym Cavius. Altan would also reveal the identity and potential travel patterns of any spies or assassin agents. Altan knew that at the time that this was wrong, but he felt no remorse. He spoke to Yaba, his father

"I am not sorry for my actions of spying, I did this work so that the family would grow even more powerful."

The Hun chieftain was also interested in the internal organizational structure of the Roman military command. During the summer, Altan was seen drawing military field operational plan and soon was arrested and held by the Hun guards. Altan admitted to illegally acting as an agent for the Roman Empire. The Roman war council of justice charged him guilty and sentenced him to ten years in an underground limestone work prison. His father, Yaba pleaded that his son Altan

"deeply regrets the mistakes he has made. The truth is that my son always loved the Roman culture and society. Altan never intended to cause the emperor any harm." As he sat with remorse in his eyes, Yaba said in a loud voice to the tribunal consisting of Pretorian soldiers, "Altan hopes to put this matter behind him and move forward with his life."

The tribunal knew that Hun relationships came with many rewards. The Huns paid for Slavic blue-eyed comfort slaves and caravan journeys to warm resorts. On several occasions, the Hun Chieftain paid him gold coins. Relatives of Altan also received payments from the large numbers of high Roman officials that Altan had influenced to learn about their policies and battle plans. Altan was given land estates with over one hundred livestock.[49]

ATTILA LEADER OF THE HUN

It is speculated that Attila the Hun, 5th-century Supreme leader of the Hunnic Empire, given birth (AD 406) in the area that is Hungary. He destroyed Roman Estates starting from the Black Sea to the Mediterranean Sea. Romans named him, "Flagellum Dei" ("Scourge of God"), as he used brutal force killing all Romans living in the final period of the Roman Empire. Attila murdered his own brother after sleeping with brother's wife so that he was the only ruler of the Huns. Attila marched his Army to Germania to recruit into his army hundreds of Germanic ethnic groups before launching battles of the genocide of the Eastern Roman Empire's population. Attila was never to be believed when in 434, Roman Emperor Theodosius II paid gold and silver to Attila for a lasting peace. In actual barbarian behavior, Attila abandoned the Roman peace treaty and attacked the Roman villages that bordered the Danube river. Next, he moved his vast Army of barbarians into the Roman Empire's cities of Naissus (Niš) and Serdica (Sofia), burning homes and hanging all inhabitants. Attila's eye sites were then focused on Constantinople (Istanbul), defeating the main Eastern Roman forces that left the high walled forts to meet Attila in veracious hand to hand battles. Attila marched to the sea both North and South of Constantinople, the high walls of the capital unscalable by his Army of horseback riders with their bows and arrows. He then reversed his course to destroy what of the Eastern Roman Empire's Army. Seven years after he began his conquest, Attila repositioned his vast barbarian Army to the Balkans.[50] Emperor

Richard Theodor Kusiolek

Theodosius who ruled both Eastern Empire and Western Empire from AD 379 to AD 395 paid Attila tripled tribute of diamonds, gold, and silver for peace. Unfortunately, Emperor Theodosius died in AD 395 at the end of his reign. Fifty-two years later, the Hun Emperor attacked the Eastern and Western Empire. Then again barbarian Attila negotiated for a better treaty and more tribute. When the new Eastern Roman emperor, Marcian, and Western Roman Emperor Valentinian III, refused tribute payments. Attila the Hun recruited an army of 500,000 barbarian warriors and invaded Gaul. Flavius Aetius the son of a master of the Roman cavalry was as a teenager held hostage by the Visigoth barbarian leader Alaric, and the Huns. He was treated remained fairly and learned the culture of the various barbarian ethnic groups. Flavius rose to be a Roman general of the closing period of the Western Roman Empire. After victorious battles in Gaul against the Visigoths and the Franks he was regarded protector of Rome. General Flavius Aetius organized the Visigoths to fight with the Roman Army. In the AD451 Battle of the Catalaunian Plains, Aetius ended forever the Attila the Huns bloody invasions of the Roman Empire. For many years of war, the Roman population fearful and believed that the Huns attacked the Roman Empire because their Roman God of War, Mars, was angry with the people as they were sliding into moral depravity with no connection to the Gods. Mars did not give his power to the Roman Legions to stop the Hunnic invasions. Attila died in March AD453. Thereafter, the threats to the empire by Attila gone and General Flavius Aetius's joint Roman and Barbarian forces renewed Rome's divine destiny as a strong military and economic power.[51]

When Theodosius begged for terms, Attila's tribute tripled, but, in 447, he struck the empire again and negotiated yet another new treaty. When the late Eastern Roman emperor, Marcian, and Western Roman Emperor Valentinian III, refused to pay tribute, Attila the Hun massed an army of 500,000 warriors and invaded Gaul (now France). Flavius Aetius "son of a magister equitum ("master of the cavalry"), Aetius in his youth spent some time as a hostage with the Visigothic leader Alaric, and later with the

Huns, thus acquiring valuable knowledge of the leading tribal peoples of his day. From 423 to 425 he supported the usurper John in Italy. After victorious battles in Gaul against the Visigoths and the Franks. Rome accepted its power and destiny.[52] "However, the seed and origin of all the ruin and various disasters that the wrath of Mars aroused (Mars was the Roman God of war and second only to Jupiter in the Roman pantheon) were the invasions of the Huns. Attila the Hun was defeated at Chalons in 451 by the Roman General Flavius Aetius who had banded together with the Visigoths."[53] In the destruction of the Hunnic Empire by the successor of Attila and the Visigoths, the Balkans became a political wasteland and economic disaster. For one hundred years of Roman imperial rule, the numerous barbarian hordes relentlessly attacked the Greatest Empire to exhaustion.[54]

GERMAN - VISIGOTHS (GOTHS)- 3ᴿᴰ CENTURY C.E.

What was the origin of the Visigoths? Scholars believed they came from the western Germania tribe of the Goths. In the 3rd century C.E., they broke away and set up villages west of the Black Sea. According to the historian Herwig Wolfram, the Roman writer Cassiodorus coined the term Visigothi to mean `Western Goths.' However, he understood the word Ostrogothi to mean `Eastern Goths,' sometime in the 6th century C.E. Cassiodorus wrote that two different Gothic ethnic groups existed and had to have distinct names, namely, Visigoths and Goths.[55]

The designation Visigoth seems to have appealed to the Visigoths themselves, however, and they came to apply it to themselves. When the Huns invaded the area, the Visigoths appealed to the Roman Emperor Valens for sanctuary in the Roman Empire. Valens consented, and the Visigoths settled in an area near the Danube. Mistreatment by provincial Roman governors soon led to widespread discontent among the Visigoths and, by 376 AD, open rebellion had broken out. The Visigoths plundered the neighboring Roman towns, growing in power and wealth as they went.[56]

THE VISIGOTH ALARIC I

During the reign of the Roman Emperor Theodosius and until 395AD, Alaric I was the sole commander of the Visigoth forces within the Roman military. Alaric known among his tribe as a glorious and imposing war headman. The Roman leaders in Rome promised vast tribute to Alaric for his troop's contribution to the Roman Army. Rome continued to not make the payments and thereafter Alaric led his forces against Roman stockades. With the Visigoths of like mind, he surrounded the city of Rome and no food or water was allowed in. In 410 AD, the city's population simply open the gates thinking that they would be given food and water. Instead in barbarian fashion the Visigoth forces simply stole anything of value, raped women, took many slaves leaving only a burning city. Roman Empire ceased to exist. The Visigoths under Alaric went on a rampage of killing, stealing, burning, and pacifying the former Western Roman territories. The Roman Empire was gone forever it seemed.[57] In 452 AD, Attila's Huns invade Italy, but the hand of God results in Attila's death. The Vandals led by Dengizich burn and rob the city Rome. In 469, Attila's son Dengizich is attacked, placed in chains, and executed on a cross. Seven years later, Odoacer, a mercenary and leader of Germanic barbarian troops within the Roman forces, uses his strengths to remove the Western Roman Emperor. The final death of Rome occurs in 476 AD. Early on, the entire Roman Empire consisted of one hundred million people. Rome was a vital capital and center for trade, government, and finance. At his empire greatness, the city of Rome had an estimated one million inhabitants but by 513AD only 98,890 people living in the city.[58]

THE GOTHS

The majority of historians have no idea where these people originated from. All that seems to be known is that the "Goths were a Germanic tribe who are frequently referenced for their part in the fall of the Roman Empire and their subsequent rise to power in the region of northern Europe, initially in Italy. The first referenced by Herodotus as Scythians or Alans, but Herodotus inclined to sweeping definitions of people whom he considered "barbarians" and perhaps designated the Goths as "Scythians" simply because they lived in the regions surrounding the Black Sea, traditionally Scythian territory. Modern scholarship has rejected the identification of the Goths with the ancient Scythians." The only primary source of Gothic history is attributed to Jornandes, a six century Eastern Roman bureaucrat of Gothic extraction. On his retirement, he took to writing historical fiction creating the Goths as mystical people who possessed vast physical, spiritual, mental powers, unlike space aliens. Then there was Cassiodorus, a Roman bureaucrat who was a court member of Theodoric the Great, a Gothic King who ruled from 454 to 526 AD. Cassiodorus also used his fictional writing skills. He also used his imagination to create the Goth's glorious erstwhile foundation of the Goth's past and the visionary rule of Theodoric the Great.[59]

In 238AD, the first Gothic invasion of Rome attacked the city of Histia in modern-day Hungary, which had been part of the Roman Empire since 30 C.E. What drove the Goths to this invasion is not fully understood? Perhaps, Rome's Empire was the weakness in its provincial cities like Histia and Thuse attractive targets for the Goths and other tribes. Roman's military could not respond with the large numbers of troops it once had. Rome, at this time, was going through a period known as mob street unrest. The Roman Empire from 235 to 284 CE was faced with mob rule and eventual to please the population forced the Roman Senate to set up three distinct regions. As a result, the Goths moved further into the areas of Roman. In 251 CE, The Roman legions were to face total defeat at the Battle of Abrittus with Emperor Decius and son were hacked to death in the battle. The Goths created their own naval ships and became pirates along the coast of Rome. The Romans still did not think that the Goths were superior to them and referred to them as vermin that were merely annoying.

THE DAYS OF ROMAN UNREST

In A.D.253, events continued; namely, a general could not win a battle against the barbarians, clocked in purple, and then marches with his Army against another general who seeks the same ruling power as emperor. In the 3rd century, a "revolving door" existed in which emperors did not have time to mint their coins before they were killed or imprisoned. The Persians captured the Roman Emperor Publius Licinius Valerianus and murdered him in 260AD, at Bishapur, Iran. According to ancient chronicles, Shapur king of Persia forced Emperor Valerian to swallow molten gold; another account states Valerian was killed by being flayed alive and skinned. His skin was stuffed with straw and preserved as a trophy in the main Persian temple. History records that a long chain of Roman Emperors was murdered by close Roman guards or forced to commit suicide during this period.

Alaric sack of Rome by Visigoths- Courtesy of FineartAmerica

ALARIC THE GREAT

Alaric, the first was a Visigoth noble and war chieftain. He served as a commander of Visigoth troops for the Roman Army until the death of Emperor Theodosius in 395" C.E. When payment from Rome continued delayed, Alaric led his forces against Roman strongholds. One of the most famous barbarians, Alaric the Goth. On December 18, 371AD., he was the first barbarian who successfully captures Rome's City in 410 AD. Although his troops spared most of the residents and the architecture (Alaric was a known lover of beauty and literature), they pillaged and looted Rome." The Goth Emperor Alaric had a vision as he slept that if he attacked Rome, he would be victorious. After his victory, his navy navigated toward Africa, but a severe storm occurred, and Alaric the Great Goth suddenly took ill and died. He was buried close to the river Busento. Other legends emerged that Alaric only faked his death as the Vandals and Romans were attacking the Goths. He thus set up a Visigothic kingdoms that he ruled until he died at 98 years of age in 470AD. The historical speculation is Visigoths known as Alaric's descendants migrated to the Iberian Peninsula, and their blue eyes, light hair, and dark skin are indicative of present-day Northern Spaniards.[60]

ROMAN EMPIRE - HISTORICAL PERSPECTIVE

The Roman Empire historically began when Augustus Caesar, the great-grandson of Julius Caesar. Augustus became the first emperor of Rome (31 Before the Common Era (BCE)). He ended, in the West, when the last Roman emperor, Romulus Augustulus, was deposed by the Germanic King Odoacer (476 Common Era (C.E.)- Flavius Odoacer (433–493 CE), also known as Flavius Odovacer (Italian: Odoacre, Latin: Odoacerus. "German: Odoaker, was a soldier who is 476"[61] CE became the first King of Italy (476–493 CE). Western Roman Empire died after 493.[62]

Map of Noricum the Roman Empire Acknowledgement ancient.eu

AUGUSTUS CAESAR (RULED 27 BC-14 AD)

The Noricum land itself still governed by people who viewed themselves as Romans, but their language, religion, government, and culture would continue to evolve past the point of recognition as part of Roman life. In 113 BC, the peoples in Noricum asked the Rome Senate for help from the Barbarian invaders. Senator Carboni led an army to Noricum and requested a meeting with the barbarian ambassadors to see the Roman Army's armament and discipline Army. Carboni made a significant mistake by letting savage barbarians leave in peace. However, the Roman generals worked up a plan to have a total victory of the Germania barbarians. Carboni sets up a plan to attack the barbarian Army before their ambassadors can return to their camp. In the end, the ambassadors killed, and the remnants escaped and arrived to tell of the Roman treachery. In a vengeful rage, the barbarians attacked the Roman Army with great fury and mayhem. Carboni later loses battles with the savages and commits suicide. More Romans Armies arrived in action against the barbarians at Tolosa, Burdigala, and Aurasio. The barbarians were unpredictable on the battlefields. In 113, 107, 109, 106, 105, and 103 BC, the Romans lost every Battle with the German tribes. The Roman Legions were defeated. A new commander selected by the Senate, Marius, a proven commander, and fighter. In 101 BC the fierce 120,000 Northern Barbarians meet the 50,000 Roman Legions in a final battle. The Romans succeed and kill over 120,000 of the "Cimbri" Barbarians. The Cimbri were an ancient people, either Germanic or Celtic who, together with the Teutones and the Ambrones, fought the Roman Republic between 113 and 101 BC. The Cimbri initially successful, particularly at the Battle of Arausio, in which a large Roman army outed, after which they raided large areas in Gaul and Hispania. In 101 BC, during an attempted invasion of Italy, the "Cimbri (people)," were decisively defeated by Gaius Marius, and their king, Boiorix, killed. Some of the surviving captives are reported to have been among the rebelling Gladiators in the Third Servile War.[63] It is an excellent win for Marius. In 104 BC, Rome suffers a critical troop shortage. After recruitment of the poor to join the Legion, the Army sets off for Gaul. Marius promoted Consul. The barbarians instead leave Gaul and attack Hispania. Marius builds fortresses and can repel the barbarian Army of 150,000 men. The Roman soldiers fight for their honor and homeland. The barbarians always outnumber the Roman legionnaires. The Roman Army kills over 100,000 German evildoers in a famous battle. Later the wild bands breakthrough the Alp passes at Noricum as Marius is in Rome. The barbarians reach the Northern part of Italy and plunder and burn all Roman homes. The Korka IV is a descendant of the "Star stones" orders that all warriors bring their families on the march. Korka IV knows that his barbarian fighters would fight harder, and the women would come into the Battle with their warrior fighters. The barbarians only want lands to grow. They believed that women had special powers and could communicate with their pagan gods, becoming priests and soothsayers. Rome thought that it had a mission to bring law and order to Germania- as the barbarians were unpredictable, savage, dangerous. Barbarians skilled in ambush and stealth.

ROME'S CIVIL UPHEAVALS (111–71 B.C.)

Spartacus (Greek: Σπάρτακος Latin Spártakos) Spartacus; was a Greek Thracian gladiator who, along with the four Gladiators from Gaul; namely, Crixus, Oenomaus, Castus, and Gannicus, was one of the escaped slave leaders in the Third Servile War, a time of significant slave uprising against the Roman Republic. Due to the human resources shortage and the revolts in Hispania and the Third Mithridatic War, there existed no force to neutralize Spartacus's Army of gladiators and liberated slaves. The Roman Senate and the Emperor never viewed Spartacus's uprising as a war, but a governmental policy has gone amuck. In 71 B.C., courageous Spartacus defeated near "Senerchia on the right bank of the river Sale. The area includes the border with Oliveto Citra up to those of Calabritto, near the village of Quaglietta."[64] Roman General Marcus Licinius Crassus, a member of the First Triumvirate and the wealthiest man in Rome, had his legions find and imprison survivors of the Spartacus Army. They located over six thousand survivors and had them crucified on a cross and placed on the road along the military Appian Way from Rome to Capua.[65]

REIGN OF GAIUS JULIUS CAESAR "VENI, VIDI, VICI"

In 49 B.C., perhaps on January 10, C. Julius Caesar led a single legion (Legio XIII Gemina) south over the Rubicon from Cisalpine Gaul to Italy to make his way to Rome. Dalan, son the Tiger Claw Chieftain, migrates to Greece with members of the Tiger Claw tribe. Dalan is recruited and joins the Legion of Legio XIII Gemina and changes his name to Crassus Biondo. "Caesar's decision for swift action forced Pompey, the lawful consuls (C. Claudius Marcellus and L. Cornelius Lentulus Crus), and a large part of the Roman Senate to flee Rome in fear. Caesar's subsequent victory in the Roman Civil War ensured that punishment for the infraction would never render.[66]

Farsala was a Greek city and also known as Pharsalos. The Romans called the City Pharsalus. The town was a Roman province located in southern Thessaly and its boundary, the Southern Larissa region. Farsala was the largest city in Greece. According to Plutarch's, he wrote that Crassus Biondo witnesses the assassination attempt and alleges screams out to Caesar,

"Run, they are assassins!"

Biondo cannot reach Caesar to attack them, as over 60 men rush Caesar, but to no avail as Caesar lies in a pool of blood. Julius Caesar killed. At the same time, Publius Servilius Casca Longus produced his dagger and made a glancing thrust at the dictator's neck. Caesar turned around quickly and caught Casca Longus by the arm., and he said in Latin, "Casca, you villain, what are you doing?" Casca, frightened, shouted, "Help, brother!". Within moments, the entire group, including Brutus, was striking out at the dictator. Caesar attempted to get away, but, blinded by blood; he tripped and fell; the men continued stabbing him as he lay defenseless on the lower steps of the portico. According to the Roman historian Flavius Eutropius that sixty or more men participated in the assassination. Emperor Julius Caesar stabbed 23 times before bleeding to death on the steps of the Roman building.[67]

AFTER CAESAR'S ASSASSINATION

Roman historians wrote that Crassus Biondo made himself available night and day to citizens who needed to petition services. He always made sure that he is alert and sincere when voters spoke to him. Crassus became very popular, and voters began to believe that Crassus cared, but did not. As a result, this assassin of Caesar, achieved popularity for he had a persona that leaders always deliver what they promise. To achieve celebrity status, Roman leaders would have their togas bright white. Wherever they walked amongst the crowds, they would stand out and thus attract attention. The social crowd-pleasing campaigns of Julius Caesar and Gaius Octavius Thurinus (Augustus) featured their large painted images in all public locations. After the election, the Roman Leaders ordered that coins be made off their facial features and profiles on coins to further enhance their celebrity. Julius Caesar was a skilled politician who knew what to say to the crowds. His soldiers admired and loved him. Unfortunately, insiders began to hate Caesar as they believed that he was egotistical and acted like a god. Roman senators joined the insiders in his government administration to kill him.[68]

JULIUS CAESAR – THE BEGINNING

In the 1st century BCE, at the time of violence is everywhere in a state of anarchy. In 65 BC Julius Caesar is 30 yrs. Old and sent to Hispania to put down a rebellion. In the 2nd Century, the first barbarian invasion of the Roman Empire began. In 68 BC, Julius Caesar appointed to Spain. In 60 BC, Caesar forms a "triumvirate" with Crassus, who was the richest man in Rome and Pompey the Great. In 59 B.C., as 300,000 Germania barbarians move south, looking for lands is quickly elected by the Roman Senate as Consul.[69]

GALLIC TRIBAL CONFEDERATION

The next year large number of Helvatians (Footnote: the Helvetii were a Gallic tribe or tribal confederation occupying most of the Swiss plateau at the time of their contact with the Roman Republic in the 1st century B.C.) with a 5 to 1 ratio, attack Caesar's

Army. Still, Caesar's military skills always win the Battle.[70] The Barbarians keep moving south, and in 57 B.C., the Barbarians move into pastoral Gaul.

BATTLE OF THE SABIS RIVER

Roman Provinces in Asia Minor — Map courtesy of BibleStudy.org

In present-day France, Belgium and Luxembourg, Caesar would conquer the northern tribes by diplomacy or by the sword. His Army had conquered the Helvetii confederation in 56 B.C., and he was determined to conquer any other rebel factions. What stood before him was the tribal coalition of the Belgic Nervii tribe. The coalition consisted of the Gallic Warrior Chief Boduognatus's Nervii, Aduatuci, Atrebates, and the Viromandui. The Nervii Tribe alone massed over 60,000 warriors. Even before the other three tribes arrived, Boduognatus had a basic plan to hide in ambush and attack each individual Legion in sequence from the gaps that existed between the baggage train that followed each of the individual eight legions; namely, VII, VIII, IX, X, XI and XII plus a new Belgae/Gallic mercenary force under Legions XIII and XIV or estimated at 42,000 men. If the barbarian tribe could strike hard and fast, they could easily defeat the Roman force. Boduognatus strategized that if he could disrupt the baggage train, the Roman troops would panic and Caesar then would only have the option to retreat and return to his winter quarters. In August, the eight legions left their stockade fortress and marched down a narrow road preceded by a Recon force to discover Boduognatus's main warrior screening elements. After two and half day's march, the Romans located the Gallic warriors of the Nervii clan and their allies about ten miles near the Sabis River (present-day Selle River in northern France from the Belgian border). However, they met Boduognatus's main Nervii cavalry who charged the Roman force, withdrawing, and then charging again in a hit and run tactic that helped Boduognatus to learn of the strength and composition of Caesar's Legions. Caesar's Belgae-Gallic tribal barbarian cavalry contingent began to desert in large numbers and Caesar was greatly concerned. Now the Roman Army has lost a key ability to seek intelligence and monitor the movements of the Nervii. Gaius Julius Caesar immediately consolidated his six legions and placed them forward and moved all the baggage trains into one single column of eight baggage trains and placed Legions XIII and XIV as rearguards. Caesar moved his legions on a Command Post (C.P.) on the highest hill overlooking the Sabis River. Still, the foliage was thick with hedgerows and thus would restrict any Roman maneuverability. Caesar's orders were to dig trenches around the campsite and to send out scouts. Unknown to Caesar, the main force of the Nervii and all of their coalition tribes hid south of the Sabis River. The Roman scouts met the main screening cavalry force that used the tactic of striking and then quickly moving back into the woods and hedgerows. As the baggage carts reached the Roman camp, the Gallic warriors plunged from the thickets crossed the knee-deep river and attacked headlong up the hill towards the (C.P.). The Roman legions had no advanced warning or preparation were standing with no armor or helmets but still engaged in hand-to-hand combat. The Legions fought and circled their defenses around their standards. It appeared that the Roman Legionnaires were doomed to die. Caesar wrote in his History of the Gallic Wars,

"As the enemy was so near and advancing so swiftly, the officers did not wait for further orders but on their responsibility took the measures they thought proper." All legates and centurions took control and urged a counterattack and not to lose hope. On the left flank Legions, IX and X engaged the Atrebates using barrages of Pila (javelins). The exhausted Atrebates died in great numbers and retreated across the Sabic River with the legions pursuing and killing them as they ran. In the center of the field, Legions VIII and XI attacked by the Viromandui learned of the plight of the Atrebates retreat across the river with legionnaires in fast pursuit. However, the right flank was now exposed, and Boduognatus and the Nervii saw this battle opportunity and moved against Legions VII and XII. The Battle was chaotic, and many Roman soldiers lay dead or dying. Caesar then ordered Legions VII and XII to pivot and fight back to back. With the right flank thus secured, hope and a sense of strength ushered into the minds of the legionnaires. The Belgae/Gallic fought but the Nervii slowly pushed them back. As if by heavenly wishes, the fresh and stronger Legions XIII and XIV arrived and seeing the dire straits of their fellow Roman brothers in arms, moved forward with the reorganized Legion X and surrounded the Nervii on three sides, slashing and stabbing as they moved within their ranks until every Nervii Gallic warrior slaughtered. The day ended as Boduognatus Gallic Warrior confederation lay in the blood-soaked Sabic River. This Battle on the Sabis River could have been Caesar's waterloo. Caesar's military skills as a general were clear by then. However, any campaign against the fierce Gaul could be won by a professional, well-trained and equipped, and highly disciplined army with quick decision making by officers. In addition, disciplined rank and file soldiers could defeat any courageous highly motivated barbarian army. Planning, strategy, and tactics are important elements in Battle. Caesar asked himself the question, what does it take to win?

"First, you have to have the will to kill. You cannot win without killing the enemy. On the other side of the nummus aureus coin, you have to have the will to die."

Caesar's Army conquers all of Gaul, killing 50,000 thousand of the various tribes. Julius Caesar is brutal and has a sword in hand, and He kills the barbarians as they attack his legions. Not being satisfied with his bloodlust, Caesar murders all members of the Ario Vistus' family except for one, who he and takes has his slave. Julius takes over Gaul, and Airo Vistus manages to swim across the Rhine back to Germania to fight another day. In 55 BC, Caesar wrestles with the German tribes by crossing the Rhine. Overtime, Julius grows in wealth but not crucial within the Roman Aristocracy. In politics, violence becomes the norm, and as a result, the "triumvirate" (Pompey, Gratus, and Caesar) does not last long. In 51 BC, Caesar crushes the revolt of Vercingetorix in Gaul. Mark Anthony, Caesar's adjunct, arrives in Gaul's with 200,000 troops. In 52 BC, Gaul gives up its independence after the Romans win the Battle.

According to Commentaries on the Gallic War (1st Century B.C.) by Julius Caesar and speculated by ancient historians, the Romans killed one million people in Gaul, enslaved one million, and captured over 800 cities. Towns that refused to surrender, Caesar ordered crucifixions, chopped the hands of all males who fought against him, plus sending their women and children into slavery for the rest of their lives. Later, in his commentaries, Caesar describes the German warlike tribe, Suebi, as nurturing young boys to learn duty and discipline. They are taught not do anything against their self-will. They live in extreme cold and only wear only thin animal skins in the coldest of climate conditions and only bath in rivers.

Now Northern Europe, including Britain, becomes part of the Roman Empire. In 49 B.C., When the Roman Senate asks for his resignations, Caesar invades Roma by a small river called the Rubicon. (Cilicia was an early Roman province, located on what is today the southern Mediterranean "coast of Turkey) Cilicia was annexed to the Roman Republic in 64 B.C. by Pompey, as a consequence of his military presence in the East, after pursuing victory in the Third Mithridatic War. The province subdivided by Diocletian in around 297, and it remained under Roman," and subsequently Byzantine, the rule for several centuries, until falling to the Islamic conquests.[71] In 48 BC, Caesar defeats Pompey at Pharsalus and becomes the sole dictator of Rome, calling himself "imperator." In 47 BC, Caesar invades Egypt and proclaims Cleopatra queen (ethnically a Macedonian Greek). Julius Caesar's reign as Emperor ends in 44BC when stabbed to death in the Senate by several senators led by Marcus Brutus.

ROMAN TACTIC'S OUTCOMES TO SEIZE THE TEMPLE IN JERUSALEM

"The Roman legions surrounded the city and slowly squeezed the life out of the Jewish stronghold. By the year 70AD, the attackers had breached Jerusalem's outer walls and began a systematic ransacking of the city. In victory, the Romans slaughtered thousands. Of those sparred from death: thousands more were enslaved and sent to toil in the mines of Egypt, others were posted throughout the Roman Empire butchered for public amusement."[72] Jew's Slaves of the Roman Military "dispersed to arenas throughout the Empire. The temple's sacred relics taken to Rome displayed in celebration of the victory. The rebellion sputtered on for another three years and finally extinguished in 73 A.D. with the fall of the various pockets of resistance including the stronghold at Masada. "the Jews let out a shout of dismay that matched the tragedy."[73]

JOSEPHUS FLAVIUS

Josephus Flavius was a Jewish historian who appeared to be the only eyewitness of the Roman legions' assault of the Jerusalem Temple. Josephus, a former leader of the Jewish Revolt, surrendered to the Romans and had won favor from Roman Emperor Vespasian. In gratitude, Josephus took on Vespasian's family name of Flavius. According. Josephus, the Jewish separatist, decided to attack the Roman legions and Jewish guards of the retreat and the Romans who were helping to put out a fire that occurred in the inner court.

A bloody confrontation resulted in the temple guards running into the holy temple with the Roman legions several paces behind them. Josephus writes that a Roman soldier grabbed a burning log and threw it into the rooms that surrounded the worship refuge. The flames grew in intensity, and the Jews saw the smoke in the city. This Roman intrusion angered all those who had strength, but the Roman troops only became aggressive. The people rushed into the inner sanctuary, but trampled at the entrance and died in flames. As they came closer to destroying the temple, the Roman soldiers threw more fiery embers that only raised the temperature, smoke, and destruction. Like the Jews, both men and women rushed to save their sacred temple and documents. The Roman troops pretended that they did not hear the commands of Emperor Julius Caesar to stop and withdraw. As the innocent and non-violent crowds stood gazing at the burning temple, they butchered as they stood praying by the soldiers. The armed Jewish separatist could do nothing, but instead, they ran away from the carnage. Josephus narrates that the numbers murdered were stacked higher than the altar, and blood flooded the steps of the temple entrance. Caesar was powerless to stop his men or the fire. As he entered the building with his generals, he viewed the sanctuary's splendor and its richly carved furnishings. Only the outer sacred private room was not burning, but only the chambers that circled the holy place were on fire. Titus Vespasianus Augustus could see that the building could still be saved and dashed out to urge his men to extinguish the flames and tell a centurion by the name of Liberalius centurion who was his bodyguard to lance any of the men who disobeyed his orders. The rage they felt towards the Jewish rebels, their hate for Jews, and their mentally unbalanced state for the killing was more potent than their love for Caesar or the fear of being lanced. They believed that inside the temple was a treasure of gold, silver, and precious stones. The rooms covered with gold ceilings, and as they moved towards the inner holy altar, they became lustful for bounty. Caesar and his generals wanted to control their troops. Still, when more embers thrown into the gate hinges, they realized the futility of trying to control the enraged soldiers of the Legion. When Caesar and his officers left the scene, no one was available to stop the burning inferno. Peraea was the portion of the kingdom of Herod the Great occupying the eastern side of the Jordan River valley. Peraea and the surrounding hills seemed to echo the carnage of those innocent civilians hacked to death for no other reason than they were not intimidated by the Roman soldiers and believed in their deliverance. The Temple Mount seemed to be on the top of an active volcano with hot lava being hot blood. Today, the Temple Mount is an elevated plaza above the Western Wall in Jerusalem that was the site of both of Judaism's ancient temples.[74]

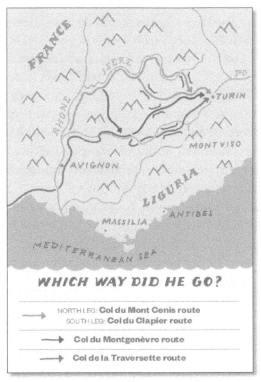

Hannibal's War Campaign route – Courtesy of
Smithsonian Magazine Margaret Kimball

ROMAN'S STRATEGY OF WINNING DEBATES

It takes a certain style to win political arguments, but facts are not required. During the time of the Roman Republic, Cato the Censor was recognized as the master of this technique. An example is that during the 149B.C. Roman Senate debate centered around how to neutralize the State of Carthage. Cato reached into a basket and pulled out grapes. Cato stood in a purple robe within the center of the Hall and said, "these grapes were picked today in Carthage!" Of course, he bought the grapes from an Italian grape vendor inside of Rome. Cato's words interpreted by the Senators that Carthage had emerged again as a threat to Rome. Cato the Censor's emotional presentation motived the Senators to build military forces to attack Carthage and destroy the nation.

Charismatic leaders are good actors. Whether facing constituents, competitors, or enemies, they present themselves as dominant and fit. When Gaius Popilius Laenas first encountered the Seleucid King Antiochus IV in 168 B.C., he used a stick to draw a circle in the sand around the king. He ordered him not to cross it until he agreed to do Rome's bidding. Intimidated by the brazen act, the king consented. Roman leaders knew that anger stunts contemplation. Opponents excoriated one another with vitriolic insults. Cicero accused Mark Antony of having been a male prostitute in his youth and of frequenting brothels later in life. Such slurs, difficult to disprove, distracted attention from Antony's achievements and Cicero's flaws. Shared feelings and actions have always been used by charismatic leaders to bring people together in common cause. At Julius Caesar's funeral Mark Antony whipped mourners into a collective frenzy by revealing the dead man's lacerated body. Overstating the threat posed by "outsiders" also reinforces the collective identity of the "insiders." (Footnote: The Roman province of Egypt (Latin: egyptus, pronounced [aj'gyptʊs]; Greek: Αἴγυπτος Aigyptos [ɛ́:gyptos]) was established in 30 BC.)

The time after Octavian (the future Emperor Augustus) defeated his rival, Mark Antony, deposed his lover Queen Cleopatra VII and annexed the Ptolemaic Kingdom of Egypt to the Roman Empire. "Octavian, the future Emperor Augustus, suggested around 33 B.C. that his rival, Mark Antony, had become the plaything of the enemy's most famous seductress, Queen Cleopatra of Egypt. Octavian warned that if Antony came to power, then a foreigner crowned Rome's queen. "As the politically savvy Quintus Pompey understood, voters are romanced more by appearance than reality. Roman leaders knew that politics is theater, and much depends on the script's power and the stardom and charisma of the performer. As seen in the 2016 USA presidential election, political figures through the age's scissor from the same bleached cloth.[75]

History records that Phoenician settlers from Tyre (Lebanon) traveled to the northern coast of Africa in 814 B.C. and called their new city-state, Carthage. The series of wars between Carthage and Rome used the Latin word Punic meaning Phoenician. Carthage located in a vital trading route, and by 265 B.C. wealth flowed in, high buildings built, making the city a magnet for open trade, and protecting itself, Carthage built a large slave navy. Carthage fought with Greece and other regional forces, but it kept a diplomatic policy with Rome. Trading treaties signed that gave both States preferred trading rights.[76]

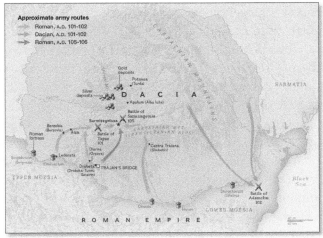

Map routes in Dacian Wars - Courtesy of weapons and warfare.com

Beginning in 264 B.C. and ending in 146 B.C. with the burning of Carthage. By 264 B.C., Rome had become the world's dominant power. By the time the First Punic War broke out, Rome had become the dominant power throughout the Italian peninsula. In contrast, Carthage–a powerful city-state in northern Africa– had established itself as the leading maritime power in the world. The First Punic War broke out in 264 B.C. when Rome interfered in a dispute on the Carthaginian-controlled island of Sicily; the war ended with Rome in control of both Sicily and Corsica and marked the Empire's emergence as a naval as well as a land power. In the Second Punic War, Hannibal invaded Italy and scored great victories at Lake Trasimene and Cannae.[77] History records confirm that Genera Hannibal Barca, was an exceptional leader of a vast army that occupied Italy in 218 B.C. He organized "war elephants" that traveled over the frozen snow encased Alps. General Hannibal's troops consisted of African and Spanish who spoke many languages and yet he won defeated an experienced and superior numbered Roman Army in three pivotal battles. General Hannibal's field battle plan was to kill as many Roman troops and cause horrific casualties on imperial Rome.[78] In 216 B.C., the Battle of Cannae, records wrote that over 50,000 Roman soldiers killed in action in a few hours. Rome was determined even with these battle causalities, sent General Scipio with legions with fresh troops. General Scipio had similar military skills as General Hannibal and was able to pursue Hannibal from southern Italy to Hannibal's headquarters in Northern Africa. Scipio made a final blow to Hannibal's Army at a town called "Zama near today's Algeria and Tunisia." In 202 B.C., the Roman legions destroy Hannibal, who surrendered in Carthage. After that period, Rome gave "control of the western Mediterranean and much of Spain. In the Third Punic War, the Romans, led by Scipio the Younger, captured and destroyed the City of Carthage in 146 B.C."[79] The entire landmass of Africa became a province of the deadly military power of the Roman central authority. What was it that drove Hannibal's lifelong anti-Roman crusade? According to historians Polybius and Livy, Hannibal himself described to a king who employed him, late in life, how his father Hamilcar Barca, took the hand of this boy of age 9, to a solemn sacrificial rite and bade him swear eternal enmity to Rome.[80]

ROME'S FOREST OF DEATH - 4ᵀᴴ CENTURY BC

The great uncle of Julius Caesar, Gaius Octavius Thurinus, a Roman statesman and military general who was the first Emperor of the Roman Empire. Thurinus controlled Imperial Rome from 27 B.C. until his death in1 A.D. Tiberius Julius Caesar another of Rome's greatest generals' marches to Pannonia (Modern day Hungary & Austria) to quell an uprising of the Germania Barbarians. The life of Rome consisted of trade, commerce, and more substantial communities. In 9AD, Tiberius gains victory in Pannonia over the German barbarians. After pacification, the German leader Arminius realizes that his people were Roman slaves and orders his clan to take up arms against the Roman troops who felt a sense of security and could defeat the barbarian tribe. Tiberius returns to Rome. However, the reality is that Rome is stretched for resources and hence build a massive fort in the Kalkris woods (i.e., Tuborg forest). Legions numbered 17, 18, and 19 ordered to leave the fort's safety and due to Arminius treachery. The barbarians skilled in ambush and stealth tactics destroy the three legions and brutalize their corpses. The barbarians who, in a spiritual ceremony, cut off the hands, tongue, and eyes.[81]

The eagle standard, which is a Roman religious symbol, is taken by Arminius. All of the tribe's former lands restored. By 9AD, Emperor Augustus learns that 3 Roman Legions consisting of 60,000 men killed without mercy in the Kalkris woods. The Barbarians march south to raid or destroy Roman towns. In 14 AD, Tiberius masses 8 Legions of 160,000 soldiers and journeys back to the Germania borders. Armanius is now King over all the other tribes. In 17AD, Emperor Augustus who is 77 years old sends "Germanicus" to Germania, but Augustus suddenly dies. Tiberius voted as Emperor. After six years with the memories of the three legions that destroyed, Arminius is angry that the Romans legions had come back without a victory. In

19AD, Germanicus dies, and the barbarian leader Armaniius is killed by his people as they only wanted freedom and not a King.

BARBARIAN WARRIOR QUEEN OF THE CELTS

The warrior queen of the Celts, Boadicea, who ruled in England during the 1st century C.E., was one such female barbarian. In 61 C.E., Boadiceo, clad only in deer skin, led a revolt against the Roman invasion of Britain in retaliation for the rape of her daughters by two drunken Roman soldiers. Her Army of Celts victorious at first and pushed the Romans back to London, which Boadicea and her forces sacked and burned to the ground, randomly killing men, women, and children past 16 years of age. The remaining children were sold to Celtic families. Boadiceo did not lose a battle until the Battle of Mancetter, where she and her Army defeated by the Roman general Suetonius Paulinus. She died by being bitten on the neck by a poisonous snake administered by one of her faithful druids. Boadiceo, rather than suffer the ignominy of capture by the Romans and paraded in the streets of Rome she committed suicide.

A KORKA RENEWAL

To seek money and power and under the cloak of disguise, Levak Korka paints his face blue and becomes a Druids Priest seeking intel on Roman's troop tactics and gains friendships with generals and senators of Rome. The Tatars live in tents made of animal hides and life centers around the horses that can pull carts that are made of wood and have wooden wheels. The Tatar Chieftain Radik captures a white, green-eyed fifteen-year-old girl with white as the snow on the mountaintops. Radik thinks about his nagging wife Alfiya and decides to push his wife, Alfiya down a cliff. Radik thoughts are now on the making love to the captured girl. After many months in which the young girl spends in Radik's tent, she becomes pregnant. In March, Radik's temporary comfort partner gives birth to a baby boy with green eyes. Inside the camp lurks a spy by the name of Altan who contacts the Radik's enemy rival tribe to sell his information on Radik and his forces. The Tatar Chieftain Radik decides to kidnap this slave woman Nataliya and give her to his son, Yasher.

They then attack the Red Dawn Hun Tribe, and a brutal battle occurs. The family members hide but the wife, Khutulan of the Red Dawn warlord Nasan dies in the struggle, and the Warlord Nasan loses his right arm. The blue-eyed girl Nataliya is then taken as a "love slave." To avenge his parents and to rescue the girl, Temunder, the son of Nasan, the Hun Chieftain, waits until night and saves the girl Nataliya. Radik's son Luarka killed by an arrow to his chest and the Red Dawn Tribe leave the vast prairie soaked with blood where the attack took place. The Red Dawn's valley had an abundance of animals that consisted of mammoths, small Horses, and Uintatherium, an herbivorous mammal of thirteen feet long and about 2 tons, grazed upon the hills and plains. Above the plain ten large flying carnivorous reptiles flew looking to attack with their 5-foot razor-sharp beaks and spear the horses and take them up in the air and drop the prey upon the rocky cliffs surrounding the prairie plain. Thus, their victim efficiently killed. The other meat-eating, flesh-eating, predatory; beast was the saber-tooth tigers, and the bear dogs stalked and brought down Mammoths and horses. The rescued girl Nataliya soon gives birth to a baby boy called "Nasan Khan of the Sky Star."

Nasan Khan grows up to unite the tribes, and he travels with over 350 warriors to the East and meets five scouts of an advanced Hun warrior. He befriends them, and they agree to take him to reach the Hun Leader. He meets the Hun Chieftains daughter, Chen LiJuan. Nasan Khan then stays with Chen for two years, and they have two children, a girl, Zhen and a boy Kun Shan. Nasan Khan, the Sky Star, then joins the Hun Barbarian Army. Soon, Nasan recognized as a great warrior who is unmatched with a sword. On a horse, Nasan Khan can kill many at full gallop with his bow and arrows. For those enemies who fight on foot, Nasan Khan can use his sword to slow his horse, and completely severe the heads of those who attack him.

Richard Theodor Kusiolek

THE INVASION OF BRITANNIA- DRUID TRIBES

The invasion of Britannia forced the legions to fight the druid tribes into inland forests and swamps. Druids (Catalonians) attack with savagery and stealth. The Druid's spiritual beliefs held water to be sacred and would protect them in Battle. For six centuries, Roman conquest resulted in trade and a society that lived-in luxury. In 41AD, the Roman Pretorian Guard kills the insane Emperor "Kolingula" Emperor and selects his cousin Claudius as the new Emperor. Roman troops reward for their courage by allowing all the battle bounty that they can carry. "Emperor Claudius arrives in Britanni. It enters recorded history in the military reports of Julius Caesar, who crossed to the island from Gaul (now named France) in both 55 and 54 BCE. The Romans invaded the island in 43 C.E., on the orders of Emperor Claudius, with battle elephants, and Plautius invaded with four legions and auxiliary troops, an army amounting to some 40,000 Legion soldiers. Emperor Claudius who crossed over to oversee the entry of his general, Aulus Plautius, into Camulodunum (Colchester), the capital of the most warlike tribe, the Catuvellauni. At the end of the 4ᵗʰ century C.E., the Roman presence in Britain threatened by "barbarian" forces. The Picts (from present-day Scotland) and the Scots (from Ireland) were raiding the coast, while the Saxons and the Angles from northern Germany were invading southern and eastern Britain. By 410 CE, the Roman Army had withdrawn."[82]

THE DACIAN WARS - DOMITIAN'S REIGN (81-96AD)

Military power lies in the Roman Army. Roman Dacia was a province of the Roman Empire. - An area north of Macedon and Greece and East of the Danube. In 80AD, King Decebalus manipulated the tribes against each other, so they are not strong enough to defeat Rome. Roman Emperor Titus rules for two years, but he dies from the plague. In 83AD, Roman governor Agricola leads an Army along the Danube and Rhine Rivers to remove the Germanic Barbarians. Barbarian King Decebalus surrender and accept unfavorable peace terms. Soon the Dacians mass large numbers to attack the Roman Army and raid the province of Moesia. In 84AD, the Dacians kill the Roman Governor Agricola. Roman Emperor Trajan led the Roman legions across the Danube, penetrating Dacia and focusing on the critical area around the Orăştie Mountains. The Romans defeated the Army that Emperor Domitian sent against them. In 89AD, Roman legions, auxiliaries composed of conquered barbarians, launch another attack on the Dacians led by King Decebalus. Romans defeated in several key battles. Emperor Trajan goes with 9 Legions (90,000 troops) back to Dacian who had grown in military power and nationalism. Rome always considered Dacian a threat to the Empire.

Tracea Roman provinces of Illyricum −TotalWarCenter Forums.net

In 101AD, Trajan was ready to advance on Dacia. The Roman offensive was spearheaded by two legionary columns, marching right to the heart of Dacia, burning towns and villages in the process. The Dacian's led massive assaults on the Roman legions. (When Dacian capture Roman soldiers alive, they hand them over to the woman who tortures them and kills them) The battles fought in locations in present-day Romania. Dacian barbarian troops captured by the Legions take poison rather than be slaves by the Romans. In 102AD, "Emperor Trajan moved his Army down the Danube to Oescus. There the Roman armies converged for a final assault and defeated the Dacian Army at the Battle of Tapae. After the Battle, plus some additional conflicts, Trajan, worried by the upcoming cold winter, decided to make peace. The war, spanning months, had concluded with a peace treaty with harsher terms for King Decebalus. When King Decebalus broke these terms in 105AD, the Second Dacian War began. In 106AD, Romans are victorious, but King Decebalus kills himself in defeat. Romans find over 250 tons of gold and 500 tons of silver. The Roman Emperor overjoyed over replenishing the Roman Treasury.[83]

On June 24, 79 CE Titus Flavius Vespasianus succeeded his father, Vespasian, as Emperor of the Roman Empire. Emperor Titus adopts two sons from aristocratic families; namely, Marcus Aurelius is serious about the privileges of his new title, but his adopted brother Lucius Verus does not. By 160AD, the Roman Empire stretches nine continents. Rome protects its borders with 300,000 soldiers, but the barbarians continue to strike the edges. Emperor Aurelius dies. Marcus Aurelius and Lucius Verus share the throne with the Praetorian Guards. The Roman Praetorian Guard gives the two co-emperors their protection and loyalty, knowing that they will receive gold and silver bonuses. Vachir, son the warlord Nasan become a member of the Praetorian Guard.[84]

THE ROMANS -IMPERIUM AND PROPRIETORIAL COMMANDERS

Emperor Hadrian (117 A.D.) ascended the crown and is known for building a wall from coast to coast in Northern England. Hadrian survived only by cooperating with the elites who lived in the Roman provinces. Locals in the regions could become Roman citizens, and some advanced to the rank of knight or equestrian and could become a Senator or even an Emperor. To become Emperor, he would have to come from the family royalty or minimally a Senator. Most of the critical posts in the administration or Army went to one of the six hundred Senators. Emperor Hadrian provoked a rebellion in Judaea and stayed independent for a period. However, that was the example of provinces seeking to create their state and not ruled by the Roman Army. At the end of the Roman period, Judaea remained vast, sturdy, and unmatched by those outsides of its borders. By 113AD, Rome controlled the entire Mediterranean basin. The further North they expanded, they came upon barbarian people who were formidable and did not want them to go to Italy. The barbarians only wanted land and to live near the Romans. They did not speak classical Greek or Latin and thus considered backward, less civilized peoples. The mountains of the Alps kept the Germania barbarians with little offensive capabilities. What kept them at bay was the Roman Army that was an all-volunteer body armor militia and protracted war-making spear, swords, assault machines, and not led by a centralized dictator. Rome's National Rome at that time was a Republic ruled by the Senate. Security was the critical responsibility of two Consuls who ruled the Army. They were vital as they set the legislative agendas. As conquest expanded, wealth flowed into Rome's and created a separation between the wealthy elitist and those who lived a life of poverty. The population of Germania was huge, and they had a thirst for savagery in Battle. The barbarian armies headed for Noricum, the village that guarded the Roman Alpine Passes against the barbarians.

ROMAN EMPIRE – 600 YEARS -THE BEGINNING AND END

Rome lasted for over 600 years. At its apex, after fifty years of expansion, the Roman Empire stretched from London to Baghdad. By 6AD, Germania to the River Elbe was temporarily pacified by the Romans as well as being occupied by them. In 9AD, the Roman plan to complete the conquest and incorporate all of in Magna Germania into the Roman Empire. Rome's global continuation as power was frustrated when the German tribesmen defeated Rome's legions in the Battle of the Teutoburg Forest. Emperor Augustus then ordered Roman troop withdrawal from Magna Germania (completed by 16 A.D.) and established the boundary of the Roman Empire as being the Rhine and the Danube."[85] "The Romans under Augustus began to conquer and defeat the peoples of Germania Magna in 12 A.D., having the Legati (generals) Germanicus and Tiberius leading the Legions."[86] The Roman Empires' effect on the expansion of the Slavic Tribes was substantial. Dalan, one of the sons of Nasan, a warrior God of the Slavic tribe, becomes a spy to help his father and members of the tribe. Dalan decides to conceal his primitive roots, thus changes the name to Crassus Biondo and later a member of the Senate where he witnesses the killing of Julius Caesar. Temunder is a young prince of a Slavic tribe who goes to Rome to become an auxiliary commander but holds resentment towards Rome and seeks to destroy Roman life and culture. In 162AD, the Parthians attack Armenia, an ally of Rome. Parthian Orodes II, with the Parthian Army, defeated the Armenians. Parthian forces attacked critical Roman positions and Roman garrisons. Lucius Verus is part of the Roman Legions but stays far from the battlefront. In 165 AD, the Roman legions reach Ctesiphon (modern-day Baghdad) and conquer the Great Parthian Empire (but many Roman soldiers' contract bubonic plague by sexual contact with those infected). However, along with the Northern German borders, the Barbarians continue to prey on the Roman forts. By 166AD, 25% of the Roman population is dead by the plague that the soldiers brought back from the Eastern stretch of the Roman Empire. In 167AD, 60,000 barbarians attack border towns. "Pannonia, a province of the Roman Empire, corresponding to present-day western Hungary and parts of eastern Austria, as well as portions of several Balkan countries," becomes the focal point of Marcus Aurelius campaign. Still, Lucius Verus dies, and Marcus returns to Rome with his step-brother's body. With no money to fund the campaign in Pannonia, Emperor Marcus Aurelius organizes an auction to gain funds for the attack. Marcus returns to Pannonia loses 20,000 troops with the Germania barbarians. Marcus also fights along the Danube to keep the barbarians from entering Italy. In 170AD, Marcus Aurelius abandons the classical Roman battle formations with fixed garrison fortresses along with the areas of the Goth and Visigoth Barbarian attack points. In 175AD, Marcus Aurelius suddenly takes seriously ill and expected to die, but by a miracle, he becomes well but unable to rule. Commodus, his only son, becomes co-emperor with his father, Marcus Aurelius. Catius beheaded by his troops, and the rebellion of the Roman soldiers is over. This time Emperor Marcus Aurelius focuses on conquering the German barbarian tribes. In 178AD, the rebels' leaders are isolated and put to death. Two years later, Emperor Marcus Aurelius dies from the plague. Commodus has no vision or desire to fight the Germans. Germania abandoned after thirteen more years of bloodshed. The beginning of the end for Rome has now becomes a real outcome. [87]

CHRISTIANITY VERSUS THE ROMAN PAGAN GODS

By the 3rd century A.D., Christianity, this religion believes in one God versus the many Roman Pagan Gods. In 249AD, The Roman Army picks their commander Commodus, the son of Marcus Aurelius, who plotted to replace Emperor Phillip1, but Commodus assassinated by his troops and another commander picked, General Traianus Decius. Decius is proclaimed Emperor by the Danubian legions and defeats but does not capture Emperor Philip1 in Battle. In 251 AD, Emperor Decius decides to make his son Herennius Etruscus co-emperor with Trajan Decius as the joint ruler. The joint Imperial rulers then embarked on an expedition against Chieftain Cniva of the Goths to punish the invaders for raids into Roman territories. Emperor Phillip1 takes his Army to Verona to meet Decius's mutiny troops of the Danube. Decius's legions triumph over Emperor Phillip, who dies after the Battle. Decius went to Rome and crowned Pagan Emperor. The Christian population grows in numbers. Emperor Decius decrees all must sacrifice to the Pagan Gods or face pain and death. The fearful Christians are given a Roman Certificate that they sacrificed to the Roman Pagan Gods. Many Christians leave Rome and live in the forest, but they are brutally murdered or put into slavery. The northern barbarians enter the imperial Rome town of Moesia. South of the barbarian border lies immense wealth, coined money, treasures, and slaves. The Roman road system along the Danube makes it easy for barbarians to travel to Roman towns and then return to the North of Germania that the Romans viewed as a place to steal and have a booty that they take home.

Thracian Sea- Courtesy of WorldAtlas.com

Decius and his Army intercept the Goths on their way to Rome. Decius agrees with the Goth Chieftain not to attack the THRACE city of Philippopolis. However, Goth Chieftain Cniva decides later to move the barbarian Army to THRACE city of Philippopolis. Roman women sold into slavery, and over 100,000 Romans murdered. After the Battle, Trebonianus Gallus, Governor of the Province, lets Cniva the Gothic chieftain to leave with his spoils and aided the Goths' departure. He then makes a deal with the leader of the barbarians to attack a shared enemy; Emperor Trajan Decius. In 251 AD, Battle of the City of Nicopolis Adistrom Kaniva fought between the Roman Army of Emperor Decius and his son, Herennius Etruscus, and the Gothic Army of Chieftain Cniva. Decius and Herennius Etruscus killed in the Battle of Abrittus fighting against the Goths and Sarmatians.

THE BURDENS OF ROMAN CITIZENSHIP

Rome's population destroyed by bubonic plague, Christians murdered to bring back the Roman Gods, upheavals, and the first Emperor killed by a Barbarian Army. Marcus Aurelius then takes charge of the Army, and in 269AD barbarians are moved south. Break-away provinces now rule the Western and Eastern regions. Emperor Claudius the 2nd then seeks the advice of Marcus Aurelius, who was known for his quick mind and weaponry skills. Claudius forced to move against the Alamanni Barbarians (a confederation of Germanic tribes on the upper Rhine River) at Lake Garda. In 270AD, the Roman legions march to the Balkans to increase the Roman presence. However, Emperor Claudius is stricken by the plague and dies. Marcus Aurelius then takes charge when the Army declares himself as Emperor. Aurelius makes a sacrifice to the God of Soldiers and the God of Victory. They march to meet the Alamanni Barbarians at Placenza, but Marcus Aurelius defeated by the Alamanni Barbarians. Alamanni beasts enter Rome approximately 180 miles from the capital, but the barbarian hordes are defeated. The reality for the Roman central authority from 213AD to 367AD was never-ending attacks by the barbarians. At the 357AD Battle of Strasbourg, Emperor Julian entered into peace agreements with the Franks of Gaul, who took their gold and women's tribute and marched out of Rome. The Franks increased their birth rates and expanded their military power. In 496AD, the Christian Frankish King Clovis conquered the Pagan Barbarian Alemanni tribes and absorbed them into his kingdom. The Alemanni tribes, even Christianized, kept their German pagan language, culture, and names.[88]

OCEANS OF BARBARIANS

The barbarians who made their home in the vast sand deserts attack the Eastern edge of the Roman Empire (Palmyra) Syria and cause a rollback of the frontier and then ask for payments from Rome. Palmyra's Army then tired of Rome not protecting them formed the "Palmyrene Nation" and absorbed Egypt and the abundant grains silos controlled by Queen Septimia Zenobia. Then, they decided to restrict all shipments to Rome. Zenobia was a wise leader of her people and carved out an empire, encompassing Syria, Palestine, Egypt and large parts of Asia Minor. As Africa and Egypt were the breadbaskets of Rome, Rome's population began to starve, which caused a rebellion in Rome. Palmyrian cavalry attacked the Roman cavalry along the road to Antioch but defeated, and the way is then secured. Emperor Aurelian captures Queen Zanobia. Emperor Aurelian takes over the East Region and then gives free bread to the Roman citizens. Emperor Aurelian's legions marched to take all the Gaelic lands that were once Imperial Rome. The legions had a Latin war-cry, namely, Sol Invictus or bring back the areas for the Gods.

They meet Gaius Pius Esuvius Tetricus, Emperor of the Gallic Empire of France. In 274 AD, Emperor Aurelian unites the Empire. In September 275AD, it was Emperor Aurelian's military goal to reach Persia. However, historians note that he was murdered by his guards while waiting in Caenophrurium Thrace (Turkey) to march into Asia Minor.[89] The high-ranking Roman officers feared Aurelian's strictness and severe punishment for extortion and corruption by key army commanders and local officials. Eros Zosimus, a conspirator, and Aurelian's secretary hatched a plot. At night as Emperor Aurelian slept with a local official's wife, Eros forged Aurelian's signature on a document listing the names of high officials and officers marked by the Emperor for execution and showed it to his corruption collaborators. Senior officers Marcellinus and Praetorian Guard officer Mucapor read the document and feared crucifixion punishment from the Emperor, crept into his tent and murdered him as he slept.[90]

Map of Roman Empire – Courtesy of CIAGov world factbook

THE LATE ROMAN EMPIRE-EAST & WEST UNITED

Diocletian proclaimed Emperor by the Roman Army after the death of Emperor Numerian, and in opposition to his older brother Carinus; adopted Maximian as senior Co-Emperor in 286 AD. By 302 AD, four Regions exist, namely, Gaul, Illyricum, Italy, and Nicomedia. Christianity grows, but Emperor Diocletian thinks it is a threat to Rome and proclaims that all soldiers must make a sacrifice to the Gods, and if they refuse, they will die. In 305AD, Emperor Diocletian falls ill, and Christianity movement stalls. Constantine is cut from the succession of emperors and escapes to Boulogne Gaul to meet his father, who controls Spain, Gaul, and Britain-York Britain. In 306AD, Constantius, the father of Constantine, dies. The Roman Army makes Constantine the Roman Emperor. There is no peace for Rome in the 3rd century Rome as the Barbarians continue to attack Rome without let up. Constantine the Great ruled Rome from 306 to 337 AD as the first Roman Catholic Emperor. Constantine engaged in a series of civil wars against the existing co- Emperors Maxentius and Licinius and victorious. By 324 AD, he ruled both the West and East of the Roman Empire. In the next year, to solidify the Roman Empire as a Catholic society, Constantine summoned the First Council of Nicaea at which the Nicene Creed is read by Christians to profess their faith in Jesus Christ.[91]

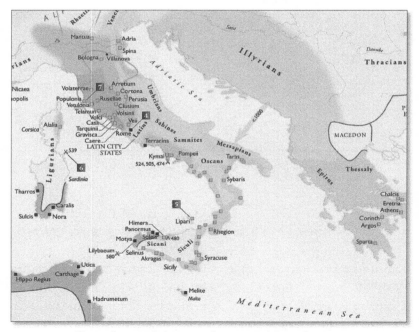

Illyria Roman Colonies — Courtesy of Eupedia.com

During the reign of Constantine, The Great, the Roman Army is reorganized into mobile fighting units, and heavily armed internal garrison soldiers are primarily to respond to internal security threats and any further invasions by barbarian tribes. Further, Emperor Constantine mounts highly successful military campaigns against the border barbarian tribes of the Franks, Alamanni, Goths, and Sarmatians. All of the Emperors who lost Imperial lands during the emergency of the Third Century are restored under the rule of Emperor Constantine. Emperor Constantine and his Army march from Britain to meet the Franks in Gaul and wins the Battle and parades his captives in the villages of Germany. Constantine reclaims territories abandoned by his predecessors during the Crisis of the Third Century. However, Constantine threatened from within his governing body. Rome's politicians decide to proclaim an Emperor of both East and West. Maxentius, son of a co-emperor, declares himself Emperor and takes over Italy and North Africa. Rome is now in significant economic and political crisis. In 311AD, citizens of Rome revolt due to high taxes and limited grain for the poor while low fees & unlimited grain to the rich.

Emperor Maxentius puts down the revolt with a lethal force. Emperor Constantine I goes to Milan to ally with another co-emperor to consolidate his military forces joined with Licinius I, who in 308 A.D. is appointed as "Augustus" in the EAST by Emperor Galerius. In 311 A.D., Constantine, in opposition to Maxentius, became WEST "Augustus" after the death of Galerius Maximianus. In 313 AD, Licinius 1, who defeated Maximinus in the civil war, became sole EAST "Augustus." To solidify his power, Licinius 1 marries Flavia Julia Constantia, half-sister of Constantine the Great. Now Rome faced with four emperors; namely, In the EAST Licinius I and Maximinus who fought each other for supremacy and in the WEST Constantine began a war with Maxentius. Next Constantine and Licinius I trick Maxentius co-emperor in the West. With Rome's battle won, Constantine and Licinius both plots to take over all of Rome.[92] Emperor Constantine marches to the City of Rome and lays siege to the town where Maxentius is hiding. A pagan priest tells Maxentius's future by examining the entrails of sheep. The pagan priest consults a spirit guide to the Oracles that an enemy of Rome will die tonight."[93] Maxentius thought that he would live, and Constantine will die then decides to meet Constantine in battle. Constantine then gets worried that he has a smaller number of troops than Maxentius. At night, Constantine prays to Pagan Gods and receives a vision of a cross in the clouds with the name of Christ and also a voice, "you will conquer by this sign-Christian Kiro or an X and a vertical line with the P on the top."[94] The Battle will be a test of religion between Pagans versus Christian. Maxentius and Constantine meet at the Milvian Bridge (Oct AD 312) that crosses over the Tiber River. Although superior in numbers, Maxentius pushed towards the edge of the Tiber River. As he tries to escape by swimming across the Tiber River, his heavy armor causes him to die in the swirling waters.

WESTERN & EASTERN ROMAN EMPIRE

Constantine the Great controls half of the Western Roman Empire, proving the Christian God is more potent than the Pagan God. His co-Emperor Licinius I gave the Eastern Part of the Roman Empire and their power sealed with the natural Roman way of sealing an alliance with marriage. Constantine then adopts Christianity, and persecution of Christians ends. Constantine proclaims the Edict of Milan that religious freedom will exist for all in the Empire. Unfortunately, Licinius I ambitious and threatens Constantine in the West, which resulted in 9 years of peaceful shared rule, but their rivalry drives Rome to the Civil War. However, Licinius I then view Christians as a "5th column" and begins to kill all Christians within the Roman Empire designated as the Eastern part. Licinius, I order all churches and holy text to be burned. In August AD 316, Constantine attacks with all of his forces at Cibalae in Pannonia. Constantine the Great defeats Licinius's more massive

Army, forcing a retreat. Instead of maintaining the realities of his battlefield loss, Licinius I announce Aurelius Valerius Valens as the new Emperor of Rome West, but it becomes a failure. Soon after Licinius's ploy, another battle at Campus Ardiensis begins in Thrace. (footnote: Aurelius Valerius Valens (died 317) was Roman Emperor from late 316 to March 1, 317. Valens had previously been dux limitis (or Duke of the frontier) in Dacia.) In the first civil war between Licinius and Constantine I, the latter won an overwhelming victory at the Battle of Cibalae on October 8, 316[2] (some historians date it in 314). Licinius fled to Adrianople, where, with the help of Valens, gathered a second army. There, early in December 316, he elevated Valens to the rank of Augustus, presumably to secure his loyalty. Much later, Licinius would use the same trick (with just as little success) in the second civil war with Constantine, by appointing Martinian co-emperor).[95]

However, the Battle is a stalemate. On March 1, 317AD, a treaty allows Licinius1 to surrender all Danubian and Balkan provinces, except Thrace (modern-day Turkey), to Constantine The Great, who had already conquered and controlled all three territories. In a weaker strategic perspective, the treaty allows Licinius 1 to have complete sovereignty over his entire Eastern Region. Also, as part of the settlement, Licinius' alternative for Western "Augustus," Aurelius Valerius Valens, was put to death by hanging. The third and final part of the treaty agreement reached Serdica creates three new Caesars; namely, (1) Flavius Julius Crispus, (2) Constantine II, and (3) Licinius the Younger. The Treaty arrangement becomes meaningless. From AD 320, Licinius, I begin to restrict the Christian church in his eastern provinces and purges any Christians from his government posts. Instead of consulships in which emperors would groom their sons as future rulers, the Serdica treaty made consulships appointments by agreement. Licinius harbored the belief that Constantine would be biased towards his sons when granting these positions. To counter his view, and a clear violation of the terms of the Serdica agreement, Licinius appoints his two sons and himself as consuls for the eastern provinces. His actions stand as a violation of the trust between Constantine and Licinius1. In the year 323 AD, Constantine created yet another Caesar by elevating his third son Constantius II to this rank. Constantine, while campaigning against Gothic invaders, strayed into Licinius' Thracian territory. Licinius declares war in spring 324 A.D. In the battle, Constantine attacks first in 324 A.D. with 120,000 infantry and 10,000 cavalries against Licinius' 150,000 infantry and 15,000 cavalries based at Hadrianopolis. On July 3,324, A.D., Constantine severely defeats Licinius' land forces at Hadrianopolis. Licinius 1 flees across the Bosporus to Asia Minor (Turkey). Still, Constantine, having brought with him a fleet of two thousand transport vessels, ferries his Army across the water and achieves a decisive battle of Chrysopolis. On September 18, 324 A.D., Licinius 1 is defeated, imprisoned, and then executed by archers. Constantine the Great as the only real Emperor for the Roman worlds of East and West, outlaws' pagan sacrifices, the treasures of pagan temples are confiscated and used to pay for new Christian churches. Barbaric gladiatorial contests outlawed and harsh new laws issued prohibiting sexual immorality. Jews, in particular, were forbidden from owning Christian slaves.

NEW LAWS MAKING CONSTANTINE NULL

Constantine's laws and regulations were quite severe. For example, Edicts were passed by which the sons were forced to take up the professions of their fathers. Thus, male sons could not deviate and seek, and another career and military recruitment required that could lead to death.

TAXATION WITHOUT REPRESENTATION

Taxation reforms were necessary for the Roman Empire and, in some cases, could result in hardship. City dwellers were obliged to pay a "chrysargyron" tax in gold or silver. This tax levied every four years, beating and torture being the consequences for those too unfortunate to pay. Although unproven, historians speculated that parents sold their daughters into prostitution to pay the "chrysargyron." Under Roman Catholic Constantine laws, any girl who ran away could be burned alive. Any boyfriend who should assist in such a matter might have molten lead poured into her mouth. By the height of the Roman Empire, Gold, Silver, and precious stones are critical elements of value and wealth. Researchers of the Roman Period also speculated that rapists burned at stake. Also, their women victims punished if they had raped away from home, as they, according to Constantine, should have no business outside the safety of their homes.

In the East, Christian persecution in Constantinople caused Emperor Constantine to convene three hundred Bishops to resolve the conflict between the Western and Eastern Church beliefs so that one definition exists as to what Christians believe. Constantine's wife, who gave birth to three other sons, appeared to lie about Constantine's son so that her sons from a previous marriage would have better career positions in the future. She plotted and told Emperor Constantine that his son tried to have sex with her. The Roman Emperor believed his wife and immediately ordered his son's execution before discovering his wife's betrayal. Upon learning of the truth, he also executed his wife. Later, Emperor Constantine so engulfed in mental pain that he traveled by ship to the Eastern Empire and began a major construction project of Christian Churches in Jerusalem. Constantine the Great was to build a church over St. Peter's tomb named the Basilica of St Peters, thus believing that all of his sins forgiven by God the Father, and for all eternity, his crimes absolved. "Byzantium had first been reconstructed in the time of Septimius Severus not just as a Roman city, but modeled on Rome itself, on and around seven hills." Later, Constantine the Great chose it as his new capital, renaming Constantinople, the central city of the eastern part of the Roman Empire. At Constantine's death at Nicomedia in 337

A.D., three sons and two of his nephews were destined by the late Emperor to succeed him.

THE RISE OF THE BARBARIAN GENERAL

By 371 A.D., over 45% of Roman Officers are of barbarian Slavic descent, and Imperial Rome defined by West and East regions. Roman Empire Collapses. In 378 A.D., Gothic Barbarians launched an attack on Adrianopolis and marked the final melt-down of the Roman Empire. The Battle of Adrianople fought between an Eastern Roman army led by the Eastern Roman Emperor Flavius Julius Valens Augustus, and Gothic rebels, The Greutungs, non-Gothic Alans, and various local insurgents led by Fritigern, a Thervingian Gothic chieftain. The barbarians are savage and relentless fighters. Flavius Julius Valens Augustus dies in the Battle against the Goths. By 382 A.D., the Roman militias depleted in their ranks and Emperor Theodosius I (Son-in-law of Valentinian I, appointed as "Augustus" for the East by Emperor Gratian. After the death of Emperor Flavius Julius Valens "Augustus", Theodosius became sole "senior Augustus" after the end of Valentinian II, makes a decision that marks the start of the decline of Imperial Rome to recruit the Goths Barbarians as legionnaires to fight for Rome. Emperor Theodosius negotiates land for the barbarian Goth's military service.

ROME'S WESTERN REGION

In 392 A.D., the Western Region shocked by the murder of the Emperor of the West. His barbarian guards murder him based on orders from the Frankish General Arbogast. In 394 A.D., headquartered in Constantinople, the Eastern Emperor Theodosius I betray the Gothic General and uses the barbarian Army on the front while he holds his Roman troops in reserve, and then attacks the Goths under his command killing thousands.

Theodosius I an emperor of all of the Western and Eastern Regions of the Roman Empire. However, the Goths take their vengeance as they battle in the Balkans to rob the grain from the Romans. The Roman garrisons cannot stop the barbarians and slowly put to death by torture or beheading. The Goths then name General Alaric I as their King and Ruler. Frankish Generals Arbogast and Eugenius removed as military leaders. Theodosius, I appoint his younger son, the Honorius Western Augustus, with half of the Roman Empire. Once again, the faltering Roman Empire divided into West and East with Theodosius sons commanding the Army. Roman Emperor Theodosius I, also known as Theodosius the Great, dies and becomes "the last emperor to rule over both the eastern and the western halves of the Roman Empire." In the Balkans, the Barbarian Wars do not end.[96]

KORKA'S BARBARIAN CLAN INFILTRATES ROMAN MILITARY

Temunder, son of the Korka Druid high priest, the young barbarian prince can see that the Roman Army is all-powerful, and Rome rules vast territories, takes his sword, and joins the Roman Army in the Balkans. Temunder is a fighter without equal, who eats the flesh of each of his murdered fellow barbarian warriors, is recognized as a warrior leader, and appointed as an auxiliary commander. Soon, after so many victories, he is granted leave to travel to Rome. Temunder is paraded in the streets of Rome and hailed with flowers. When Temunder is allowed to give a speech in the Roman Senate, the Senators cheer him. The Senators rushed to his side and embraced him with cheers and the citizenship of a Roman. He given the Roman name of Atilius Regulus Lupus. Emperor Honorius awarded Lupus the title of General and given the command of ten legions. Roman emperor Honorius is a great Roman military commander in the West. Honorius, with the help of General Lupus, fights together in several campaigns against the barbarians, opposing the invading Visigoths under Alaric in the

Balkans and Italy and repelling an Ostrogothic invasion of Italy in 406 AD. Lupus had the skills to understand logistics.

"One of the chief logistical concerns of General Lupus was feeding his men, cavalry horses, and pack animals, usually mules. "Wheat and barley were the primary food sources. Meat, olive oil, wine, and vinegar also provided." His assigned Army consisted of four legions or 40,000, including soldiers and other personnel such as slaves, would have about 4,000 horses and 3,500 pack animals. His Army ate daily about 60 tons of grain and 240 amphorae of wine and olive oil. Each man receives a portion of about 830 grams (1.8 lb.) of wheat per day in the form of un-milled grain, which is less perishable than flour. Hand mills used to grind it. The supply of all these foodstuffs depended on availability and was hard to guarantee during times of war or other adverse conditions." As the Roman military advanced in Battle, it attracted merchants who sold various items, including foodstuffs with which the soldier might supplement his diet. Further, General Lupus urged the living off the land and to increase the supply lines to ensure that his soldiers had an adequate food supply."[97]

BARBARIAN KORKA HUN ROMAN GENERAL LUPUS

Atilius Regulus Lupus is half-Roman, a half-Hun barbarian by birth, finds the Army as a career, in 383AD he serves on an embassy to the Persian king Shāpūr III, afterward marrying Soraya, the favorite niece of the Emperor Theodosius. He is appointed the manager of the domestics (commanding the Emperor's household troops) 385 and before 393, master of both services (i.e., General Lupus military exploits are well known by 395. He became the enemy of Flavius Rufinus, because of a difference of opinion about the treatment of some barbarian. The Emperor appoints Lupus "to be the guardian of his son Honorius in the West and Rufinus to be the guardian of his son Arcadius in the East. Lupus had a tremendous military advantage over his rival, for the Army Theodosius had assembled to crush the usurper Eugenius. He was still concentrated in the West under Lupus's command when Theodosius died. Before either Lupus or Rufinus could attack the other, the "Visigoths, a Germanic tribe living in Lower Moesia who had suffered severe losses in the campaign against Eugenius, rebelled under the leadership of their chieftain Alaric and began to devastate Thrace and Macedonia."

General Lupus, who claimed for the Western Region Government the prefecture of Illyricum, "disputed between the emperors, went with his Army to Thessaly. About to engage Alaric there; however, he was ordered by Arcadius, acting on Rufinus' advice, to send a number of his troops to Constantinople. General Lupus obeyed and thus enabled Barbarian Alaric to penetrate Greece, but the forces sent to Constantinople murdered Rufinus on November 27, 395." In 397, General Lupus took another army to Greece but failed again to bring Barbarian Gothic Warlord Alaric to Battle and withdrew to Italy. In that same year, Gildo, the governor of Africa, rebelled against the Roman government and refused to allow African grain ships to sail to Rome. Lupus promptly imported grain from Gaul and Spain. In the following year, he sent "Gildo's brother, Mascezel, to Africa with an army. Mascezel overthrew Gildo and put him to death. General Atilius Regulus Lupus contracted professional Korka family assassins to murder Masrezel so that he would not become a rival to his power base.[98]

Eastern Emperor Arcadius (teenager) son of Theodosius I then invites Alaric the Visigoth in 397 A.D. to Constantinople, but the Romans citizens only wanted to kill Alaric the Visigoth. Still, they cannot agree to peace because the Goths are viewed as devilish by the Roman Christians. Alaric the Visigoth goes to Italy to negotiate a better deal there and, at the same time to plan for the barbarian Huns attacks on Rome from the North and for the other Barbarian tribes to attack the Western Region. As the ranks of the Roman Army depleted, General Lupus forced to recruit barbarians. Lupus's daughter Marianna is married to Emperor Honorius, and Lupus arranged for himself to become Consul in

400. As all-powerful Consul, Lupus married Sadira, the niece of the Emperor Theodosius I.

Consul Lupus is quite muscular and stands 6feet and 4inches. At 49 years of age, he had jet black long hair, closely cropped beard, when not in body armor, he enjoys the casual style of wearing a tunic and snakeskin sandals. To stay athletic, the Consul lifts ten-pound stones for his arms and legs. Each day, he would run bare-footed along the sandy track that circles on the outside of the gladiator arena. After his work-out, Lupus drove in a chariot to a cold bath and steam baths. As Consul, Lupus enjoys practicing every day with his favorite weapon, the javelin. The overall length of the spear is 103.2 inches, and it weighs 1.9 pounds. In Battle, Consul Lupus would throw it 436 feet and let is spear over five to six barbarians or at least two mounted horses. Consul Lupus learned to be meticulously prepared and innovative in his military strategies and tactics at a young age. As mounted in battle or standing with his foot soldiers, he inspires all who see him, and they recognize that he is an exceptional military leader. General Lupus never drinks wine to intoxication. He is always encouraging his legions by his physical appearance and his deep, piercing eyes. He spoke only when to inspire.

ROMAN GENERAL ALARIC THE VISIGOTH

Rome would do anything to shore up the ranks in the Roman Army. Thus, the Roman military grows very desperate as the causalities mount from all the incursions from numerous Barbarian tribes. To secure more troops, General Lupus travels to Moesia and recruits more soldiers. General Lupus gave the command to attack the Western Region. The Republic of Serbia was under Roman (and later Byzantine) rule for about 600 years, from the 1st century B.C. until the Slavic invasions of the 6th century. General Lupus agrees that Alaric the Visigoth will be paid, but the Roman Emperor will not honor General's Lupus agreements with Alaric. The Goths demand 4,000 pounds of gold paid immediately. If he does not pay, then all Goths' soldiers in the Roman Army will revolt. Alaric the Visigoth overruns the Balkan Peninsula. In 497AD, Alaric militarily restrained by General Flaviuset Lupus. Alaric gave Illyria that was inhabited in the western part of the Balkan Peninsula by the Illyrians.

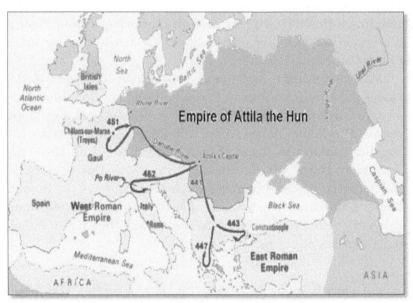

Map of Empire of Attila the Hun – Courtesy of freeenglishsite.com

Emperor Constantine III begins spreading rumors against Barbarian Roman Atilius Regulus Lupus as not being one hundred percent vandal barbarian. He was married to Serena, the niece of the Emperor Theodosius. The Roman Army at Ticinum mutinied on August 13, 408, killing at least seven senior imperial officers. Roman politicians made up coordinated coup d'état organized by Lupus's political opponents.[99]

In 408AD, over 10,000 Goths, men, women, and children, are killed in all the Roman cities by the Roman Army. Goths who escape join Alaric's Barbarian Army. The Roman General Lupus's promises of land and gold. In 409AD, known by his friends and troops as "Florentissimo Invictis Simoque".[100]

Lupus dies five days after eating fresh berries given to him by Sadira. The man who was a barbarian, Korka's Hun shadow agent, is carried in a religious procession dedicating him as a God elevated to sitting on the right-hand side of Mars. Temuder, known as the Roman General Lupus, lay within a heroic carved 1000 square foot marble enclosure with his muscular depicted statue standing with his hand on the spear in a throwing position. Sadira is arrested and crucified upside down. She dies twelve days later from an agonizing death.[101]

Alaric's powerful Barbarian Army attacks Rome in 410AD. Under pressure from Roman Senators, Emperor Honorius signs an agreement to give Alaric the 4,000 pounds of gold if he stops the siege of Rome. In good faith, the Roman Emperor, with his legions, marches to Ravenna Italy to seal the deal. However, "barbarian thugs" attack Alaric's Army. With this act, Alaric the Barbarian believes betrayal and lack of honor of the Roman Emperor Honorius. The Barbarian Chief Alaric goes back to Rome to begin another siege. The Goths break down the gates of Rome, burn and sack all towns.[102]

LAST ROMAN BARBARIAN EMPEROR ATTILA THE HUN

Italy Historical Regions- Courtesy of time maps U.K.

Attila the Hun is ruthless and becomes the bloodletting barbarian that Rome has ever fought in a battle. In vicious intensity, Attila's many armies lay waste to what left of the Roman Empire in the East. In 449 AD, the western region of Pannonia is succeeded to Attila the Hun. Orestes, who is on the high court of Attila, comes up with a plan to merge the Huns and Roman armies. The merger set to be signed when Attila's blood vessels on his legs begin bleeding, and Attila, the Hun dies immediately. Rome begins to disintegrate as a sovereign ruling State.[103]

BARBARIAN TRIBES

Burgundians were a large East Germanic or Vandal tribe or group of tribes, who lived in the area of modern Poland in the time of the Roman Empire. Burgundians tribe (Footnote: Scandinavians) from North-settle in southern Gaul is given more land in the West. Rome gives more land to the Barbarians, and their tax base diminishes, creating economic disasters. In 473AD, Burgundian King made a Master of Soldiers, and the Turks, Germans, and other Barbarian tribes make up the Roman Army. Flavius Orestes starts as the sole General Military Commander, but from the town of Herculian named Flavius Odoacer is also picked. (Footnote: Flavius Odoacer (433 – 493AD), also known as Flavius Odovacer, was a soldier who in 476AD. Probably of Scirian descent, Odoacer was a military leader in Italy who led the revolt of Herulian, Rugian, and Scirian soldiers that deposed Romulus). Co-commanders now exist; namely, one Roman and the other a Barbarian. Still, Rome suffers from the Visigoths and Goths. The Roman Army cannot be one unit as fights break out between Roman and barbarian soldiers. The Roman Army soldiers no longer fight for the Rome Empire but only themselves. Italy suffers from barbarians attacking along the coast of Italy, but the Roman Empire capital of the East, Constantinople, is prosperous. The Western Empire is an economic disaster.

MONGOLS HISTORICAL FOOTPRINT

As a tribe from Central North Asia the Mongols. Their area of habitat was on the steppe and lived a life of moving from place to place with no set base camp location. They only loved their horses as this was their primary means of movement. They saw spiritual life in all forms of animate and inanimate forms. Even with these limitations, the Mongols created a large empire and lived in harmony with the tribes of Northern China and Central Asia with the Turkic and Tatars. The Mongol warriors lived for war and thus engaged in battles with their neighbors. It was in the reign of Emperor Shi Huang (247-221 B.C.) that the Great Wall of China was built to keep the warring Mongols out of China. Throughout history, they were usually at war with their neighbors. China to the south, in fact, built the Great Wall of China during the reign of Emperor Shi Huang (247-221 BC) as a means to keep the Mongols and others away from their villages.[104]

EAST MEETS WEST

The Eastern Emperor appoints Julius Nepos in Constantinople to the Regional Command. Emperor Glycerius is the Emperor of the West and mounts an army to meet Julius Nepos army from the East. The barbarian leaders Odoacer and King Widimir in the West decide to desert the Emperor of the East. Further, the Roman militias and the Barbarian forces will not fight for the Western Emperor. The Western Roman army surrenders, and Glycerius is made a Bishop and sent to exile. Julius Nepos then crowned Emperor of the West. Both Germanic Odoacer and Flavius Orestes gave the highest of commands in the Julius Nepos Court in Rome. All along, Visigoths continue to attack Gaul. Roman territory in the West continues to shrink from the Visigoth's bloody attacks. Flavius Orestes then tries to undermine the Germanic Odoacer. Gaul lost to the Visigoths and Odoacer with his Army tries to attack Rome and capture the Emperor and Flavius Orestes, but both flee to Piacenza.

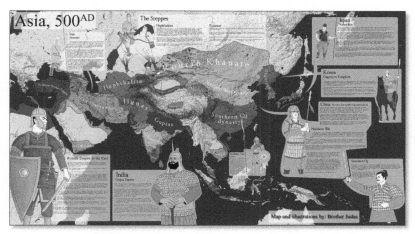

Asia AD 500 – Map Courtesy of Judas i.imgur.com

ROMAN EMPIRE DISINTEGRATES

In 475 AD, Romulus Augustus, youngest son of Flavius Orestes, is named Emperor, but he will not attack the barbarians. Instead, he remains in Ravenna, a walled defense barrier to protect Roman City, but the Barbarian Army stops its siege and demands property, and gold promised. Flavius Orestes does not have land or gold to give to the Heruli, Scirian, and Torcilingi mercenaries. In 476AD, the uncivilized turn to Odoacer for help, and he agrees to join the barbarians to take over all power from General Flavius Orestes.[105] Since the uncivilized cannot get land or gold, and they will kill all Roman citizens. Flavius Orestes fearing for his life escapes to Northern Italy and leaves his son in Ravenna, but Odoacer takes over the Army, and Flavius Orestes tries to mount another Army. The barbarians' battle savagery overtook Flavius Orestes and knifed to death by the Barbarians who take over all of Rome and mount attacks on Ravenna. The fourteen-year-old boy Emperor

Romulus Augustus exiled, and Herculian Odoacer becomes the First Barbarian King of Rome, but not the Emperor. After only 500 years, the Roman Empire ends. Barbarians now get the land promised to fight for the Roman Army. In the former Western Empire, the massive immigration of the barbarians begins. As the barbarians entered Rome, Romans viewed them as a devilish negative force. The barbarians retained their tribal culture and refused to assimilate into Roman customs and laws.[106]

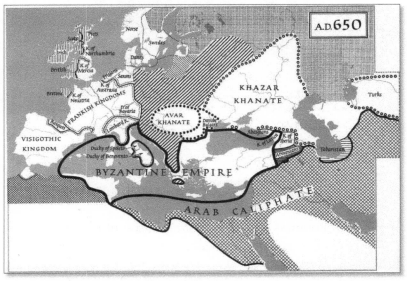

Byzantine Empire AD 650 -Courtesy Micah Course Columbia Education

EGYPT -PROVINCE OF AEGYPTUS

Aegyptus was by far the wealthiest Eastern Roman province and governed in 30 B.C. to 641 A.D. after Emperor Augustus battled and defeated Mark Antony and removed his Queen Cleopatra VII, who ruled the Ptolemaic Kingdom of Egypt to become part of the Roman Empire. The province was a major producer of grain for the Empire and had a highly developed urban economy.[107]

In Alexandria, its capital, ancient Egypt, possessed the largest port and the second-largest city of the Roman Empire. Even early on, but less frequently than in later times, the miners were according to Ptahhotep was the city administrator and vizier (first minister) during the reign of Djedkare Isesi in the 5th Dynasty credited with authoring The Instruction of Ptahhotep, a prime piece of Egyptian "wisdom literature" meant to instruct young men to follow appropriate behavior.[108]

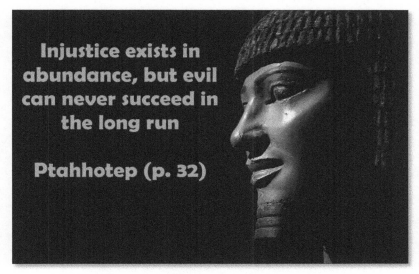

Injustice exists in abundance, but evil can never succeed in the long run

Ptahhotep (p. 32)

Ptahhotep Quote – Courtesy of storemypic.com

The good-will of the gods was of importance to the Egyptians, who often built shrines near the mines. Sanctuaries of Hathor, (Goddess of the sky, dance, love, beauty, joy, motherhood, foreign lands, mining, music, and fertility) the principal protector of miners, have been found at Timna in the Negev, in the Sinai desert at Serabit el Khadim, and other places. Ameni, who led a small expedition of about thirty men to Wadi Maghara in the 42nd year of Amenemhet III's Egyptian Reign, left an inscription "… The treasurer, assistant of the chief treasurer, Sesostris--seneb-Sebekkhi, favorite of Hathor, mistress of the malachite country, of

Soped, lord of the East, of Snefru, lord of the highlands, and of the gods and goddesses who are in this land. -were made for Hathor, all beautiful mine-chambers."[109]

ANCIENT METAL MINING

Copper - Atomic number: 29 - Melting point: 1984°F (1085°C)

Copper is the first metal worked in Egypt during the Neolithic (6th millennium BCE -5300 to 2600 BCE). Copper was generally mined under dreadful conditions. The miners were the least fortunate captives from Egypt's wars of expansion, enslaved and worked to death in the mines in western Sinai, Timna, and other locations in the Arabah Valley, which stretches from the Gulf of Aqaba to the Dead Sea.

TIN - ATOMIC NUMBER 50 - BOILING POINT 2270 °C

Tin, a necessary ingredient for bronze, was not mined in Egypt and had to be imported from Syria. Existing iron ore deposits not exploited in ancient Egypt until the Late Period, but the metal was occasionally found in its meteoric form and put to use as early as the 4th millennium BCE.

GOLD- ATOMIC NUMBER 79 - MELTING POINT 1062 °C

Gold was one of the first metals to be exploited. The gold of the mountains, as the scribes of "Ramses III called it, was found mainly in the Eastern Desert and Nubia. Agatharchides' description dates from the second century BCE. Diodorus Siculus reported that 'The galleries which they dig ... are not straight, but run in the direction of the metal-containing vein, and as the workers are in the dark in these winding tunnels, they carry torches which affixed to their foreheads ... non-nubile children enter these underground galleries and lift with great pains the loosened chunks of ore and take them outside."[110]

ROMAN COLONY OF EGYPT

In Egypt, an adjunct of gold, silver was in the very early days of metalworking rarer and dearer than the gold itself, later, during the New Kingdom, its value was about half of that of gold. The Sinai malachite (sehmet) and turquoise (mafaket) deposits have attracted miners since the sixth millennium BCE. Near Serabit el-Khadim, a few kilometers inland from the western coast of the Sinai Peninsula, turquoise deposits were discovered by the middle of the fourth millennium BCE and taken over by the Egyptians a few centuries later.

CHAPTER THREE

EAST & WEST - MONGOLS, CRUSADERS, & ISLAM

"Don't ask to be loved, seek to be feared." Machiavelli

CHINA AND MONGOL HISTORICAL CULTURE CONNECTIONS -TRADITIONAL VALUES OF CHINESE HAN FAMILY

FOR NEARLY 2 000 years, the family's very foundation has been the organizing principle of Chinese society. "Confucian values" is shorthand for the idea that a peaceful community built on the family as an extended, stable unit of several generations under one roof, each with a distinct social role and status.

Kalmyks were the descendants of the Mongolian tribes that remained along the lower Volga. Their distinctive "Konfederatkas" was a new type of "Czapski" (helmet or crown) that was universally used by Lancers.

MING DYNASTY 1368–1644

The Ming dynasty was the ruling dynasty of China or the Empire of the Great Ming (1368–1644) following the collapse of the Mongol-led Yuan dynasty. Empire of the Great Ming had these weapons would include early firearms. The Ming military employed various cannons and swiveled guns on the wall to defend against the Mongolian horsemen north of the wall. During this time, the Chinese who lived during the Ming Dynasty were also buying and learning to build firearms from the Portuguese, Dutch, and Ottoman Turks. The Ming Army also saw some use of matchlock muskets against the Mongolians. Still, the inaccuracy and slow rate of fire of these weapons limited their feasibility against nomadic cavalry. Still, matchlock muskets often used in conjunction with wagons during the many Ming campaigns against the steppe.[6] The carriage provided with wooden shields where musketeers hide behind to fire and load while blocking the arrows of Mongolian bows. During this time, the Chinese also experienced various multi-barrel guns in an attempt to raise the firing rate of gunpowder weapons. One of these weapons includes a triple barrel musket and a Roman candle weapon, which consisted of multiple charges stacked behind each other in a metal barrel, which provided continuous fire when lit.[7]

THE GREATEST OF MONGOLS -GENGHIS KHAN-1206-1227

Temujin was born into the nomadic clan of royalty but raised in slavery. Temujin fled the rugged plains of Mongolia and arrived by the Great Wall of China. In 1206, the warrior Temüjin received the title of Genghis Khan. Temujin is the last successors to Genghis as overlord of all the Mongol territories Kublai Khan, the grandson of Genghis Khan, reigning from 1260 to 1294 as the fifth Khagan of the Mongol Empire. In 1271, he established the Chinese Yuan dynasty. The Great Khan ruled until he died in 1294. The Mongol Empire ruled over the Chagatai Khanate, the Golden Horde, and the Ilkhanate. In 1368, its Confucianism was part of the Chinese social fabric and way of life; to Confucians, everyday life was the arena of religion.[1] (Bibliography: A Nation of Individuals-The Economist)

Ties were vertical and hierarchical, defined by respect and obligations flowing from the young to the old, from the kinship group to the Emperor. Family values were part of a vision the Emperor had of a harmonious China. For hundreds of years, marriage was primarily an economic contract between two families. Bonding designed to ensure heirs for the groom's clan. But in the one-child society, a child is regarded as the center of the family, so weddings are focused on the groom's parents. Putting self-interest above the collective interest was "basically illegitimate" to do so, said William Jankowiak of the University of Nevada, Las Vegas.[2]

SON OF HEAVEN

In Imperial China, the Emperor was the Son of Heaven. He had to do secret rituals to maintain the cosmic balance in society. The Chinese Imperial government had formed a committee of the right worship by his subjects. The key participant in all rituals was the Emperor, for this was his duty as Emperor. Every year there was annual worship of heaven, which was the most important day of the imperial ritual calendar. Worship not only to pray but to do rituals for all the past dynasties and emperors and their relatives. The Chinese people believed if the Emperor ritualized the ancestors, he was a noble and good form of Chinese Confucian. When the Emperor worshiped legitimacy, the idea to the continuation of past dynasties, imperial institutions.

Confucius stated at the time "that if a ruler himself is upright, all will go well without orders. Even though he gives orders, they will not listen if he is not upright."[3]

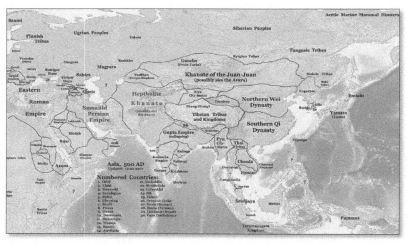

China NoWei Dynasty- Courtesy ofnationsonline.org

RED DAWN WARLORD IN WEI DYNASTY 386CE TO 534CE.

The Wei Emperor (or Khan) began to call up troops to fight the invading Mongol and nomadic tribes. If there had been a son, he could have gone to his father's place as it was only up to the family to provide one man to fight. Whether it was the father or the son did not matter; all they needed to do was offer one person to join the military. Dasoh is born the girl of Khutulan and RedDawn Hun Warlord Nasan. At twelve years of age, when she needs to express her male strengths and disguise herself as a boy, Dasoh travels to

China. Dasoh has struggled with her identity since she was five. She has these feelings and behaviors of a lesbian character. She is rejected by her brothers Dalan, Vachir, and Temuder for wanting to hunt with them and engage in the arts of war.

Dasoh suffers immense pain, anxiety, and anger. Dasoh travels alone and finally arrives in Chin, and starving meets a farmer named Li Yi, who never had a daughter or boys. They live together, and then Li Yi adopts her as his daughter. At eight years of age, Dasoh changes her name to Sima Yi, now disguised as a man. As is customary, Li Yi is enlisted at the age of seventy-one to fight with the Emperor's Army. Sima Yi takes her father's military obligation and joins in the military. Sima Yi prepared to fight against the Mongolian and nomadic tribes that wanted to invade Imperial China. Her stepfather Li Yi trained Dasoh on how to be skilled with weapons. But during her enlistment, she practiced Kung Fu and rode horses while shooting arrows. After six years of proving herself as a ruthless battlefield horse fighter, she, still disguised as a man, is given the rank of Lt. General to reward her for her battle skills. However, without her identity discovered, Sima Yi returns to her village of Yingchuan to live a solitary life. Except for her sexuality found in the communal bathhouse by her best friend, Sima Yi is praised and honored as a man. The secret kept until found in a Buddhist cave frozen to death at forty-eight years of age.[4]

NORTHERN SONG DYNASTY (960–1127)

A hereditary order flourished within the early Song society. The society Song governed by a central bureaucracy of scholar-officials chosen through the civil-service examination. Chinese Dynasty Scholars viewed themselves as the ruling elite. The result at times was friction with others in the community and then forced to retire. Soon as a form of revolt, those outcasts pursued artistic endeavors like painting and writing.[5]

Song ceased to exist, but the name of Khagan endured by the rulers of the Northern Yuan dynasty was a weaker military threat. However, when Genghis Khan became the tribe's chieftain from 1206 to 1227, the historical realities of the Mongols changed forever. Genghis Khan was a ruthless negotiator, and he united by force all the Mongol tribes and the Turkic tribes as well. The Turkic tribes originated in Mongolia, southern Siberia, Xinjiang, and East-Central Asia. Once united, Genghis Khan planned to conquer all the lands that Mongolian horseback riders could reach. When he arrived at the Great Wall, the Chinese Emperor Shi Huang gave him great gifts and honors. He given the title Genghis Khan or Prince of Conquerors. Khan conquered most of Northern China in the 1210s by obliterating the Xia and Jin dynasties. Also, subjugating Beijing and all Turkic tribes of Central Asia and Iran (Persia).

Genghis Khan pays one hundred ninety pounds of gold and silver to the Korka Clan's Eastern European network of spies and assassins. That payment for assassination and spying in Poland and Hungary, and as far as eastern Austria, in preparation for an attack into the heartland of Europe. The Korka Clan in a secret meeting held in a hotel in Warsaw Poland selects Dalan II, the great-grandson of Nasan, the warlord of the Red Dawn, and Taban II, the great-granddaughter of Nasan. They travel to Poland, Hungary, Austria, Serbia, Bulgaria, and Georgia by horse and carriage disguised as ministerial officers of King Wenceslaus I of Bohemia. The mission ordered to raise funds and troops to fight the Mongols.[8]

As the size and speed of Genghis Khan's 20,000 to 40,000 (2 to 4 lumens) Mongol cavalries' slice into Eastern Europe, attacking Kievan Rus' principalities and even the borders of Central Europe's Germania states. Kyiv sacked. Crimea's population killed by the Golden Hordes. More important than what Genghis Khan conquered was how he captured. Genghis

Khan used earlier Roman Legions' terror tactics as a weapon of war. If a city surrendered without a fight, its population would usually be allowed to live, and they had to submit to live under Mongol control. If the city took up arms, all men, women, and children murdered and their heads placed on spikes throughout the city—at least 40% of the population killed by slaughter or epidemic. Genghis Khan knew that fear of death would make him a winning conqueror. People who think of the torture and pain allow their imagination to cripple their fighting spirit, for they would die in the end. Genghis Khan's successor, Ogedei, viewed the Muslim world as a threat to his Mongol Kingdom. Still, he knew that in 1255 he wanted to conquer the desert kingdoms. The Great Khan, Mongke, convinced his brother Hulagu Khan to command an army with only one purpose. The Army conquer Persia, Syria, and Egypt. Also, to destroy the Abbasid Caliphate with Capitals in Baghdad, Damascus, Kufa, Samarra, Cairo, Raqqa, and Abbasid Samarra. Hulagu Khan, intensely hate the Koran instructed to annihilate Islamic believers. Islam preached no tolerance for Buddhists and Christians. Buddhists and Christians in the Caliphate capitals were beheaded or nailed to a cross upside down and punctured slow bleeding wounds.[9] In 1314, a Crusade in Hungary mounted against the Mongols and Lithuanians. This Crusade later renewed by the papacy in 1325, 1332, 1335, 1352, and 1354. The Mongol Negus or Chonos tribe had developed a less than a Nomadic life, but had established stockades and increased their armament to fight the Crusaders. Their tents still made of animal hides. Their life center was still horses but had carts made with wooden wheels. They existed to blunder and to raid other villages to capture a blue-eyed woman and sell them to other tribes. In some cases, they would only use their slaves for domestic activities or to feed the animals. To the Chonos, to die in battle was a sign that their god gave the tribe more excellent protection and prosperity. Violence was part of their everyday life. When they would kill other members of the tribes, they felt no guilt, but pure joy. The holy man or shaman was a vital member of the inner circle of the tribe of Chonos. Shamans administered rituals to protect tribal members. All male slaves had not worth and put to death. However, female slaves lived who gave birth to a baby boy whose father was a psychotic warrior male.[10]

ISLAMIC CALIPHATE AND THE MONGOLS

The 1200s started out looking right for the expanding Islamic caliphate, and the Mongols expanded their territorial ambitions. In 1260, the Mongols invaded Southeast Asia. With the establishment of the Yuan dynasty in 1271, the Kublaids became Yuan emperors, who were considered as Khagan for the Mongols and Huangdi (Chinese emperor) for native Chinese. By 1277, the Mongol Armies entered Burma and established their governing authority. Their reign existed until 1283 in Burma. In 1284, Mongols were on the march again. Mongols conquer the jurisdiction of China, known as Annam. A year later, Champa's armies rose and defeated the Mongol Army. Khan forced to China's safe territories. In 1292 the first Mongol naval fleet in Southeast Asia was organized to defeat Champa's armies, but the Annam-Mongol forces were defeated. The military actions of the Mongols had three main effects on the region. First, Champa and NamViet united as one. Secondly, the Burmese defeat caused the Thai Independence movement as a separate country. Finally, the Mongol campaigns to conquer new lands led to the decline of the Indian-governed Kingdoms.

OTTOMAN EMPIRE

Known as the "Turkish Empire, or Ottoman Turkey was founded at the end of the thirteenth century in northwestern Anatolia in the vicinity of Bilecik and Söğüt by the Oghuz Turkish tribal leader Osman. After 1354, the Ottomans crossed into Europe. With the conquest of the Balkans, the Ottoman Beylik transformed into a transcontinental empire. The Ottomans ended the Byzantine

Empire (known to the Ottomans as the Roman Empire) with the 1453 conquest of Constantinople by Mehmed the Conqueror. During the 16th and 17th centuries, at the height of its power under the reign of Suleiman the Magnificent, the Ottoman Empire was a multinational, multilingual empire controlling much of Southeast Europe, parts of Central Europe, Western Asia, the Caucasus, North Africa, and the Horn of Africa.

Armenian Kingdom of Cilicia- Courtesy of Pinterest

At the turn of the 17th century, the Ottoman Empire governed 32 provinces and numerous feudal states. During centuries some of these were absorbed while other countries became independent. The Ottomans held the prior Roman city Constantinople as their capital and rule the lands around the Mediterranean basin. For over sixty years, the Ottoman capital stood as the gateway for both East and West.[11] The founder Osman I began to build the Ottoman Empire when he found it in 1299. Using military force, he conquered states and demanded loyalty of the population or death would fallow. On September 27, 1371, Battle of Maritsa. Serbia made to declare allegiance to the Ottoman Empire. On September 25, 1396, Battle of Nicopolis. Bulgaria conquered. On July 20, 1402, the Battle of Ankara. Ottomans entered into a lengthy siege. On October 17–20,1448, The Battle of Kosovo II. Balkans fully began the Ottoman reign. In 1463, Bosnia conquered. In 1498, Montenegro captured. In1526, Battle of Mohács. Suleiman I, defeat Louis II of Hungary and Bohemia. In 1590, The Treaty of İstanbul between the Ottoman Empire and the Safavids, Georgia, Azerbaijan, and Armenia as well as western Iran under Ottoman rule. During 1672-76 was In the Polish-Ottoman War of 1672-1676, Ottoman defeated Kamianets-Podilskyi (Kamaniçe). After that war, the Ottoman Empire reached its highest point in the control of Eastern Europe. After 1676, revolts sprung up against Ottoman rule. The First and Second Serbian revolt uprising began in the 1800s.[12]

SYRIA DURING THE ROMAN EMPIRE

Eventually, in 539 BCE, the Persians (Iranians) took Syria as part of their empire. In 64 BCE, the Roman General Pompey the Great, captured Antioch, turning Syria into a Roman province. The city of Antioch was the third-largest city in the Roman Empire after Rome and Alexandria. The swamp that is 2018 contemporary Syria is as infinitely involved as it was when it emerged from the ruins of the Ottoman Empire. Its medley of cultures and ethnicities coexisted peaceably under the sultans. Still, the European powers that inherited the land after World War I were unfamiliar and not interested in maintaining Syria's unique brand of pluralism. Instead, following Roman rule, Syria embraced centralized rule.[13]

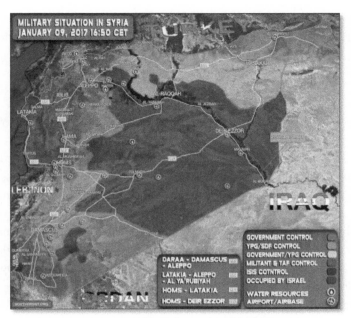

Syria war map Jan 2017 Courtesy of SouthFront.org

CONTEMPORARY SYRIA – TARGET FOR COVERT WAR

From 2016-2020, warring factions populate the Syrian battlefield. This covert operation led to the unraveling of Syria's once-cohesive society. "Identity politics strategy" of western covert military designed for civil war. Today, the lessons of the Ottoman Empire remain. Perhaps, those lessons may be the best hope for turning a failed state into a nation at once unified and diverse. Now, Syria's Civil War reached a milestone of eight years (2012-2020). After Syria's challenges over the centuries to maintain its sovereignty as a nation, the covert campaigns by the Western Powers' intelligence agencies used the historical friction between the various religious and ethnic communities to ignite the deep-seated hatred of these groups buried thousands of years ago. The Syrian Observatory for Human Rights, a British-based war monitor, wrote in October

2018 that an estimated 511,000 people killed in the Syrian Civil War. In the 1862-1865 American Civil War, 625,000 Americans buried.

BASHAR AL ASSAD'S GOVERNANCE

Even President Bashar al Assad embodied some of the Ottoman Empire respect for minority groups. Under Bashar al Assad's government, the arbitrary division of ethnic and religious groups into modern states balanced by his consideration for the needs of these communities. A few journalists witnessed firsthand in Damascus. In 2020, former colonialist empires of France, England, and Germany sought a truth. Namely, the borders drawn by the Sykes-Picot agreement a century ago may well have outlived the agreement's usefulness. Would it make sense that new boundaries drawn due to the EU/USA "Looking Glass" in light of broader social and political realities could be the beginning of a robust and lasting resolution to Syria's war? The world will have to wait as former Sovereign Nations (Libya, Syria, Iraq, Afghanistan, and Bosnia) regain their borders and cultural groups.[14]

OTTOMAN TURKS

In the sixth century, the Ottoman Turks, over 500 years, claimed to be the leader of Islam. Caliphate is the successor of the Prophet, Guardian of Islam, and therefore the power center of all world's Muslims. During the migration's era when Turks, Germans, and Slavs were migrating in vast numbers, Turks came to the Balkans in the 4th century. The Mediaeval State of Bulgaria, named after the Volga Bulgars, a Turkish people who lived for 1000 years in a Turkish state in Europe as was the Khanate of the Crimean Tatars. By the time Ottoman rule came, they had met Turks who had been living there for 1000 years. The confusion existed because these Turks called themselves Bulgar, Petcheneg, Cuman, or Hun. Ottomans came to Europe earlier than the conquest of Constantinople (1453). Following the Battle of Kosovo in 1389, the Balkans were under Ottoman control. Balkan's power much earlier than the Ottoman conquest of eastern Anatolian Beyliks, which did not come until the 1500s. Albanian, Bulgaria, and Macedonian were more Ottoman than many modern Turkish cities such as Erzurum. Greece was always impoverished economic territory., and it was the same under Ottoman rule. In 1908, the Ottoman dominance over other states ceased to exist. Without the autocratic foundation of the Ottomans, the Balkan Peninsula and the Arab East burst into violent political movements of independence. Albania, as well as Iraq, fought to protect Mecca and Jeddah in Saudi Arabia.[15]

The Expansion of Russia under Peter the Great. Peter added vital territory on the Baltic Sea to the vast Russian empire.

Territorial Expansion of Russia By Peter I — Courtesy ofSlideshare.com

The Ottoman Empire was the dominant force in the region for several hundred years. The expansion of Russia's southern frontier, begun in earnest in the late 17th century by Peter I (the Great), frequently brought the two powers into conflict. Over the next two centuries, Russia and the Ottoman Empire engaged in a series of wars for control of the Black Sea region.

Treaty of Küçük Kaynarca – Courtesy of YouTube

One of those conflicts, fought from 1768 to 1774, concluded with the Treaty of Küçük Kaynarca (1774) that ceded to Russia fortresses on the Kerch Peninsula and established an independent Crimean Tatar state. In 1783 Catherine II (the Great) annexed the peninsula, and it became Russian territory. The Islamic State of Iraq and the Levant, alternatively translated the Islamic State of Iraq and Syria or Islamic State of Iraq and al-Sham, is a Salafi jihadist terrorist group that follows an Islamic fundamentalist Wahhabi doctrine of Sunni Islam.[16]

VLADIMIR THE GREAT

"You can kill those who speak the truth, but once spoken, the truth will live forever." Leo Tolstoy

By the very end of the 10th Century, Vladimir Sviatoslavich, revered as Vladimir the Great, brought Christianity to the majority of the Rus population. The small village of Kiev (Kyiv) excelled in trading and soon an important part of Kievan Rus. Kievan Rus was an influential medieval city-state) and the largest in Eastern Europe from the late 9th to the mid-13th century. However, the ruthless and savage Mongol invasions of 1237 to 1240 destroyed Kiev as a stable trading location.[17]

MEDIEVAL KNIGHTS

In medieval times, the elite warriors were the knights and when introduced in a battle decisively changed the outcome. The army that had the largest number of knights won the contest. Only men who could prove their military skills on the battlefield were knighted. Over time, the title of a knight became reserved for sons of knights who were almost always nobles. To become a knight, a warrior had to start as early as seven or eight years of age and the training would continue until the age of twenty-one. The night before granting of knighthood, fasting and all-night prayers are completed. During the accolade ceremony, the monarch then raises the sword gently just up over the young man's head and places it on his left shoulder. The new knight then stands up, and the king or queen presents him with the insignia of his new order.[19]

THE CRUSADES MILITARY CAMPAIGNS (1095 – 1291)

The Crusades were sanctioned by the Roman Catholic Church in the Middle-Ages. A complex 200-year struggle ensued that resulted in dire consequences for the 21st Century. During the many decades that followed, Islam tribal elders and their children used the Crusades as an example of Christians seeking to eliminate the teachings of the Quran. In 1095, Byzantine Emperor Alexios I, in Constantinople, sent an ambassador to Roman Catholic Pope Urban II in Italy. Pope Urban II in Italy pleaded for military help against the growing Turkish Islamic threat. Pope Alexious I's used the Crusades to repair the 1054 break-up of the Western and Eastern branches of the Christian Church. The Pope in Rome would be the Pontiff of the united church. All Roman Catholic soldiers were expected to join the First Crusade or "going to the cross." The Muslim's controlled the holy sites in Jerusalem and the Pope wanted to ensure that the Christian Holy Sites would be protected as well as the Christian pilgrims. Christian Knights had to go to Palestine and free Jerusalem and other holy places from Muslim domination. The First Crusade was a great success for the Christian armies; Jerusalem and other cities were secured by the knights. In 1148, the Second Crusade armies of France and Germany were weak and could not destroy Damascus. In 1187, Jerusalem was liberated from the Crusaders by the Shia sect, Ismaili Fatimids. Also, a new Persian Khwarazmian Empire emerged in the region. In 1192, the Third Crusade resulted in a compromise between English King Richard the Lion-Hearted of England and the Muslim leader Saladin, who granted access to Christians to the holy places. The Fourth Crusade led to the sacking of Constantinople. In 1204, the Latin Kingdom of Byzantium was established and lasted for about 60 years. The Children's Crusade of 1212 ended with thousands of children being sold into slavery, lost, or beheaded. In 1291, the final Roman Catholic Church outpost in Constantinople fell to the sword of the Muslim fighters.[19]

FIRST CRUSADE

From 1119 to 1129 the First Crusading Military Orders were a hybrid creation combining knighthood and monasticism. The "Brother Knights" lived under a monastic rule modeled in the case of the Rule of the Templars upon the Cistercian rule. Their monastic work ethic was prayer and warfare. Like the Cistercians, the Military Orders only accepted adults into their ranks.[20]

Crusader 1600-Courtesy of Jenny Ruth

HOLY AND JUST WARS

In 400 A.D., St. Augustine of Hippo developed a benchmark for what is a just and holy war that Christians could participate in. The key was a right intention that would be an expression of the love of God and neighbor, but it must be proclaimed by a higher authority to be just and legitimate. The religious dogma for a Holy Crusade War assumed that violence and death and injury as a result of that violence is always morally neutral rather than intrinsically bad or that it was a matter of intention if that violence would be viewed as good or evil. Jesus Christ is concerned with the political order of man, and intends for his agents on earth, kings, popes, and bishops, to establish on earth the Christian Republic that was a "single, universal, transcendental state' ruled by Christ through the lay and clerical magistrates he endowed with authority. It follows from this doctrine that the defense of the Christian Republic against God's enemies, whether foreign infidel (Turks) or domestic heretics and Jews was a moral imperative for those qualified to fight. A Crusade was a holy war fought against external or internal enemies for the recovery of Christian property or defense of the Church or the Christian people. It could war against Turks in Palestine, Muslims in Spain, Pagan Slavs in the Baltic, or heretics in southern France, all of whom were enemies or rebels against God.[21]

ROME LOOTED AND DESTROYED

In the 846 A.D., a Saracen fleet of 73 ships landed at Ostia, and raided inland, sacking Rome. In doing so, they burnt the churches of St. Peter and St. Paul. The new Pope Leo IV (847-855 A.D.) ordered Rome's walls to be rebuilt and refurbished and had the walls extended to protect the Vatican hill. He also formed a naval alliance with the cities of Amalfi, Naples, and Gaeta, which drove off a Saracen fleet in 849 AD.

Three years later Pope Leo IV issued a call to the Germanic Franks, declaring -" Whoever meets death steadfastly in this fight against Muslim raiders of Italy, the Heavenly Kingdom will not be closed to him."[22]

In 950 AD., the revival of Christian trade in the Mediterranean, like Venice, Amalfi, Pisa, and Genoa successfully confronted Arab pirates; long-distance trade routes began to be dominated by Italian and Jewish merchants. Merchant guilds developed as sworn associations or confraternities of merchants to protect, avenge, and pay for the funerals of their members. The Siege of Antioch (Oct 20, 1097-June 3, 1098) proved a turning point. This long siege turned into a competitive starving match during which many crusaders refused to fight and fled. Regional tribal Turkish rulers were beaten by the Crusaders but they could not take the city.

The Turkish ruler Bohemond hatched a plot to have all the other rulers give him Antioch and once that was accomplished, he paid five gold bars to a Korka warden of a key watch tower to leave the watch tower un-guarded and allow the Crusaders to enter the city.

The Crusaders took the city by treachery. However, the Crusaders were in the city walls but caught between the main citadel and the outer walls. As a main Turkish Army led by the Kerbogha, Governor of Mosul, approached in the distance, the Crusaders had made little progress to advance and found themselves starving without re-stocking their supplies. Kerbogha now attacked and sieged the city with the Crusaders weakened inside. During the siege, "Peter the Hermit was sent as the emissary to Kerbogha by the Christian princes in the city, to suggest that the parties settle all differences by duel. Presumably feeling his position secure, Governor Kerbogha declined."[23]

SECOND CRUSADE

From 1101 to 1102, the Crusade of the Faint-hearted (coda to the First Crusade). Pope Paschal II, taking up where his predecessor Pope Urban II left off, preached another crusade to aid the fledgling Kingdom of Jerusalem. The 2nd crusade of 1101 was almost annihilated in Asia Minor by the Seljuqs (footnote: a member of any of the Turkish dynasties that ruled Asia Minor in the 11th to 13th centuries, successfully invading the Byzantine Empire and defending the Holy Land against the Crusader). Pope Paschal II called in particular upon those who had taken but failed to fulfill the crusader's vow but had not fulfilled it, whom he threatened with excommunication, and those who had left the First Crusade before it reached Jerusalem (the "faint-hearted"). The result was another large, disorganized crusade, even more, heterogeneous and far less successful than the First Crusade.

SECOND CRUSADER'S ARMY

The most massive contingents of the Second Crusader's Army were townspeople and peasants from Lombardy (northern Italy). Others came from various parts of France and Germany. Among the Crusades' leaders were Count Stephen of Blois and Count Hugh of Verminous, both seeking to restore the honor they had lost by leaving the First Crusade prematurely. Stephen of Blois, who had left the crusade just before Antioch was taken and was on his way back to his mortified wife Adela, convinced "Alexius that the Crusaders' situation was hopeless and that there was no point in coming to their rescue. When all seemed lost, a simple soldier in Count Raymond's southern French army, Peter Bartholomew, had visions in which St. Andrew told him where to find the Holy Lance. The discovery of the "Holy Lance" was greeted with skepticism by Bohemond and Bishop Adhemar of Le Puy, but it raised morale in the ranks and was an essential factor in the Crusaders victory over Kerbogha's relief army. Peter Bartholomew crucified in an ordeal by fire to prove the authenticity of the Lance. The Fatimids of Egypt, enemies of the Seljuqs, entered into negotiations with the Crusaders, whom they understood to be a Byzantine Mercenary Army, facilitating their capture of Turkish held towns in Syria and the Levant as they marched south toward Jerusalem.

KORKA CLAN'S STEP INTO A THIRD SHADOW

The Korka Family bloodlines march through the time tunnel of the decades to follow. Nasan Khan had several descendants who realized that during their migration to France that it would in their best interest to convert to Christianity and take French or German surnames. Jimena Korka and Paulo Silva become parents of two twin boys and name them Rodrigo Diaz de Vivaro and Bertrand du Gueslay. Rodrigo Diaz becomes a Knight of the Templar and his twin brother, Bertrand Gueslay, owner of a small Northern Italy winery grower of Roman wines. They will join the Second Crusade. The times that Korka's great-great-grandchildren found themselves was no different than the story of their ancestors during the time of the Roman and Barbarian periods except for now it was a time of religious upheavals between the Roman Catholic Church and the followers of the Goran. The times were indeed full of violence, cruelty, and crime. The annals abound with terrible and shameful records, bloody and desolating wars, and individual cases of oppression, injustice, and cruelty.

In Paris, Grand Master James Wells of the Holy Papal Sovereign Military Order of Malta is assassinated in his chapel during vespers with his throat cut and two of his right-hand fingers removed and placed in his mouth. The supreme officer of the Teutonic Order is proved to have received bribes to have induced a knight to allow him sex with his wife as the price of a favorable decision in not allowing him to be a mounted crusader on the march to save Jerusalem. Wealth and power led to luxury and sensuality, the weaker oppressed, the all wealthy elites and Catholic Bishops alike were themselves above the law. There are often two false accounts of the same transaction, and it is impossible to decide where the fault was, yet money could be used to gain the upper hand in the outcome.

Bertrand du Gueslay grows to be a superior lance and broadsword horseman. As he is recognized for his leadership skills as well, he given the command of a German Crusader mounted horse unit. The German Crusader soldiers suffered great miseries from sickness and their wounds, and all members lived in common; Bertrand and his group sleep in dormitories on small and hard beds; they have their meals together in the refectory, and their food is meager and of the plainest of quality. They all attend the daily services in the church and recite specific prayers and others privately.

Bertrand has them stand at attention with all their armor on and commands them after meal evening, "you are not permitted to leave your billets, nor to write or receive letters, without my permission, do you all understand? I can assure you that if I find you disobeying my orders, you will suffer severely. You will have a cut on your leg and hold a tighten a chain so that you feel the pain that Christ suffered on the cross. Do you understand? We march toward Jerusalem where our Lord preached and died for your sins. That is all, dismissed!"

Bertrand's soldiers' clothes, armor, and the harness of their horses are all of the plainest descriptions. Bertrand's order is that all gold, jewels, and other costly ornaments are strictly forbidden. The Catholic Church provides horses. As Commander du Gueslay and his Knighted horse command enter the Syrian town of Aleppo, they dismount and set up a perimeter around a former Roman Catholic Hospital that was used for Turkic warriors who were wounded. His squire and twelve knights enter the front door of the hospital. They inspect each room.

"Commander du Gueslay come here." They found bed sheets wet from blood. "Look the blood is fresh. You can see by the shield set on the chair that a very important Turkic leader was here just five or ten minutes ago. We saw three Muslim warriors and one of them was limping and trying to escape. I think they must have heard our chain messed armor and ran. They must have known that we had every intent to kill them and burn their bodies. As we ran through the deserted halls, we heard some sounds like digging under the building but we are not quite sure yet."

One of the knights spoke, "I was told yesterday by a dispatch from Rodrigo Diaz's forces that they found tunnels at this building and they destroyed them."

Commander du Gueslay stopped for a minute, "Let us not take a chance that they might come behind us in the future. Search the entire building and the well outside." After one hour, they found another tunnel. On the walls, written in Arabic, "Punishment for theft, cutting off the right hand. Punishment for alcohol consumption, 40 lashes, Punishment for adultery, stoning to death. "Look Commander up here, they appeared to use a rope ladder to move up through the well to escape!"

They heard the voices of children crying. As they traveled down the tunnel, they found three young Catholic girls ranging in ages nine, ten, thirteen, who were tied up. "Don't be afraid we are Catholic German Knights who are here to save you."

The children were untied and taken up to the first floor near the small altar. Alaina, the thirteen-year-old stopped eating and burst out in tears, "We were supposed to wear burgas, completely black. When they left us here, we took off the burgas. They raped me twice. May they go to hell. One day they took us outside. A man who was the janitor of this hospital was circled by several Turkic men and then they started to saw off his head. They held him by his hair and kept sawing."

Commander du Gueslay asked, "Were you afraid they would cut off your head?" Camila, the nine-year-old girl laughed, "No, we were too little for them."

The next day when they marched to battle, each knight had three or four horses, and an esquire carried his shield and lance. It was during the siege of Damietta that the famous St. Francis of Assisi visited the crusading army and endeavored to settle a dispute that had arisen between the knights and the foot soldiers of the military, the latter being dissatisfied and declaring that cruel exposure to danger as compared with the mounted knights. Bertrand will list those who complained to face his wrath by their sons being forced to serve for five years on trader ships.[24]

THIRD CRUSADE - 1189-1192

Richard the Lionheart led the Third Crusade. Richard also known as Richard I of England (1157-1199) succeeded his father Henry II as King of England in 1189, but he spent most of his reign abroad. Shortly after his coronation, he went on the Third Crusade (1189-1192) where he demonstrates his reputation as a great military leader. The arrival at the army of King Philip II Augustus of France in April and King Richard I of England in early June with about 18,000 soldiers between them proved decisive in the siege of Acre, which fell to the crusaders in early July after an attack of two years.[25]

Siege of Acre 1291-Courtesy of FireForge Games

In the aftermath of the victory, Richard the Lionheart made a mortal enemy of Duke Leopold of Austria when he ordered the Duke's banner, raised beside his and King Philip's, removed from the city's walls. When Philip Augustus decided to return to France because of illness and political concerns, Richard assumed sole command of the crusading army, including the French and German contingents. After massacring 2,700 Muslim captives when Saladin missed the deadline for ransom, Richard the Lionheart began a march down the coast. Richard secured the coast by marching from Acre to Jaffa, taking each port city along the way. This march was among Richard's most impressive military feats. The crusaders marching in close formation were under constant attack, as Saladin tried to lure Richard into a set battle. Richard, intent on securing the port cities as a necessary prelude to taking Jerusalem, refused to get drawn into the conflict. Using Cyprus (which he had taken on his way to the Holy Land in 1191 as a supply depot and Acre as a logistical base, Richard ordered his fleet to follow along with the coast, so that they could bring supplies and reinforcements to the troops and take away the wounded and sick. When the Crusaders' patience finally gave out near Arsuf, just shy of Jaffa, and the Hospitallers in the rearguard decided to charge the Saracens, Richard quickly deployed his troops from line of march to line of battle using prearranged trumpet signals and attacked.[26]

Although victorious in the battle, Richard chose not to pursue Saladin's army but instead continued his march to Jaffa. Richard, however, came to recognize that although he could take Jerusalem because it was inland, he would not be able to hold it. His best chance was to attack the capital of Saladin's empire, Egypt, but the army balked and insisted on marching to Jerusalem. Faced with news that his brother Prince John with the support of Philip Augustus was attempting to seize the English throne Richard negotiated a three-year truce with Saladin and a settlement that allowed Christian pilgrims' access to Jerusalem, although the city remained under Muslim control. Saladin, fearful of the threat posed to Egypt, also required that the walls of Ascalon, the southernmost port in Palestine, be leveled. Richard was unsuccessful as well in his attempt to preserve the kingship of Jerusalem for his Poitevin vassal King Guy of Lusignan. Faced with a unanimous vote by the barons of the Kingdom, Richard reluctantly accepted Conrad of Montferrat, a supporter of Philip Augustus, as King of Jerusalem. He sold Guy the lordship of Cyprus as a consolation prize. Before his coronation, Conrad was assassinated by two members of the Ismaili Shiite sect the Hashshashins. Suspicion immediately falls on Richard. Conrad belonged to a well-connected family, having been a cousin of the Emperor Henry VI of Germany, King Philip Augustus of France, and Duke Leopold of Austria. All of them held Richard responsible for his murder. On his return to England, he was captured and handed over to the Holy Roman Emperor; however, released after a ransom paid in 1194. After a brief period in England, he went to France where he fought against Philip II of France. Richard the Lionheart died in 1199 after he was hit by an arrow while besieging the Chalus-Chabrol castle.[27]

ANCIENT SUMER

Sumer was the southernmost region of ancient Mesopotamia that some historians believe was the cradle of Western Civilization. The region of Sumer first inhabited around 4500 BCE. The name comes from Akkadian, the language of the north of Mesopotamia, and means "land of the civilized kings". The Sumerians called themselves black people. In the Book of Genesis, Sumer is known as Shinar. When the gods gave human beings the gifts of a productive society, they shined down from heaven and created the city of Eridu in the region of Sumer. At that time over thousands of years ago, Mesopotamians believed that it was the city elders of Eridu who laid down the rules for a peaceful civil society. Mesopotamians believed that their gods had set everything in motion, and that human beings were created as facilitators with the gods to maintain order and hold back chaos.

In 1244, Jerusalem was lost to Muslims yet another time. Jerusalem sacked by the Muslim Turkic Khwarezmian mercenaries. The Ayyubid Sultan Salih Ayyub, in Egypt, hired these Turkic warriors whose empire had extended over Iran and Iraq until destroyed by the Mongols sought to fight against his uncle, Salih Ismail. The Khwarezmiyyas, heading south from Iraq towards Egypt, invaded Christian-held Jerusalem along the way. Two Crusader Knights with their lance esquire are lost in a wind storm and captured near the city of Jaffa. They are surrounded by fifty Warriors. The three men attempt to plead for their lives.

The French Crusader Knight Jules cries out that "We are only following the orders of the Pope."

The Turkic Sunni warrior leader demands, "Kneel. Do you pray I am asking? Do you pray I am asking? Do you pray to Allah or Jesus Christ? Allah the Great Said to us, Fight the Infidels just as they fight you. Now Get up! Kneel here on this ledge properly facing Jerusalem as if you are praying to your Infidel GOD." As the three prayed out loud, "Our Father in heaven, hallowed be your name. Your kingdom come, your will be done, on earth as it is in heaven."

As the three Turkic Warriors stood behind them, each raised their swords and with one swift movement each of the Crusader's heads rolled down bouncing until they lay in a small ravine. They then wiped their sword blades on their tunics and facing the sun shouted, "Let Allah the Great and merciful be praised!" Jerusalem was to be lost by the West and was not recaptured again until 1917.

ORDER OF TEMPLAR -ROMAN CATHOLIC SUPPRESSION

From 1307 to1312, the Roman Catholic suppression of the Knights Templar began. In 1307, King Philip IV ordered the arrest of all the Knights Templar in France, charging them with heresy (including rites of spitting on the cross and worshipping the head of an idol called "Baphomet" for sodomy, and witchcraft. Under torture, Templars confessed, which King Philip used to pressure the pope to suppress the Order. Philip's motivation was unknown. Threatened with military force by King Philip, Pope Clement VI dissolved the Order of Templar in 1312.

In 1314 the last Grand Master of the order, Jacques de Molay, and Geoffrey de Charny, Preceptor of Normandy, faced with life imprisonment, recanted their confessions and were burnt at stake. Rodrigo Diaz due Vivaro disguises himself as a Bilbao Spanish shepherd and has five children with a Roma Gypsy woman. Korka's descendant, Bertrand du Gueslay, returns to his vineyards and produces high-quality wines for the European Catholic Church.

CHAPTER FOUR

LIBERTY, EQUALITY, FRATERNITY -NAPOLEONIC WARS

"THE BATTLEFIELD IS A scene of constant chaos. The winner will be the one who controls the chaos, and both are our own and the enemies."

A fiery French nationalist wrote, "We confess that one of the periods of French history that we find most interesting is that of the First Empire, le Premier Empire. The idealism of the new République defended brilliantly by Napoleon against the onslaughts of all the rest of Europe determined to restore royalty." Against the revolutionary Jacobins, the Corsican raised General organized a coup d'état on November 9, 1799. However, he held close to his heart the revolutionary values of equality before the law and personal property protection, as in the Roman Era, the Gallic vision of reaching global dominance via brutal military force. Bonaparte did not waste time and crowned himself Emperor as a substitute to the decapitated Monarch. Napoleon alleged that I no longer regarded myself as a simple general, but as a man called on to decide the fate of peoples. After Napoleon rose as a royal figure, his power corrupted by his ego, Napoleon ushered in a period of high hopes and beautiful dreams for the best for humanity. It was as if the heavenly angels had not reached down against the Gaul's ancestors, and only given brutality, madness, and Napoleon's complete defeat by the Czar's Russian Imperial Army. The Napoleonic Wars' casualty rates rose over the years from fifteen percent at Austerlitz, to thirty-one percent at Borodino and the final blow of forty-five percent at Waterloo. The military defeat closed the last door that would lead to a world of ideas that would have perfected the dream of all humanity to live in glory as equals in love for all.[1] In the end, Frenchman of that era believe that national fame and a stable economy was more important than individual freedom

MIDDLE AGES - 5TH – 15TH CENTURY

In Europe's history, the Medieval Period lasted from the 5th to the 15th Century and categorized by feudal or aristocratic social structures. The first tower, the Western European Roman Empire, fell, and its bricks picked up to become part of the Roman Catholic Renaissance and the Period of Discovery. There was no set timetable and especially in Western Europe, as monarchies lasted for thousands of years. Even in 2018, countries like Britain, Sweden, and 27 other monarchies rule forty countries. The first French King's foundational rock was Clovis (King of the Franks) and then to Henry Tudor, who nationalized the Plantagenet bloodlines. The land was taken over by the monarchies of the Middle Ages and became a tax base and their wealth for thousands of years.[2]

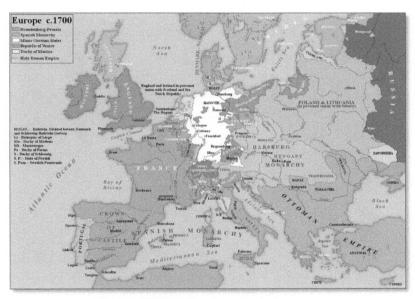

Europe 1700 – Courtesy of edmaps.com

The medieval world connected with the Royalty Empire Era of the European Middle Ages thrived under the foundational territorial boundaries of the Holy Roman Empire. The Medieval royal houses of England and the European continent existed under the heredity rights of Kings and, in few cases, Queens. All aspects of the society, such as the religion of the Roman Catholic and Orthodox Eastern Church, paintings, and societal norms, influenced by the royalty ruling classes. The vital issue for kingship families was how to stay in power, create spheres of power, and to extend their territorial boundaries? They found a way to stay in control for centuries via intermarriage, wars, and treaties. Some have speculated that this form of Imperial Families ruling the masses always existed from the barbarian Roman era to the early 20th Century. However, the destructive trigger for the European Imperial families was the French Revolution that had the slogan, liberty, equality, and freedom. The Poles, Italians, Germans, and French were to fight against the Russians, Prussians, members of the German treaty alliances, and the Habsburg Empire.

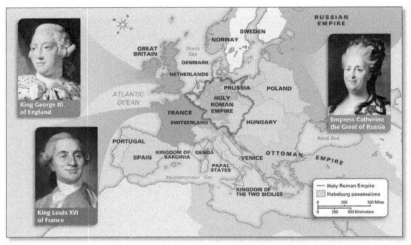

Europe Monarchy Map – Courtesy of unofficialroyalty.com/monarchs

EARLY EUROPEAN ROYAL DYNASTIES

ROTHSCHILDS DYNASTY

From modest beginnings, the five brothers founded banking houses in Frankfurt, London, Paris, Vienna, and Naples. They achieved renown as the most important - and most successful - bankers in the world. Rothschild ventures have become the stuff of legend: the financial investment made for Wellington's armies, the California Gold Rush, the building of the Suez Canal, the arrival of the National and Global Railroad, and the search for global oil reserves.

EUROPE'S BANKING MONOPOLY

The Rothschild recognized as the best of all European banking dynasties that, for some 200 years, exerted significant influence on Europe's economic and, indirectly, the political history. The wars, for the Rothschilds, made them enormous profits by providing loans to warring princes. Also, smuggling as well as legal trading in critical products such as wheat, cotton, colonial produce, and arms; and transferring international payments between the British Isles and the Continent that Emperor Napoleon hoped to close British trade. Peace transformed the growing Rothschild business. War is good for business elites. The Rothschild Banking Group continued its international business dealings. By the last quarter of the 19th Century, the Rothschild Banking Group lost its markets with other banking groups in the U.S.A. and Europe that were financially more powerful and enterprising.[3]

RURIK DYNASTY

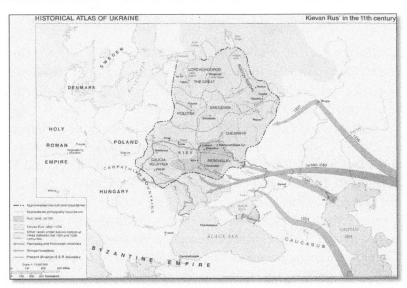

Kievan Rus in 11thCentury — Courtesy of Historical Atlas of Ukraine

Rurik Dynasty's early start was with the princes of Kievan Rus and, later, Muscovy. They were descendants of the Varangian (Vikings) prince Rurik, who had been invited by the people of Novgorod to rule that city (c. 862); the Rurik princes maintained their control over Kievan Rus and, later, Muscovy until 1598.

Settlement Varangians (Vikings) in Eu – Courtesy of griffith.edu.au

Rurik's successor Oleg (d. 912) conquered Kyiv (c. 882) and established control of the trade route extending from Novgorod, along the Dnieper River, to the Black Sea. Igor, believed to be Rurik's son, reigned from 912 to 945). He succeeded by his wife, St. Olga, the regent from 945 to969. Next, their son Svyatoslav reigned from 945 to 972, who further extended their territories. Svyatoslav's son Vladimir I or St. Vladimir reigned from 980 to 1015, and he consolidated the dynasty's rule. Vladimir Svyatoslav "compiled the first Kievan Rus law code and introduced Christianity into the country." Vladimir established the Kievan Rus lands into a cohesive confederation by distributing the important cities among his sons. The eldest, a grand prince of Kyiv and the brothers were to succeed each other, moving up the hierarchy of cities toward Kyiv, filling vacancies left by the advancement or death of an elder brother. The youngest brother was to be succeeded as a grand prince by his eldest nephew, whose father had been a noble prince. A succession pattern frequently followed by the various reigns; namely, Svyatopolk (1015– 19); Yaroslav The Wise (1019–54); his sons Izyaslav who reigned for three periods (1054–68; 1069–73; and 1077–78), Svyatoslav who reigned from 1073 to 1076, Vsevolod ruled from 1078 to 1093, and Svyatopolk II (son of Izyaslav) who reigned 1093–1113.[4]

HIERARCHICAL SUCCESSION TRIGGERED THE CIVIL WARS

The successions were accomplished, however, amid continual civil wars. The princes' unwillingness to follow the hierarchical rules-driven to achieve their regal positions by using force. The population and the administrators would naturally rebel against the usurpers who did not support the accession ladders that designated the proper city ruler. The princes would further have undermined the legitimacy of the traditional steps to move from town to town to become the Prince of Kyiv when they would decide as one voice to rule instead in regions that they established as their own. In 1097 all the princes of Kievan Rus met at Lyubech (northwest of Chernihiv) and decided to divide their lands into male ruled estates. The succession for the Grand Prince, however, continued to be based on the generation pattern; thus, Vladimir Monomakh succeeded his cousin Svyatopolk II as Grand Prince of Kyiv. During Vladimir's reign (1113–25) tried to restore unity to the lands of Kievan Rus; and his sons (Mstislav, reined 1125–32; Yaropolk, 1132–39; Vyacheslav, 1139; and Yury Dolgoruky, 1149– 57) succeeded him eventually, though not without warring sides. Nevertheless, distinct branches of the dynasty established their own rule in the major centers of the country outside Kyiv—Halicz, Novgorod, and Suzdal. The princes of these regions vied with each other for control of Kyiv. Still, when Andrew Bogolyubsky of Suzdal finally conquered and sacked the city (1169), Andrew returned to Vladimir (a town in the Suzdal principality). He transferred the seat of the Grand Prince to Vladimir. Andrew Bogolyubsky's brother Vsevolod III succeeded him as Grand Prince of Vladimir (reigned 1176–1212); Vsevolod followed by his sons Yury (1212–38), Yaroslav (1238–46), and Svyatoslav (1246–47) and his grandson Andrew (1247–52). Alexander Nevsky (1252–63) succeeded his brother Andrew, and Alexander's brothers and sons succeeded him.

The Rurik Dynasty lacked organizational cohesiveness. None of the princes move to the principality of Vladimir. To protect their own families' center of power, they stayed within their regional seats of power. Alexander's son, Daniel, founded the House of Moscow. After the Mongol invasion (1240), the Russian princes obliged to seek a" contract right" from the Mongol Khan to rule as Grand Prince. Rivalry for the "contract" for leadership in the grand principality of Vladimir developed among the royal houses, particularly those of Tver and Moscow. Gradually, the princes of Moscow became dominant, forming the grand principality of Moscow (Muscovy). By 1598, males had died off, leaving no one to carry on the bloodline and the Rurik Dynasty ceased to exist. Women were not considered worthwhile and not bestowed sovereign power to rule.[5]

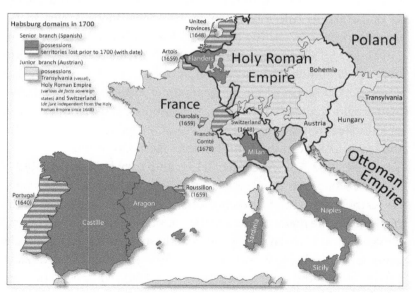

Habsburg Dominions 1700 – Courtesy of reddit.com

HABSBURG DYNASTY

House of Habsburg, also spelled Hapsburg, also called House of Austria, a German royal family, one of the principal sovereign dynasties of Europe from the 15th to the 20th Century. The Habsburg Dynasty sprawled from Central and Eastern Europe and acted as a physical and psychological boundary wall for its hundreds of minorities and interests. Albert IV's son Rudolf IV of Habsburg was elected German King as Rudolf I in 1273. It was he who, in 1282, bestowed Austria and Styria territories on his two sons, namely, Albert (German king Albert I) and Rudolf (Rudolf II of Austria). From that date 1282, the age-long identification of the Habsburgs with Austria begins at that point. The family's custom was to vest the government of its hereditary domains, not in individuals but all male members of the family in common. Though Rudolf II renounced his share in 1283, difficulties arose again when King Albert I died (1308).

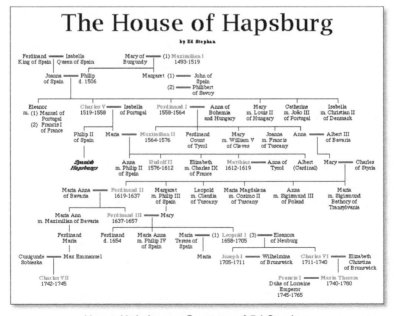

House Habsburg - Courtesy of Ed Stephen

After a system based on fairness rights, Rudolf IV of Austria was not a stupid man, and he and his younger brothers acknowledged the principle of equal rights. Still, they all agreed that Rudolf IV supremacy over the Habsburg house. However, upon his death the brothers Albert III and Leopold III of Austria agreed on a partition of Austria; namely, (Treaty of Neuberg, 1379): Albert took Austria; Leopold took Styria, Carinthia, and Tirol.[6]

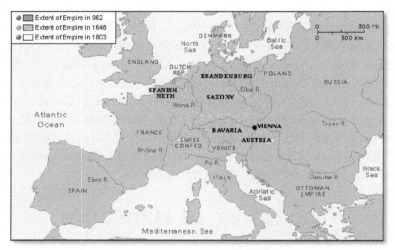

Holy Roman Empire AD 1648- Courtesy of Grolier online Atlas

BOHEMIA

Rudolf III of Austria had been King of Bohemia from 1306 to 1307, and his brother Frederick I had been German King as Frederick III from 1314 to 1330. Albert V of Austria was in 1438 elected King of Hungary, German King (as Albert II), and King of Bohemia; his only surviving son, Ladislas Posthumus, was also King of Hungary from 1446 to 1452) and of Bohemia from 1453. Once again, with Ladislas, the male descendants of Albert III of Austria died out in 1457. Meanwhile, the Styrian line descended from Leopold III had been subdivided into Inner Austrian and Tirolean branches.

HOLY ROMAN EMPEROR - FREDERICK III

Frederick V, the senior representative of the Inner Austrian line, was elected German King in 1440 and crowned Holy Roman Emperor, as Frederick III, in 1452. A descendent of the Habsburg crowned in Rome and recognized as imperial secular attainment. The Bohemian, Hungarian, and German kinships voted on. If Habsburg Kingship was to succeed with Charles VI's accession in 1711, the hereditary lands of the Habsburgs had to be immense and wealthy. Thus, the Habsburg kinships could force all Germans to vote for them. As kings of Bohemia, the family line remained protected. The Hapsburg could not control the Bohemian and Hungarian kingdoms. For over 70 years, with the death of Ladislas Posthumus in 1457 and the Swiss territories, they were renounced in 1474. Frederick's control over the Austrian inheritance was slim. In 1453, Frederick ratified the Habsburgs' use of the unique title of Archduke of Austria. The anachronism A.E.I.O.U. Meant Austriae est imperare orbi universe, meaning that Austria destined to rule the world. Also, the meaning Alles Erdreich ist Österreich untertan' or the whole world is subject to Austria. Fredrick lived long enough to see his son Maximilian achieve the most magnificent marriage in European history. Besides, he also saw the Austrian hereditary lands reunited when in 1490 Sigismund of Tirol abdicated in Maximilian's favor.

THE WORLD POWER OF THE HOUSE OF HABSBURG

The time allowed the Habsburgs to gain recognition in Germany and central Europe by arranged marriages to heiresses. Frederick's son Maximilian carried that matrimonial policy to the level of intelligent planning. In 1477, he married the heiress of Burgundy, Charles the Bold's daughter Mary. This move allowed the House of Habsburg the birth of their son Philip to inherit valuable part of Charles the Bold's large spheres of influence, namely, Artois, the Netherlands, Luxembourg, and the County of Burgundy or Franche

Comté. Maximilian's wife died in 1482, allowing him to marry the Breton heiress Anne in hopes of obtaining Brittany. In 1496, they arranged Philip's marriage to Joan, the prospective heiress of Castile and Aragon. With unions, the Habsburg's controlled Spain, Naples, Sicily, Sardinia, and the lands conquered in America. Since Philip I of Castile died prematurely, Maximilian's son was already ruler of the Burgundian heritage and Spain when, in 1519, he succeeded Maximilian as ruler of the Habsburgs' Austrian territories. In 1519, Maximilian's son was elected Holy Roman Emperor as Charles V.[7]

CHARLES V

To secure Maximilian's son's right to be elected Holy Roman Emperor, huge bribes in gold paid, and as a last effort, military force would threaten. Few of the German princes had no desire to have the entire idea of sovereignty as a burden upon them. Time of the Rise of the Roman Empire, France saw itself as a victim nation that was encircled by its enemies from the northeast to the southwest. The French Kings viewed the Habsburgs as imperialist and not in tune with their liberal values. From the 17th to the 18th Century, European countries only felt sympathy for the people of France.[8] Immediately, Charles V realized that as Emperor, his responsibilities were enormous, and he decided to share them. With the passage in 1522, the Treaty of Brussels allowed Charles V to give the Habsburg-Austrian ancestral lands to his brother, Ferdinand I. In 1521, Ferdinand had married Anna, daughter of Louis II of Hungary and Bohemia. In 1526, Louis II killed in the Battle of Mohács. Ferdinand the first elected as Louis II successor.

HABSBURGS' POWER AND CORRUPTION

By the end of the 16th Century, the Habsburgs reached the zenith of their power. The Duchy of Milan, annexed by Charles V in 1535, was assigned to his son, Philip II of Spain. In 1540, Philip

II conquered Portugal. In 1580, and the Spanish dominions in America were ever-expanding. There were three faults in the power structure—two of them historical accidents and the third an effect of the Habsburg dynasty's self-preservation measures. The first was the ascendancy of Charles V that coincided with the outbreak of the Protestant Reformation in Germany. As Charles V, from his Spanish upbringing, was imbued with ideas of Catholic uniformity. Maximilian II, also sought to realize those ideas, religious resistance to the Habsburgs' authority came to aggravate or to camouflage political strength. Ferdinand's accession to Hungary meant that the Habsburgs had to bear the brunt of the Turkish Ottoman drive from the Balkans into Central Europe, just as Habsburg Spain had to confront Turkish incursions into the western Mediterranean. The great victory of Lepanto (1571), won by Charles V's natural son, Juan de Austria, did not end those troubles against the dynasty, by the Hungarian rebels, and by the French. Habsburgs won power and territories by marriages that would stop any rival families from taking away their gains. They decided to stay in control by intermarrying within themselves. In a few generations, inbreeding brought the male line of Charles V to its natural end.

BLOODLINES AND CONFLICT

By a series of abdications toward the end of his life, Charles V transferred his Burgundian, Spanish, and Italian possessions to his son Philip II and in 1558, his functions as Emperor to his brother Ferdinand. The division of the dynasty between Imperial and Spanish lines was definitive. Ferdinand's male descendants were Holy Roman Emperors until 1740, Philip's were kings of Spain until 1700. The Imperial line was inevitably concerned to maintain its position in Bohemia and to assert itself against the Turks in divided Hungary. Also, if their holdings in Swabia and Alsace were lost, the consequence would lower their opportunity to continue to be elected to the German kingship. The Revolt of the Netherland was not winnable. The English and French sent arms and supported terrorist in the Hapsburg's holdings. Philip II of Spain remained the greatest sovereign in the Western world until he died in 1598.

DEATH OF THE HABSBURG DYNASTY

In only 30 years, the Habsburg Dynasty's claim to European hegemony had lost its brilliance. It did not take time for the French Monarch to attack the weakness of the Habsburgs. In 1667, Louis XIV of France, occupied territory after territory from the Spanish Habsburgs that consisted of Flanders, the rest of Artois, and other areas in the Netherlands, as well as the whole Franche Comté. In 1683 Turkish siege of Vienna was defeated by the Imperial Habsburgs. Louis started the War of the Reunions to conquer Luxembourg in 1683. In December 1683, Luxembourg bombarded with French mortars. About 6,000 bombs and grenades fired. In 1684 as the inhabitants suffered from no food or water, Luxembourg fell. The Habsburg Dynasty could no longer defend the German frontier west of the Rhine.[9]

FRENCH BOURBON DYNASTY

From 1689 t0 1697, the War of the Grand Alliance, the rising powers the Dutch and English, pushed for those supporting the Habsburgs against Louis XIV. Apart from the Bourbon ascendancy, other powers dreamed of the collapse of Spain. The physical frailty of Charles II of Spain, who could not assist in the birth of a male heir, would end the bloodline. With no apparent heir, the European powers were concerned about the power vacuum and how to keep the Grand Alliance's continuity. Up to 1699, Charles II's crown would pass to the electoral Prince of Bavaria, Joseph Ferdinand. That arrangement was acceptable because transferring the Spanish inheritance to the Bavarian House of Wittelsbach would not necessarily upset the balance of power between the imperial Habsburgs and Bourbon France. In 1699, Joseph Ferdinand died. When that happened, Charles II's next natural heirs were the descendants of his half-sister. His half-sister had married Louis XIV of France. His father's two sisters were heirs, of whom one had been Louis XIV's mother and the other the mother of Emperor Leopold I. The Imperial Habsburgs. Nor their British and Dutch friends, could consent to their Bourbon France enemy's acquiring the whole Spanish inheritance. Neither Bourbon France, British, or Dutch opponents would tolerate the Imperial Habsburgs reunite in one pair of hands most of what Emperor Charles V accomplished. Charles II, in the meantime, regarded any partition of his inheritance as a humiliation to Spain. In 1700 as Charles II lay dying in cold upstairs castle room, he named as his sole heir a Bourbon France prince, Philip of Anjou, the second of Louis XIV's grandsons.[10]

THE HABSBURG DYNASTY SUCCESSION IN THE 18TH CENTURY

To allay British and Dutch misgivings, Leopold I and his elder son, the future Emperor Joseph I, in 1703, renounced their claims to Spain in favor of Joseph's brother Charles. They strategized that Charles could then create a new line of Spanish Habsburgs but not Imperial. Joseph I, died, leaving only daughters. In 1711, his brother became Emperor (Charles VI), and as ruler of the Austrian, Bohemian, and Hungarian lands, the British and the Dutch lost interest and plotted with France. When Charles's brother Joseph died, the Spanish Habsburg's blood died as well. Therefore, in 1711, Charles was the last male Habsburg. Since no woman could rule the Holy Roman Empire, and the Habsburg succession in some of the hereditary lands was assured only to the male line, Charles had a creative solution.

On April 19, 1713, as Emperor of the Holy Roman Empire, Charles decreed the Pragmatic Sanction, stating that "in the event of Charles dying sonless, the whole estate should pass to a daughter of his and her descendants but not to his late brother's daughters.

However, if his nieces' line were extinct, then the inheritance would go to the heirs of his paternal aunts."

The 1713 Treaties of Utrecht recognized the Bourbon accession Spain and to Spanish America, virtually forced the hand of the reluctant Charles. He made peace with France by the Treaty of Rastatt in 1714. Charles pleased with his possession of southern Netherlands, the former Spanish possessions on the mainland of Italy, Mantua (footnote: annexed by him in 1708), and Sardinia.

In 1717, Sardinia exchanged for Sicily, which the peacemakers of Utrecht had assigned to the House of Savoy. Charles's character defect was that he was a hardheaded man, and he only stayed at war with Spanish Bourdon until 1720. Finally, in 1725, the Bourdon accession was recognized by Charles. Beginning in 1716, Charles VI only wanted to gain recognition for the Pragmatic Sanction when his only young son died.). By 1738, at the end of the Polish Succession War, Charles VI lost both Naples and Sicily to a Spanish Bourbon but rewarded with Parma and Piacenza for the Habsburgs. England and France agreed to honor the Pragmatic Sanction upon Charles VI's death in 1740. Maria Theresa, Charles VIs daughter, crowned as his heir, ordered the Army to repel the Prussian Silesia invasion that was the fire strike for the War of Austrian Succession.

WAR OF THE AUSTRIAN SUCCESSION

Bavaria promptly challenged the Habsburg position in Germany. France's support of Bavaria encouraged Saxony to follow suit and Spain to try to oust the Habsburgs from Lombardy Britain. They came late enough to support Maria Theresa somewhat out of hostility toward France out of loyalty to the Pragmatic Sanction. Maria Theresa in the War had her holdings in the majority of Silesia, Lombardy, Parma, and Piacenza duchies, but retained her father's remaining lands. Maria married Phillip Marten, a genetic link to the Korka's treasurer Giovanni Francesco Albani. In 1737, Philip's uncle Francis Stephan ascended to the throne of the Holy Roman

Emperor, given the title of Francis I. Maria was to divorce Phillip and remarry Francis Stephan of Lorraine., thus ensuring that he and all descendants of the House of Habsburg–Lorraine, would continue the Habsburg dynasty of lands. Prussia was not satisfied with the seizure of Silesia from the Habsburgs. They wanted to recover Silesia to protect their outlying possessions in the Netherlands against the continuing danger of French attack. The Diplomatic Revolution revealed that Britain had no interest in working with Austro-Russian and favored Prussia. Even though France was the enemy of the Habsburgs, they decided to reconcile their difference. From 1770 until 1792, peace existed between the French and Austrians.[11]

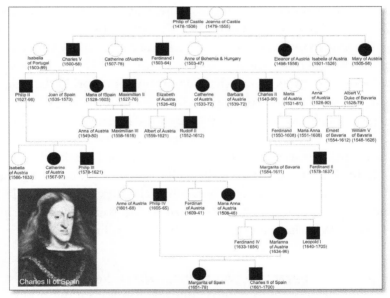

Habsburg family tree – Courtesy of powerofthegene.com

The Habsburg' wanted to maintain their imperial status in Germany versus Prussian businesses. Therefore, they consolidated and expanded their holdings in Central Europe. It was clear that the assets of Tuscany and the Netherlands had little value. Tuscany was no longer imperial and not connected to the ancient Habsburg vast holdings. In 1765, the Roman Emperor Francis I died, and his eldest son, Emperor Joseph II, became co-regent with his mother of the Austrian dominions. Still, Joseph's brother Leopold became grand duke of Tuscany. In the succession process of 1790, Leopold received all of Joseph's titles and his second son succeeded in Tuscany as Ferdinand III. From 1790, the Habsburg's Tuscany branch was distinct but not of imperial hereditary significance.

RUSSO-TURKISH 1774 TREATY OF KÜÇÜK KAYNARCA

The northeastward expansion of Habsburg central Europe, which came about in Joseph II's time, was not the result of the 1772 First Partition of Poland. The partition allowed Galicia and Lodomeria to be under Joseph II's control but was only due to his mother's remembrance of Silesia and Joseph II's 1775 acquisition of Bukovina. It was logical that Silesia would be a bridge between Joseph II's Transylvanian and the Galician lands. Joseph II planned to go through Bavaria as the gateway for his westward expansion. This made sense as Joseph II could fortify his western frontier and gain political status among the German princes. Prussia's decision to fight this strategic move limited his improvements during the 1779 War of the Bavarian Succession to the Innviertel. If his plan succeeded, Joseph II would have given the Netherlands to the House of Wittelsbach in exchange for Bavaria in 1784.[12]

FRENCH REVOLUTION AND NAPOLEONIC WARS

The French Revolutionary and Napoleonic Wars brought numerous changes in the power make-up of Western and Eastern Europe. The House of Habsburg was soon to disintegrate based on three events; namely, (1) the Holy Roman before its dissolution was "a rambling, multiethnic configuration that was only an empire in name only." (2) Leopold II was Holy Roman Emperor and King of

Hungary and Bohemia from 1790 to 1792, as well as given the title as Archduke of Austria and Grand Duke of Tuscany from 1765 to 1790. (3) In 1806, the elitist nobility created a formal dissolution of the Holy Roman Empire.

In anticipation of this action, Habsburg's Leopold II's successor Francis I plotted to build a new empire. In 1804, Francis I gave himself the title as the Hereditary Emperor of Austria. Francis II thought by doing this, and he could regain the southern Netherlands. As Emperor of Austria, Francis I regained Lombardy, Venetia and Dalmatia, and Tirol. Habsburg Ferdinand III of Tuscany recovered his Grand Duchy. A Habsburg's Emperor of Mexico member of the Dynasty of Habsburg crowned sovereign Duke of Modena, because in 1771, his father, a brother of the Holy Roman emperors Joseph II and Leopold II, married the heiress of the House of Este. Napoleon's second wife, Marie Louise, received the Duchies of Parma and Piacenza until she died. However, Napoleon took it away and gave it back to the Bourbons, who had ruled France and Navarre in the 16th Century.[13]

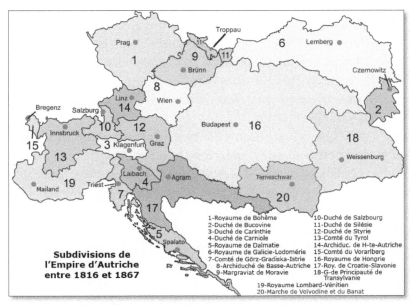

Subdivisions of Empire of Austria 1816-1867 – Courtesy of Medium.com

Richard Theodor Kusiolek

HOUSE OF HABSBURG PARALLELS THE AUSTRIAN EMPIRE.

In 1803, the territory of Salzburg acquired, but in 1809 Bavaria gained the region. However, seven years later, the domain became part of Austria. In 1795, Poland cut into three partitions, and the Congress of Vienna recognized Western Galicia as part of Habsburg's lands. A small region of Western Galicia was the territory of Cracow that was annexed by Austria in 1846. In 2014 following the precedent set by the 1795 Congress of Vienna, the Crimean Peninsula was annexed from Ukraine by the Russian Federation and peacefully administered as two Russian federal subjects—the Republic of Crimea and the imperial city of Sevastopol. The history of the House of Habsburg, a fortress of Kingly Conservative thought, for the Century following the Congress of Vienna slowly eroded. In 1859, the first sign of the erosion of the power of the Habsburg began when Austria forced to cede Lombardy to Sardinia–Piedmont, a nucleus of the new kingdom of Italy and could do nothing to prevent the bureaucrats in the Congress of Vienna from dispossessing the Habsburgs of Tuscany and Modena. German nationalism that connected with the start of the 1866 Seven Weeks' War gave Austria no choice but to give up Venetia. In 1867, Habsburg Emperor Franz Joseph granted the Hungary Kingdom equal status with the Austrian Empire in what was, henceforth, the co-Monarchy of Austria–Hungary.

The Magyars had become a very well-organized tribal alliance of seven tribes and one hundred eight clans. Magyars originated in the Urals and migrated westwards to settle in the Carpathian Basin as late as the seventh Century. Historians believed that they had ancestral roots with the Huns. The Magyars viewed themselves in parity with the Germans and their superiority over the non-Magyar peoples of their kingdom. Thus, they would never humiliate themselves by pacifying the Slavs and the Romanians of the Dual Monarchy by similar parity they had with the Germans. The ardent German nationalists of the Austrian Empire, versus those who were naturally loyal to the Habsburgs, took the same posture as the Magyars.[14]

EMPEROR OF MEXICO

Remote from Austria's national concerns but still wounding to the House of Habsburg was the fate of Franz Joseph's brother Maximilian who in 1864 set up by the French as Emperor of Mexico. During an uprising, Maximilian was executed by a Mexican firing squad in 1867. In 1889, Crown prince Rudolf thinking his fitness for the imperial and royal succession was questionable, committed suicide. Also, gross misconduct of certain archdukes and archduchesses, in the Imperial and the Tuscan lines further impaired the Habsburgs' prestige. The assassination of Franz Joseph's Wittelsbach consort Elizabeth in 1898, followed by the dire consequences of World War I in 1918.

ROMANOV DYNASTY

In 1565, Oprichnina, private court or household, created by Tsar Ivan IV the Terrible that administered those Oprichnina Russian lands that had been annexed from the rest of Muscovy and placed under the Tsar's direct control. During this early time of poverty and crime, the organized clandestine police forces were similar agents to the Roman Catholic Church's Venetian Inquisition and the Oprichnina of Czar Ivan IV of Russia. Romanov dynasty ruled Russia from 1613 until the Russian Revolution of February 1917 -1918. As descendants of Andrey Ivanovich Kobyla (Kambila), a Muscovite Boyar who lived in the 13th Century during the reign of the Grand Prince of Moscow Ivan I Kalita. The Romanovs acquired their name from Roman Yurev. Upon his death by a poison mushroom in 1643, Roman's daughter Anastasiya Romanovna Zakharina-Yureva married Ivan IV the Terrible who ruled as Tsar from 1547 to 1584.[15]

THE GENESIS OF THE RUSSIAN STATE

The Russian State, built by Vasily III and his son, Ivan IV, would become an influential global power. Vasily III was the first Russian sovereign crowned as Czar or the meaning, Caesar. Russian Government mythology as a sovereign he could trace his ancestry back to Augustus Caesar. Augustus was the Roman Domain founder and considered the first Roman Emperor, controlling the Roman Empire from 27 B.C. until he died in A.D. 14.

Philotheus wrote, "Two Rome's have fallen. The Third (Rome) stands, and there shall be no fourth."

Under Ivan IV, The Terrible wars were raged in the West and the East, spread imperialism, and deadly purges occurred. Anastasiya's brother Nikita's children took the surname Romanov in honor of their grandfather, father of a Tsarina. After Fyodor I (the last ruler of the Rurik dynasty) died in 1598, Russia endured fifteen chaotic years known as the Time of Troubles (1598–1613), which ended when a Zemsky sobor or "assembly of the land," elected Nikita's grandson, Michael Romanov, as the new Tsar. The Romanovs established no regular pattern of succession until 1797. During the First Century of their rule, they followed the Rurik's custom of passing the throne to the Tsar's eldest son or, if he had no son, to his closest senior male relative. Alexis, who ruled from 1645 to 1676, succeeded his father, Michael, who ruled from 1613 to 1645, and Fyodor III, governed from 1676 to 1682, succeeded his father, Alexis. But after Fyodor III died, both his brother Ivan and his half-brother Peter demand the throne for themselves. Although a Zemsky sobor chose Peter as the new Tsar, Ivan's family were supported by the streltsy or Russian guardsmen who were authorized to carry guns and shoot law-breakers. A palace revolution came into play, and in 1682, Ivan V and Peter I jointly assumed the throne.

In 1696, Peter named Emperor, and he decided to create the Law of Succession on February 5, 1722. This law allowed the Monarch the right to choose his successor. Peter the Great decided to modernize Russia and forcibly removed the Byzantine Robes of young men and sent them to Europe to learn navigation, engineering, and modern science. Peter succeeded the throne to his Romanov wife, Catherine I. In 1727, upon Catherine I's demise, the throne reverted to Peter I's grandson Peter II who died three years later. Ivan V's second surviving daughter, Anna, became Empress. In 1740, Anna died; thus, her elder sister's daughter Anna Leopoldovna, whose father belonged to the house of Mecklenburg, assumed the regency for Anna's son Ivan VI, of the house of Brunswick-Wolfenbüttel. In 1741 Ivan VI was deposed in favor of Elizabeth, daughter of Peter I and Catherine I. With Elizabeth, who reigned from 1741 to 1762, she could not give birth to a boy, and the Romanovs of the male line died out in 1762. The name Romanov preserved by the branch of the Swedish house of Holstein-Gottorp. Later, the Russian throne extended to Elizabeth's nephew, Peter III. From 1762 to 1796, Peter III's widow, a German princess of the house of Anhalt-Zerbst, ruled as Catherine II.

As she was known, Catherine the Great decided to liberalize Russia and make it more like Western Europe. It appeared that under her reign, the "Third Rome Empire of Russia" ceased and became Europeanized.

Catherine the Great, described by Romanovs-Simon Sebag Montefiore, as "Far from being the nymphomaniac of legend, she was an obsessional serial monogamist."

Peter III's son, a Romanov of Holstein-Gottorp, named Paul I, became Emperor again and ruled from 1796 to 1801. On April 5, 1797, Paul I changed the succession law, establishing a definite order of succession for members of the Romanov family. He died by conspirators supporting his son Alexander I (reigned 1801–1825). The sequence following Alexander's death was confused because the rightful heir, Alexander's brother Constantine, secretly declined the throne in favor of another brother, Nicholas I, who ruled from 1825 to 1855. After that, the succession followed Paul's succession rules. In

1861, four years before the end of the American Civil War, Czar Alexander II, who reigned from 1855 to 1881, freed the serfs, created local governments, and jury trials. Nicholas I and his grandson, Alexander III (1881-1894) immortalized in Russia's identity under the motto, Orthodoxy, Autocracy, and Nationality or Russian, Православие, Самодержавие и народность. Unfortunately, Nicholas II, who ruled from 1894 to the Russian Marxist Revolution of 1917 was to be murdered with his children to end the Romanov Dynasty forever.

Nicholas II children – Courtesy of Hulton Archive/Getty Images

FRENCH REVOLUTION AND NAPOLEONIC WARS (1792-1815)

War raged between 1792 and 1815 that misaligned France against shifting alliances of other European powers, and that produced a brief French hegemony over most of Europe. Revolutionary wars, concluded by 1801, were initially undertaken to defend and then to spread the effects of the French Revolution. Napoleon became the absolute power. However, on Napoleon's downfall, the Congress of Vienna (1814–15) inaugurated the restoration, from which the battered House of Habsburg naturally benefitted. The Congress consisted of two emperors, five kings, 209 reigning princes, and 20,000 officials.

KEY NAPOLEONIC STRATEGY AND BATTLES

On May 15, 1796, Napoleon Bonaparte began his inspiring spiritual journey as he marched his troops into Milan and led his young and robust Army across the bridge at Lodi. Now after over three centuries, Napoleon morphed as a general greater than Caesar and Alexander the Great. With each battle, his tactical skills as a military field commander and his vision to uproot the old order led his armies to victory. Napoleon had many advantages so that no army could defeat him. The French conscripts could march farther and with high speed along roads that no other army could move. The opposition generals could not respond or anticipate what tactic Napoleon would use. Napoleon spent considerable time studying the terrain that his troops would march. At 24-years-of age, his mind quickly evaluated the routes and, with an intuitive vision, knew exactly what the battle outcome would be. In Toulon's battle, he occupied the high ground and used his revolutionary artillery to force the British Fleet to retreat, thus leaving the town without any protection. The anti-revolutionary troops gave up without a shot fired. Napoleon's tactic was to be unpredictable and not follow the conventual diplomacy or of war.

SIEGE OF MANTUA (1796-1797)

The Siege of Mantua began on June 4, 1796, and ended on February 2, 1797. French Revolutionary General Napoleon Bonaparte's first Italian campaign and the successful siege of Mantua eliminated the Austrians from northern Italy. The city was easy to besiege, and the only access to it was via five causeways over the Mincio River. The two Austrian commanders, Count Dagobert Siegmund Graf von Wurmser and Baron Josef Alvintzy made a tactical mistake by putting all their resources to stop the city of Mantua from Napoleon's siege. They continued to make the same mistakes from over four attempts. Military historians thought that the Count and the Baron should have first attempted to destroy Napoleon's 40,000-man Army of Italy and of deploying their troops too far apart to coordinate their attacks effectively. Napoleon utilized his central position and greater mobility to "divide and conquer." The French conquest of northern Italy completed with the forced surrender of Mantua on February 2, 1797. Napoleon had solidified his genius and respect as a great general with this episode of 1797.[16]

BATTLE OF THE NILE

Before entering with his expeditionary Army, General Bonaparte reminded his troops that Alexandria was a city founded by a young Macedonian King, Alexander the Great. In 332 BC, this young King entered Egypt with his triumph troops, and now in 1798, they were paralleling this Macedonian triumph. Napoleon spoke to these troops that they were European civilization heroes and would wake up the East into the new French enlightenment and new trading routes. In 1798, Napoleon Bonaparte mapped out his plans for an invasion of Egypt to impede Britain's trade routes and threaten its possession of India. The British Admiralty heard that a large French naval expedition was to sail from a French Mediterranean port under Napoleon's command. In response, it ordered the Earl of St. Vincent, to organize a fleet to find and destroy the French Fleet. The Battle of Aboukir Bay was one of the most significant victories of the British Admiral Horatio Nelson. It fought on August 1, 1798, between the British and French fleets in Abū Qīr Bay, near Alexandria, Egypt. Fierce fighting ensued, during which Nelson wounded in the head. The climax came at about ten o'clock at night, when French Admiral Brueys' one hundred twenty-gun flagships, L'Orient that anchored in the bay, blew up with most of the ship's company, including the admiral. The fighting continued for the rest of the night; just two of Brueys's ships of the line and a pair of French frigates escaped destruction or capture by the British. The British suffered about nine hundred casualties, the French about nine thousand wounded and killed. The Battle of the Nile Napoleon's Army in Egypt was isolated, thus ensuring its ultimate disintegration. The confrontation a great disaster for the French Navy as Malta lost to the British, and Britain would gain prestige as a great naval power and complete control of the region surrounding the Mediterranean Sea.[17]

BATTLE OF MARENGO

On June 14, 1800, the Battle of Marengo allowed a narrow victory for Napoleon Bonaparte in the War of the Second Coalition. The battle engagement occurred on the Marengo Plain about 3 miles southeast of Alessandria, in northern Italy, between Napoleon's approximately 28,000 troops and some 31,000 Austrian troops under General Michael Friedrich von Melas. Consequence led the French occupation of Lombardy up to the Mincio River and secured Napoleon's military and civilian authority in Paris. Napoleon led his Army across several Alpine passes in May and cut Melas off from communication with Austria. Melas concentrated his troops at Alessandria to meet the French. Napoleon mistakenly thought Melas was at Turin, more than fifty miles (80 km) to the west, and his troops widely separated when Melas attacked. The initial French force of about 18,000 men was at first overpowered by the Austrians and was pushed back four miles (6.4 km) by three in the afternoon. Melas, believing victory was secured, gave the command to a subordinate, and retired to Alessandria. The slow Austrian pursuit enabled Napoleon to hold his forces together until the arrival of some 10,000 reinforcements, mainly General Louis Charles Antoine Desaix de Veygoux corps. At five in the late afternoon, the furious French counter-attack, in which Desaix died almost immediately from a bullet that penetrated his heart, compelled the Austrians into a massive retreat. Austrian losses included about 7,500 dead and wounded and some 4,000 captured, while French damages were nominal.[18]

Richard Theodor Kusiolek

BATTLE OF COPENHAGEN

The Battle of Copenhagen occurred on April 2, 1801, when Admiral Horatio Nelson gained a British naval victory over Denmark in the Napoleonic Wars. The armed-neutrality treaty of 1794 between Denmark and Sweden, to which Russia and Prussia adhered in 1800, was considered a hostile act by England. In 1801 a detachment of the British navy was sent to Copenhagen. After a fierce battle in the harbor, Admiral Horatio Nelson, ignoring orders to withdraw from the fleet commander, Sir Hyde Parker, instead continued to destroy most of the Danish fleet. Danish losses amounted to some 6,000 dead and wounded, six times those of the British. Denmark subsequently withdrew from the neutrality treaty. The Battle of Austerlitz was "the first engagement of the War of the Third Coalition, and Napoleon's most significant victories occurred on December 2, 1805. His 68,000 troops defeated almost 90,000 Russians and Austrians nominally under General M.I. Kutuzov, forcing Austria to make peace with France (Treaty of Pressburg) and thus keeping Prussia temporarily out of the anti-French alliance. The battle took place near Austerlitz in Moravia (or Slavkov u Brna, Czech Republic) after the French had entered Vienna on November 13, 1805, and then pursued the Russian and Austrian allied armies into Moravia.

The arrival of the Russian Emperor Alexander I virtually deprived Kutuzov of supreme control of his troops. The allies decided to fight Napoleon west of Austerlitz and occupied the Pratzen Plateau, which Napoleon had deliberately evacuated to create a trap. The partners then launched their main attack, with 40,000 men, against the French south force to cut them off from Vienna. While Marshal Louis Davout's corps of 10,500 men stubbornly resisted this attack and the allied secondary attack on Napoleon's northern flank repulsed, Napoleon ordered Marshal Nicolas Soult, with his 20,000 infantries, to attack up the slopes to smash the weak allied center on the Pratzen Plateau. Marshal Nicolas Soult captured the plateau and, with 25,000 reinforcements

<< 164 >>

from Napoleon's reserve, held it against the allied attempts to retake it. The partners were soon split in two and vigorously attacked and pursued both north and south of the plateau. They lost 15,000 men killed and wounded and 11,000 captured, while Napoleon lost 9,000 men. The remnants of the allied Army were scattered. Two days later, Francis, I of Austria, agreed to a suspension of hostilities and arranged for Emperor Alexander I to use trains to take his Army back to Russia.

Battle of Austerlitz – Courtesy of Francois Gerard
(Galerie des Bastilles, Versailles)

At Ulm, a city in the south German state of Baden-Württemberg, founded in medieval times, General Bonaparte achieved a great triumph. Napoleon's forces of 210,000 trained and hardened warrior men faced an Austrian Army of close to 72,000 men and at its head was Baron Karl Mack von Leiberich. The battle of Ulm began on September 25, 1805, and ended on October 20, 1805. In fighting, political aspects and strategies were more than just the killing of soldiers. As the Holy Roman Empire was gasping for life, a new order created by the Deutscher Bund or the German Confederation. The context of the battle of Ulm rested on the design behind the German Confederation, namely, to institutionalize the Franco-Russian ambitions while not allowing one state's dominance over the other. The eleventh article of the Confederation required members to come to provide mutual assistance in case of an invasion. In 1805, the German Confederation, namely, to institutionalize the Franco-Russian ambitions while not allowing predominance of one state over the other.

Napoleon Battle of U.L.M. – Courtesy of alchetron.com

The eleventh article of the Confederation required members to come to provide mutual assistance in case of an invasion. In 2018, the NATO North Atlantic Treaty Organization pact of twenty-nine countries copied the same provision of mutual aid in case of an attack upon a member. After two hundred years, the U.S. backed NATO's historical animosity against Russia continues with little logical sense. As in 1805 with the German Confederation, Germany defended with a rapid military force from Prussia, Austria, and other smaller states. In 2018, Poland, Norway, Romania, and Ukraine would be packaged militarily into a rapid response force. Besides, the defense of Germany existed fortresses of Ulm, Mainz,

Landau, Luxemburg, and Rastatt. Austria given the Presidency overseeing the Diet at Frankfurt Germany. All political coordination within Germany and the members of the Confederation was the responsibility of the Diet. If Prussia's leader, King Frederick William, could be convinced to join the Confederation, Napoleon would not be able to influence Germany's internal politics. Napoleon made a strategic and tactical plan to make the battleground Germany. Napoleon Grand Army had only one goal: to ultimately defeat the Austrian forces before Tsar Alexander I could arrive in support of Baron Karl Mack von Leiberich. On September 25, 1805, the wave of French troops crossed the Rhine River north of the Black Forest and forced marched at sixteen miles a day, crossing the principal Danube river. In a month, the Austrian Army crushed, and Napoleon emerged as a god-like victor.

BATTLE OF JENA

Napoleon gained tactic advantages on the battlefield when he inherited an officer corps that was both militarily professional and transformed by the revolutionary cry of liberty, equality, and fraternity. The regiment based on the bedrock of the revolutionary principles of merit, talent, and elections amongst peers for promotion. While he adopted the first two reforms, Napoleon halted the anarchist policy of elections. Anarchist, who attacked Napoleon, only extended his ability to encourage loyalty to himself, and he promoted those who performed well regardless of their social background. Now, the French officers' economic welfare linked to Napoleon's triumph and the extension of his power. The Battle of Jena took place on October 14, 1806. The military engagement of the Napoleonic Wars, fought between 122,000 French troops and 114,000 Prussians and Saxons, at Jena and Auerstädt, in Saxony (modern Germany). In the battle, Napoleon smashed the old Prussian Army inherited from Frederick II the Great. The military action resulted in the reduction of Prussia to half its former size at the Treaty of Tilsit in July 1807.

BATTLE OF EYLAU – FIRST DEFEAT

Battle of Eylau raged February 7 to the 8 1807 was "one of the engagements in the Napoleonic War of the Third Coalition. The first significant deadlock suffered by Napoleon, the battle fought around the East Prussian town of Eylau (i.e., Bagrationovsk, Russia), 23 miles (37 km) south of Königsberg (Kaliningrad). The 76,000 Russians and Prussians under Leonty Leontyevich Bennigsen confronted 74,000 men under Napoleon after the Russians launched an unexpected winter offensive. An initial unplanned battle on February 7, 1807, cost each side about 4,000 casualties without accomplishing anything. On the morning of the 8th, Napoleon had only 41,000 men to the Russians' 63,000, and he fought a delaying action until his reinforcements arrived. Napoleon tried to stem the Russian advances in cavalry attacks. The first of these was beaten back in a blinding snowstorm, with heavy losses.

Meanwhile, three Russian columns headed for the weak French lines, threatening to overwhelm them. Napoleon ordered a 10,700-man cavalry reserve under Joachim Murat to charge the advancing columns and the Russian center. In one of the most historical cavalry charges in history, they halted the Russian attack, slashed through the Russian center in two columns, re-formed in a single column in the Russian rear, and plunged through the organized lines again. This attack enabled Napoleon to hold his center and overcome the crisis. During the next six hours, both sides received reinforcements. After ten hours, the Army lost between 18,000 and 25,000 men. German General Count von Bennigsen made a retreat at eleven in the evening.

BATTLE OF FRIEDLAND - KALININGRAD, RUSSIA

On June 14, 1807, the Battle of Friedland fought at Friedland (i.e., Pravdinsk, Russia), 27 miles southeast of Königsberg (i.e., Kaliningrad, Russia) in East Prussia. Another victory occurred for Napoleon on July 5-6, 1809, at Wagram. Austria had no choice but to sign an armistice that was a precursor to the October 1809 Treaty of Schönbrunn that gave the French control of Germany. The battle fought on the Marchfeld (a plain northeast of Vienna) between 154,000 French and other troops under Napoleon and 158,000 Austrians under Archduke Charles. Overall, Napoleon felt somewhat compensated for his loss at Eylau, and the victory resulted in the Treaty of Tilsit between Napoleon and Alexander I of Russia.[19]

INVASION OF RUSSIA

"A favorable situation will never be exploited if commanders wait for orders -Helmuth Von Moltke, 1866."

On Aust 26, 1812, Napoleon launched his invasion of Russia. During the attack, a horrific battle was fought about 70 miles west of Moscow, near the river Moskva. The resources were great between Napoleon's 130,000 troops, which had placed 500 cannons and 120,000 Russians who had 600 guns. Napoleon's succeeding and the French forces marched to occupy Moscow. The Russian General M.I. Kutuzov ordered the Russian retreat to stop at the town of Borodino and built fortifications, to block the French advance to Moscow. Napoleon feared that an attempt to outflank the Russians might fail and allow them to escape, so he executed a bloody frontal attack. For six hours, the fierce fighting seesawed back and forth along the three-mile front. By noon the French artillery began to tip the scales, but the successive French attacks were not robust enough to overwhelm Russian resistance. Napoleon refused to commit the 20,000-man Imperial Guard and 10,000 other practically fresh troops to win the battle. Napoleon had no knowledge that Kutuzov had already committed every available man; thus, Napoleon might have gained a decisive, rather than a nebulous victory. Both sides became exhausted during the afternoon, and the battle subsided into a cannonade, which continued until nightfall. Kutuzov withdrew during the night, and a week later, Napoleon occupied Moscow unopposed. The Russians suffered about 45,000 casualties, including the death of the Russian General Pyotr Ivanovich Bagration, commander of the 2nd Russian Army, and was a Russian general and prince of Georgian origin. The French lost about 30,000 men. The cold weather aided by one hundred seven Cossack and eighty irregular Cavalry units destroyed Napoleon's Grande Armee. Bonaparte described the Cossacks that included the Bashkir, Kalmyk, Khirghiz, and Tartar horseback riders as the best of light troops he had encountered, adding that he had them in his Army, he could have ruled the world.[20]

KORKA'S NAPOLEONIC CHILD

Napoleon's Army engaged in a flanking battle plan outside the small village of Semenovka that lay on the outskirts of the principal city of Sloviansk in Russia. Korka's descendant Jimera and Paublo Silva, are parents of two sons, Diaz de Vivaro, Bertrand du Gueslay, and daughter, Tatiana, who has golden hair and blue eyes that she inherits from her parents and the psychopathic genes of Nasan Korka. They all enjoyed a serene pastoral life on their small thirteen-acre corn and vegetable farm. At 32, Tatiana's shapely body of 5'4" does not go unnoticed by locals as well as the local mayor. Her best friend Tanya is four years older than Tatiana. They trust one another and freely express their thoughts and concerns to each other.

Tanya is very depressed on this cold afternoon.

"Tatiana, my husband soon was sleeping with a neighbor of ours. A few days later, he returned to the log house of 1987 square feet that he had built with his own hands. So, Tatiana, I asked him when he finally entered the living room, "why were you gone for two days as I was anxious about you?"

Viktor answered, "I was sleeping with our neighbor's wife for the last two days. Her husband had gone on a long trip. I think he joined the Russian Army as it was moving west against the French, but I am not certain."

She pleaded with me to have sex with her. She was so lonely and needed a warm, sensual love moment. I felt compassion for her. I then compelled to take off her clothes, but I was still thinking of you. I am so sorry."

Tanya crushed by this news. She had never thought that her husband Viktor would ever cheat on her, and now that time had come. Tanya cried out! "You rotten bastard how could you do this to our family?"

Viktor sat down and took a deep breath. "Tanya, I made a terrible mistake. If you can forgive me, I will make it up to you. I do not like her. You are my only love."

Tanya stood up and walked to where he was sitting and slapped him. The blow was sharp, and she could see that Viktor's eye was red. His cheek began to gain redness. Then she walked silently out of the living room leaving Viktor to process this first event of anger that his wife never showed in their six years of marriage. He knew that Tanya would never leave him. It was a dark moment in his life, and he thought of joining the French Army into their march towards Moscow. Six months had passed from that day of revelation and bitterness. Viktor had important news. He entered their bedroom to tell Tanya that Verona, their neighbor woman of 43, was pregnant. He could do nothing, and he did not want to admit that he was the father of this baby.

On July 30, 1800, a baby boy was born to Verona. He was an active baby, he cried to seek attention and at times would act aggressively for no reason. He would take his food and throw it at his mother. The baby continued to show a behavior of anger and hate for his mother. Time began to pass, and the boy turned twelve years of age. His mother named him Isaac. Isaac started to immediately show his anger and hateful tendencies to fight with other students at this school. He would steal their pencils and tear up their assignments. The school principal would call his mother

Verona to come to the school and take him out. Isaac, the Korka prodigy, continued to fail in his school, and his mother Verona would be called every week. Verona learned that when Isaac was fifteen, his father, Viktor, was killed in the battle of Waterloo. From that point, his behavior was uncontrollable.

Verona became despondent, and her health deteriorated. At fifty-eight, she died and buried in a small grave behind her home. The Svetlana's, Igor and Galina, lived two miles away from Verona's small village home. The Russian Orthodox Father George pleaded with Igor and Galina to please god and give Isaac a home. After Sunday service, they then agreed to care for Isaac and make him their son. By the time Isaac reached his third year in high school, he always fought with other students and would break into homes to rob them. He was a terror, and many in the small village were afraid of him.

On a cold night in November 1817, he was drinking vodka with several boys along the ridges behind the town's hills. Soon an argument broke out between Isaac and a larger built boy called Vladimir. Isaac attacked Vladimir with his knife and stabbed him twenty-five times. Isaac continued the rapid movement of his knife hand into the chest and stomach of Vladimir even as the blood flowed onto the wet snow. Vladimir laid dead, and Isaac stood over him, laughing. Isaac just walked away and returned home. He did not speak at all to Galina. She noticed that he had blood on his trousers. When she asked, what happened, Isaac said nothing but only stared into the fireplace flames.

At seven in the evening of the next day, two policemen knocked on Igor and Galina's wooden door and entered the home. Isaac was sitting by the fireplace. He heard the front door open and sprang up! He saw the two uniformed policemen walking towards him and jumped like a wagon wheel spring to the back door with the policemen in hot pursuit. Isaac opened the back door, but by then, the two policemen grabbed him and pushed his face into the cabin's hard wooden floor. They grabbed his legs and arms, placing a massive steel chain around them and dragged him to a waiting horse wagon. After the court hearing, the local and regional officials sentenced Isaac to 45 years in a prison located in the Donbas Ukraine Region. Galina was never to hear from Isaac, and she learned five years later that he died in a gang fight with prison inmates.

KORKA'S GENERAL LA GAILLARDE

Jacques La Gaillarde rises to the rank of General after a humble beginning. La Gaillarde directly related to the Sunni Terrorist leader Taha Falanha, a distant Korka cousin of Nasan Khan, the grandson of the RedDawn warlord Nasan. La Gaillarde was born on November 15, 1770, near Dunkirk, France. General La Gaillarde died July 30, 1830, but not before an appointment as a military commander under Napoleon's direct command.

Jacques, of humble origins, enlistment in the French Army as a private in a 1788 regiment serving in Martinique. Two years later, he deserted and returned to civilian life as a baker in Paris, France. In 1791, as a supporter of the French Revolution, he enlisted again in the French Army as a private. He raised a company of volunteers and was named its captain. When war broke out in 1792, he traveled to the Army of the North. A staunch supporter of the Revolutionary government, he was rapidly promoted and by September 1793 had been named a general of a brigade. In 1794, General Jacques La Gaillarde fought in the Low Countries, 1795 on the Rhine, and from 1796 to 1799, he saw battle in Germany. When the British and the Russians invaded Holland, in 1799, he was sent to serve under Gen. Guillaume Brune and played a significant role in defeating the Allied forces.

In 1805, at the Battle of Austerlitz, La Gaillarde and General Louis-Vincent-Joseph Le Blond, count of Saint-Hilaire, led their division onto the Pratzen Heights and broke the center of the Russian Army, which led to Napoleon's most significant victory. In 1806, Jacques la Gaillarde rewarded with the title Count of Unebourg. Following the Prussian Army's destruction in 1806,

General La Gaillarde successfully laid siege to the major cities in Silesia (Golgau, Breslau, and Brieg). He commanded a division during the 1809 Wagram campaign and given command of the Seventh Corps of the Army that, under Napoleon, invaded Russia in 1812. However, early in the campaign, he quarreled with Jérôme Bonaparte, King of Westphalia, and was removed from the Army's command and ordered back to Paris. The 1813 Dresden phase of the Leipzig campaign was a disaster for General La Gaillarde when given the authority to block the retreat of the Austrian Army that defeated at the Battle of Dresden several months earlier. The Army encircled by the Russian Army and his entire corps of 10,000 killed in the battle. Napoleon realized that for the first time his troops faced troops who were as motivated as his French nationalist conscripts.

General La Gaillarde was taken prisoner and sent to Russia, where he spent the next two years. While interned in the Samara prison of war camp, La Gaillard developed a close personal relationship with a French Cavalry officer by the name of Paul Berthier. The food consisted of only two potatoes and a small bowl of fish soup twice a day. The temperatures would drop to minus twenty each night. Paul and Jacques decided to save scraps of food and attempt to cut through the wire fence and seek to travel through the forest and reach the Volga River and transit to Astrakan and from there to the Caspian Sea. They had to keep their escape secret and to rest as much as possible after each day that they cut trees to build more prison housing. They crawled out of their bunks after two years and slid through the sewerage underground system until they reached 300 yards under the prison fence.

When La Gaillarde and Paul returned to France in 1817, he was not well received by the restored Bourbon government and discharged. However, he and Paul became a close civilian-military consultant for the second in command at Borodin's battle. Paul Berthier's niece, Tatiana, who he inherited, confirmed all the traits of a sociopathic teenager. Berthier could not concentrate on the strategy for the campaign that was soon to happen as he was so concerned about his niece Tatiana: who left his cousin's small vegetable farm in Southern Russia.

Jacques, "I can't understand the girl, no matter how hard I try. It's not that she seems dangerous or exactly what she means to do wrong. She can lie with the straightest face, and after she's the most outlandish lies, she still seems entirely comfortable. However, she attacks any man that approaches her. Two weeks ago, she took a letter opener and stuck it into one of our serf's wagon drivers. She did it and said nothing. She laughed and just stared at the blood squirting from his neck. Of course, we gave medical care to the Slavic serf, but she said nothing. What am I to do? The battle plan must complete in the next 8 hours. I fear she will even attack me."

Jacques La Gaillarde knew that when a woman was not of sound mind, it would be best to jail her or outright kill her on the battlefield. Jacques looked deeply into the eyes of his friend. "General Berthier, you must think of France, and victory for the Republic. Let me talk to her, and I think that I can solve this problem immediately."

Paul looked at his close friend who had shared so much war episodes, and said, "Jacques, do what you must. I respect your decision, whatever befalls this mentally imbalanced niece of mine. Make it reasonable so that I can protect myself and France."

Jacques bowed and left the headquarters tent, lifted himself on his horse, and rode to Paul Berthier's family estate. From a distance, he could see a blonde teenager wearing a black cape and a white dress. As he rode closer, he saw Tatiana sitting on a tree trunk broken from a Russian cannonball. She sat staring out into the distant formations of 40,000 French cavalry troops and 200 Italian field cannons. She did not hear his horse approaching. He dismounted and reached into his waistcoat and pulled out a dagger. As silently as the flowers moved back and forth that surrounded the tree log, Tatiana fell and bled to death. The wind rose sharply, and the cannons began pounding the enemy positions.

BATTLE OF LEIPZIG

On August 26 and 27, 1813, Napoleon's final major victory fought near the Saxon capital of Dresden. However, the Battle of Leipzig was to become a negative precursor to the Battle of Waterloo. The French Army consisted of only 185,000 troops facing an overwhelming force of 320,000 f Austrian, Prussian, Russian, and Sweden. The loss removed France as a power base in Germany and Poland. General Napoleon Bonaparte gives up the field and agrees to an exile to the Island of Elba.[21]

NAPOLEON THE NEVER DEFEATED EMPEROR

On March 1, 1815, Napoleon returned to France, landing near Cannes with 1,000 men. He won support from the rural peasantry as he marched toward Paris, and Louis XVIII fled the country. On March 20, 1815, Napoleon arrived in the capital of Paris. In a treaty of alliance signed on March 25, 1815, Great Britain, Prussia, Austria, and Russia each vowed to maintain 150,000 men in the field until Napoleon's overthrown forever. Shortly after that, the allied armies comprising about 794,000 troops, plan to assemble along the French frontier, and march on Paris by convergent routes. The time needed for the Russians to reach the Rhine would delay the invasion until early July 1815, and that allowed Napoleon the opportunity to organize his defenses. Napoleon could command over 160,000 first-line troops, but forced to relegate many of them to border defense.

Because Louis XVIII, restored to the throne upon Napoleon's first abdication, had abolished conscription, Napoleon was not immediately able to draw on the vast number of trained men who had returned to civilian life. To address that lack of trained conscripts, Napoleon quickly set about raising troops for an early campaign. All undischarged soldiers summoned to arms, and in eight weeks, 80,000 men added to the Army for a total of 240,000. At the beginning of June 1815, too late for use in the Waterloo campaign, the conscription class of 1815 ordered to mustering points, and Napoleon hoped to have more than 500,000 men under arms before the autumn of 1815. By April 27, 1815, Napoleon had decided to attack Wellington and Blücher in the southern Netherlands (now Belgium), hoping to defeat them before the Austrians and Russians could bring their larger forces to overpower the French contingent.

NAPOLEON'S FINAL BATTLE

On June 18, 1815, France had been at war for twenty-three years. It fought during the Hundred Days of Napoleon's restoration as Caesar, between Napoleon's 72,000 troops and the combined forces of the Duke of Wellington's English coalition army of 68,000 that consisted of British, Dutch, Belgian, and German units, plus 45,000 Prussians, the main force of Gebhard Leberecht von Blücher's command. Napoleon's return from Elba and his seizure of power in 1815, Vandamme was given command of an army corps and took part in the Waterloo campaign, fighting in Belgium at the Battle of Ligny and Wavre. The allied campaign against Napoleon began in earnest in early June, but the armies that had assembled in Belgium were of dubious quality. Blücher's four corps included many inexperienced conscripts among their 120,000 men. Wellington, whose forces numbered more than 93,000 before the campaign began, characterized his Army as "infamous." Of the 31,000 British troops under his command, most had never been under fire. Many of the 29,000 Netherlanders under William, Prince of Orange (later William II), were unreliable, having served under Napoleon little more than a year before. The remainder of that polyglot Army comprised 16,000 Hanoverians, roughly 6,800 Brunswickers, and the 6,300 men of George III's German Legion. Only the last contingent, veterans of the Peninsular War, could be safely trusted to battle to the death. Thus, the majority of the troops arrayed against Napoleon did not match the highly enthusiastic and mostly veteran French force. Wellington and Blücher had agreed to come to each other's assistance should either be attacked.

Still, the lack of any real preparation before June 15, 1815, shows that little close attention had viewed as to such a possibility. The first French troops crossed into the southern Netherlands on June 15, 1815, and by day's end, through skillful and audacious maneuvering, Napoleon had secured all of his essential strategic needs. His Army deployed compactly, presenting front some twelve miles wide, separating the Prussian and British forces and ready to operate against either.

Early on June 16, 1815, Napoleon had planned to shift the bulk of his Army to the left-wing against Wellington along the Charleroi–Quater-Bras–Brussels road. Still, he soon became aware that the Prussian forces assembled at Ligny were vulnerable. To contest the crossroads at Quatre-Bras, Napoleon dispatched a holding force under Marshal Michel Ney, a commander whom Napoleon had dubbed "the bravest of the brave" for his conduct during the retreat from Russia. Marshal of the Empire Michel Ney and 1st Duke of Elchingen, 1st Prince of the Moskva advanced cowardly with limited aggression on the allied position; thus, allowing Wellington the opportunity to reinforce his outnumbered troops, and held on to Quatre-Bras after a day of inconclusive fighting. Allied casualties numbered roughly 4,700 killed and wounded, while the French lost 4,300. Napoleon himself led the attack on Blücher's force at Ligny, and the Prussians escaped destruction mainly as a result of miscommunication between the divided French commands. Blücher had deployed three corps that consisted of 83,000 troops on a forward slope, a position that gave him control of the valley below but subjected his people to fierce artillery bombardment. Napoleon's plan of attack was based on the use of a corps under Marshal Jean-Baptiste Drouet to shatter the Prussian right flank. Drouet's brigade was attached to Ney's command; however, Ney and Napoleon gave conflicting orders for his march. Drouet's brigade became exhausted on June 16, 1815, marching and countermarching between the two battlefields. Blücher's troops fought stubbornly, but they lacked the skill and stamina of the French veterans, and by late afternoon Napoleon was ready to administer a finishing blow to the Prussian center with the arrival of Drouet's corps. At that moment, an active enemy column reported in the French rear, and sections of the French left-wing began to withdraw in the face of that apparent threat. Blücher took advantage of the confusion by launching a massive attack but rebuffed by a detachment of Napoleon's veteran Imperial Guard. At that moment, the turning point of the battle's victory or defeat chiseled in stone. Blücher's troops had spent their force, and Napoleon had confirmed that Drouet's mysterious enemy column was. The French Drouet column began to withdraw by orders from Ney.

Two hours later than he had intended, Napoleon ordered the Guard to assault the Prussian center. The Imperial Guard charged through Ligny soon after 7:30 in the evening, followed by vast cavalry, and the Prussian line collapsed. Adolf, Baron von Lützow, spurred his cavalry unit into a failed countercharge that led to his capture by the French, and the seventy-four-year-old Gebhard Leberecht von Blücher had his horse shot from under him while securing the Prussian retreat. Pinned by the dead animal and with the cavalry battle continuing around him, Blücher was saved by his trusted aide-de-camp, Count Nostitz, who pulled him from under the dead animal and placed Blücher on the back of his horse. They both raced away at full gallop from the field of battle. After using root ointments for his crushed leg and a bottle of liquor, Blücher returned to the battle.

Darkness and the stubborn resistance of the two Prussian wings prevented Napoleon's success in the center from turning the defeat of the Prussians into a rout. The French victory was considerable. Prussian casualties were more than 12,000, while the French lost approximately 10,000. During the night, a further 8,000 Prussians, recruited from former provinces of the French Empire, deserted Blücher and fled east toward Liege, away from the French and the more massive engagement to come. Blücher's forces, temporarily under the command of Count Neidhardt von Gneisenau, continued their retreat toward Wavre on June 17, 1815, leaving the French free to turn against Wellington. Napoleon was uncharacteristically slow to seize upon the advantage he had gained, however. At midday on the 17th, Marshal Emmanuel de Grouchy, with 33,000 men of Napoleon's 105,000 strong force, wastefully pursued the revived Blücher that would remove his Army from the action to come. On the left flank, Ney did nothing to hinder Wellington's orderly withdrawal from Quatre-Bras, and the last French response stymied by a torrential thunderstorm and a skillful rearguard action by the coalition army. As they repositioned their forces, Wellington and Blücher remained in regular communication. With the promise of reinforcement by the Prussians the following day, Wellington ended June 17, 1815, bivouacked in a strong defensive position along a ridge south of Mont-Saint-Jean.

Napoleon still hoped to defeat Wellington before the Prussians could arrive in force. Two cavalry divisions sent to form a screen in Bülow's path, and a corps under Georges Mouton, Count de Lobau, was built against the allies by 1:30 in the afternoon those arrangements completed. The battery near La Belle Alliance opened fire, and 18,000 infantrymen under Ney and Drouet advanced on the allied center a half-hour later. No cavalry accompanied the attack, and the British infantry met Drouet's men with maximum firepower. Many of the attackers marched in an unusual formation: in three divisional columns, two hundred soldiers full, twenty-four, and twenty-seven ranks deep. Thus, they were unable to return fire efficiently and were very vulnerable to artillery. La Haye Sainte attacked. Papelotte occupied the town only. Wellington's cavalry commander, Henry Paget, Earl of Uxbridge, now threw his horsemen against the disorganized French columns and the numerically inferior cavalry coming up behind. The French withdrew from Papelotte in good order, but elsewhere, they failed to stem the English cavalry's advance. Flushed with success, Lord Edward Somerset and Sir William Ponsonby's cavalry ignored Uxbridge's call to return and charged the French lines. Ponsonby killed a third of the French column, but 2,500 English horsemen lay dead. Despite that reverse, Wellington had surmounted the first crisis. Drouet's corps had been driven back from the slopes before the British lines.

On June 17, 1815, at 3:00 in the afternoon, the battlefield showed no activity except for Hougoumont, where 1,200 coalition troops continued to hold off their number of French many times. Napoleon ordered Ney to quickly seize La Haye Sainte in preparation for an assault by Drouet's and Reille's corps and elements of the Imperial Guard. Ney dispatched the two brigades of infantry to La Haye Sainte repulsed, and Ney then committed the bulk of the French cavalry to a fatally dangerous course of action. Ney lost the Battle at Waterloo by his lack of understanding that the movement of wounded men and empty ammunition wagons from Wellington's center was a clear sign of Wellington's weak front. He thought that to be the case, at 4:00 pm, Ney brought up Édouard-Jean-Baptiste Milhaud's two divisions of cavalry to seize a chance of deciding the outcome of the battle. Charles Lefebvre-Desnouettes ignored the chain of command and ordered his cavalry division to follow Milhaud. The British responded by forming Infantry squares that were hollow defensive formations several ranks deep that had proven to be especially useful at breaking cavalry charges.

Waterloo battlefield re-enacting- Courtesy
of William Sadler (Pyms Gallery)

"Between a battle lost and a battle won, the distance is immense and there stand empires" Napoleon.

Although the French horsemen were extremely determined, a massed cavalry attack had little chance of success when delivered virtually without infantry and close artillery support against unbroken English squares. English gunners took a heavy toll of the 5,000 cuirassiers or heavily armed cavalry mounting the slopes between Hougoumont and La Haye Sainte. Driven off by Uxbridge's remaining cavalry, the cuirassiers reformed their ranks, but their second attack also failed. Although very critical of Ney's first use of unaccompanied cavalry, Napoleon decided to stand by Ney's action. François-Étienne Kellermann's two cavalry divisions were sent to support Ney and joined by Claude-Étienne Guyot's division of cavalry from the Imperial Guard. There were now a 9,000 cavalry about to attack a front reduced to 500 yards by the zones of fire around Hougoumont and La Haye Sainte.

Meanwhile, on the French right flank, at about 4:30 in the afternoon and after an eleven-hour march through difficult country, Bülow's leading divisions opened fire from Paris Wood on the French cavalry screen. Lobau resolved to engage the Prussians before Bülow could deploy the rest of his force, and he held his ground. Although increasingly outnumbered. Blücher, who had accompanied Prussian General Freidrich Wilhelm Freiherr von Bulow's corps, switched the Prussian attack to Plancenoit. Lobau forced to fall back and detach a brigade to defend the village. Sheer numbers eventually forced the French out of Plancenoit, and Napoleon dispatched Philippe-Guillaume Duhesme's division of the Young Guard to recover it. Duhesme's success there relieved the pressure on the French right flank for the moment.

After Napoleon's final defeat at the Battle of Waterloo, Vandamme was exiled and sought refuge in the United States, where he lived in Philadelphia (1816–1819). In 1819 he was allowed to return to Europe and settled with his family in Ghent, Belgium. Reconciled with Louis XVIII, he was able to go back to Cassel, his birthplace, where he died.

Napoleon could see that his Army was in retreat and unable to mount a counter-attack. With a detachment of cavalry detachment of 300, he returned to Paris France on June 21, 1815. With great emotional agony, General Bonaparte gave up his throne on June 22, 1815. On July 5 and 6, 1815, the once-great French Army began a reluctant march south of the Loire River and disbanded. The allies entered Paris on July 7, 1815, and Louis XVIII restored to the throne on July 8, 1815, Napoleon journeyed to the west coast and planned to escape to the United States.

However, he was betrayed to the English by a Korka double agent, Conrad Graveland. The War of 1812 fought between the United States and the United Kingdom. The English and James Madison, the President of the United States, did not want Napoleon to seek refuge in the U.S. as it would politically hinder the on-going peace treaty. Under the direction of the Madison White House, Graveland was paid 150,000 dollars in gold to contact a British Naval Squadron at sea. He reported to the British Admiralty that Napoleon would leave on an Italian ship from the port of Cherbourg on the French West Coast. The plan was to sail directly to the New York port and contact President Madison for refugee status. After two hours at sea, Napoleon found his plans for an escape to the United States, frustrated by an armed British naval squadron. He had no choice but to surrendered himself to the commander of the H.M.S. Bellerophon on July 15.1815.

Sadly, Napoleon spent the remainder of his life in exile on the coast of Africa on the island of St. Helena. The "Great Caesar of the Gauls," statesman and revolutionary ruler of Europe, Napoleon Bonaparte died on May 5, 1821, at the young age of fifty-one from stomach cancer. Nine years later, his body returned to Paris, interred in the Hotel des Invalides-a retirement home and museum for French veterans.[22]

CHAPTER FIVE

PEOPLE'S DREAMS – CRIMEAN WAR

"A Nihilist is a person who does not take any principle for granted; however much that principle may be revered." – Ivan Turgenev

HISTORICAL PERSPECTIVES - CIMMERIANS

HISTORIANS BELIEVE THAT CRIMEA colonized by the Cimmerians (Cimmerians (sĭmēr´eənz), ancient people of South Russia. The Greek Homer, the author of the Iliad and the Odyssey, mentioned them, but the Cimmerians were known to live in the 8th century B.C. and forced to leave by the Scythian people near Lake Van a Salt Lake in East Turkey. What is known is that around the 7th century BCE, the steppe area conquered by a nomadic tribe that was of Iranian derivation. The people in this area were then called Scythian, or Scyth, Saka, and Sacae. In 2018 terms, the geography of Scythian included present-day Central Ukraine, South-Eastern Ukraine, Southern Russia, Russian Volga, and South-Ural regions, also to a smaller extent north-eastern Balkans and around Moldova.

Before the 9th-century BCE, this nomadic tribe migrated westward from Central Asia to southern Russia. They reached Ukraine in the 8th and 7th centuries BCE. The migration of the Scythians from Asia eventually brought them into the territory of the Cimmerians, who had traditionally controlled the Caucasus and the plains north of the Black Sea. In a war that lasted 30 years, the Scythians destroyed the Cimmerians. They set themselves up as rulers of an empire stretching from west Persia through Syria and Judaea to the borders of Egypt. leaving them finally in control of lands, "which stretched from the Persian border north through the Kuban and into southern Russia." The Scythians formed families and established great wealth and a mighty empire known as Crimea. Today, Crimea is part of the Russian Federation. The empire prospered for several centuries before in 4th-century BCE to the 2nd-century C.E. laid waste and annexed to the Sarmatians, a broad alliance of Iranian warrior clans. The Scythians were great warriors and justly feared and admired by the Cimmerians and Sarmatians for their prowess in war and their battle horsemanship. They were among the earliest people to master the art of riding, and their mobility astonished their neighbors. The Scythians were remarkable not only for their fighting ability but also for the sophisticated culture they produced. They developed a class of wealthy aristocrats whose only example of their importance and power is the Kurgans tombs in the Valley of the Tsars or Caesars near Arzhan, 40 miles from Kyzyl, Tyva. The excavation of these graves revealed opulent worked articles of gold, beads of turquoise, carnelian, amber, and rubies. The Royal Scyths established themselves as chieftains of the southern Russian and Crimean territories. It is at the Kurgans that the richest, oldest, and most-numerous relics of Scythian civilization found near Tyva. "In 519 BC, King Darius attacked the Scythians east of the Caspian Sea and a few years later conquered the Indus Valley." In 513 BC, the Scythian horse nomads devastated the country of grains and animals as they retreated from Darius's army. Darius could not supply his army and withdraw. The Scythians used guerrilla tactics to kill many as Darius fled back to Persia.

ROYAL SCYTHS - ARSIAN KORKA- THE LION

The Royal Scyths headed by Arsian Korka- the Lion, an Ottoman Turk, who on his mother's side, was also a direct Korka descendant of the French Royalist la-Gaillarde who fought in the Napoleonic Wars. Arsian Korka's father was simply known as, Korka the Turk, and by his first marriage related to Monsieur Vitry, a Major in Napoleon's Hussar light cavalry. Korka, the Turk, was a former Scythian Warlord who stood at six feet and seven inches. His eyes were piercing, and he rode a white horse that was able to carry his body weight of two hundred ten pounds. With his armor of padded double elk and horse skin plus a bronze back and chess breastplate to ward off arrows and lances, he struck a dominant figure on the battlefield. In battle, he wore a red cape lined with mink fur to keep his head warm. It was important for those horse warriors to see their leader and inspired by his physical presence on the battlefield. When he attacked at full gallop, he held in the right hand the Korka family Shashka passed down for over 900 years. Besides, he had a bow strung over his back, and the quiver with bronze tipped arrows on the left side of his saddle. He could quickly shoot an arrow and then grab his Shashka to finish-of who he was attacking.

According to the stars, upon Arsian's death, his authority transmitted to his son, Timer Korka, - Man of Iron. Eventually, about the time of Herodotus, the royal Scyth family intermarried with Greeks. In 342 BC, the ruler, Arsian-the Lion, was killed by an arrow while fighting Philip II of Macedonia. He was 92 at the time and stood 6'9" with a muscular body that showed no signs of aging. The Korka Scyth Crimea clan eventually dispersed into the vast Asia Minor in the 2nd-century BCE. Arsian Korka being the last Ottoman Turk sovereign Royal Scyths. The Korka family members within the Scythian army viewed themselves as men of liberty who received no wage other than animals and clothing, but if they wanted more riches won in battles, they had to bring the head of the enemy they killed to the sovereign's general. With their women, they celebrated the virtue of warfare, fearlessness, aggression, cunning, strength under fire. Their daily realization as they moved from place to place was that they had to conquer the peoples that they found and expand a save circle of land. Many warriors in battle wore Greek-style bronze helmets and chain-mail jerkins. Their principal weapon was a double-curved bow and trefoil-shaped arrows; their swords were of the Persian type. Every Scythian had at least one personal horse. Still, the Arsian Korka-the Lion had owned large herds of horses, chiefly Mongolian ponies that kept intact for they adjusted to the harsh climate of the steppes, the Mongolian horse derived from millennia of ruthless natural selection. Scythian horses were small, and its toughness is legendary to the Korka family, and the horses accompanied the Scythians' nomads in their daily lives.

The Scythians evaded the Persian Army, using feints and retreating eastwards, all the while destroying the vegetation of the countryside. Darius's army chased their enemy deep into Scythian lands, where they sent word to Arsian and his father, Arsian Korka -the Turk, urging them to fight or surrender. Arsian and his father refused as they knew that with their horses, the Persian Army would tire once they reached the banks of the Volga river and moved toward Thrace around the banks of the Volga River and headed towards Thrace and attempted to subjugate all those who resisted.[1] The year was 513 BCE, and the battle with Darius was a significant campaign in European Scythia history. The campaign was satisfying Darius's revenge for a previous conflict during the reign of Cyrus, where the Scythians had attacked Medes. The Scythians were very savage and brutal and continuously committed horrible cruelties upon their more civilized neighbors. Their war tactics were laying waste the country, destroying crops, carrying off cattle, burning towns, and villages. The Scythians would murder all the inhabitants with circumstances of extreme atrocity, often burning their captives alive as sacrifices to their star god as in Neolithic times.[2]

Arsian-the Lion had raised over 25,000 of his best-mounted warriors to prepare a battle in the vast steppe and trap Darius's unique rear-guard army with both horses mounted archers and foot warriors with spears and swords. Arsian took his four daughters to watch the battle from a high ridge overlooking the battlefield below. Still, Darius learned of the Arsian's location from a Scythian who rode five miles to find Darius's camp and requested twenty gold bars. Darius was pleased by this messenger and gladly gave him the gold. Darius ordered his general to send his one-hundred and twenty-five of his lone assassins to surround the ridged citadel. The fight did not take long as, Arsian-the Lion, and 600 of his 6' 9" tall, muscular, powerful men, could not stop the onslaught, but savage fighting took place, and 400 stabbed and hacked to death, and one hundred thirty-nine had the top of their heads removed. With sixty-one warriors, Arsian-the Lion rushed to protect his daughters, but the large numbers of Persian warriors were too much for him, and he also was hacked to death with his head decapitated. His daughters were taken to the cliff edge to stand; then their throats were sliced with the full length of the sword and thrown down over the forty-foot-high hill that overlooked the vast plain below. Arsian the Lion, and his four daughters, Culpan, Golcacak, Guzzi, and Tansilu, were dead and never to come back. Once Arsian's son, Timer Korka, -the Iron, organized a group of his best warriors, they set off to find his father and sisters. They found the bodies and carried them to the temporary village and laid them above eight-foot wooden platforms dressed in their distinctive attire stitched with gold and precious stones. Next, they placed the sacred Korka glowing green Star Stones below the platform in a circle and lit huge bonfires near the deep common grave for all five. Five horses were taken and sacrificed for the fallen members of Arsian's family. A bronze knife designed with a broad, square blade placed next to Arsian with his shield. The bronze and gold dagger and sword set to Arsian's left and his gold ring and necklace, a symbol of his royalty, to the right. His Boar Tusks helmet laid on where his head had been and the hands across his chest. The girls were arranged two on Arsian's right side and two on his left side. Their mirrors adorned with carved ivory and jade at the bottom of their feet. They placed flowers in their hair and gold dust on their closed eyes. Their ivory combs lay on a bronze basin above their heads. Large stones set in a rectangular arrangement around the grave, and the grave lay in ten feet below the surface.

Arsian Lion's father, Korka, the Turk, took his dagger and cut a triangle upon his chest. He let the blood flow over the center of the bodies. Next, soil and rocks pushed over the opening, and with each stage, the members of the Korka Clan cried and gave out warrior chants and screamed death to the Persians. The band of Scythian warriors and their families all mounted their horses and wagons and took up their animal skin shelters.[3]

They moved slowly moved northward toward the land of the Slavs. Their hearts and bodies were heavily laden with grief. As wealth created complacency of the warrior class, the Medes, who ruled Persia, attacked the horsemen of Scythian clans and forced them out of Anatolia or Asia Minor. Asian Turkey, the Anatolian peninsula, or the Anatolian plateau, is the westernmost protrusion of Asia, which makes up the majority of modern-day Turkey.[4]

ScythiansAncientHistory -Courtesy of Barry Cunliffe Oxford UnivPress

GREEK ISLAND'S HIDDEN STATE

Greece viewed by early historians was a hidden state. Greek live in the existence and actions of "actors" within their democratic state, not only intelligence and defense but Government bodies' influential figures outside of government. All members in the inner hidden state immune from being known but controlling all politics, economics, and wars. The early history of Greece can easily understand by dividing it into periods. The region already settled, and agriculture initiated during the Paleolithic era, as evidenced by finds at Petralona and Franchthi caves. From 3200 to 1100 BCE, the Cycladic Civilization flourished in the islands of Aegean Sea, Delos, Naxos, and Paros and demonstrated the earliest evidence of continual human habitation in that region. During the Cycladic Period, houses and temples built of finished stone, and the people made their living through fishing and trade. This period divided into three phases: Early Cycladic, Middle Cycladic, and Late Cycladic, with a steady development in art and architecture. The latter two stages overlap and finally merge with the Minoan Civilization, and differences between the periods become indistinguishable. From the 5th and 4th centuries BCE onward, Greeks established colonies along the Crimean coasts, the first colonies being at Chersonesus, near modern Sevastopol, and Panticapaeum, where the city of Kerch connects the Russian the Black Seaport. In fifteen BC, Rome colonized these islands, and they survived a series of attacks by eastern nomadic Asian Mongol and Hun Hordes.[5] The Mongol Tartars army that overran eastern Europe in the 13th century established a khanate in Russia and maintained suzerainty there until the15th century. The Russian Cossack forces twice defeated the Golden Hordes and then occupied the steppe region for hundreds of years.[6]

CRIMEA

For over nine centuries, Prince Vladimir I of Kievan Rus proclaimed that the Crimea coastal cities were Russian sovereign territory and not under Ukraine's control. He surmised that Ukraine never had the political will or military strength to retain Crimea from various warring tribes. Crimea fell to the Tatars of the Golden Horde and later the Kipchaks, a Turkic nomadic people, and confederation who lived on the Eurasian Steppe. In the 13th century, the Republic of Genoa established a trading post with their headquarters situated at Feodosiya and created a Black Sea trade monopoly.[7]

Crimea early 1400 – Courtesy of the leftbankcafe. blogspot

Islam ushered into the Tatar villages, not along the coastal regions but in the Crimean interior under Öz Beg, a Khan of the Golden Horde who had converted to Islam. The remnants of the Golden Horde came to be known as the Khanate of the Crimea. Ottoman rule was harsh, and in 1475, the Khanate bowed to Ottoman jurisdiction. However, from the Tatars capital of Bakhchisaray in southern Crimea, the large Muscovite agricultural and horse breeding estates were raided for economic gain.

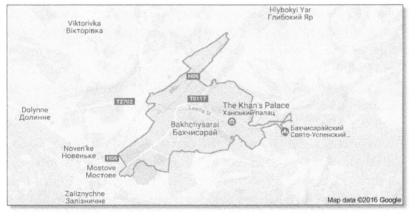

Bakhchisaray Crimea early - Courtesy of Map data Google

The Russian Tsars and the Ottoman Sultans were more often at points of dispute. From the 16th to the early 20th century, twelve wars fought between them. Historical documents reveal the memory of Nikolai Yudenich and the titanic battles he fought in wild places like Van and Erzurum, with genocide for those on the wrong side. In 2018, it became common to assert that the Middle Eastern boundaries now being challenged by the Sunni Terrorist State (ISIS) versus those markers by the 1916 Anglo-French Sykes-Picot agreement.[8] Scholar Sean McMeekin wrote that it was an Anglo-Franco-Russian agreement making Russia the senior country. Sean McMeekin wrote "the fighting spirit of all the forces battling for the Tsar, a coalition which at certain times and places included local Armenians. Whether with disgust or approval, that emphasis will certainly understand as a way of vindicating or explaining away the mass deportation of Armenians, decreed in 1915, which was a death march." Further, Sean believed that Talaat Pasha, the Turkish Sultanate overlord, did not view the "the survival of the Armenia deportees as the priority" in the Sykes-Picot agreement.

Today, Armenians regard Pasha as guilty for the Armenian genocide. International relationships are as volatile and essential as that between the Russians and the Turks. Although they were a formidable combination when they occasionally teamed up to fight the French from 1798 to 1799, the tsars and the sultans were often in disagreements. They clashed in twelve wars between the 16th and the early 20th century. Starting in 2014, under Recep Tayyip Erdoğan, Turks and Russians have veered between warm commercial relations and war conflict by proxy over the Syrian Civil War.[9]

Words can cleverly mask the damnation of Mehmed Talaat. Rafael de Nogales Méndez, a Venezuelan soldier of fortune, reported he saw on a mountainside "thousands of half-nude and bleeding Armenian corpses, piled in heaps or interlaced in death's final embrace ..."[10]

Crimea Talaat Pasha – Courtesy of spe-pp.britishgasco.uk

How can one-witness validate this Armenian version of their genocide? Did they die under the hands of the Ottoman Empire? No other person saw this carnage. No genocide picture ever recorded.

California Congresswoman Anna Eshoo, who is of Assyrian and Armenian heritage, worked with Adam Schiff on January 30, 2007, a proposed Armenian Genocide resolution a measure under consideration in the U.S. House of Representatives that would recognize the 1915 Genocide. The Democratic Party of the USA believes that the United States' foreign policy reflects appropriate understanding and sensitivity concerning issues related to human rights, ethnic cleansing, and genocide documented in the United States record relating to the Armenian genocide for other purposes. United States foreign policy must reflect appropriate understanding and sensitivity concerning issues related to human rights, ethnic cleansing, and genocide documented in the United States record relating to the Armenian genocide.[11] The proposed Armenian Genocide resolution was a measure under consideration in the U.S. House of Representatives that would recognize the 1915 Genocide. It was officially called H. Res 106[1] or the Affirmation of the United States Record on the Armenian Genocide Resolution. It never passed in the House.

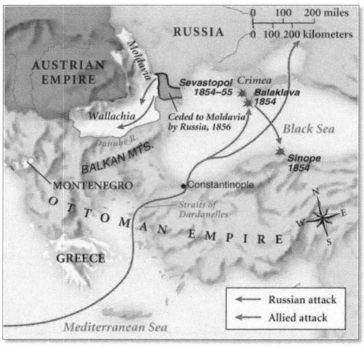

Crimean War (1853-1856)- Courtesy of crimeahistory.org

Historians viewed the 1853 to 1856 Crimean War as Great Britain, France, and Turkey ganging up on Russia. Some believe that the war was unnecessary as it revolved around political and diplomatic fallaciousness. It should have never fought in Crimea except for Austrian manipulations. The Middle East and Turkish internal politics were the driving force for the war. In June 1854, the Russian Czar accepted the Austrians' demands that his troops withdrew from the "German Danubian principalities." Immediately, Austrian troops entered and replaced the Russian army. With Austrian troops now in Ukraine, the French and English decided not to enter Ukraine.

The Czar had a plan to march and capture Istanbul, and some speculate that the Russia accord with Austria stopped the action. The Russian army had earlier saved Austria when in 1849, the Hungarians rebels attempted a coup. The Czar felt that the Austrians showed no excellent will and deceived Russia. With the British and French unable to attack the Danubian principalities, their government decided instead to send a large naval force to Crimea to destroy the Russian Sevastopol naval base. The massive maritime bombardment was the beginning of the Crimean War, but the Russian high command was unable to transport and supply Sevastopol.

SIEGE OF SEVASTOPOL (1854–1855)

This battle well documented. Historical realities cannot change so quickly. The combined force consisted of 50,000 British and French troops and 10,000 Piedmontese troops during 1855, commanded by Lord Raglan and Gen. François Canrobert, besieged and finally captured the main naval base of the Russian Black Sea fleet. Sevastopol's defenses built by the military engineer Colonel Eduard Totleben and the Russian troops commanded by Prince Aleksandr Menshikov. The siege lasted three hundred thirty-one days because the allies lacked heavy artillery to effectively smash the defenses, while all Russian efforts to break the blockade failed. Once again, the severe weather saved Russia from a major defeat. The cold brought on severe suffering and heavy casualties among the allied troops, whose commanders had made little or no provision for a winter campaign. This situation produced several crises within the British government. On September 8, 1855, French troops took and held the Malakhov, a vital defensive position at the southeast end of the city. On September 11, 1855, the Russians decided to retreat and block the port by sinking their ships in the harbor, destroying their fortifications, and empty Sevastopol. The French and the English occupied Sevastopol and allowed the Russians to retreat in safety.

British firing on Sevastopol – Courtesy of britishbattles.com

After Austria threatened to join the allies, Russia accepted preliminary peace terms on February 1, 1856. The Congress of Paris worked out the final settlement from February 25 to March 30, 1856. The resulting Treaty of Paris signed on March 30, 1856, guaranteed Ottoman Turkey's integrity and obliged Russia to surrender southern Bessarabia at the mouth of the Danube. The Black Sea neutralized, and the Danube River opened to the shipping of all nations. The Crimean War causalities amounted to 250,000 dead from disease and starvation. Still, through Russian bravery and perseverance, Russia won victories over the Turks in the Caucasus, and after twelve months, the defense of Sevastopol held and considered a great military achievement. However, Russian forces decided to abandon the naval base to save the population of the city. After the Crimean War, the Crimean descendants of the

power of Moscow's principality. In 1448, the Russian bishops elected their patriarch without recourse to Constantinople, and the Russian church was thenceforth could appoint its Head and not subject to the authority of an external patriarch or archbishop. In 1589 Job, metropolitan of Moscow, elevated to the position of the patriarch with the approval of Constantinople and received the fifth rank in honor after the patriarchs of Constantinople, Alexandria, Antioch, and Jerusalem.

In the mid-17th Century, the Russian Orthodox patriarch Nikon came into violent conflict with the Russian Tsar Alexis. Nikon, pursuing the vision of a theocratic state, attempted to establish the Orthodox church's spiritual direction over the State in Russia. He also undertook a thorough revision of Russian Orthodox texts and rituals to bring them into accord with the rest of Eastern Orthodoxy. Nikon deposed in 1666, but the Russian church retained his reforms and shunned those who continued to oppose them; the latter became known as Old Believers and formed an energetic body of resisters within the Russian Orthodox church for over two centuries. After Constantinople fell to the Muslim Turks in 1453, Russia continued for several centuries to develop a national art that had grown out of the middle Byzantine period. After the dominance in the world of Orthodox Christianity shifted to Muscovite Russia, Moscow believed as the new third Roman city of Emperor Constantine, and the center of culture and importance. From 1475 and 1510, Moscow's planners built the Kremlin and commissioned Italian architects to rebuild; namely, The Assumption (Uspensky) Cathedral and the Cathedral of St. Michael the Archangel. Builders believed that they designed after the churches of Vladimir.

Soviet United We Are Strong -Courtesy of Kherson Ukraine Museum

SOVIET OF WORKERS' AND SOLDIERS' DEPUTIES

On March 1, 1917, the Petrograd workers' party issue protected the homeland immediately and thoroughly executed by all men in the Guards, Army, Artillery, and Navy and made known to the Petrograd workers. (1). In all companies, battalions, regiments, batteries, squadrons, and separate services of various military departments and onboard naval ships committees shall immediately elect from among representatives of the ranks of the previous units. (2). In all groups which have not yet selected their representatives to the Soviet of Workers' Deputies, one representative from each company elected. All representatives, carrying appropriate identity cards, are to arrive at the building of the State Duma by ten in the morning, March 2, 1917. (3). In all their political actions, units subordinated to the Soviet of Workers' and Soldiers' Deputies and their committees. (4). All orders issued by the Military Commission of the State Duma shall be carried out, except those which run counter to the laws and decrees issued by the Soviet of Workers' and Soldiers' Deputies. (5). All kinds of weapons, namely rifles, machine-guns, armored cars, and so forth, shall be placed at the disposal and under the control of the company and battalion committees and shall by no means be issued to the officers, not even at their insistence. (6). In military formation and on-duty soldiers shall strictly observe military discipline; however, off-duty and in military alert formations, in their political, civic, and private life, soldiers shall thoroughly enjoy the rights granted to all citizens. In particular, standing to attention and obligatory saluting off duty shall stop. (7). Likewise, officers addressed as Mr. General, Mr. Colonel, etc., instead of Your Excellency, Your Honor.[2]

OPEN REBELLION

On March 8, 1917, bread and potatoes were in short supply, and demonstrators poured into the streets of the Russian capital of St Petersburg or Petrograd. As more common people rushed to the streets, they joined by factory workers who walked out of their employment. It did not take long before the police organized and met the street mob. The large numbers of demonstrators would not leave the street but began to throw street bricks at the police. Two days later, the factory strike included all the plant workers, and the street mobs attacked the police stations. In the evening, gun shoots heard as the police and military attempted to stop the violent crowds. A period of calm erupted, and factory managers tried to give the workers a voice. Based on the model created during the 1905 revolution, deputies from the various factories elected to the Petrograd Soviet, Council, or workers' committees.

PETROGRAD ARMY EMBRACES DEMONSTRATORS.

On March 11, 1917, the 150,000 troops of the Petrograd army garrison called out to quell the uprising. In some encounters, regiments opened fire, killing demonstrators, but the protesters kept to the streets, and the troops began to waver. That day, Nicholas II again dissolved the Duma. On March 12, 1917, the Revolution triumphed when regiment after regiment of the Petrograd garrison defected to the demonstrators. The soldiers subsequently formed committees that elected deputies to the Petrograd Soviet.

ROMANOV IMPERIAL GOVERNMENT RESIGNS

The Romanov imperial government forced to resign, and the Duma formed a provisional government that peacefully worked with the Petrograd Soviet for control of the new Revolution. On March 14, 1917, the Petrograd Soviet issued Order No. One, which instructed Russian soldiers and sailors to obey only those orders that did not conflict with the Petrograd Soviet's directives. On March 15, 1917, Czar Nicholas II abdicated the throne in favor of his brother Grand Duke Michael Alexandrovich Romanov. He refused the Romanov crown as he had no desire to become a part of the czarist autocracy. From that point, the Romanov years of kingship ended forever.

Michael Romanov – Courtesy of the Russian Orthodox Church Moscow

As an Orthodox Christian, Michael caused a commotion at the imperial court when he took Natalia Sergeyevna Wulfert, a married woman, as a part-time lover. Czar Nicholas II sent Grand Duke Michael to Orel, to avoid scandal, but this did not stop Michael, who openly and frequently traveled to see his aficionado who became pregnant.[3] In 1910, Natalia gave birth to their son who they named George. Michael arranged for Natalia to live with him and their son in St. Petersburg. The imperial household ignored her and refused to associate with her. To make the morality slate clean, in 1912, Michael married Natalia with the hope that he would never be named Czar. After that, Michael and Natalia left Russia to exile abroad in France, Switzerland, and England. Later, thinking that he could be an ordinary citizen, he returned to Russia, where he was arrested and murdered by the Bolsheviks. In July 1918, the Bolsheviks also executed Czar Nicholas and all his immediate family executed at Yekaterinburg. George lived to be twenty years old until his Chrysler sports car crashed, hitting a tree, and he died from broken thighs and internal injuries. He is buried in Paris and was the last male-line descendant of Alexander III of Russia.[4]

RUSIAN KORKA VYACHESLAV'S COSSACK REGIMENT

It is the Rusian Korka Vyacheslav's Cossack Horse Regiment of two battalions White Russian Forces that are politically supported and armed by the British and French. Vyacheslav's regiment financed by the Ainsworth National Bank of Portland and 119th National Bank of Tokyo. Bolsheviks who seized power from the Romanovs were financially supported and armed by the Germans. In late 1917, Woodrow Wilson, a staunch progressive European ordered 3500 Americans of the 339th Infantry Regiment that consisted of factory workers, accountants, lawyers, farm laborers, and conscripts to the cold port of Archangel. When they arrived on September 4, 1918, the Cossack White Russian, French and British forces had removed all Bolshevik soldiers who fled across the North Dvina River.[5]

During a mounted patrol, the Vyacheslav Regiment consisting of 1600 men and officers captures two Marxist Duma members in Petrograd; namely, Volkonskij Vladimir Mikhailovich and Urusov Dmitrij Dmitrievich. They spend one night camped in a rural area twenty miles Southeast of Petrograd. In the early morning, the two men are woken and feed on bread, fresh eggs, deer meat, vodka, and hot tea. At 10:14 in the morning, both are put on horses and ride toward a small dilapidate farmhouse. Volkonskij and Urusov enter the front door; they are surprised to find their families. Both men are more than thrilled that they can sit with their loved ones and have a long day of meals of sausages and caviar, and their five children run around the house playing the game "catch me if you can."

After dinner, they are escorted by the armed men to the two bedrooms near the kitchen. In the early morning hour of 6 AM, awaken and in a single file led down to a damp basement of dacha house in Krasnoyarsk. First, the parents ordered to stand with their backs towards the wall and summarily shot. Next, the children began screaming. However, shot in the head where they stood or crouched with their fingers in their ears. The bodies are taken and pushed into a common grave. There are no prayers for them. Each corpse tossed into the ground hole like potato sacks.

Thaddeus Sikorski was a Russian American who was a war correspondent for the German magazine Der Spiegel. Thad's assignment was to travel with General Rusian Korka Vyacheslav and his Czar's Cossack Regiment. General Vyacheslav was known as a member of the Kings of Scythia, an ancient region of Eurasia extending from the mouth of the Danube River on the Black Sea to the territory east of the Aral Sea. Regional nomadic people of flourished from the 4th Century to the 8th BC but conquered by the Sarmatians and merged into other cultures. Thad was to write about the Cossacks (Ukrainian: козаки́, kozaky, Russian: казаки́) that as a group was predominantly East Slavic people who formerly were members of democratic, semi-military communities in Ukraine and Southern Russia. They inhabited sparsely populated areas and islands in the lower Dnieper and Don basins and acted as an essential player in the historical development of both Ukraine and Russia.[6] Without knowing the editors of Der Spiegel and the White Army, Thad is paid $150,000 US Dollars by the Bolshevik Red Army's secret police to spy on the Cossacks plans of attack and extent of support that they were receiving from the Americans and Japanese financial and political institutions.

After the assassination of the Duma members and their families, the Cossack Regiment bivouacs 25 miles northeast from the murder scene. Later the next day, a terrible battle occurs in which the Bolsheviks outnumber the Cossack forces. In the firefight, Maxsym Korka, the Marxist Regimen's leader, finds himself in a one-on-one fight as his militia force of 350 are killed or captured. Maxsym Korka is alone and bleeding in a small horse barn that serves as his refuge and hiding place from the Cossack warriors who look for him. He thinks about his son, Rodzianko, who he has not seen for over two years. General Rusian Vyacheslav enters the barn and, without an escort, sees Maxsym bleeding from six bullet wounds. He no longer cares about living. Rusian pointed his Colt Python, a 1917 S&W Model 22 revolver, and prepared to deliver the final bullet to the heart of the bleeding Bolshevik Maxsym. Just when he is ready to pull the trigger.

He stops and puts the revolver in his holster and speaks, "I am not going to relieve your pain, you son of a Bolshevik dog. Just bleed to death. You executed my entire family in Kyiv, and now you will suffer the flames of hell."

The Cossack General Vyacheslav stands up and then realizes that a bullet smashed into his stomach from Maxsym's sidearm. His men run-up to the barn and catch their leader as he collapses from the loss of blood. Sergeant Dimitry Korka walks up to Maxsym, points his pistol to his forehead, and pulls the trigger.

He then shouts to the five Cossack soldiers standing behind that General Vyacheslav has been shot, "Take him men and put him in the horse wagon. We will not let him die."

Cossack unit charges – Courtesy of Agefotostock

During the Russian Civil War, Cossack regions became centers for the Anti-Bolshevik "White Movement," a portion of whom would form the "White Emigration." The Cossack's were light infantry cavalry warriors and a constructive code of honor to defend the Orthodox faith and the Russian Czar State. They lived in a semi-military community and had a passion for freedom and self-government. The Cossacks even formed short-lived independent states, the Ukrainian State, the Don Republic, and the Kuban People's Republic. November 8, 1917, to October 25, 1922, the Russian Civil War was a twenty-five multi-party war in the former Russian Empire fought between the Bolshevik Red Army and the White Army, the loosely allied Cossack-driven anti-Bolshevik forces. Many armies warred against the Bolshevik Red Army, notably the United States, Great Britain, Germany, and Japan.

SUPREME RULER - ALEXANDER VASILYEVICH KOLCHAK

Alexander Vasilyevich Kolchak was a Russian naval commander and the Supreme Ruler of the counter-revolutionary anti-communist White forces during the Russian Civil War. From 1918 to 1920, Kolchak was Supreme Ruler of Russia as he was recognized in this position by all the heads of the White movement, namely, according to law, Kingdom of Serbs, Croats, and Slovenes, and the Anglo-Russian Entente. Initially, the White Army forces under Kolchak's command had some success. However, Kolchak was unfamiliar with combat on land and gave the majority of the strategic planning to D.A. Lebedev, Paul J. Bubnar, and his newly appointed staffer, Thaddeus Sikorsky. Kolchak had put around 110,000 men into the field, facing nearly 96,000 Bolshevik Red Army troops.

Thaddeus Sikorski established his credentials from a forged letter from General Rusian Vyacheslav. Thus, Admiral Kolchak trusted the advice Thad gave to have good relations with British General Alfred Knox. With orders from David Lloyd George, Knox ensured that Kolchak's forces to be armed, uniformed, supplied with food and whatever else they needed. The Northern White Army under Anatoly Pepelyayev and the Czech Rudolf Gajda seized Perm in late December 1918, and after a pause, other forces spread out from this strategic base. The Kolchak battle plan was for three main advances to take place with Czech commander Rudolf Gajda to take Archangel, commander Khanzhin to capture Ufa. The third advance consisted of over 1500 Cossacks under Captain Alexander Dutov to capture Samara and Saratov. As a result, in March 1919, the White Army forces took Ufa, the capital city of the Republic of Bashkortostan, Russia. They pushed on from there to seize Kazan and approach Samara on the Volga River. Anti-Communist Orthodox Christian uprisings in Simbirsk, Kazan, Viatka, and Samara assisted the White Russian military campaign. Each strategic and tactical plan that Kolchak devises is copied by Thadeous Sikorsky and using local communist agents, secretly rush to the Red Army's commanders.[7]

Charge of the Red Army Cavalry – Courtesy of world history

RED ARMY

The recruits of the Red Army proved unwilling to fight and quickly retreated, allowing the White Army to advance to a line stretching from Glazov through Orenburg to Uralsk. Kolchak's territories covered an extensive geographic area and held seven million people. In April 1917, the fearful Bolshevik Central Executive Committee issued a ruling that Kolchak be defeated and killed. The spring thaw brought mud making movement impossible, and the British, Japanese, and Americans unwilling to supply Kolchak's Army adequately. Using threats of killing their family members, the Bolshevik's saw a one hundred thirty-five percent increase in army recruits. After one month in training, the recruits board trains to meet Kolchak's exhausted Christian forces. As in all wars, politics rules the outcome of battles. Kolchak viewed the Czechoslovak Legion and the Polish 5th Rifle Division as ethnically inferior. The Czech and Polish commanders were angered and retreated, leaving Kolchak's inability to fight off the expanding Red Army troop levels.

Thaddeus Sikorski, by the secret carrier, advises the Red Army's General staff that the White Forces starving, lacked ammunition, and not able to fight. Further, the Czech and Polish forces withdrawn and probably will not fight for Kolchak. Thaddeus, a descendant of Korka, receives $150,000 in US dollars deposited in the French-American Banking Corporation (FABC).

Inspection of Company M. 339th infantry. United States army. at Archangel. Russia. Nov. 20, 1918.

RU Civil War General William S. Graves – Courtesy
of USARMY 31st Infantry archives

Richard Theodor Kusiolek

"PEACE WITHOUT VICTORY"- PRESIDENT WOODROW WILSON

During the movement of European Socialism, Woodrow Wilson was a leader of the American Progressive Movement. From 1913 to 1921, he served as the first socialist President of the United States. Working with his Secretary of State, Robert Lansing, a Democrat lawyer, the US Commander in Chief sent 7,500 American troops to Siberia. The American Commander, General William S. Graves, gave specific instructions that the forces were strictly neutral regarding internal Russian affairs and only served to maintain the Trans-Siberian railroad's operation to preserve trade in the Far East. In 1919, when the Red forces managed to reorganize and turn the tide of attack against Supreme Ruler Kolchak, the White Russian forces quickly lost ground.

Thanks to the American Progressive Movement's strong embrace of Marxism and the destruction of tradition and liberty epitomized by the Cossacks and their White Army, the Red Army grew stronger. The American commander, General William S. Graves, allowed his animus of Kolchak to lead to the defeat of the White Russian Army. It recorded that Graves viewed Kolchak as an Autocratic despot who wanted the Orthodox Russian Czar structure to become a reality again. Historians believe that the Progressive President Wilson had the same view. Wilson and Graves worked together to give no supplies or troops for the 80% Cossack White Russian Army to defeat the Red Army.

Thaddeus Sikorski sent dispatches to the Red Army Central Committee that Kolchak was an instrument of the British. The Americans would not help him and that the Japanese only wanted to occupy Far Eastern Russia to support the Bolsheviks. The Imperial Japanese only wanted the Cossack forces to create a buffer state to the East of Lake Baikal. The Japanese had 5,000 troops in Russia, but would not help Kolchak. The end was coming to White Russia because of the Sovereign Nation States wanting to gain mineral rights in Russia. They believed that progressive movements would give economic freedom and prosperity. In other words, one economic model and bounty for all under the red banner of Communism.

Russian Front — Courtesy of General Maurice Janin

AGENTS AND TRAITORS

General Kolchak promotes his key staffer, Thaddeus Sikorski, to a full colonel's rank. Thad arranges that Kolchak granted safe passage by an armed Czechoslovakian army unit to the British military mission in Irkutsk. Five miles from the British Irkutsk mission, his wagon escort stopped. General Kolchak is ordered out of the carriage, handcuffed, and handed over to a Red Army unit of fifty armed soldiers. Their Major read an order from the supreme council immediately jailed in Irkutsk for trial. Thirty days later, on January 14, 1920, Admiral Alexander Vasilyevich Kolchak accepted as the Supreme Commander of the White Russian field Army brought before a military court. On February 7, 1920, he was found guilty of crimes against the Russian Communist Party and ordered to be shot by a firing squad within forty minutes and dies of multiple wounds.

Colonel Thaddeus Sikorski, former Chief of Staff to Admiral Kolchak, who witnessed the execution, wrote in his diary. "Kolchak, Kornilov, Denikin, and Wrangel were first of all Russian patriots with a deep love for their country and worked for its salvation without any regard for self-advancement."

Sikorski further wrote that "Political intrigues were unknown to them, and they were ready to work with men of any political party, so long as they knew that these men were sincere in their endeavors to free Russia. I never betrayed anyone. I worked strictly for money and not for a political position."

In 1922, with the civil war coming to an end, the Red Army formed a National Assembly, chosen by the people, to decide the character of the future Government of Russia. After the treasonous murder of Admiral Kolchak, all Cossack lands subjected to public domain laws, troops are allowed to billet in their home, famine occurs, and 18,000 inhabitants die from starvation, extensive governmental repression by the Central Communist Government. Many thousands of Cossack's family members leave Russia and migrated to Great Britain and America, hoping to hide from Communist's Red Army agents. The White Army Cossacks try to start new lives in Chicago, Boston, Pittsburg, Indianapolis, and New York City by creating new name identities so that they could simply raise families and disappear into standard American life patterns.

THE POLITICS OF NATIONALISM

During Russia's 1890s and early 1900s, abysmal living and working conditions, high taxes, and land expansion led to more frequent strikes and agrarian disorders. These activities prompted the bourgeoisie of various nationalities in the empire to develop a host of different parties, both liberal and conservative. Socialists of different nationalities formed their parties. Russian Poles, who had suffered significant administrative and educational retraining, founded the nationalistic Polish Socialist Party in Paris in 1892. The Party's founders hoped that it would help reunite a divided Poland with the territories held by Austria–Hungary, Germany, and Russia. Vladimir Lenin was the most politically talented of the revolutionary socialists. Although the Germans and French viewed Karl Marx and Friedrich Engels as foundational experts of Marxism, the Russians did not. In post-Czar Russia, the foundational socialist was Pyotr Nikitich Tkachev, a Russian writer, critic, and revolutionary theorist. Vladimir Lenin based his revolutionary ideas on the writings of Tkachev. During the time of the Czar, Lenin exiled in Siberia from 1895 to 1899. Lenin viewed as the nationalist master organizer and tactical expert of the Russian Social Democratic Party.[8] Even Nikolai Bukharin viewed Lenin as their leader.

Nikolai Bukharin was an early Moscow University communist student activist, and he saw Lenin as his spiritual leader. Later, Bukharin became an editor of Pravda, Izvestia, author of The Politics and Economics of the Transition Period, Imperialism and World Economy, co-author of "The ABC of Communism", principal framer of the Soviet Constitution of 1936. In 1938, under Joseph Stalin's orders, Bukharin was executed by a firing squad.

BOLSHEVIK REVOLUTION: 1917 - 1920

The German Government never wanted Russia to be a factor in any European War again as it had been in World War I. They wanted a rebellion in the Czar's Army and to destroy the Romanov Dynasty. To meet those goals, the Germans sent covert agents to incite riots in Russia. The German politician, Theobald Theodor Friedrich Alfred von Bethmann-Hollweg, viewed Stalin and Lenin as key socialist to meet those goals. Thus, Joseph Stalin and Vladimir Lenin received train tickets to return to Russia from their exile in Germany secretly. In the upheaval of the February Revolution, power shared between the weak provisional government and the Petrograd Soviet. On October 24 and 25, 1917, leftist revolutionaries led by Vladimir Lenin launched a coup d'état against the provisional government. With Lenin in front of hundreds of Bolsheviks, army soldiers, peasants, and factory workers, the armed mob occupied government buildings, and other strategic locations in Petrograd declared a government with its new Marxist Czar and iconic dictator of the world's first Marxist State. The new Marxist State government organized with Lenin as its Head. Lenin became the virtual dictator of the first Marxist State in the world. Lenin immediately signed a peace treaty with Germany, his benefactor. Next, lands were taken away from the wealthy and distributed to the peasants and workers who converted from Orthodox Christianity to the Marxism religion. All private means of production nationalized to serve the Marxist State. In 1918, the Cossack driven anti-Bolshevik White Army forces launched a bloody two-year battle but lost in 1920.

Two years later, the Union of Soviet Socialist Republics (USSR) became a reality with the magnitude of millions killed for their beliefs in democracy and the Russian Orthodox Church. As some of the brave Slavs escaped serfdom, they ended up in the land of the roaming Kazaks, intermarried, becoming the Slav Cossacks. They were very free men, and their worst mistake was when after a few years of fighting the communists after Lenin took over, they went home. They went home because none of the Tsar's family remained as the "Caesar of Christian Orthodoxy". Communists didn't win that war as they claim. The Cossacks simply went back to their villages. Stalin hated Slav Cossacks and deported those who did not escape, to Siberian concentration camps to die.[9]

"The Revolution is Dead, and You Must Die with It." Maximilien François Marie Isidore de Robespierre

For 304 years, the Romanovs ruled Russia. In the early morning hours of July 17, 1918, Czar Nicholas II, the father of Russia and the last monarch of the Romanov dynasty, was shot along with his wife, Alexandra, and their five children by their Bolshevik Communist captors in the basement of a house in Yekaterinburg.

Also, their staff members, Eugene Botkin, Anna Demidova, Alexei Trupp, and Ivan Kharitonov murdered in the basement. In the official Bolshevik count, eleven executed by order of the Communist Committee.

Nicholas II children - Courtesy of Hulton Archive/Getty Images

The Chairman of the Central Executive Committee, Yakov Sverdlov, sent a message to Oleg Korka Yurovsky noting the murder plot only after he had told the alleged Jacob Schiff. Jacob was a New York Jewish banker, businessman, and who gave generously to charitable causes that would lead to the death of the Romanovs. The New York Jew embraced numerous radical Marxist movements in the USA. Jacob Schiff was a German Jew, and he helped with monies to finance the US Union Pacific Railroad and gave millions to Leland Stanford. The latter founded Stanford University in Palo Alto, California. Also, Schiff funded the Russo-Japanese War allowing the Japanese attacks against the Tsarist Russian forces.

In New York and knowledge of the approach of the White army, "Sverdlov had received orders from a wealthy investment banker to liquidate the Tsar and his entire family at once."[10]

This order was delivered to Sverdlov by the American Special Consulate in the town of Vologda. Sverdlov ordered Oleg Korka

Yurovsky to carry out the order. On the next day, Yurovsky wanted to check whether the written request should apply to the Czar's children or just to the Head of the family, Tsar Nicholas II. Although Sverdlov did not verify the demand with the New York Jewish banker, he decided that all family members die immediately. Oleg Korka Yurovsky was made responsible for the order.

In November 1924, Sokolov told a close friend that his publisher was afraid to print these raw facts in his book. Sokolov showed his friend the original scripts and the deciphered translations. Sokolov poisoned by his mistress and died thirty days later. He was to have traveled to the United States to give evidence in favor of Henry Ford in Jacob Schiff's Kuhn, Loeb & Co's lawsuit against the car magnate who had published his book "The International Jew." Sokolov's book "The Murder of the Tsar's Family" was published in Berlin in 1925 without the information mentioned earlier.

"These facts were made public only in 1939, in the exile periodical Tsarsky Vestnik that Jacob Schiff had the alleged role in those murders described in Russia only in 1990."

Russian Imperial Family with Officers — Courtesy of NYTimes archives

For many years the exact location of the bodies of the murdered family of Nicholas II remained a mystery. Still, false rumors drummed-up by the New York newspapers quickly spread that a few of the Romanovs had survived. Fifty-eight years later, Russian scientists uncovered the remains of Nicholas, Alexandra, and three daughters, but they kept it a secret until the Soviet Union collapsed. In 1979 amateur historians discovered the bodies of Nicholas, Alexandra, and daughters Olga, Tatiana, and Anastasia. Two bodies were still missing, however, in 2007, thirteen-year-old Crown Prince Alexei and his sister Maria discovered. One of the dead Bolshevik assassins left clues in a letter where the bones of Alexei and his nineteen-year-old sister Maria lay. The Romanov remains were removed and relocated to a room in the Bureau of Forensic Examination in Ekaterinburg. The Russian Orthodox Church expressed lingering doubts resisted calls that those were their remains interred with the rest of the family in Peter and Paul Cathedral.[11]

RED CENTURY, JULY 10, 1917-BREST-LITOVSK

On March 3, 1918, three months before the massive murder of Nicholas II and his family, the Bolshevik government signed the Treaty of Brest-Litovsk. The Treaty was an enormous land-grab that ceded vast areas of the former Russian Empire to the Central Powers of Germany, Austria-Hungary, and the Turkish Ottoman Empire. On March 7, 1918, Michael Romanov and his secretary Johnson were arrested on the orders of Moisei Uritsky, the Head of the Petrograd secret

Russian Brian Johnson & Mikhail Alexandrovich — Courtesy of Siberian Times

police, and imprisoned at the Bolshevik headquarters in the Smolny Institute.[12]

MYASNIKOV'S MURDER PLOT

Grand Duke Michael Alexandrovich of Russia was the youngest son and fifth child of Emperor Alexander III of Russia and the youngest brother of Czar Nicholas II of Russia. On March 2 or the 5th of 1917, Nicholas II abdicated the throne in favor of his brother Michael, who refused it the following day. As the local Bolsheviks sat around a conference table at the Smolny Institute on June 12, 1918, the leader of the local secret police, Gavril Myasnikov, mapped out a plan to murder Grand Duke Michael Romanov.

Myasnikov assembled a team of four men, who all, like him, were former inmates of the Czar's forced labor camps - Vasily Ivanchenko, Ivan Kolpashchikov, Vasily Korka Kalpashkov, and Nikolai Zhuzhgov. Using a forged order, the four men gained entry to Michael's hotel at 11.45 in the late evening. At first, Michael refused to accompany the men until he spoke with the local Chairman of the secret police, Pavel Malkov. The latter was ill and refused to help and save the lives of Michael Alexandrovich and Brian Johnson. Michael did not want to go but got dressed anyway to accompany the men. Brian Johnson insisted on accompanying him, and the four men plus their two prisoners climbed into two horse-drawn three-seater carriages. They drove out of the town into the forest near Motovilikha, Russia.[13] It was in the early morning of June 13, 1918, when Michael asked of their destination. The men replied that they would catch a train at a remote railway crossing and not to worry. One hour later, the horses stopped, and everyone left the carriage to stand in the middle of a forest.

Accounts reported that Vasily Korka Kalpashkov fired immediately upon Brian and the n Michael and then the others, but since they made their bullets, some of their guns jammed. Michael gravely wounded moved towards the injured Johnson with arms outstretched, then shot at point-blank range in the head.

Both Ivanchenko and Zhuzhgov claimed to have fired the fatal shot. Johnson was shot dead by Vasily Kalpashkov. The bodies were pulled from their clothing and buried. Anything of value stolen, and their clothes were taken back to Perm as proof to Myasnikov that they died. The Ural Regional Soviet Director, Alexander Beloborodov, and Vladimir Lenin approved the execution. Michael was the first of the Romanovs to be executed by the Bolsheviks, but he would not be the last as one month later, all of his family members shot and their bodies burned. The bodies of Michael and Johnson's buried in an unmarked grave.[14]

Oleg K. Yurovsky – Courtesy of Soviet Era Archive Gulag prisoners

THE FATE OF OLEG YUROVSKY

The drunken murderers who stabbed and shot point-blank the family led by the paid Korka assassin plotter, Oleg Korka Yurovsky, would face a horrible fate. The hand of God appeared to punish him. All grandsons of Oleg Yurovsky, who was in charge of the execution of Nicholas II's family, died tragically, and all of his granddaughters killed in their early years. Thus, "Iron Commandant" Oleg Yurovsky left a dark imprint not only in Russian history but also brought trouble to his family. His great-grandson Vladimir Yurovsky quoted in the Express-Gazeta paper. One child of his beloved daughter Rimma perished in a fire, her second son fell from the roof, another son got poisoned with mushrooms, the fourth son hung himself, and the fifth son died while driving. "Rimma was also misfortunate, Vladimir further said, she was arrested in 1935 and sent to the camp for political convicts.

Vladimir Korka Yurovsky was sorry for his daughter but didn't do a stroke of work to free her." Vladimir's granny, Yurovsky's niece Maria ran away with a Gypsy, who soon left her alone with their son Boris. Boris's life was complicated. As a boy, he cared for and then buried all of his stepbrothers and sisters who all died from cold and hunger.

Boris's son Vladimir Yurovsky II said. "Neither good undertakings nor honest living of his descendants can redeem what Oleg Korka Yurovsky did with Romanovs, Yurovsky said, I am concerned with the future of my son and daughter."

Oleg Yurovsky complained of chest aches last year of his life. He suffered from respiratory distress, hypersomnia, swollen ankles, and high blood pressure. The "Bolshevik Commander" died miserably alone from blood and lung cancer. Many of the Russian Orthodox faith believed that God gave Oleg pain deserving of his genocide of a Russian family.[15]

Czar's Okhrana to the Committee for State Security (KGB)

The coup to overthrow the Czar resulted in Czar Nicholas I's order to form a ruthless clandestine police force. The Third Department of the Czar's Chancery created a complicated and robust censorship regimen, and the purpose was to suppress subversive actions and even thoughts. The Third Section used its agents posing as Marxist revolutionaries and, in many cases, led to assassinating the Czar's government officials who were supporting the overthrow of the Romanov Dynasty. The Czar created "thought police" forces in every city and village. Before 1945, Japan's Imperialist created secret "thought police" to arrest those who had extremist views against Emperor Shōwa (Hirohito), a direct descendant of the sun-goddess Amaterasu. Before 2019, Silicon Valley's modern American electronic social media Cartels, namely, Facebook, Google, and Twitter, also created employees as "network thought police social media monitors."

BOLSHEVIK POLICE STATE

Feliks Dzerzhinsky, a Bolshevik revolutionary, was the founder of the Cheka or All-Russian Extraordinary Commission for the Suppression of Counterrevolution and Sabotage, soon to be called the KGB. From 1917 to 1922, Dzerzhinsky's primary responsibility was to oversee the tens of thousands summarily shot without proof or trial. In 1922, Cheka instituted as GPU and then changed again as OGPU or the United State Political Administration. In 1934, the operations of the OGPU relegated to the NKVD or the People's Commissariat for Internal Affairs. The NKVD had the charter for all forced Gulag labor camps and the non-secret police.[16]

NKVD - LAVRENTIY PAVLOVICH BERIA

From 1936 to 1938, Joseph Stalin, Supreme Czar, orchestrated a wave of terrorist purges by naming his close friend Nikolai Yezhov as leader of the NKVD and the "Yezhovshchina" or Stalin's wave of terror. Nikolai created many enemies, and in 1938 he was judged in the Moscow treason trials. On February 4, 1940, book accounts stated that Yezhov was shot by the future KGB chairman Ivan Serov in the basement of a small NKVD station on Varsonofevskii Lane (Varsonofyevskiy Pereulok) in Moscow. Lavrentiy Beria was appointed to become the new leader of the NKVD. Under "Lavrentiy Beria's long tenure of the vast apparatus of the NKVD Soviet security organs, it became the most powerful and most feared section of society." In 1943, the NKVD merged into the NKGB of the People's Commissariat for State Security. Still, NKVD kept its role for all internal security. In 1946, the NKVD morphed into the MVD or Ministry of Interior. In the same year, the NKGB rebranded as the MGB or Ministry of State Security. In 1953, Beria arranged to have the MVD and the MGB under his sole command. Stalin accused his close friend Beria of treason. As with Nikolai Yezhov, Beria arrested on charges of conspiracy.

In December 1953, eight months after the death of Joseph Stalin, Beria was shot through the forehead by General Pavel Batitsky who had to stuff a rag into Beria's mouth to silence him from crying.[17]

COMMITTEE OF STATE SECURITY (KGB)

After Beria fell from power, the Soviet security service organized under the KGB or known as the Committee of State Security. Although the KGB's functions resembled those of its predecessors, it employed terror to a far lesser degree. Party control remained as an umbrella while the KGB's primary duties focused on internal intelligence and to locate British, American, and French spy agents, as well as Sunni Terrorist Organizations within the Russian Federation. Much of the information about Soviet Union secret police was made public in reports by President Khrushchev, who had arranged the murder of Lavrentiy Beria. From 1985 to 1991, Mikhail Sergeyev ich Gorbachev, a former Soviet politician and elected as General Secretary of the governing Communist Party of the Soviet Union, given the powers of Joseph Stalin. Under Gorbachev's administrative capabilities and after a coup for his appointment as General Secretary, he realized that the KGB leadership and the power of the KGB was a threat to his administration and pruned. Mikhail renamed the KGB and significantly restricted its agents to counterintelligence, economic crimes, and air and rail security. Gorbachev then placed all Foreign intelligence gathering and transferring under the scope of the new Central Intelligence Service. With the collapse of the Soviet Union, Russia absorbed the KGB's remnants, combining most of them under the Security and Internal Affairs Ministry. President Boris Yeltsin served as President from 1991 to 1999. In 1993, he ordered that the KGB's ministry replaced with a new (FSK) Federal Counter-Intelligence Service. In 1995, Yeltsin gave the FSK expanded powers and renamed the Federal Security Service or FSB. After the collapse of Communism and the Soviet Union,

Man of Seven Shadows

many thousands of documents made concerning the activities of the Russian secret police.[18]

FEDERAL SECURITY SERVICE (FSB)

The American FBI conducts investigations and authorized intelligence collection to identify and counter the threat posed by domestic and global terrorists and their supporters within the United States and to arrest and bring to international trial terrorists. In furtherance of this function, the FBI designs, develops, and implements counterterrorism initiatives, which enhance the FBI's ability to minimize the terrorist threat. The Russian Federal Security or (FSB) works under the executive branch in areas of national security. It has a broad range of authority for all intelligence and espionage activities inside border protection, protection waterways, inside and outside of the Russian Federation, and counterintelligence.[19] An example of (FSB)'s operations were on July 23, 2018, that involved an action for gun smuggling, 380 domestic- and foreign-produced firearms (25 machine guns, 30 assault rifles, 70 submachine guns, 94 carbines and rifles, 158 pistols and revolvers, two anti-tank guns were found and removed. Also, 45mm infantry mortar, AGS-17 automatic grenade launcher, an improvised explosive device, fifteen hand grenades, and more than 4,500 rounds of ammunition for the weapons) were taken to protected FSB's warehouse.

Duma passed legislation to focus on CIA operatives doing covert operations in the Russian Federation. For example, the definition of "spy hardware" was legislated by the Russian Duma; namely, illegal turnover of individual devices destined for the clandestine gathering of information can face criminal charges with punishments ranging from fines up to $3,220 to prison terms of up to 4 years. In 2018, Russian military intelligence officers were celebrating their professional holiday for the Main Directorate of the General Staff of the Armed Forces of the Russian Federation. The organization is best known by its Soviet-times name the GRU or the Maine Intelligence Directorate, even though the agency has changed its name to simply GU many years ago.

JOSEPH STALIN – MASS MURDERER COMMANDER

Joseph Stalin's internal value system was as a purist Bolshevik, namely, create a rigid society that will follow the State's doctrines and orders. If this is not possible, then remove those members and start all over.

Further, Stalin is known for the following beliefs, namely, "Death is the solution to all problems. No man - no problem"; "A single death is a tragedy; a million deaths is a statistic"; and "It is enough that the people know there was an election. The people who cast the votes decided nothing. The people who count the votes decide everything."

Joseph Stalin was the man who turned the Soviet Union from a backward country into a world superpower at an unimaginable human cost. Stalin was born into a dysfunctional family in a poor village in Georgia. Permanently scarred from a childhood bout with smallpox and a deformed arm, Stalin always felt unfairly treated by life. As he grew into manhood, he developed a robust and romanticized desire for greatness and respect. Plus, Stalin possessed a streak of calculating cold-heartedness towards those who had insulted him. He always felt a sense of inferiority before educated intellectuals and particularly distrusted them. Sent by his mother to the seminary in Tiflis or Tbilisi, the capital of Georgia, to study to become a priest, the young Stalin never completed his education and was instead soon wholly drawn into the city's progressive revolutionary circles. Stalin never a fiery intellectual polemicist orator like Lenin or Trotsky. He specialized in the humdrum nuts and bolts of revolutionary activity, risking arrests every day by helping organize workers, distributing illegal literature, and robbing trains to support the cause. Lenin and his bookish friends lived safely abroad and wrote original articles about the plight of the Russian working class. Although Lenin found Stalin's boorishness offensive at times, he valued his loyalty and appointed him after the Revolution to various low-priority leadership positions in the new Soviet Government.

In 1922, Stalin appointed to another such post as General Secretary of the Communist Party's Central Committee. Stalin understood that "cadres are everything" that meant control the personnel; you control the organization. Stalin shrewdly used his new position to consolidate power in precisely this way, namely, managing all appointments, setting agendas, and moving around Party staff in such a direction that eventually everyone who counted for anything owed their position to Stalin. By the time the Party's intellectual progressive core realized what had happened, Stalin had his ordinary revolutionary people in place, while Lenin, the only person with the moral authority to challenge him. Lenin frequented prostitutes and contracted a venereal disease. Also, Lenin had numerous heart strokes and was dying from the venereal disease. He could not challenge Stalin as he could not speak. Stalin even appointed who could see Lenin. Therefore, as General Secretary of the Party, Stalin stood as the de facto leader of Russia on up until Mikhail Gorbachev.[20] In 1922, the German military made a secret agreement to establish military bases, factories, and R&D centers to rearm Hitler and the Soviet Army. Germany also tested their tank prototypes and designed to fit railway cars used in France and Belgium. In 1939 the Molotov-Ribbentrop Pact was signed to continue military collaborations. Stalin transported tons of crude oil, grain, and resources used against France and Great Britain. Also, Stalin attended Germany army ceremonies located on Soviet territory.

In 1924, after Vladimir Lenin died, Joseph Stalin methodically went about destroying all the old leaders of the Party, taking advantage of their weakness for standing on arcane intellectual principle to divide and conquer them. At first, these people were removed from their posts and exiled abroad. Later, when he realized that their blasphemy tongues and pens were still capable of inveighing against him even from far away, he took action.

In the 1930s, Stalin switched tactics, culminating in a vast reign of terror and spectacular show trials during which the founding fathers of the Soviet Union unmasked as "enemies of the people." Stalin proved that his enemies were agents employed by the US's CIA and UK's MI 15-MI 16 covert Intelligence Services, and if uncovered, they would be tortured and then summarily shot.

Leon Trotsky 1924 – Courtesy of IMBD.com Photo Gallery

In 1929, Stalin exiled his former associate Leon Trotsky to Mexico City. However, the energized Leon Trotsky (Lev Davidovich Bronshtein) continued to write attacking articles and heckle Stalinism from Mexico. In 1940, Stalin had enough of Trotsky and plotted to have him silenced with an ice steel mountaineering instrument. It was as if Trotsky was part of a criminal mafia family and knew that Stalin was the type of man who attempts an assassination of his critics. On August 21, 1940, Trotsky allowed Ramon Mercader to ask for financial help from a former Bolshevik. Mercader, who was paid by Stalin to be Trotsky's killer, did not waste time. Upon entering the library study, Mercader struck the Marxist theorist and creator of the Red Army in the Head from behind with the shortened pick he had hidden under his clothes. Leon did not die immediately but fought off Mercader until his bodyguards arrived. He was taken to a hospital and died from shock.

STALIN'S PURGES

The purges, or "repressions" as known in Russia, extended far beyond the Party elite, reaching down into every local Communist Party cell and nearly all of the intellectual professions since anyone with higher education suspected of being a potential counter-revolutionary. The purges depleted the Soviet Union of its brainpower. To fill that gap now that he killed his chief Marxist critic, Joseph Stalin used his propaganda media to project himself to the Russian as the sole Marxist intellectual force in Russia

RAPID INDUSTRIALIZATION

Due to the disastrous WW I out-of-date Russia military, Stalin pursued an economic policy of mobilizing the entire nation to achieve rapid industrialization so that it could stand shoulder-to-shoulder with the Capitalist powers of Germany and the United States. In 1917, as a critical policy doctrine, Bolsheviks' stole the land from the aristocracy and gave free land to the peasants. Soon after the Marxist created a new program Stalin called collectivization, the Marxist took it back from peasants and efficiently reduced them to the status of serfs again. Stalin created the Five-Year Plans to coordinate all investment and production in the country and undertook a massive program of building heavy industry. Although the Soviet Union boasted that its economy was booming, millions lost their lives in forced labor. It was at this time that the Global Depression erupted, and Stalin's propaganda highlighted the virtues of Stalinism and Communism. The Marxist miracle was yet a "nebulous dream" demonstrated in World War Two.

Key drivers of the Soviet System consisted of the violent expropriation of the grain harvest by the Government, the forced resettlement, and murder of the most successful peasants as counter-revolutionary elements. The system of Communism needed cheap labor that was plentiful from the millions of Russian citizens arrested, placed in labor camps of the Gulag, and starved to death working for the glory of Stalin's worker paradise on earth and not in heaven. A man must live like a brilliant high flame and burn as brightly as he can. In the end, he burns out. But this is far better than a meaningless little spark.

STALIN-HITLER NON-AGGRESSION PACT

In 1939, it was precise war drums sounded the alarm, Josif Vissarionovich Dzhugashvili felt that he had scored a coup by striking a non-aggression pact with Hitler, in which they both agreed to divide up Poland and then leave each other alone. The Red Army attempted the invasion of Finland that failed miserably. Stalin discharged and or arrested over 30,000 army officers. Stalin believed that he and Hitler had an understanding that he refused to listen to his military advisors' warnings in 1941 that the Wehrmacht was massing for an attack. If his close military advisors spoke the warning, arrested, and imprisoned. Stalinism had become a religion replacing the Russian Orthodox church, and to speak against the German pact was blasphemy. When the attack came, the Soviet Army was utterly unprepared and suffered horrible defeats. Stalin hid in his barricaded office complex and refused to believe that Hitler would take away his trust.

German soldiers grodny-june-22-23-Byelorussia –
Courtesy of history/images.blogspot

The millions lost in First World War, a murderous three-year war with the White Army, and purges of the 1930s, left Russia with limited trained troops, no financial resources, and backward strategies, and tactics to eliminate German forces control of Ukraine and Belarus. In 1941, massive Nazi artillery pounded the Kremlin, and Leningrad surrounded without food supplies. At that moment, it appeared that the Germans would accomplish what Napoleon could not namely conquer and subjugate the vast Soviet Union. However, after two years of bloody battles, the Germans have turned away from Stalingrad. The population of 197 million mobilized in a patriotic frenzy, and in 1943, the German forces weakened as their supply lines destroyed, and the sub-zero temperatures killed many. With the US military working with the British and attacking Germany on the East, the expanded and industrialized Military fighting machine of the Red Army began to liberate all Eastern Europe from the West.[21]

Richard Theodor Kusiolek

WORLD SUPERPOWERS

During the Teheran, Yalta, and Potsdam Conferences, Stalin proved a worthy negotiator. He managed to negotiate with Roosevelt and Churchill and arrange for the countries of Eastern Europe, which the Red Army controlled, to remain in the Soviet sphere of influence. Next, he secured three seats for the Soviet Union in the newly formed United Nations. The Soviet Union now recognized world superpower, with its permanent seat on the Security Council, and the respect that Stalin had craved all his life. Still, he sought more blood. Russian soldiers and refugees returned found themselves arrested and either shot or sent to the labor camps as traitors— deportation conducted in Estonia, Latvia, and Lithuania to force agricultural collectivization through terror. The Soviet authorities removed more than 92,000 people from the Baltics to remote areas of the Soviet Union Siberia to die or survive in sub-zero temperatures.

KORKA DESCENDANT

Dmitry Korkasky's stepfather Vasily Ivanchenko had done much to remove the Government of the Czar and defeat the White Army. His wife, Nina, had an exceptional mathematical mind and worked for Stalin's secret police chief Lavrentiy Pavlovich Beria. Infuriatingly, that brought her under suspicion when members of his staff shot Lavrentiy Beria as he sat by his desk reading reports. Beria's attraction was power and sex. In his office, Beria held batons for the torture of prisoners and a mountain of lingerie, sex toys, pornography. His staff found eleven pairs of silk stockings, eleven teddy bears, seven silk nightgowns, a women's sports uniform, blouses, silk scarves, an endless number of sexual love letters, and a vast amount of male leather masochistic clothing and whips. Beria had his staff kidnap pretty girls on the street and brought to him for sex. He idealized them. Staffers asked many if Beria's sex performance was any good with his partners.

The answer was a resounding no! Lavrentiy was an ordinary man with a small sex organ that created laughter when viewed by his abducted teenage girls. Stalin had died six months earlier, and so many others had to settle the revenge book of Stalin's terror, by locating his small-minded chieftains and killing them one by one. Nina killed herself two months after Lavrentiy killed in his office.

Nina had a secret love affair with her boss, and they had a secret daughter by the name of Nataliya.

When Beria would drink, he would lay on his office couch and whisper to Nina, "You know, Nina, how lonely I am. I have a wife, too, Nina, a beauty, but we do not live together as her character is diabolical. I have no one."

Nina believed that he loved her and cried.

She thought to herself, "Lord! I'd rather have him like a bad dream, and I loved my husband. I want to live, and if I did not love him, he would kill me."

Dmitry Korkasky gave Nataliya a home, but she was miserable at school as she was growing up. Nataliya was very depressed as a teenager. Nataliya walked with a limp and bowed-legged. She hated living with her grandfather, and she spent so much time worrying about being lonely and unmarried.

Dmitry tried to move to Moscow from their village of Asbest but refused a Communist Residence Permit. Nataliya had fantasies about killing the three men that killed her birth father. The purges continued after Stalin and Beria died. Nataliya had written in a diary of her plan to kill members of the new Soviet Communist State. The NKVD did a house search and found the journal, and she and Dmitry sent to the Gulag for three and a half years. When they returned to their home, a different family has taken over the house, but they forced to find a new shared home in Moscow. Nataliya just wanted to live a happy life, and she married Olesky, a retired naval officer who had a good pension.

Her father, Dmitry Korkasky, hired by the NKVD, rose to a prominent position in the organization. Nataliya became 45 years of age as an office worker, a conventional housewife, happy in her job, and her son, Kolya, who was a good student and an avid anti-nationalist but arrested as a subversive who was giving information on Soviet military bases to the United States. Nataliya's depression came back as she had to queue up on Wednesday to find news of Kolya holding in a cage in the basement of the Secret State Police's Moscow headquarters. Each day Kolya hung naked up by his feet for thirty minutes. Kolya had nothing to reveal as he created his fantasy and made the mistake of telling his Moscow University roommates about his covert work for the USA. The interrogators struck his buttocks and back so many times in a three-day session that the flesh peeled off and became infected. Kolya died two days later. Nataliya was never able to find her son's grave.

On a wintery evening in a massive snowstorm, she took her husband's revolver and shot herself. Dimitry had little sorrow for his stepdaughter or her son Kolya. Dimitry believed that they were flawed from the very beginning as subversives hiding under the disguise of pretending to be new Soviet revolutionaries. Soon Dimitry met Anastasia Dubovak, who had a hard life but never complained and connected to the Soviet thinking that it was hard to give up her convictions that life will always be hard. The Soviet government made career choices for its citizens to build their economic system? Dmitry's second wife, Anastasia, was first removed from her village as the daughter of the alleged Kulak (i.e., wealthy peasant) and then trained to make cakes and drive like a chauffeur for the KGB. She believed that if Stalin did not force and remove those Orthodox Christians from power, she would have remained a poor peasant. Also, she felt at times living another person's life when she married Dmitry Korkasky. The killing of the Czar, his family, and his brother all made sense now. Anastasia would never suffer from a lack of food or live without firewood during the winter.

CRIMEA TATARS

In 1917, the Bolshevik Revolution and the destruction, by brutal assassinations of the Romanov Dynasty. Those Tatars who survived and remained loyal to the Czar immediately formed the People's Crimea Democratic Republic. From 1918 to 1920, the Czarist White Russia anti-Bolshevik Army used Crimea to be their safe staging and secure military territory. In 1920, the White Army defeated by the traitorous actions of the military and political commanders of the Czechoslovakian, Americans, Greeks, Balkans, and Japanese troops numbering approximately 175,000. Red Army forces overran Crimea, and as a result, the People's Crimea Democratic Republic did not exist any longer. In 1921, the Crimea Peninsula reorganized as the Crimean Autonomous Soviet Socialist Republic. The Soviet collectivization process unusually harsh in Crimea caused tens of thousands of Crimean Tatars to perish during Joseph Stalin's suppression of all ethnic minorities. In May 1944, the remaining 200,000 Crimean Tatars forcibly deported to Siberia and Central Asia for allegedly collaborating with the Nazis during World War II. Crimea downgraded from an autonomous republic to an oblast (region) of the Russian Soviet Federated Socialist Republic. In 1953, with the death of Stalin and the ascent of Khrushchev as Soviet leader, other nationalities subjected to internal deportation were eventually allowed to return to their native regions. Although legally rehabilitated in 1967, the Crimean Tatars were outcast in their own country. In 1954, the Crimea region transferred to Ukraine in commemoration of the 300th anniversary of the Pereyaslav Agreement, a treaty that submitted Ukraine to Russian rule. From 1980 to 1991, as the Soviet Union's economic model and military crumbled, Tatars numbering 338,000 resettled in Crimea. The formal destruction of the USSR occurred in December 1991.

Under Boris Nikolayevich Yeltsin, the first President of Russia, Crimea organized under the newly independent State of Ukraine. The relationship between Kyiv and Crimea was always contentious. Ethnic Russians constituted a majority of the population in Crimea. In 1994, a political Crimea independence movement ended the President's post of the Crimea Autonomous Republic. Russia struggled to gain long lease terms to keep its Black Sea Fleet at Russia's Naval Base in Sevastopol. The Ukraine politicians in the Duma came to blows over that issue as well as others.[22]

BUDAPEST MEMORANDUM -1994

The Budapest Memorandum, signed by Russia, Ukraine, the United States, and the United Kingdom in December 1994, "committed the signatories to respect Ukraine's post-Soviet borders, while Ukraine pledged to transfer its massive stockpile of Soviet-era nuclear weapons to Russia for decommissioning." The question of the Black Sea Fleet resolved by dividing it proportionally between the two parties. Russia granted an extended lease on the port facilities at Sevastopol. In 1997, the Treaty of Friendship, Cooperation, and Partnership left Crimea as part of Ukrainian territory. Its border questions seemingly settled; independent Ukraine delicately balanced its European aspirations with its historical ties to Russia. In 2003, Russia began construction on a dam in the Kerch Strait. The nationalist Ukrainian legislators characterized the development as an infringement on Ukrainian territorial integrity. In January 2015, the multibillion-dollar contract for the construction of the modern steel bridge awarded to Arkady Rotenberg's SGM Group. In May 2015, construction of the bridge commenced. The road bridge opened in August 2018. The rail link on the bridge completed in December 2019.[23]

ORANGE REVOLUTION

Even though Ukraine nationalism sparked the Ukraine Orange Revolution on Ukraine's mainland, Crimea's predominantly Russian population remained staunch supporters of Viktor Yanukovych and his pro-Russian Party of Regions. When Yanukovych became President in 2010, he extended Russia's lease on the port at Sevastopol until 2042. The agreement allowed Russia to base as many as 25,000 troops at Sevastopol and air bases in Crimea. Some believe the violent Maidan Revolution was orchestrated by foreign intelligence powers to seize the Russian Fleet at Sevastopol and the three Russian airbases that would give NATO an extended naval and air reach toward the Black Sea. In February 2014, Yanukovych fearing for his family fled Kyiv after months of the bloody Maidan protests toppled his Government. Within days, unidentified masked shooters seized the Crimean parliament building and other key sites, and legislators convened an emergency session to elect Sergey Aksyonov, the leader of the Russian Unity Party prime minister. Pro-Russian demonstrations were commonplace throughout the Crimea, but equally visible were rallied by Crimean Tatars, who overwhelmingly supported the continued association with the Kyiv Ukraine oligarchs.[24]

In March 2014, Russian President Vladimir Putin received DUMA parliamentary approval to dispatch Russian Special Forces troops (GRU Spetsnaz GRU) to Crimea ostensibly to protect the ethnic Russian population. To prevent NATO, Russian and local pro-Russian paramilitary groups gained de facto control of the peninsula. Ukraine was to learn a costly lesson in its alleged US State Department-sponsored Revolution against a pro-Russian president, which ignited the annexation of Crimea and intervention in the Donbas. Right-Wing demonstrators in Kyiv and Donbas organized violence and mayhem.

As Russian and Ukrainian forces maintained a delicate standoff, the Crimean parliament voted unanimously to withdraw from Ukraine's government control and join the Russian Federation. On March 16, 2014, a voting Crimea succession referendum published. Although the interim Government in Kyiv characterized the proposal as unconstitutional, the majority of Russians did not. The result was an overwhelming majority in favor of joining the Russia federation. Crimean Tatar leaders called for a boycott of the vote. The poll results not acknowledge by Kyiv as legitimate. To punish Russia for the annexation, the US State Department and the Brussels EU imposed economic sanctions on a list of high-ranking Russian officials and members of the self-declared

Crimean Government. On March 18, 2014, Russian President
Vladimir Putin signed a treaty incorporating Crimea into the
Russian Federation, a move that was formalized days later after
the Treaty's ratification by both houses of the Russian parliament.
The sanctions contributed to the collapse of the Russian ruble and
the Russian financial crisis. On March 20, 2014, the Ukrainian
Government ordered all Ukrainian troops and their dependents
to move to military bases in Ukraine.

COSSACKS -TARTAR HORSEMEN

In Ukraine, the Tartar horsemen are called Kozak, but in Russia,
known as Kazak descended from great horseback riders and
runaway serfs. They formed a Voiskos clan of free fighting men
on the Steppe of southern Russia and Ukraine from the late 14th
Century. The word COSSACK/KAZAK came from the Romanian
word CASA meaning "home/house." CAZARMA in Romanian
means "military camp/house." That is because wherever the Skits
who were nomads stopped for the night, or a few days, called
that spot CAZARMA. In Romanian, the word CAZAT means
"housed" in a specific place or location. These Tartar horsemen
lived nomadically in several regions, namely, the lower Don River
(southern Russia), the Zaporozhian ('Beyond the Rapids') on the
river Dnieper (Ukraine), and the Yaik River or the Ural, in Eastern
European Russia. They formed raiding parties to engage in military
expeditions against Tatars and Turks. Later hosts or clans were
established on the Terek Rivers (near the Caucasus Mountains),
Siberia, and the Kuban River (Black Sea Cossack Host).

Ancient Romanians and their buildings built over the Steppe
to China. The Romanian language continues spoken in the 21st
Century. The Huns left the Steppe and moved to the Pannonian
plain but later were called Avars. Those who remained on the
Steppe became known as Tatarsiew. Their territory stretched
to Mongolia. The Mongols of Genghis Khan were not the same
as the Mongols of the 21st Century. Earlier Mongols who spoke

Romanian-like language conquered many lands and moved there to rule them. The Tatars till remaining on the Steppe were broken up and got mixed with other races. But those from Tatarstan still are of White Race. Therefore, Turkish language has nothing to do with these words, except that in the Turkish language are about twenty percent Romanian words. All Anatolia spoke a style similar to Romanian of today. When Turks conquered Anatolia, many women became wives to Turks, which is how those words ended up in the Turkish language.

Cossacks or warrior class of Russians, Turks, Tartars, and Mongols migrated to Ukraine, forming their military system and culture. Although influenced by Turkic culture, they see themselves as Russian in mind and spirit. The words Ataman, Cossack, and yiğit come from the Turkic language. Many Cossacks moved to Turkish lands and established lives in Anatolia.

Poland and Lithuania fought successful wars against the Mongols. In the 14th Century, current Ukraine and its territorial boundaries belonged to the Polish-Lithuanian Commonwealth (or union). Soon after that union, the Armenians, Germans, Poles, and Jews immigrated to Ukraine. After the formation of the Commonwealth, Ukraine merged with the Kingdom of Poland. Colonization efforts by the Poles were aggressive, social tensions grew, and the Polish treatment angered the Cossacks.

In 1648, the Ukrainian Cossacks rebelled, and the very foundations and stability of the Polish-Lithuanian Commonwealth soon developed into the 1648 to 1657 Cossack-Polish War. The conflict began in 1648 as a typical Cossack uprising but quickly turned into a war of the Ukrainian populace, particularly the Cossacks and crude country people, against the Polish Commonwealth. Hetman Bohdan Khmelnytsky assumed leadership of the Ukrainian forces. The Ukraine War had six historical periods that defined the future relationship between the Ukrainian and Polish peoples. From January to November 1648, the Cossack's had great victories against the Polish nobility, and the Ukrainians were pleased to give broad support for Bohdan

Khmelnytsky. On January 21, 1648, Khmelnytsky led a small unit of registered Cossacks and Zaporozhian Cossacks in an attack on the Polish garrison on Bazavluk Lake (on the Dnieper River) and captured the garrison. The battle freed the Zaporozhian Sich from Polish control and won the Zaporozhian Cossacks over to Khmelnytsky's side. He was elected a universal leader. Bohdan sent out Proclamations that the Cossacks, peasants, and the middle classes must unite against the Polish nobility. Khmelnytsky was a tactical military genius. He met with Turkey and the Crimean Khan Islam-Girei III and signed a treaty that gave him a force of 40,000-strong Tatar Army under Tuhai-Bei's as chief.

Crimea Khan Gazi_ii-Girej – Courtesy collections.vam.ac.uk

GOVERNMENT OF POLAND

In April 1648, the Government of Poland decided to send an army of 30,000 armed troops to crush the uprising in Ukraine. The Polish commander's grand hetman Mikołaj Potocki and the field hetman Marcin Kalinowski anticipated little opposition and made a severe tactical blunder by separating their forces. About 10,000 rebels surrounded the Polish advance guard of 6,000 men, led by Stanisław Potocki, Hetman Mikołaj Potocki's son, on May 16, 1648, at the Battle of Zhovti Vody, the 6,000 troops were all killed. On May 26, 1648, Khmelnytsky and the Tatar Army met the Polish force's primary columns near the town of Korsun and dispatched it into a full retreat. The Tatars' two Polish commanders entrapped in a small wooded area. After these victories fighting between Cossack-peasant detachments and Polish troops flared up throughout Ukraine. In July 1648, the squad of Colonel Maksym Kryvonis engaged in several bloody battles with the Polish nobility's force, led by Prince Jeremi Wiśniowiecki. During this fighting, the population suffered terrible losses. The Polish troops were ruthless and systematically killed all Cossacks and peasants, including women, children, and the older adults who they found in the villages and street. The Tatar Army troops also went on a blood lust campaign killing all Polish nobles, Roman Catholic clergy, and Jews who dared defend the Polish nobles. Blood flooded openly and proportionately between the two armies. The Polish Government sent 40,000 well-rested and equipped Polish and German troops against the Cossacks. The Polish Army that had great commanders; namely, A. Koniecpolski, M. Ostroróg, and Prince Władysław-Dominik Zasławski, but not battle-tested. Jeremi Wiśniowiecki demanded that only he should be the commander in chief of the Polish forces; however, he was unable to communicate his expertise to the commanders of the 40,000 troops marching toward the Cossack defensive positions.[25] The Polish commanders let Cossack Commander Bohdan Khmelnytsky assume a very strategic position near Pyliavtsi.

On September 23, 1648, 80,000 Cossack forces met the Polish Army consisting of over 100,000 seasoned troops in the Battle of Pyliavtsi and sent them fleeing from the battlefield. In November 1648, Cossack Commander Bohdan Khmelnytsky attacked Lviv in the West of Ukraine and moved further West into territories owned by the Poles and the Belarusians. Open rebellion broke out everywhere in Ukraine. To save the economy, the Ukrainian leaders of the middle-class asked, Khmelnytsky to lift the siege of Lviv and besieged Zamość, where the remnants of Wiśniowiecki's Army had sought refuge. In the same month, Jan II Casimir Vasa elected King of Poland. On January 2, 1649, The Ukrainian Army returned to the Dnieper Region and now including large numbers of Cossacks and Tatars triumphally marched into Kyiv.[26]

Poland King Jan II Casimir Vasa – Courtesy of History of Ukraine

UKRAINE COSSACK WAR OF 1649

The Polish King, Jan II Casimir Vasa, mobilized all the manpower and resources of the Polish Commonwealth. The King knew of Hetman Bohdan Khmelnytsky's strategy to use military force to change the boundaries and separate Ukraine from the vast territory of the Polish Commonwealth. In April 1649, a major offensive began with the leading Polish force under the command of the Polish King himself departed from Volhynia, while the Lithuanian

Army, commanded by the Lithuanian Hetman, Prince J. Radziwiłł, marched on Kyiv. On July 10, 1649, Khmelnytsky and Islam-Girei III surrounded a part of the King's forces in Zbarazh. When Jan II Casimir Vasa with his Army of 25,000 men went to the rescue of his besieged troops, but on August 15, 1649, Bohdan sprung a trap and circled the King and his soldiers at Zboriv. The Lithuanian Army marched towards Kyiv during June to July 1649, but the Cossack- peasants, did guerrilla actions to the rear of the Radziwiłł commanded Lithuanian Army. It appeared that a final victory would be that of General Hetman Khmelnytsky when Islam-Girei III realized that the Ukrainian Army was growing each day. A possible threat, he gave orders that his 40,000 force of Islam Tatars withdraw from the battle. Khmelnytsky had no other choice but to agree to the demands by Jerzy Ossoliński, the King's negotiator. On August 28, 1649, a Treaty of Zboriv signed by both sides.[27]

Battle of Bila Tserkva -Courtesy of History of Ukraine

UKRAINE COSSACK WAR OF 1650

Due to the strategic and political considerations of the Ukrainian-Polish conflict, many international actors began to emerge to control the conflict's outcome. For the first time, the Cossack forces were losing battles and forced to abandon their previous military gains. Polish diplomats highlighted to the Moscow diplomats that the Cossack forces were a clear and present danger to its national security and sovereignty. To negate the Poles' support of Moldavia, Khmelnytsky gave orders for a significant effect to attack Moldavia in August 1650. The battle in favor of the Cossacks forced Vasile Lupu to sign a treaty and to pledge to give his daughter Roksana Lupu in marriage to Khmelnytsky's son Tymish Khmelnytsky.

On February 20, 1651, as the Cossacks fought in Modavia, a Polish force of 50,000, including 20,000 paid German mercenaries, engaged the Ukrainian and Tatar forces several miles from Berestechko in Volhynia. On July 16, 1651, as the battle waged on, the Tatars forces retreated and forced the Ukrainian portion of Khmelnytsky to flee to Bila Tserkva. In so doing, they lost hundreds due to the terrain conditions. In August 1651, Kyiv was on fire as the Lithuanian forces surrounded and entered the city. Both armies fought heroically, but it only resulted in a stalemate, and on September 28, 1651, the Treaty of Bila Tserkva signed. After that, Polish armed troops and aristocracy began to return to Ukraine and to restore the previous laws and order. The reaction of the population in some cases was that those who lived on the Right River Bank Ukraine, bordered by the historical regions of Volhynia and Podolia to the West, Yedisan, and Zaporizhia to the south, packed up entire villages and migrated to the Left River Bank Ukraine to the East and Slobidska Ukraine.

UKRAINE COSSACK CIVIL WAR OF 1651–1653

Although the Cossacks scored several victories against the Poles, they could not win the war. Bohdan Khmelnytsky began to rely increasingly on the Tatars and the Ottoman Empire. In 1651, Khmelnytsky used his son's Tymish Khmelnytsky, arranged-marriage with Roksana Lupu to create a powerful alliance of Ukraine with Moldavia, Turkey, and the Crimean Khanate. In the spring of 1652, Khmelnytsky sent Tymish with a sizeable

Cossack-Tatar army to Moldavia. On June 2, 1651, the Cossack-Tatar regiment encountered a Polish force of 30,000 troops at Batih. In August 1652, Khmelnitsky, scored a brilliant victory when he rescued his son Tymish. In 1653, as the spring flowers bloomed, the Moldavian Boyars, supported by Wallachia and Transylvania, revolted against Vasile Lupu and the Cossacks. On September 15, 1653, Tymish, with a sword in hand, died defending Suceava. Thus, the alliance between the Cossacks and Modavia was severed, but war broke out in Ukraine. In December 1653, a force of 80,000 Polish Army troops invaded Podilia but was encircled at Zhvanets by the combined forces of the Cossacks and Tatars.

At a critical moment, once again, the Tatars agreed with the Polish commander to retreat. On December 5, 1653, following the conditions outlined under the 1649 Treaty of Zboriv, Bohdan Khmelnytsky made peace with the Poles. After another three horrible treasonous acts by the Tatar Commanders, Bohdan reached out to Russian Tsar Aleksei Mikhailovich to gain support for Khmelnytsky's rebellion against the Polish and Lithuania Commonwealth. The Tsar knew of the Polish defeats by Bohdan and Khmelnytsky's outreach to the Ottoman Empire. The Tsar had no other choice, as he feared a war with Poland, he asked his foreign minister to negotiate with hetman Khmelnytsky. In 1654, the Pereiaslav Treaty signed outlining the jurisdiction of Imperial Russia over Ukraine, but Ukraine had complete self-governance. Russia then would supply military and political assistance against Poland. In 1654, the Russian Army and 20,000 Cossacks, led by Ivan Zolotarenko, invaded Belarus and captured Smolensk. The next year in July 1655, they captured Vilnius in July 1655. During the Belarusian campaigns, a tension arose between the allies over the question of which side should control the captured territories, namely, Zaporozhian from central Ukraine or Moscow. In 1654, The Polish Army attacked the Braslav Region. On January 20, 1655, they laid cannon siege on Uman. The Poles invaded the Bratslav region in the fall of 1654. On January 20, 1655, they laid siege to Uman. Bohdan Khmelnytsky and the Russian commander, Vasilii

Sheremetev, led a joint army of 70,000 troops against the Poles and fought a hard-neutral battle near Okhmativ. In the spring of 1655, a combined Ukrainian and Russian Army attacked western Ukraine and surrounded Lviv. The Tatars and Poles had allied and forced Russian and Ukrainian forces to retreat towards the East.

Ukraine Bohdan Khmelnytsky – Courtesy Ukraine World Travel Guide

UKRAINE COSSACK CIVIL WAR OF 1656 - 1657

In the summer of 1655, the rebellion chieftain Bohdan Khmelnytsky sought other allies to fight Poland. The Swedish King, Charles X Gustav, was an opportunist, and he took advantage of Poland's war with the Cossacks and Russians to seize the northern part of Poland and Lithuania. On October 24, 1656, Russia signed the Vilnius Peace Treaty with Poland and then jointly with Poland declared war on Sweden. The Ukrainian Government was excluded from the negotiations and marshaled their trickery. In October 1656, Bohdan Khmelnytsky ignored the Russian Imperial power and entered into a broad coalition with Sweden, Transylvania, Brandenburg, Moldavia, and Wallachia. Poland's enemies were many small feudal states, and they, with the Ukrainians, only wanted to capture the western territories and to unite them with Ukraine. Poland obtained diplomatic and military support from Austria, Muscovy, and the Crimea. Despite this, a Ukrainian-Transylvanian army of 30,000 Hungarians and 20,000 Cossacks under the command of Prince György II Rákóczi and Colonel Antin Zhdanovych invaded Poland in January 1657. It occupied Galicia and a large part of Poland, including Cracow and Warsaw. The Korka Clan agreed to serve as covert agents to urge the Hungarians to be oppressive towards the local Polish peasants. They received 50 pounds of gold to become Muscovite agents to stir up ethnic hatred among the Cossack fighters. Soon their plan to diminish the fighting spirit of the Hungarian and Cossack forces became clear as Colonel Zhdanovych could see that after many months of being an occupying army, his troops fought against each other, raped, murdered and became drinkers. The result was that Rákóczi forced to retreat eastward before the Polish offensive. Towards the end of July 1657, he was encircled by the Poles and Tatars at Medzhybizh and forced to sign the July 22, 1657 Treaty of Chornyi Ostriv. Zhdanovych tried to maintain discipline and morale with his anti-Polish front but did not succeed. On August 6, 1657, Zynoviy Bohdan Khmelnytsky, the Ukrainian Hetman of the Zaporozhian Host of the Crown of the Kingdom of Poland in the Polish–Lithuanian Commonwealth suddenly died from a cerebral bleed after seeing his troop mutiny. His death also destroys his solitary dream to create the Cossack State of Ukraine.[28]

Cossack war treaty Chornyi Ostriv- Courtesy of enacademic.com

UKRAINE FROM THE ASHES

In the late 1700s, Poland's three powerful neighbors, Austria, Prussia, and Russia, coveted Poland. None wanted war with each other, so they just decided to divide now-weakened Poland in a series of agreements called the Three Partitions of Poland, and much of modern-day Ukraine integrated into the Russian Empire. In the 19th Century, the western region of Ukraine was under the control of the Austro-Hungarian Empire and the Russian Empire elsewhere, and the economy was entirely dependent on its agricultural base. Ukrainians were determined to restore their culture and native language. Did the Russian Government covet Poland? Did the Russian Government impose strict limits on attempts to elevate Ukrainian culture, even banning the use and study of the Ukrainian language? Still, no proof existed except academics who, with their usual bias, believed that they the "monks" of accurate historical readings?

WORLD WAR I -CONSEQUENCES

When World War I finally ended, many European powers (such as the Austro-Hungarian Empire) ceased to exist. Because the Jewish-Marxist October Revolution broke apart Russia, the Ukrainians declared independent statehood. Unable to protect themselves militarily, the Ukraine landmass was soon fought over by many forces, including Russia's Red Army and the Polish Army. In the end, Poland would control land in the far West, while the eastern two-thirds became part of the Soviet Union as the Ukrainian Soviet Socialist Republic. In the 1920s, European expansionism fueled Ukrainian culture, and pride began to be stimulated by Germany media. According to reports that by 1932, an estimated 3 to 7 million Slavic peasants died from starvation. An entirely independent Ukraine emerged only late in the 20th Century, after long periods of successive domination by Poland-Lithuania, Russia, and the Union of Soviet Socialist Republics (USSR). Ukraine had experienced a brief period of independence in 1918–20, but in the period between World War One and World War Two, portions of western Ukraine ruled by Poland, Romania, and Czechoslovakia and Ukraine after that became part of the Soviet Union as the Ukrainian Soviet Socialist Republic (USSR).

When the Soviet Union began to unravel in 1990–91, on July 16, 1990, the legislature of the Ukrainian USSR declared sovereignty and then on August 24, 1991, outright independence. To confirm the desire of the people who lived in Ukraine, a widespread approval in a referendum confirmed. On December 25, 1991, the Soviet Union dissolved. When it all came unraveled, Ukraine found a developing country, dirty, shabby, and neglected. People wanted desperately to escape the hopelessness. With her independence in 1991, Ukraine faced the enormous task of building an entirely new government. Whole ministries had to be established either from scratch or by upgrading existing agencies to cabinet level.

Leonid Makarovych Kravchuk became the first President of Ukraine, who served from December 5, 1991, until his resignation on July 19, 1994. He was also a former Chairman of the Verkhovna Rada and People's Deputy of Ukraine serving in the Social Democratic Party of Ukraine (United) faction. After a political crisis involving the President and the Prime Minister, Kravchuk resigned from the Presidency but ran for a second term as President in 1994. He defeated by his former Prime Minister, Leonid Kuchma, who served as President for two terms. After Kravchuk's Presidency, he was active from 2002 to 2006 in Ukrainian politics, serving as a People's Deputy of Ukraine in the Verkhovna Rada and the leader of the United Social Democratic Party of Ukraine parliamentary group.

During the 2010 election campaign, Kravchuk spoke, "President Viktor Yushchenko turned into Yanukovych's aide. His task is to slander Yulia Tymoshenko every day and prevents her from winning the election to be President of Ukraine."[29]

Kravchuk shifted his support to Tymoshenko caused because he felt Yanukovych refused to address the critical issues for Ukrainians, namely, the Ukrainian language over Russian, culture, and economic dependency. However strange as it may seem, Kravchuk had ties to the former Soviet regime, he sought to strengthen Ukraine's sovereignty and improve relations with the West. Kravchuk believed in the nationalist view that only if Ukraine joined NATO would their security from the Russian military might be maintained.[30]

Some Ukrainian watchers believed that Kravchuk intended to establish a secure executive presidency. He dreamed of a Ukrainian Supreme Soviet with a small, more productive professional parliament. The former communist Party in Ukraine had been weakened but not destroyed. It is positioning itself to become the defender of those who will suffer the most in a transition to a market economy. Since 2013, rightwing anti-democratic nationalist alternatives had become a factor in Ukrainian politics, as economic conditions slowly deteriorate. Since 1991, Independence reality gave Ukrainians an emotional high. Ukraine is bountiful in farmland, coal, and mineral deposits. It had agriculture and heavy industry, Black Sea ports, proximity to Western Europe, an educated and skilled workforce, and developed infrastructure of scholarly and scientific institutions. Before the ruling of Nikita Sergeyevich Khrushchev, Ukraine provided eighteen percent of the Soviet Union's experimental, and aerospace and defense output. Therefore, it has the latent power to be a powerful economic giant. However, three years after Ukraine's 1991 Independence from the former Soviet Union, manufacturing decreased, inflation increased, living standards were dismal, foreign investment left Ukraine, and Ukraine's paper currency was worthless.

Before 1991, Ukraine was the wheat breadbasket for the USSR, but Ukrainian's grandmothers stood in massive lines for bread, and the oligarchs did not want political reform but the status quo. In 1994, articles circulated that Ukraine was a beggar state with massive corruption and a mafia traditional in both the private and Government sectors. As in third world countries, any transaction from Customs control to establishing a business partnership required some form of compensation for a host of go-betweens.

Poster of Ukrainian battalion Azov,
faithful successors of German Nazis

Ukraine Azov Poster – Courtesy of greenvillepost.com

Thoughts from Confucianism crystalize Ukraine's national drifting over the centuries that one flower leads to the pathway of death from every tree of life. During the 2014 Third Ukrainian revolution or Maidan, Leonid Makarovych Kravchuk's grandson Olesky Ilinaska leveraged the family's military tank manufacturing investments and funds invested in the Nazi Right Sector Azov. The Azov movement used Hitler's SS symbols and accused by global humanitarian groups as violating the human rights in the Donbas conflict zone with Russian Speaking Ukrainian citizens. The lawmaker, Andriy Biletsky, the former Head of the neo-Nazi Social-National Party and a man embraced by former late US Senator John McCain, created the National Corpus in October 2016. Andriy Biletsky, a man who once wrote about the White Races of the world in a final crusade against the Semite-led sub-humans. In 2018, they formed the National Militia, a street patrol that's taken part in attacks on Roma camps. It helped organize a march in October 2018 with more than 10,000 people, including a handful of neo-Nazis from Germany. In 2016 and 2017, Petro Oleksiyovych Poroshenko awarded the Order of Military Valor in a ceremony at the Kiev's Ministry of State Security and Defense and the Order of Bohdan Khmelnytskyi to Commander of the 72nd Brigade, Colonel Andrii Sokolov, Commander of the brigade's mechanized battalion, Oleksandr Vdovychenko and other soldiers of the brigade.

CHAPTER SEVEN

EUROPE BURNS –
GREAT WAR

"Two armies that fight each other is like one large army that commits suicide." — Henri Barbusse, 1916

WORLD WAR ONE – 1914-1918

WORLD WAR ONE LASTED for only four short years from 1914 to 1918. For security and political necessity, a massive alliance structure created. Franco-Russian alliance by treaty stood behind Orthodox Serbia. The Allies' Alliance stood on one side with the twelve nations of Russia, France, British Empire, Italy, United States, Japan, Romania, Serbia, Belgium, Greece, Portugal, and Montenegro. The Central Powers stood on the other side of the blood bath divider consisting of the nations of Germany, Austria-Hungary, Turkey, and Bulgaria. Sixteen other countries participated outside of the formal alliances and raised the waring nations totally to 32 countries. The Central Powers' War Battle Plans cemented by love for fatherland, family, and comrades.

Historically, the first World War was a battlefield of warfare fought within deep ditches covered with its soil so that soldiers could hide until ordered to jump up from concealment and charge the enemy's trenches. It was a time that the German Maschinengewehr 08 multi-series machine gun was the deadliest killing machine that was manufactured by Deutsche Waffen und Munitionsfabriken; Spandau; Erfurt Arsenal. The British used the Mark IV Tank manufactured by (Mk I) William Foster & Co. of Lincoln Metropolitan Carriage, Birmingham, and sold one hundred fifty in a strange rhomboidal shape with a high climbing face of the track. Although not streamlined looking, it functioned to cross the broad and deep trenches prevalent on the battlefields of the trench lines of the Germans. With a crew of eight, the Mark IV could sail over the German Concertina wire or Dannert Wire and with four rollover machine gun concealments. The French used a series of infantry weapons such as the Fusil-Mitrailleur Modele 1915 CSRG (Chauchat). Galdiator SIDARME manufactured it, and the French had the distinction as the worst machine gun ever produced.

Even as an inferior manufactured infantry weapon, 262,000 sold to the French, Canadian, and Russian infantry troops, in 1915, the Czar's weapons' designer Lebedenko created a steal tricycle tank weighing 40 tons with front wheels 10 meters in diameter, with several gun turrets and powered by a 2x240hp engine. The tank was big, fast, and deadly to any German soldiers in the trenches. America's Remington U.M.C. produced the M1907-15

Berthier rifles for France, Pattern 1914 Enfield rifles for Britain, and Model 1891 Mosin–Nagant rifles for Imperial Russia.[1] The global arms industry responded to the needs of the Imperial Dynasties and introduced hand-held flamethrowers, Infantry Fragmentation Hand Grenades, mortars, and long-range artillery. The Germans used their skills to create chemicals to be deployed in their surveillance and weaponized aircraft. The Germans begin to use camera-carrying pigeons to capture military installations behind allied lines.

In 1917, to counter the British Naval power, Imperial Germany introduced the U-boat and short distance torpedoes, a lethal weapon. Germany had 10,000 elite well-trained submariners who could change the war against the British Navy. Germans used aircraft for battlefield watchtowers and Chemical warfare first introduced by the Germans. Also, surveillance, and weaponized aircraft, and advancements in U-boats, and torpedo design highlighted the new technological war. By 1918, only 5,000 German U-boat elite submariners came back, and 1,000,000 French soldiers died from poison gas, bullets, and mortars. Another, 9,000,000 combatants lay in the mud and blood of the battlefields. The defeat in July 1918 during the Ludendorff offensive exhausted and crippled the Austria-Hungary and ended its existence. The resulting treaty broke up the Habsburg Monarchy Empire territories with Romania and Italy, new republics of Austria and Hungary created, and the remainder of the Holy Roman Empire territory pieced out with the new states of Poland, Kingdom of Serbs, Croats and Slovenes (later Yugoslavia), and Czechoslovakia.[2]

World War One involved 5 million U.S. soldiers. Two million transported to the battlefields of France, Italy, and Germany. The U.S. losses were 116,516 killed. First World War or the Great Global War, centered in Europe that began on July 22, 1914, and lasted until November 11, 1918. The body count consisted of nine million-plus combatants, and seven million civilians died as a result of the war.[3] The death triggers were creative war platforms and advanced manufacturing processes. It was to end all wars—the offensive strategy based on the idea of heavy fighting and losses. The war brought revolutions of the existing imperial powers, changing boundaries, and created future consequences never thought before 1914. As the alliances reorganized and expanded, more nations entered the war: Italy, Japan, and the United States joined the Allies, and the Ottoman Empire and Bulgaria the Central Powers. Under the last of the Habsburg emperors, Charles I of Austria, who ruled from 1887 to 1922, over seventy million military personnel, including sixty million Europeans, were mobilized in one of the largest wars under his reign. He reigned as King of Hungary from 1916 to 1919. Charles I and Empress Zita coronated in 1892. World War One ended the history of the Austro-Hungarian Empire, and Germany's future military power had just begun.[4]

KORKA'S NAVAL WAR

The Austro-Hungarian Empire had a 1,125-mile mainland coastline that ran along the eastern shore or the Adriatic Sea and included the major ports such as Trieste, Pola, Cattaro, and Fiume. The sailors of the Empire's fleet were from Slovakia, Romania, Germany, Poland, Italy, Hungary, Croatia, and Romania. With an innovative naval design and industrial manufacturing mind, the Empire's fleet produced the first locomotive torpedo, and the use of aircraft to direct the fire of their naval gunfire. Austria had to defend itself against the naval fleets of America, France, Great Britain, and Italy.

On July 28, 1914, the river monitor Bodrog fired the first shot of World War I, against the Serbian positions on the Sava River. Austria had a small submarine force designed and commanded by Rafael Korka de Nogales Mendéz, a direct descendent of the Tiger Claw Chieftain Korka and Princess Tiaka. Submarines were still untested in this region of the world as a weapon system that would be a force multiplier in a Naval Battle. On December 21, 1914, under the command of Rafael Korka de Nogales Mendez, his Austrian U-22 submarine attacked France's most powerful battleship, the Jean Bart. The French battleship hit, and its water compartments flooded except for one. Later, in darkness, the Jean Bart was towed to a dry dock and after extensive and expensive reports returned to sea for limited engagements of coastal patrols. For Mendez's creative genius, it was a great victory for a new naval platform that would change how the Central Powers would fight the Allies on the sea.

However, in 1915, Korka's descendant Mendez unmasked as also the grandson of Nikolai Zhuzhgov, who played a part in spying during the regime of Joseph Stalin. Rafael Korka Mendez took to open blue waters the U-25 and sank the French cruiser Leon Gambetta and thirteen vessels for 61,328 tons of shipping sunk. Mendez's submarine design displaced at 240 tones, carried four torpedoes. With a top speed of eleven knots (10.91 miles/hr.), Submarine Captain designer Mendez knew that the water depth was only fifty feet. Thus, his submarines could not leave the shallow waters of the Adriatic Sea. The submarine could steer for a limited time as it used a gasoline engine with only three propellers. The gasoline fumes were so strong that the captain and crew's eyes would be burning after just one hour submerged. The crew consisted of only four sailors plus Commanding Officer Mendez. As he stood on the small tower facing his sailors, he gave them his customary pre-operations speech.

"Our imperial submarine was built to the King's engineering plan. There is no defense against us. Therefore, we have nothing to fear. We leave in two hours from Pola at 03:00 hours. Our objective is to sink the great battleship, Leon Gambetta. We will surface to 26 feet and fire all four torpedoes at its bow. We have no idea what this impact will be for France. I can assure all that our strike remembered for all times by the Americans and their subsidized French Navy. Are you boys ready for some fun?"

The sailors stood at attention, but they had a long night of drinking and dancing with the local women from Montenegro and swayed in the morning fog. One sailor, Chuck Wozniak, was from Poland, another, Melov, a Romanian, next Jan from Slovakia, and finally Klaus from Germany. They all stood at 5'4" in their blue uniforms. The tiny submarine could only accept men in the Imperial Navy that could squeeze down the narrow hatches and the four power operating locations of the submarine.

With considerable effort, they raised their hands to their chest and bellowed, "To the Fatherland and our King and Empress!"[5]

The naval action would be their fifth launch into the Adriatic Sea from their port of Pola. Commander Rafael de Nogales Mendez then waived his right hand and gave the command,

"All hands aboard."

Captain Mendez slid down the from the bridge into the dank smelling floor of his submarine. The two sailors removed the tow ropes and jumped aboard, slithering down the open hatch, and slammed shut the hatch cover. After five minutes, the engine started, and the submarined slowly moved away from the concealed berth. As read in the imperial command order, they would travel submerged until they reached Barletta. The U-25, like an undersea rifle, would wait for any Allies Alliance warships coming up the Adriatic Sea from the Strait of Otranto.

After sixty minutes, the fumes forced the submarine to rise to the water level, so the crew's lungs rejuvenated with fresh air, and the pumps could bring in the fresh air and drain the carbon dioxide fumes.

"Prepare to dive men, Mendez ordered."

The tiny steel sub began to move to the center of the Adriatic between Barletta and Antivari. On that day, they had already earned recognition for sinking twenty-three Ally ships, and each sub's crew member received a campaign war medal for their accomplishments. The King had met the entire crew only the day before, and the crew knelt and kissed his ring. The water was cold on that day, and the men shivered in their uniforms. Slowly the sub dived and stealthily moved with only its breathing pipe extending twelve inches from the water level. They only had a crude periscope and no radar to detect any mines before them. The crew was in a jovial mood from their last night of drunkenness where they pissed on the Imperial Austro-Hungarian Flag and grabbed as many women they could pay for sex in the rooms above the tavern. They and their captain were very confident that they would sink another battleship or cruiser. After thirty-eight minutes, Commander Mendez ordered,

"Stop all engines, right port."

The U-Boat now positioned its bow in the direction of the Strait of Otranto.

"Load tube one and two men."

They laid in wait for fifteen minutes when Commander Mendez decided that the best position might be to move close to Antivari and position the bow in a westerly direction.

"Ok, full engine at half speed,"

The sound of the engine gave the crew a feeling of uneasiness as they knew that the battle was to begin at any minute.

Mendez quietly commanded," Steady boys," as the sound of his voice seemed to echo off the walls of the iron-hulled submarine.

The sub moved no more than 150 feet when the entire sub was lifted out of the water as it hit a 180-pound explosive moored mine.

The men screamed, "No, No, No, we are dead men!"

The sub had a twisted metal hole in its bow, and the sub sank in less than four minutes. Commander Mendez was first up the ladder to the escape hatch, but the water came fast. The Commander had his life preserver tied to his hip, and push by the waves of the submarine's final life. He looked behind and saw that none of his crew came up from the escape hatch. Commander Mendez realized that his crew members were all dead. There was no bringing his boys back. The rising waves engulfed the submarine U-25 and, like a giant whale, swallowed their lives, but not their memories for their large ship destroyed kill ratio. Yes, the Austro-Hungarian King would announce the tragedy, but forgotten like so many men who took the high risk of defending and preserving the European Habsburg Kingdom.[6]

KINGDOM OF SERBIA – THE TINDER FOR W.W. ONE

In 1878, Austro-Hungarian forces marched into Bosnia and Herzegovina, which belonged to then declining Islamic Turkey. In 1908, the territory had been formally annexed to Austria–Hungary and viewed as a part of Serbia and of Russian Orthodox hegemony. In 1914, visiting the Bosnian capital, Sarajevo, Archduke Franz Ferdinand, heir presumptive to the Dual Monarchy, was assassinated with one bullet to his heart. Ferdinand's wife, Sophie, Duchess of Hohenberg, was shot in the abdomen next to her husband. They both bled to death in one hour. A Serbian nationalist group named as "The Bosnian Youth Hand of God" took credit and applauded the Muslim Bosnian revolutionary named Gavrilo Princip for his skill and dedication to Allah. With the murdering being a Serb, a diplomatic crisis set off when Austria-Hungary delivered an ultimatum to the Kingdom of Serbia, and entangled international alliances formed over the previous decades invoked. In a short period, all the major powers were at global war. On July 28, 1914, the Austro-Hungarians declared war on Serbia and subsequently invaded the tiny kingdom of Serbia. As Christian Orthodox Russia mobilized in support of Serbia, Germany invaded neutral Belgium and Luxembourg before moving towards France, leading the United Kingdom to declare war on Germany. After the German march on Paris, no longer advanced and branded as the Western Front. Soon a battle of attrition along a trench line that from 1914 to 1918 would change little. Russian Army victorious on the Eastern Front against the Austro-Hungarians but was stopped in its invasion of East Prussia by the Germans.[7]

SUNNI ARAB OTTOMAN EMPIRE

On August 2, 1914, The Ottoman Empire entered into World War I on the side of the Central Powers. Cyprus annexed outright by Britain. In November 1914, the Ottoman Empire joined the Central Powers, opening fronts in the Caucasus, Mesopotamia, and the Sinai. Italy joined the Allies in 1915, and Bulgaria joined the Central Powers in the same year, while Romania joined the Allies in 1916, and the United States joined the Allies in 1917. On March 3, 1924, the abolition of the Caliphate by the Grand National Assembly of Turkey was a reality. During WW I, an estimated two million Armenians lived in an area later known as Turkey. Armenians were an Orthodox Christian minority who lived under Islam. Their history reached back thousands of years. By 1922, just 400,000 remained. According to historical accounts, over a million Armenians were killed by mass extermination. They were marched into the desert and hacked to death by the bloodthirsty Sunnis, who slaughtered men, women, and children.

DEATH OF THE MULTICULTURAL OTTOMAN EMPIRE

It was eight months into World War I. Europe had begun to cannibalize its political territories and citizens. According to Toba Hellerstein, the multicultural Ottoman Empire was dying in terrible spasms. The Ottoman Turkish Sunni majority wreaked revenge on their ancient neighbors, namely, minority Assyrians and Greeks, but mostly Armenians. They accused the Armenians of being infidels, disloyal and siding with the (Ottoman)'s Empire's encroaching foes, namely, the Russians and colonial Europeans. Kurds shot and hacked Armenians to death in exceptional mass executions. Kurdish villagers seized Armenian property (consisting of) farms, flocks, and homes.[8]

TREATY OF BREST LITOVSK – W.W. ONE ENDS

The Russian reorganized pro-democratic government collapsed in March 1917, and a subsequent revolution in November 1917 brought the post-Czarist government to sign the Treaty of Brest Litovsk. The Marxist leaning German government allowed Joseph Stalin and Vladimir Lenin (Vladimir Ilyich Ulyanov) back into Russia to take Russia out of the conflict. It thus would ensure Germany had a great victory. During this period, the German secret service worked with the Mexican government to attack America, giving Arizona, New Mexico, and Texas back to the Mexican government. However, that was nullified by 1918 with the Allies winning World War One. After a brilliant Spring 1918 German offensive along the Western Front, the Allies rallied and drove back the Germans in a series of successful assaults. On November 4, 1918, the Austro-Hungarian empire agreed to a truce, and Germany, which had trouble with revolutionaries, agreed to an armistice on November 11, 1918, ending the war as a victory for the Allies.

Henry Johnson WW I Hero – Courtesy of History.com

DEATH TO DEATH COMBAT

American losses in World War One were 50,000 died in combat, and due to the influenza epidemic of 1918 to 1919, more than 50,000 died. In June 1918, 1,800 U.S. Marines in the Belleau Wood died in combat and 8,000 wounded. The USA's progressive Woodrow Wilson added 5,300 American troops from the 339th Infantry Regiment headquartered near Detroit, Michigan, to sail to the Russian port of Archangel, and he placed the troops under British command. The 369th Infantry from New York placed under French command, and on April 15, 1918, arrived in the Champagne region of France's Fourth Army. These two regiments were strict to be expeditionary forces and not the one million troops that President commanded and held in reserve. The American Expeditionary Forces detached the all-black regiment to bolster an ally and preserve racial segregation in the American command. The French were less concerned about racial inequality and welcomed the African American regiment that would earn its nickname as the Hell Fighters from Harlem. After weeks of combat patrols, raids and artillery barrages, Pvts. Henry Johnson, twenty-six of age, from Albany, N.Y., and his buddy Needham Roberts, seventeen of age, of Trenton N.J., from the regiment's 1st Battalion, Company C, stood to watch near a bridge over the Aisne River at Bois d'Hauzy during the night of May 15. 1981. A German patrol with an estimated twenty-four troops was determined to eliminate the outpost and bring prisoners back to learn about the all-black American force that had recently arrived. At 1:33 in the early morning, shots rang out, and the sounds of wire cutters alerted the two African American soldiers. Johnson, opening a box of grenades, told Roberts to run back and alert the mainline of the French defense. Nevertheless, at that moment, the first enemy grenades landed in their position. Johnson stalled the German patrol with grenades of his own, as Roberts struck down with shrapnel wounds to his arm and hip. When out of grenades, he took up his French Labelle rifle that carries a magazine clip of only three cartridges. "Johnson fired his three shots - the last one almost muzzle to the breast of the German soldier bearing down upon him. As the German fell, his comrade Jorge jumped over his body, pistol in hand, to avenge his brother's death. There was no time for reloading. Johnson swung his rifle around his head and threw it down with a thrown blow upon the German head.

The German went down, crying, in perfectly good Bowery English, "The little black pigmy has got me!"

As Johnson looked over to assist Roberts, he saw two Germans lift him to carry him off towards the German lines. "Johnson reached for his Army-issued bolo knife and charged. His aggressiveness took the Germans by surprise. "As Johnson sprang, he unsheathed his bolo knife, and as his knees landed upon the shoulders of that ill-fated German, the blade of the knife buried to the hilt through the crown of the German's head."[9]

Habsburg DynastyAustro-HungarianStaging – Courtesy of alamy.com

U.S. Army adopted the bolo knife and was heavily weighted along the back of its curved blade, and was devastating for close-quarter combat. Turning to the face the rest of the German patrol, Johnson struck by a bullet from an automatic pistol but continued to lunge forward, stabbing and slashing at the enemy. The Central Alliance enemy patrol panicked. Overwhelmed by Johnson's ferocity and the sound of French and American troops approaching, the Germans ran back into the night's muddy darkness. The German raiding party abandoned a considerable quantity of firearms, automatic pistols, and flame throwers. As the sun rose, the carnage was evident, even after suffering twenty-one stabbing and bullet wounds in hand-to-hand combat. Henry Johnson had stopped the Germans from approaching the French line or capturing his fellow Soldier.

HABSBURG EMPIRE DISINTEGRATES

Charles IV of Hungary was the last Emperor of Austria, the last King of Hungary, the last King of Bohemia, and the last monarch belonging to the House of Habsburg-Lorraine. After his uncle Archduke Franz Ferdinand of Austria was assassinated in 1914 by a Bosnian terrorist, Charles I became heir of Emperor Franz Josef. World War I led to the dismemberment of the Habsburg Empire. While Czechs, Slovaks, Poles, Romanians, Serbs, Croats, Slovenes, and Italians were all claiming their share of the spoil, nothing remained to Charles, the last Habsburg Emperor, and King, but the "German" Austria and Hungary region. On November 11, 1918, Emperor Charles issued a declaration that would recognize Austria's right to determine the future form of the state and renouncing any share in affairs of state ever to be his. Two days later, on November 13, 1918, Charles I issued a similar proclamation to Hungary. How could he abdicate his hereditary titles either for himself or the Habsburg dynasty?

Consequently, the national assembly of the Austrian Republic passed the Habsburg Law of April 3, 1919, remove all Habsburgs from Austrian territory unless they renounced all dynastic pretensions and loyally accepted the status of private citizens. With the collapse of the Hungarian republican regime at the end of 1919 raised firm royalist hopes of a Habsburg restoration, and after the conclusion of the June 1920 Treaty of Trianon. In March and October 1921, Charles I tried to return to the throne. Under pressure from the other European powers, especially those of the smaller powers, Czechoslovakia, Yugoslavia, and Romania, the Hungarian parliament on November 3, 1921, decreed the abrogation of Charles's sovereign rights and sanctions against him if he tried to renew those rights.

Charles I of Austria — Courtesy of trc-leiden.nl

The last of the Imperial ruler of the House of Habsburg was Charles I of Austria, who ruled from 1916 to 1919 as King and supported by his wife, Empress Zita. Zita lived until 1989, and Charles I died in 1922 or three years after his final reign. Still, the land rights for the Habsburg legislatively removed in 1919. World War I was coming to an end in July 1918. Private Adolph Hitler, who was part of the 16th Bavarian Reserve Regiment, had captured two German- American prisoners. In his discussion with them, as he led them to a military prison, his ideas of a new dominant race were germinated. Private Hitler viewed the two men as clear descendants of healthy German immigrants who had returned to Germany with a war vendetta, which led to Germany's defeat. Those meetings led to Hitler's vision of the Third Reich. The elimination of all Jews who destroyed the purity of the Aryan Race by inter-marriage. His idea of Lebensraum or a "Manifest Destiny" to conquer and colonize all of Europe and Russia.

In 1925, while Hitler was in prison himself, he wrote "Mein Kampf" and called America a foundational brick of the white race. In 1928, Hitler wanted the German people and nation to have the same living standard as Americans. Germany suffered from starvation and economic depression as the Allied Powers demanded massive war reparations in gold and a large percent of Germany's GDP. Hitler organized a political party that he called the National Socialist German Workers' Party, akin to an American political party. The core of Hitler's party was capitalism and monopolies that served the Nazi State's domestic and foreign policy agendas exclusively. By the first week of March 1933, Adolph Hitler had gained a substantial voting majority. With the Nationalistic Nazi Party movement gaining headwinds, the German Reichstag passed the Enabling Act. This legislation gave extra-ordinary power to German Chancellor Adolf Hitler to negotiate treaties with the National States directly. Also, the Act gave power to the S.A. and S.S. to repress any opposition to the Nazi Party.

In 1935, Hitler restored all House of Habsburg property rights. However, three years later, Hitler revoked the restoration of Habsburg's vast properties and gave them to the Nazi National Socialist State. After the First World War ended, the Allies decided in January 1945 that the Austrian government would become a State under the 1955 Austrian State Treaty.[10] In June 1961, Archduke Otto, master of the House of Habsburg and son of the last Austrian King, applied to the Austrian government to be allowed to return to Austria as an ordinary citizen. The application denied. In 1963 Otto received a favorable ruling by the Austrian Administrative Court, but he was denied a visa until three years later. The tension between the remaining

Habsburg's over their properties continued well into the 1970s and 1980s. The resolution of the Austrian government ownership of the Habsburg assets and liabilities was never to be resolved favorably for the Habsburg heirs. By the end of the war, the German Empire, the Russian Empire, the Austro-Hungarian Empire, and the Ottoman Empire had ceased to exist. National borders were redrawn, with several independent nations restored or created.

WINNERS AND LOSERS

By 1923, the winners and losers had become apparent. Germany entered the economic growth phase of the mid-1920s burdened by a vast reparations bill, shorn of territories, and shackled by a punitive disarmament regime. Hungary felt a deep grievance over the loss of more than half its territory. In contrast, Austria, deprived of its natural forest land and refused unification with Germany, felt on an island within the new order. Turkey, though, emerged victorious from its struggle with Greece and managed to use political control over Anatolia.

TRENCH WARFARE

Digging deep warfare is a type of fighting where soldiers dig deep trenches in the ground to defend their enemy soldiers. World War One trenches could stretch many miles and made it almost impossible for one side to advance on the other. The majority of these trench battles located in France's Western Front. From June 28, 1914, to December 1914, the trenches snaked from the North Sea and through Belgium and France. From October 1914 to March 1918, the Germans and the French could not advance but looked for technology to kill as many of one's enemies as possible.

Trench war WW1british — Courtesy of MilitaryMachine.com

According to estimates at the time, there were about 150 miles of trench lines dug during World War One. Most trenches were between three to six feet wide and ten feet deep. Life in the trenches quite difficult because they were unsanitary and flooded with stench water in rain or snow weather. Rain and bad weather would flood the trenches, making them boggy, muddy and could even block weapons and make it hard to move in battle. The sustained exposure to the wet, muddy conditions could cause "Trench Foot," which sometimes would result in the foot amputation. Cold weather was dangerous, too, and soldiers often lost fingers or toes to frostbite. Some soldiers also died from exposure in the cold. Soldiers rotated through three stages of the frontline. Most soldiers would spend anywhere from one day up to two weeks in the trenches at a time. They spent some time in the frontline trenches, time in the support trenches, and time resting. Even when not fighting, soldiers had to repair the ditches, moving supplies, cleaning weapons, undergoing inspections, or guard duty. The World War One trench built as a system, in a zigzag pattern with many different levels along the lines. They had paths dug so that soldiers could move between the levels. Many of the trenches also had pests living in the trenches, including rats, lice, and frogs. Rats existed as a problem and ate Soldier' food as well as the actual soldiers while they slept. Mites also caused a disease called "Trench Fever" that made the soldiers' itch terribly and caused fever, headache, sore muscles, bones, and joints.[11]

Stuart Maldoon, an officer of the 9th Battalion, the Cameronians -Scottish Rifles, was known to lead the way out of a trap during the spring battles of 1917. He was decorated for bravery but lost his foot to trench foot. He later died from a grenade attack in the fall of 1917. Trenches typically had an embankment at the top and barbed wire fence. Often, trenches in World War One reinforced with sandbags and wooden beams. In the trench itself, the bottom covered with wooden boards called duckboards, to protect the soldiers' feet from the water inside the trenches.

NO MAN'S LAND

The land between the two enemy trench lines was called "No Man's Land." No Man's Land sometimes covered with landmines and barbed wire. The distance between enemy trenches was anywhere from 50 to 250 yards apart. The trenches dug by soldiers, and there were three ways to dig them. Sometimes the soldiers would dig the trenches straight into the ground. The method is known as entrenching. Entrenching was fast, but the soldiers were open to enemy fire while they dug. Another method was to extend a trench on one end. It was called sapping and was a safer method but took a lot longer. Tunneling accomplished by digging a tunnel and then removing the roof to make a trench when it is complete became the safest method, but it was the most difficult too.

It was challenging to sleep in the trenches. The noise and uncomfortable surroundings made it very difficult to sleep in trenches. Soldiers were always tired and in danger of falling asleep. Sleeping on the watch is why the guard shift was kept to 2 hours to prevent men from falling asleep while on watch. There were several cease-fires or truces in the trenches during World War I. In 1914, around Christmas time, both the British and German soldiers put down their weapons, to celebrate the birth of Jesus Christ their weapons rising from their trenches and exchanged gifts and sing carols. The friendship of enemy soldiers is now known as the Christmas Truce. If all of the trenches built along the Western Front in World War One were laid end-to-end, an estimation recorded would be more than 25,000 miles long. Trenches needed repairing continuously to prevent erosion from the weather and enemy bombs and gunfire. It took 450 men six hours to build around 820 feet of British trenches. The majority of raids in W.W. One happened at night when soldiers would sneak across "No Man's Land," dodging mines, to attack the enemy in the darkness. Every morning, soldiers would stand at attention and then parade rest. The command resulted in standing and preparing for battle because many attacks would take place first in the morning. A typical World War One soldier would have a rifle, bayonet, and a hand grenade while fighting in the trenches.[12]

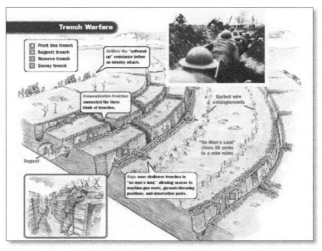

Trench warfare – Courtesy of infographically.com

KORKA'S FAMILY TIME OF BLOOD AND DEATH

War was a time of blood and death. America entered the war after the British passenger liner the Lusitania was sunk on May 7, 1915, by an Imperial German submarine U-20. The vessel's capacity was 552 first-class, 460-second class, 1,186 third class, or 2,198 total passengers. The vessel had 7,000 tons of coal aboard. Over one hundred twenty-eight USA passport holders killed or one percent of the passengers, America's President Wilson would wide-up be sending 1,000,000 soldiers to the European Campaign. The war ended with President Wilson forcing the terms of the Treaty of Versailles in June 1919. As a child, Dimitry Korka is weak and constantly ill. Dimitry rejected from joining the Russian Imperial Army, so he is finally able to join the German Imperial Army. However, he cannot shoot very well or lift a rifle. Therefore, given jobs of running messages to commanders along the trench line between German lines and the French and Allied lines. In a 1916 major battle, the trench warfare continues along the Argonne-Meuse.

On the battlefield of November 13, 1918, at 6:18 am, Dimitry Korka comes face to face with an English soldier who points his rifle at him, but he does not shoot, and the two stares at each other between the "no-man's land" trench lines. Dimitry's mind is racing for he wants to flee, but without the ability of strong leg muscles, he is transfixed and prepares to accept the bullet and die where he stands in utter fear. In that brief thirty-two seconds, the British Soldier hesitates and lowers his rifle. The English Soldier achieved yesterday's weekly quota of killing German soldiers, and he no longer wants to kill the German courier. The British Soldier turns left and then runs back to his trench location. Dimitry Korka knows that his "star stone" that is in his knapsack has saved him for higher intelligence-gathering missions ahead. Dimitry turns to the right and falls in a trench escape tunnel. His legs ache from the fall, but Dimitry accepts the pain or has been part of a battlefield miracle. Dimitry has many souls searching to do. He almost killed, and he was a non-combatant. He did not want to kill anyone, but he realizes that he had to embrace the values of his comrade soldiers: "kill or be killed." In the late morning.

Sergeant Dimitry Korka reports to the Commander of his unit, Captain Alvin Trummp. The captain stood six feet two inches and a muscular man for his height. He always carried a Colt M1911 sidearm strapped across his chest in a leather holster. Dimitry went to the rear headquarters situated in a rock cave about a quarter of a mile from the frontline trenches.

"Sergeant Dimitry Korka is reporting Sir, as he stood before Captain Jack Trummp. "What is it Sergeant, and it better be good as I am busy making plans for another assault on those snail-eating sons of bitches? Sit down, Sergeant!"

Dimitry took off his helmet and placed in between his legs.

"Sir, I had a near-death experience earlier today, and I have decided to kill or not die. I want to be transferred to a fighting unit with the 63rd Infantry Division near Verdun France." OK, Sergeant, I hope you know what you are doing. I will sign the transfer papers this afternoon. Have all of your equipment and weapons ready to go at 0500 tomorrow morning and the best of luck."

Dimitry stood up and saluted. He then reached down and picked up his helmet, made an about-face, and left the rock cave German headquarters. A horse-drawn wagon met Dimitry at the rendezvous point the next morning. The air smelled of the stench of dead bodies and gunpowder from the exploding artillery shells of the night before. He was glad to get out those rat-infested trenches that he shared with the two dead bodies of his friends, Gerard and Helmut. He had placed each body face down into the mud of the floor of the trench. He could not view looking at their faces swollen and with the slight death smiles on their faces. The experience was going to be different. He was going to be a hero and earn medals for his bravery.

Dimitry arrived at company E's headquarters and reported to the company Commander's Chief Master Sergeant, Hector Lula, with his orders. Company E was known for its one hundred percent marksmanship awards.

"Ok Sergeant Korka go find a place to crawl into and be prepared for hell as the French are advancing at our Meuse River positions. Best of luck."

Dimitry was assigned a 1903 Springfield infantry bolt action rifle capable of firing ten or more rounds per minute, 160 rounds of ammunition, an M1918 trench knife with a thin blade, and the handle had brass knuckles attached to the handle and a German helmet. His enemies probably carried German manufactured 7.92 Mauser rifle, which was good for close face-to-face penetration. The company commander was Captain Siegfried Tannin. As a German-American, he decided in 1914 that his allegiance belongs to his native European roots. Siegfried's mother and father had migrated to the USA from booking a ticket on an old steamship from the port of Bremen-Haven. He had grown up in Harrisburg, Pennsylvania, and attended the West Point Academy. His wife Alla and son Konrad were staying with his in-laws in the Midwest on a farm. Alla had grown tired of reading letters that Siegfried sent from his various base camps. The local German paper always wrote about the battles of Captain Siegfried Tannin's Company.

"So, tell me, Sergeant Dimitry Korka, why is a conscious objector like you doing in my fighting unit." Sir, I want to kill English, French, and American. I have no intention of being killed by them. I will shoot first and ask questions later."

Captain Siegfried Tannin looked at Dimitry Korka with a smile and thought, well, this guy is on a suicide mission, or he is going to be one French soldier killing machine. Perhaps he should use a cache of captured US M1917 Browning machine guns.

"OK, Sergeant go-to supply ammo dump, and you will be issued the M1917. Just do not shoot off your toes. Ok, your dismissed, now get your fat sorry ass out of my office!"

At the dawn of February 21, 1916, Dimitry arrived near the headquarters of the 64th located near the Meuse River. The Americans had used artillery shelling and mortar firing most of the night. He ordered by Sergeant Lula,

"Dig man, dig, dig a foxhole."

Each time when Dmitry reached four feet, the hole would fill up with water, and he would bail-out the water and mud and start again. French machine guns started to rain hot lead on his

Man of Seven Shadows

position. The division commander was running from foxholes to trenches shouting,

"Fire with power."

Suddenly, a sniper smashed into his helmet and crumpled into a curled-up position by a tree motionless. His name was Colonel Joseph Wozniak, a high school graduate from Hamlet Indiana and an early volunteer in the Imperial German Army. He stood six feet 5inches with a muscular body from his many youthful years helping his father run the 1200-acre farm. With their leader dead and the troops massively wounded, newly field commissioned Sergeant Dimitry Korka had to rally the troops to continue the fight and hold their position along the Meuse River. Then he heard a loud voice ordering,

"HOLD YOUR FIRE!"

He looked to the right and saw Lieutenant Reinhard Volks, a recently minted officer or a "thirty-day wonder," holding up a rifle with a white shirt tied to the end of a broken tree branch waving it as a form of surrender. Not only was Sergeant Dimitry Korka angry, but he was aiming to kill Lieutenant Reinhard Volks, but before he could pull the trigger, the German platoon surrounded by fifty French soldiers. They ordered to get out of their trench and foxholes and move to the rear with the Germans. Sergeant Dimitry Korka laid down his Bergmann MP18-I (Maschinenpistole 18/I) Submachine Guns and Mauser Model 1888 (Gew 88 / Model 1888 Deichsgewehr) Bolt-Action Service Rifle within an escape tunnel before he stood up. Dimitry Korka slowly moved out of his foxhole, intending to move along the river back to his unit across the river. He turned and almost bumped into a British soldier. He could see the British and French milling around the dead German soldiers' dead bodies, so he decided to lay flat on his face and pretend to be dead. A French soldier kicked him, but he remained still. For some reason, a French soldier took his boot and rammed it up to his butt and genitals. Dimitry let out a piercing cry. He got up in agonizing pain and put his hands up. Dimitry forced along a muddy path that consisted of more German and Hungarian soldiers who now

« 277 »

prisoners. He tripped over a dead body and fell on this face and just laid there. He laid still for over thirty-five minutes until he did not hear any more voices. When Dimitry Korka got up, he felt safe and moved quickly back to his unit and stopping every couple of minutes from listening for sounds. He traveled to the Meuse River and found a German unit still dug in. They were out of ammo, and it was clear that no one was coming to rescue them. They had lost many men.

Then when he slipped into an open foxhole, he heard a strong voice yell, "Aufstehen!"

Dimitry had a nestle bar of chocolate in his jacket and a German officer in an impeccably clean uniform, and shiny black boots reach in and take it. He then said, "Mein Einheitsheld!"

Of course, he had no idea what or why the German officer was talking about, but nobody else did. The French and American soldiers appeared forced, lined them up, and had them turn their backs away from the French's guns. Dimitry closed his eyes, knowing that he would be part of a firing squad that was to kill the remaining German, Ottoman, and Austria-Hungarian troops. He heard a great sound but felt nothing, then he turned around, and the American and French soldiers were laughing as they just hit their legs to make a sound. The allied soldiers were laughing hysterically. Sergeant Korka's birthday was on this day, and he will remember it for this day when he met his capture and liberation. Major Jan Strum, the company commander, came back to the banks of the Meuse River, where his platoons had dug their foxholes and realized that so many lay dead and so many had to be captured by the allied troops. French machine guns were still in place, and they fired into the middle of the Meuse River, and the blast crashed into the Major Strum's hip. He did not fall until struck in the legs and arms.

He fell and cried out, "Medizin, Medizin!"

A corpsman medic heard his cry and moved on his belly to patch up his wounds but gasping, and the blood was gushing from the injuries.

Sergeant Dimitry Korka spoke, "Look, Major Strum, we do not have enough bandages to fill all of these holes. We are going to drag you back. Your warfighting days are over. Now hold this tourniquet while I tie it up."

The thick fog and smoke from the American artillery. They were not as safe as they could not see anything ahead of them to escape. Soon he heard French voices again and appeared to be saying,

"Give up or be killed."

All the men who had been hiding came out with their hands up. The French took their weapons and moved them in a circle. The French Soldier guarding Sergeant Korka saw a can of red beans and biscuit rations and asked Dimitry to open it up. He then, with one hand, began to eat. Suddenly, a shot rang out, and the French Soldier dropped his machine gun. Nevertheless, the French soldier quickly recovered, and before he knew it, the German Sergeant had grabbed the machine gun and pointed it at the French Soldier who shouted,

"Non, Non, Non-Camaraderie!"

Dimitry fired point-blank, and the French Soldier lay dead with bullets entering his throat and stomach. He then ran again and found two of his troops running the same way. As they moved toward the river edge, a French machine gun opened up, and they were forced back into the forest edge. They tried again and failed. The three of them know that staying in a French POW camp would mean starvation and death, so they took off their shoes and heavy jackets and waded into the cold Meuse River. French bullets kept splashing near their heads until they got to the other side of the river. They ran barefooted for half a mile before coming to an A7V Sturmpanzerwagen armored unit of the German Army. Sergeant Dimitry Korka's feet were bleeding and almost with frozen toes as he had no choice but to jump into the icy river and swim for his life. His uniform was muddy. Dimitry's entire body was shaking like a sycamore tree in a fierce wind. A German corpsman walked by and placed a woolen blanket off his shoulders. The battle on the German side of the river was over. Sergeant Korka reached into his dirty pockets to find his "star stone" and a note handed to him by the dying German courier. The paper was still dry in his pocket.

"I need to report to your commanding officer, where is he?"

The A7V Sturmpanzerwagen tank gunner pointed to the rear of the tank, "you will find him back there in the rear, Major Jörg Newsome."

Dimitry walked past the five-tank formation that set up along the river's edge. Korka found Major Newsome in a tent going over some diagramed tank formations on a map with the stamp, "Top Secret" on each of the four edges.

He saluted. "What is it, Sergeant?" Sir, we lost many troops on the other side of the river. The Americans and French will give us three hours to pick up the wounded and have declared a truce."

The American and French generals made a mistake in attacking the well-fortified German river positions. They lost over 600 dead and 419 wounded. It was a disaster for the allied forces. A second attack was scheduled the next day at dawn.

The Commander-in-Chief of the French Army, General Joseph Joffrea canceled the order and only sought to determine what went wrong with his offensive operations across the river. Later, the French and American Generals concluded that it was their fault as they ordered the attack without knowing the German forces. In the morning, the dead bodies of the American and French soldiers found in various stages of death's embrace. It was clear that the American Commander Clark Abrahams, as well as the French commanders, would be relieved of their Commands after a quick board of inquiry. Thirty days later, thirty-four new officers arrived to replace the dead officers but were not enough to replace the regiment's losses. The entire disastrous order to cross the Meuse River executed by Americans only, and no French or English soldiers were involved. The battle casualties hidden until a researcher from the Washington Post found the General's orders and the battlefield causalities and deaths. The Washington Post newspaper ran the story the next day. General Abrahams later was to die from a massive heart attack when he returned to an American duty base.

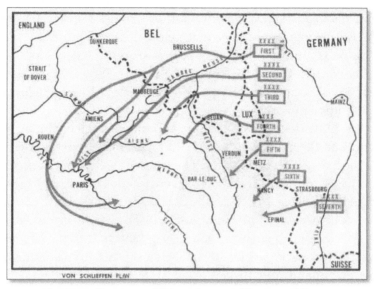

Verdun – Courtesy of Britannica.com/German Military

TREATY OF VERSAILLES

From the first month of 1919 to June 1919, The Treaty of Versailles, negotiated without the Germans present, was a treaty of paybacks. The Allies only wanted to denude the German Imperial State economically so that they could never renew war with France, the United States, and Britain. The last treaty included fifteen parts and 440 articles. Allies continued their artillery barrage up to eleven in the morning on day eleven of the 11th month of 1918, the Great War ends. At five in the early morning that cold morning November, Germany, bereft of manpower and supplies and faced with imminent invasion, signed an armistice agreement with the Allies in a railroad car outside Compiégne, located 80 miles from Paris, France. The First World War left nine million soldiers dead and twenty-one million wounded, with Germany, Russia, Austria-Hungary, France, and Great Britain, each losing nearly a million or more lives. Perhaps, another five million civilians died from disease, starvation, and weather conditions of bitter cold. The Bolsheviks focused on fighting the coalition put together by Winston Churchill to overthrow the communist regime by using the combined forces of America, Britain, Greece, and France. Czechoslovakian army troops also joined the Allies and Cossack White Russian Forces.[13]

In 1924, the Supreme Soviet Union ushered on the world's stage, and the Cold War began and in 2019 continued under the E.U. and the USA ruling elites. The historical consequences of the signing of the 1919 Treaty were many; namely, Roman Catholic Poland fought against anti-Christ Russian Bolsheviks, extreme nationalism, anti-Semitic views, and the Soviet Union and Poland would fight Ukrainian nationalism. New countries formed; namely, Austria, Hungary, Czechoslovakia, Yugoslavia, Estonia, Lithuania, Poland, Finland, and Turkey.

Several of Dimitry Korka's platoon soldiers would spend three years of starvation and trench foot in a French POW camp in L'Intermède, Camp de Würzburg. Dimitry Korka held his "star stone" and liberated with only minor injuries. German Lt. Colonel Andrei Jürgen Markov, who was born in Northern Ukraine to German parents and after capture at the Meuse River battle, would spend eighteen months interned at the Kherson Ukraine POW camp 4B. At the camp, he would meet a Turkish prisoner who made a few rings out of silver coins. Markov was going to get married as soon as he was released, and he traded five pounds of sugar for silver coins from one prisoner and then traded two pounds of flour for the Turkish prisoner to make a set of two rings. In 1919, when liberated at the end of the War, German Lt. Colonel Andrei Jurgen Markov would travel to Ukraine to marry his childhood girlfriend, Yelizaveta, in an Orthodox Church in Kherson Ukraine.

BRIDGES TO WW II

Andrei Markov has two sons, Volodymyr and Rostyslav. In 1933, World War Two, Germany started to restore its economic and military power. Before 1933, the Versailles Treaty made Germany a pauper state. Ukraine is still part of the Soviet Union, and at the ages of seventeen and nineteen, they both enlist in the Russian Soviet Army. Volodymyr assigned as an infantryman in a Russian tank battalion, and Rostyslav becomes a Russian machine gunner in the same tank battalion. Operation Unternehmen Barbarossa was the code name for the Axis invasion of the Soviet Union, starting Sunday, June 22, 1941, during World War II. The operation stemmed from Nazi Germany's ideological aims to conquer the western Soviet Union so that it could achieve repopulation by Germans; Both Markov brothers sent to defend Leningrad. Germany advanced quickly, and they use Mustard Gas against large formations of Russian Infantry. Seventeen-year-old Volodymyr fights bravely but shot in the chest. Bleeding heavily, he fights on killing three German SS troops. The mustard gas is too much for his fragile lungs, and he dies 59 miles west of Leningrad.

Nineteen-year-old Rostyslav realizes as Leningrad bombed that resistance is futile. Rostyslav defects to give the Germans the critical fortifications of Leningrad and the best points of attack. The Germans gave him a battlefield commission as a Lieutenant General in the Germany Army, directing the battle with a well-equipped Panzer division in Leningrad and, later, in the major battles to conquer Moscow. With the lack of supplies and fuel for his Panzers and heavy trucks to move the artillery guns, his unit is over-run by a killer Russian army thirsty for the blood of the German "Huns." He realizes that the advancing Russian soldiers will kill him for being a traitor, so Rostyslav disguises himself after killing a Russian Major and takes his uniform. As the Russian Army advances to take over Ukraine, Rostyslav, who speaks fluent Ukraine and Russian, is shot in the chest, arm, and legs and taken for dead on the battlefield outside of Lugansk.

He discovered by Bohdan, a small boy who is looking for war souvenirs. The boy Bohdan then calls his mother, Volya discovered a Russian doctor and Volya nurses him back to health, but he is permanently crippled and must use crutches. To avoid detection of his true identity as a traitor, Rostyslav, builds a new life with his rescuers and spends his last years on a farm with his adopted son and girlfriend, Volya.

After his release from a French POW camp, Dimitry Korka decides that Europe, both East and West, transferred into a kettle of flames and death. He then does an enlistment in the U.S. Army and spends two years at Camp Pendleton. After his two years, Dimitry decides that his survival can only happen in the U.S. Army and is assigned as a Senior Master Sergeant to a Ranger battalion that would eventually storm the beaches of Salerno Italy on July 9, 1943, and Riviera France on August 15, 1943. Dimitry Korka's ranger unit becomes the first American force to invade Hitler's Fortress Europe. SM Sergeant Dimitry Korka has the power of the "star stone" and becomes involved in constant combat operations (Rapido River, Cassino, Vosges, Colmar Pocket, Siegfried Line, Moselle River Crossing, St. Marie Pass, and Velletri.) Dimitry is recognized for his bravery and leadership skills and offered the (OCS) Officer Candidate School program as he had proven himself in battlefields and leading men. He was awarded a battlefield commission as a captain. He was to command Company E of the 24tdh Division that was to land at Anzio Beach with British 1st Division, the 504th and 509th Parachute Infantry Battalions, the 82nd Airborne Division, Darby's Rangers, and British Commandos. After only twenty-four hours of the invasion, over 20,000 troops had landed. The Germans were entirely surprised as they had no force between Anzio and Rome. German Field Marshall Kesselring immediately ordered soldiers from France, Northern Italy, and Rome to slow down the Allies advance. The Germans would make the allies pay for every inch of soil. German's 88 shelled the Allies on the beach. The Allies waited too long to move forward, which gives the

Germans time to reinforce their defenses. It would be a bloody campaign. Kesselring has at this disposal a colossal rail gun with a seventy-one-foot barrel, the K5. The weapon secretly is hidden in a tunnel. It would fire and then move back into the tunnel after shooting. Also, wooden dummies were built of the K5 and place strategically in other locations. The K5s rained hot lead on the Allies ammo dumps, supply routes, and killing hundreds on the beach. The allies were looking for the K5s. An American U.S. Army pilot from Overland Park Kansas completes his bombing run and, to his amazement, sees German soldiers running into a cave. After air surveillance of the area, the Allies spot the massive gun and immediately begin bombing the location and destroyed the K5 artillery gun. However, the allies stuck after four months, making little progress to take the high ground away from the Germans.

Dimitry's Korka's Division is now thrown into the mountains of Monte Cassino to remove the German Army. Even with the poor judgment of the pompous British and hard-drinking American General to destroy the monastery, the German Army remains strong. Beginning in 1944, the western half of the Winter Line anchored by Germans holding the Rapido-Gari, Liri, and Garigliano valleys and some of the surrounding peaks and ridges. Together, these features formed the Gustav Line. Monte Cassino, a historic hilltop abbey founded in AD 529 by Benedict of Nursia, dominated the nearby town of Cassino and the entrances to the Liri and Rapido valleys. German forces set up in a protected historic zone; it had been left unoccupied by the Germans, although they covered some positions set into the steep slopes below the abbey's walls.[14] On February 15, 1944, American bombers dropped 1,400 tons of high explosives, creating widespread damage. The raid failed to achieve its objective, as German paratroopers occupied the rubble and established excellent defensive positions amid the ruins. Between January 17 and May 18, 1944, Monte Cassino and the Gustav defenses were assaulted four times by Allied troops, the last involving twenty divisions attacking along a twenty-mile front. The German defenders finally driven from their positions, but at a high cost. The capture of Monte Cassino resulted in 55,000 Allied casualties, with German losses being far fewer, estimated at around 20,000 killed and wounded.[15]

After the final battle in which the Allies took the high points of the Monte Cassino German lines, U.S. Army Captain Dimitry Korka was to receive the silver star and campaign ribbons. At forty-two, he returned to Mykolayiv Ukraine and met 36-year-old Natalia Takovich, who stood 5'4" with long straight brown hair, at 114lbs she was considered slim. Natalia was working as a Martial Arts instructor. Dimitry thought at the time that he did not want to compete with a woman after he killed many in hand-to-hand death battles with German paratroopers that he searched for hiding in the rubble of Monte Cassino. However, she enjoyed meeting him for Sushi. Natalia's husband died five days after eating some mushrooms that Natalia cooked, and he experienced rapid heart failure.

Natalia was now alone with her eleven-year-old son, Ivan Takovich. Dimitry's Korka's son Oleksiy was nine years old, and his German mother was killed by an unexploded bomb in Berlin shortly after she gave birth to Oleksiy. Soon, they found that they had an enormous amount of chemistry between themselves, and the boys got along as if they were blood brothers. Dimitry and Natalia were married eight months later in a Russian Orthodox Church located in Radisnyi Sad. Ivan Takovich grew up to be a star soccer player and attended a local trade school in electronics. Oleksiy Korka, at eighteen years old, joined the Russian Army.

It was now 1956 and Ivan Takovich at twenty-two years of age married Slava, at eighteen years of age she had straight medium length blonde hair, petite with dark blue eyes. Slava was Russian and stood at 5'5" with a smile that would light a room. In 1957, Slava gave birth to a baby girl that they named Anastasiya. At twenty-seven years old, Oleksiy Korka was to meet Lyubov while on vacation in Crimea. Soon they were texting and meeting at local internet cafes in Kherson Ukraine. They were married two years later, and Lyubov gave birth to twin boys, Odynets and Gore. In 1959, Gore stumbled on to the 5ᵗʰ-floor apartment balcony two years later while his mother Lyubov is in bed with a man she met at the local electronics store. Gore gets too close to the edge and tumbles down six floors to the concrete steps and killed immediately. Oleksiy and Lyubov rush him to the hospital that is fourteen miles away, but the outcome is sad. Later, they place all of their attention on little Odynets, who grows up to be six-foot-two inches in height, attends the Kyiv University and achieves honors for his scholarship. After graduation in 1979 with a Master's Degree in Political Science, he becomes a staffer for Channel 5 Kyiv T.V. owned by a man who owns the concession of chocolate in Ukraine. In 1983, Odynets Korka married his teacher of mathematics, Bohuslava. Bohuslava loves Odynets, and they are a happy couple but childless until 1995, blessed with two twin boys, Boryslav and Bohdan. Odynets Korka rises to the rank of Minister of Defense for Ukraine. At the ages of nineteen, Boryslav and Bohdan Korka are two twins that become great athletics in the 2014 soccer league of Donetsk in Eastern Ukraine. They are recognized in the World Soccer league as the number one player in Ukraine and invited to play with Brazil, Germany, Russia, and Greece.

CONQUER, DIVIDE, RULE

After World War I, however, the European powers had a simple strategy used by the American Democratic Party, namely, conquer, divide, and rule. The Foreign Policy agenda followed within all the lands once ruled by the defeated Ottoman Empire. The Europeans had been gradually infiltrating the Middle East for years, enjoying the tax breaks and security ensured by capitulation contracts between their governments and the Ottomans. European powers (France, England, Germany, Italy) negotiated clear partition lines defining their spheres of influence in the region. The resulting, secret agreement, named for the British and French diplomats who negotiated it, Mark Sykes and Francois Georges-Picot created a treaty that was signed in the spring of 1916. The borders drawn within Sykes-Picot did not respect the history of the region or the political concerns of the groups within it. Instead, the agreement focused on carving-up the Middle East between the British and the French. Ottoman's Anatolia partitioned to the Eastern region controlled by British, French, Italian, and Greek military forces and the Western region semi-controlled by Muslim sympathies. Mustafa Kemal Ataturk created a Turkish force that defeated the Christian Ally powers and went on a rampage of ethnic cleansing or referred to as an exchange of population. The Christian city of Smyrna burned to the ground. In 1928, Ataturk's modernization of Turkey led to the Islam radical group, Muslim brotherhood, and other anti-European groups such as al-Qaida. Japan vis-à-vis Korea was also transformed. On May 14, 1919, the Chinese Communist Party was born. In 1919 Vietnam was a colonial possession of France. Ho Chi Minh went to Paris to negotiate with the French to establish North and South Vietnam into a united nation with the right to have freedom of speech and assembly.

Ian Kershaw noted that the 20th century was a game of two pear halves. The first saw a cataclysm that brought down empires, plunged the continent into a deep slump, and culminated in million more Slavs and Europeans in WW II. According to Kershaw, the primary catalyst was the rise of ethnic nationalism, something that helped to doom the multinational empires of Austria-Hungary, Russia, and the Ottomans. Then came demands for territorial revision, between France and Germany, in central and eastern Europe and all over the Balkans. Europe was in class conflict, as workers and a nascent socialist movement flexed their muscles against bosses and the traditional aristocratic ruling class. Finally, the stock market crash of 1929 and German's economic deprivation led to a new State Capitalism.[17]

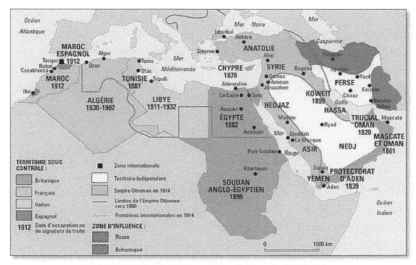

SykesPicot 1914- Courtesy of userclass.ufl.edu

OTTOMAN EMPIRE OF SYRIA -RISE AND FALL

After centuries of Ottoman rule, Syria emerged from World War I in an entirely new form. Under the Ottomans, the area known today as Syria was never a single entity but rather a collection of "wilayats," or provinces, that at times included areas of modern-day Lebanon and Israel. Nor was the population homogenous. The wilayats of Ottoman Syria each comprise an array of ethnicities, cultural identifications, and economic structures. After 400 years of rule under the Ottomans, specific particularities of the political system became ingrained. In modern-day Syria, before the civil war, cities were divided into culturally distinct quarters, namely, Armenians, another populated by Assyrians and Kurdish. Syria governed in a manner that reinforced the autonomy of these distinct ethnic and religious communities. The Ottomans enforced a policy of pluralism, intended to appease different nations and quell the rise of nationalist movements, in which Jews, Christians, and Muslims were all empowered to assert their own identities and therefore had no need to vie for power. A Religious community, known as a "millet," had a representative in Istanbul and was allowed to organize its affairs, including education, social services, and code law legal civil standards. The Goran guided millet controls all internal disputes such as marriage, divorce, inheritance, and collection of taxes.

FRENCH MANDATE

France was determined to remain a power in the Middle East, and through the French Mandate, ultimately controlled southeastern Turkey, northern Iraq, Syria, and Lebanon. The population in what had been Greater Syria was artificially divided and, at times, displaced. Under the French Mandate, life in Syria changed dramatically. The autonomy that groups had enjoyed under the Ottomans significantly diminished as the French centralized the government and restricted newspapers and political activity. France pursued a divide-and-rule policy under which some minority groups enjoyed newfound privilege while others watched their freedoms disappear. The French favored minorities, mainly the Christian Maronites, to protect themselves from the Sunni majority. Syria claimed independence in 1944, but the Millets were no longer in power. The new Syrian government adopted the autocratic bent of the French officials it had displaced, and the new rulers marginalized minorities such as the Shiites, Kurds, Assyrians, Druze, and Orthodox Christian Armenians. The Mukhabarat, the invasive Syrian intelligence services, became a prominent fact of life for the Syrian people, for whom the country's independence brought little relief.

Some operatives in the intelligence community believed that espionage is like prostitution and known as an essential job in the world. The U.S. Central Intelligence Agency (CIA), formally created in 1947, is the principal foreign intelligence and counterintelligence agency of the U.S. government. The CIA is headed by a director and deputy director, only one of whom may be a military officer. The director of central intelligence (DCI) is the chief intelligence adviser to the President of the United States. Under the U.S. President's serving as of November 2018, Gina Cheri Haspel appointed after being the Deputy of the CIA serving under Michael Richard Pompeo. George Washington University released National Security Archive CIA cables Haspel authorized by or authored torture techniques while CIA base chief at Thailand's undercover overseas sites.

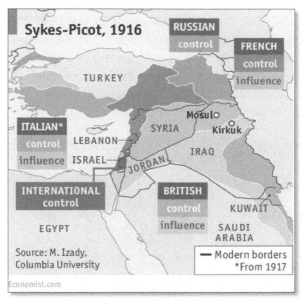

Sykes-Picot -1916 – Courtesy of M.Izady Columbia University

Without any awareness of the DNA of its employees, the Korka family begins to infiltrate global intelligence agencies. The family had made considerable headway under the shadows of high-profile USA presidents and their intelligence directors. Ramin Dadkhudak is a cousin of Dimitry Korka, who uses the disguise of a Syrian counterintelligence officer who is loyal to Syrian President Bashar al-Assad. In reality, Ramin is being paid $25,000 per month by the U.S. Central Intelligence Agency. CIA trained him in Arab dialects and gave him a cover as a battlefield hero who killed thirteen ISIS fighters. In 2015, Ramin was in the City of Aleppo, directing the (FSA) Free Syrian Army's house to house fighters. While in a Syrian hospital, wounded, and a doctor finds in the sole of his shoe a microchip that provides him CIA codes and satellite coordinates to transmit operational data back to Langley, Virginia.

Ramin immediately sent to prison, and he watches from his cell window, the Battle of Aleppo, a crucial military confrontation in Aleppo, the largest city in Syria. This battle between the CIA funded Syrian opposition (including the Free Syrian Army (FSA) and mainly other Sunni groups, such as the Levant Front and the Al-Qaeda-affiliated Al-Nusra Front), against the government of President Assad. Korka's cousin Ramin offered release only if he becomes part of the Deuzieme Bureau and spies on the CIA operating with the U.S. Special Forces in black operations in Northern Syria.

Syrian Generals — Courtesy of R.T. media on line

INTERNAL SECURITY ORGANIZATION -SÛRETÉ SYRIA

In 1963, under the Syrian Arab Socialist Ba'ath Party, the internal Security Organization -Sûreté Syria functions under martial law as the conflict continued with the State of Israel and western-inspired terrorist groups trained and armed. Syria governed under the French Mandate, had 5,000 non-military internal security forces included a National Gendarmérie of 2800, a Desert Patrol of 400 and 1800 police, or just 10,000 armed forces to combat its internal attacks from criminal gangs and extremist. The Gendarmérie and policeo were strategically located throughout the country. Their area of responsibility was Central and Eastern Syria. They possessed limited weaponry except for rifles and handguns. They had no tanks, armored personnel carriers, or RPGs. Anyone could join that had consequences from low morale and limited training. They acted like crossing road guards. They were meant not to be effective.[18] The police agencies did include the Sûreté; namely, three hundred non-uniformed officers whose job was to spy on politicians, counter-espionage, and spying on non-Syrian citizens within its borders. Unlike the US CIA and the British MI 15 and MI 16, the Sûreté's low trained informers did not produce good actionable intelligence.

The Deuxieme Bureau (Intelligence Branch) of the Syrian Army General Staff duplicated the charter of the Sûreté in the areas of espionage and counter-espionage operations, political information, and surveillance of foreigners. The Deuxieme Bureau was harmed by the lack of trained personnel and from frequent changes in top-level leadership. It appears that duplication, misplacement of effort, gathering useless information, and assembling reports proved a fool's errand. Both agencies tracked known Communists. However, the data was out of date and senseless to a trained intelligence analyst. Village security police did pay for agents to keep up to date records on Communist Party membership, organization, and activities.[19] In 2010, the four major Syrian branches of security forces were as follows: Military Intelligence and Air Force Intelligence, the Political Security Directorate (PSD), under the Ministry of Interior (MOI), and the General Intelligence Directorate (GID) that is a stand-alone institution. The four branches operate independently and generally outside the legal system's control, and all four repress internal dissent and monitor individual citizens. The Ministry of Interior monitors the four separate divisions of police forces, namely, emergency police, traffic police, neighborhood police, and riot officers. The Syrian government used its security service to employ mental pain and fear when targeting Syrians and others. From waterboarding and physical torture to giving vast sums of money or an elevation to a significant governmental position, run the technique gambit to extricate needed human intelligence information. Non-lethal methods used as in all global governments such as sanctions, removal of visa rights, 24 x 7 surveillance, threatening relatives of the human intel target, prison time plea bargaining, extended detention in a one-room cell without a judicial ruling, 24 x 7 interrogation in severe controlled environments, threats of long prison time, trials were lasting many years, and death imprisonment time for older citizens and foreigners.[20] The use of good and bad cop techniques, plus severe punishment and then rewards that make the Syrian security services so useful. After using these Syrian psychological and direct punishment techniques, people will give up their friends and family members, and will not hesitate to become champions of their tormentors.

SUNNI INTERNAL SECURITY ORGANIZATION - IIS MUKHABARAT

Under former leader Saddam Hussein, IIS Mukhabarat translates as the Department of General Intelligence or the General Directorate of Intelligence Al-Mukhabarat Al-A'ma. It was the most notorious and possibly the most critical arm of the state security system. It was the leading state intelligence body and was primarily concerned with political and security problems. It consisted of two significant departments covering internal and external activities, respectively.[21] It was the equivalent of the U.S. Central Intelligence Agency (CIA), the Federal Bureau of Investigation (FBI), the secret British clandestine MI 15, and MI 16 rolled into one powerful national and international spy agency. At the top of the pyramid, the Mukhabarat was responsible for watching the other police networks and controlling the activities of state institutions, the Army, government departments and non-governmental children, female, and labor organizations. A unique security section of the Mukhabarat commanded the Bath party's paramilitary groups. Officially, the Mukhabarat was part of the Ministry of Internal Affairs. In practice, it did come under the ministry's jurisdiction but acted instead on the direct orders of the Iraqi leader. As in the case of the U.S. State Department with embedded CIA agents, Mukhabarat agents operated in Iraq bureaucracy, in the various organizations and associations, in the diplomatic corps and abroad.[22]

In 2005, the federal government of Iraq defined under the current Constitution as an Islamic, democratic, federal parliamentary republic. It is similar to the U.S.'s three governing branches of Executive, Legislative, and Judicial with various commissions.

CHAPTER EIGHT

RIGHTEOUS GLORY -WW II

"It is not a truth that matters, but victory." - Adolph Hitler

WORLD WAR TWO (1939-1945)

THE ROMANS SOUGHT TO conquer the land of Germania made up of forest barbarians, but at the same time recognized that these fierce barbarian fighters lived in a spirit world. German life was a journey of the dominance of other tribes and nations. Spirit warriors never die on the battlefield but rise again as ground fog emanating from the forest of Germania. Germany defeated in battle after the 1918 First World War but not in its resolve to win again. As a people, the Germans felt betrayed by the November criminals made up of Jews, Socialists, Poles, and traitors within its citizenry. The allies had pushed the 68 million Germans to a low that they could not feed their families and children economically as a nation. The reparations of $33 billion in gold to France, Belgium, and Great Britain were impossible to repay. In 1923, German's trade accounts could not pay the monthly debt payments; France took the step of sending armed troops to occupy the factory assets of the Ruhr Industrial Zone. The Allies used military occupation to enforce payments, causing an international crisis that resulted in the implementation of the Dawes Plan in 1924. The payment debt stream was re-negotiated and was to continue until 1988. In 1931, the global economy collapsed. German factories were closed, and workers had no source of income. It became a multiplier effect, and ninety percent of the population grew to hate the French, English, and Woodrow Wilson's progressive Administration. In this environment, the consequences of France's Marshal Ferdinand Foch's as Supreme Allied Commander created the perfect storm for the rise of past German barbarian warriors to lead them into a global war against them their economic tormentors.

Adolph Hitler – Courtesy of historythenet.com

Germans lived under the belief that they descended from "heaven and pure." This spiritual, societal structure was how Adolph Hitler won the hearts and minds of the sixty-seven million German People. However, some Germans were skeptical of Hitler when he became chancellor in 1933. However, soon with the help of the Reich Minister of Propaganda Paul Joseph Goebbels, the Führer's propaganda and military successes soon turned him into an idol. According to Ian Kershaw, "the adulation helped make the Third Reich catastrophe possible."[1]

"TODAY HITLER IS ALL OF GERMANY"

On August 4, 1934, the Der Spiegel newspaper headline read. "Today, Hitler Is All of Germany." It was a true statement and reflected the critical shift in power that had just taken place. Two days earlier, on the death of Reich President Paul von Hindenburg, Hitler had lost no time in abolishing the Reich Presidency and having the Army swear a personal oath of unconditional obedience to him as "the Führer of the German Reich and People." He was now head of state and supreme commander of the armed forces, as well as head of Government and the monopoly party, the NSDAP. Hitler had total power in Germany, unrestricted by any constitutional constraints. The headline implied even more, however, that the significant change in the constellation of power. It suggested the identity of Hitler and the country he ruled, signifying a complete bond between the German people and Hitler. Raimund Pretzel, better known by his pseudonym Sebastian Haffner, was a German journalist and author. Haffner surmised Hitler succeeded by 1938 in winning the support of "the great majority of that majority who had voted against him in 1933." By that time, Haffner believes that by five years later, Hitler had united almost the entire German people behind him, that more than ninety percent of Germans were by that time true" believers in the Führer." Like most thinkers of the history of World War Two Germany, that no real realistic test of opinion exists to challenge official propaganda (false news) when the only public opinion which existed was that of the regime's agencies. Was ninety percent real or not? Clearly, by 1933, Raimund Pretzel wrote that beginning in 1933, the support of the National Socialist Party was due to the scripted personal "achievements" of Adolph Hitler. The State Propaganda Machine was endless and built upon the premise that Hitler was a hero and military and economic God. Even Paul Goebbels stated in 1941 that his creation of the Fuhrer Myth was the most celebrated advertising media success in the 20th Century. When a narrative repeated long enough, the population begins to believe the false narrative. Also, the human worshiped with great spiritual like gifts begins to believe the talking points after a long repetitive period. So, it was with Adolph Hitler. Those close to Hitler from 1935 through 1937 were no longer shy or withdrawn but began to act out the traits that he did not have.

Hitler's speeches were as he was Moses on the Mount, delivering his people to the Germanic-Roman Era. Hitler saw himself as the divine force that would finally allow Germany and its peoples to renew their former tribal, warlike center, and power for the world's good. This man who had fought in WW1 and thrown in prison for his political actions believed that his suffering was necessary for him to carry the cross for his defeated people. In one speech, Hitler said, "I follow the path assigned to me by Providence with the instinctive sureness of a sleepwalker."[2] Hitler truly believed that God had ordained him to lead his people to this promised land of a global Germanic foundation. Since God had prepared him for this political mission, Hitler knew that he was infallible.

HITLER'S NARCISSISM

Ian Kershaw wrote that by the entire 1930s, as Germany suffered economically, its savior magnified a narcissistic trait in (Hitler's) own personality. The extreme flattery and hero-worship that surrounded Adolph Hitler and the immense adulation of the masses repeatedly stimulated his belief that he was a reincarnation of the German tribal leader of historical Germania. Also, combined to magnify the belief that Germany's destiny lay in his own hands, and that he alone could guide his country to final victory in the ever-closer great conflict. Chancellor and Führer ("Leader") told his generals on the eve of World War Two,

"the fact that no one else will ever have the trust of the whole German people as I do. There will never be a man in the future who has more authority than me. My being is, therefore, a huge value factor. No one knows how much longer I will live. Therefore, it is better to have the conflict now."[3]

German Russian invasions — Courtesy of archive.4plebs.org

POLAND INVADED

By August 1939, the Fuhrer and his generals had achieved victories that convinced the German people that Hitler could not lose any battles against the economic tormentor nations of World War One. So, with a massed blitzkrieg force, Hitler ordered that western Poland invaded. On the early morning of September 1, 1939, the German battleship Schleswig-Holstein fired on the Westerplatte peninsula's garrison on the Baltic Sea. At the same timing, the Wehrmacht invaded Poland from the north, south, and west. The SS created a "false flag" to make it look like the radio station on the City of Gleiwitz was attacked by Polish soldiers. The SS rounded up Polish convicts and had them wear Polish Army uniforms. The convicts marched towards the battle, brutally shot by the SS. The two totalitarian regimes now cast world War II; namely, German fascist (Nazi) and the Bolshevik Soviet Communist. Hitler's policy was to expand into Central and Eastern Europe. The motivation for taking lands surrounding German was called Lebensraum or living space. Adolf Hitler believed that the German people were part of a "master or superior race," and the Italians, French, and Slavs (Poles, Ukrainians, Russians) were racially inferior.

Hitler and Joseph Stalin of the Soviet Union agreed to jointly invade eastern Poland and those Ukrainian lands controlled by Poland. After World War One, Poland did not modernize its military force. Polish troops on horseback fought back the mechanized Army of Hitler and Stalin. The Polish Cossacks fought back but were not a match and lost in just a few short days. On October 5, 1939, Warsaw, the capital of Poland, was taken as Hitler reviewed the German Army. In November 1939, the Russian Army invaded Finland and signed a peace treaty in February 1940. In the wartime years, the seemingly glorious victory gave way to poor decisions by Hitler to open up two battlefronts that required expanded supply lines. Soon defeats and not victories caused erosion of Hitler's compelling vision of a new Socialist Capitalism that would rule the world, as the Romans did, for one hundred plus years. There never was an abyss ordained except Germany could not compete with the industrial replacement of Hitler's superior fight machine. Hitler attacked Russia for fuel, grain, and recruits.

Further, before June 6, 1944, the United States created a vast media and military complex that funded a powerful anti-Hitler propaganda campaign that outspent Germany's.[4] If the people made to believe that Hitler was not a Germanic spiritual warrior, the warriors of the Wehrmacht would lose heart and give up. Still, to the bitter end, young boys and girls from Berlin fought the Russians attacking from the West and the American Army from the East. Hitler was believed as an influential leader and military general to the bitter end when he placed a cyanide pill in his mouth in parallel with his lover of fourteen years and wife of one day, Eva Braun. It was a remarkable journey of historical futility. Allied power countries that made up the forces, namely, Great Britain, France, China, Australia, Belgium, Brazil, Canada, Czechoslovakia, Ethiopia, Greece, Mexico, the Netherlands, New Zealand, Norway, Poland, South Africa, and Yugoslavia focused on defeating the Axis powers. Russia and the United States joined the efforts later in the war. More than fifty countries took part in the war, and the whole world felt its effects. Allied soldiers fought in almost every part of the world, on every continent except Antarctica. Principal battlegrounds included Asia, Europe, North Africa, the Atlantic, and Pacific Oceans, and the Mediterranean Sea.[5]

AXIS POWERS-GLOBAL ECONOMIC EXPANSIONISM

The Axis powers (German: Achsenmächte; Italian: Potenze dell'Asse; Japanese: 枢軸国 Sūjikukoku), also known as the Rome–Berlin–Tokyo Axis, were the nations that fought in World War Two against the Allies. The Holocaust occurred in 1933 when Adolf Hitler came to power in Germany and ended in 1945 when the Nazis defeated by the Allied forces. In addition to Jews, the Nazis targeted many other groups of people. Slavic peoples viewed as sub-human. Polish and Ukrainian peasants and serfs mainly targeted. People of different ethnic and religious backgrounds were at risk as were people who were handicapped or homosexual. Anyone who resisted the Nazis was sent to forced labor camps or murdered. Eleven million humans estimated killed during the Holocaust. Six million of these were Jews, and five million were not of the Jewish faith. The Nazis killed approximately two-thirds of all Jews living in Europe.

An estimated 1.1 million children murdered in the Holocaust. Although many people refer to all Nazi camps as "concentration camps," there were several different kinds of camps, including Concentration Camps, Extermination Camps, Labor Camps, Prisoner-of-War Camps, and Transit Camps.

DETENTIONS

From its rise to power in 1933, the Nazi regime built a series of detention facilities to imprison and eliminate the so-called "enemies of the state." Most prisoners in the early concentration camps were German Communists, Socialists, Social Democrats, Roma (Gypsies), Jehovah's Witnesses, homosexuals, and persons accused of "a social" or socially deviant behavior. These facilities named "concentration camps" because those imprisoned there were physically "concentrated" in one location. Millions of people imprisoned, abused, systematically murdered in the various types of Nazi camps. The Schutzstaffel (i.e., SS; also stylized as with Armanen runes; German pronunciation: ['ʃʊts͜ʃtafl̩] listen; literally "Protection Squadron") was a major paramilitary organization under Adolf Hitler and the Nazi Party (NSDAP) in Nazi Germany, and later throughout German-occupied Europe during World War II."[8]

One of the first concentration camps was Dachau, which opened on March 20, 1933. Some people are familiar with the names of the major concentration camps, namely, Auschwitz, Buchenwald, Dachau, and Treblinka. Treblinka was an extermination camp built in German-occupied Poland. The SS and collaborationists' auxiliary police, mainly Ukrainian, controlled the Treblinka Nazi Gas Chambers from 1942 to 1943 and murdered 875,000 Polish Jews. Ninety-nine percent of those who arrived at Treblinka by train executed within three hours of arrival.

Each of the twenty-three main camps had subcamps, nearly 900 of them in total. These included camps with euphemistic names, such as "care facilities for foreign children," where pregnant prisoners sent for forced abortions. The Nazis established about one hundred ten camps starting in 1933 to imprison political opponents and other undesirables. The number expanded as the Third Reich expanded, and the Germans began occupying parts of Europe. When the US Holocaust Memorial Museum first began to document all of the camps, the belief was that the list would total approximately 7,000.[6] However, researchers found that the Nazis established about 42,500 camps and ghettoes between 1933 and 1945. This figure includes 30,000 slave labor camps; 1,150 Jewish ghettoes, 980 concentration camps; 1,000 POW camps; 500 brothels filled with sex slaves; and thousands of other camps used for euthanizing the elderly and infirm. - "Germanizing" prisoners or transporting victims to killing centers. Berlin alone had nearly 3,000 camps.[7] These camps used for a range of purposes, including forced-labor camps, transit camps, which served as temporary way stations and extermination camps, built primarily or exclusively for mass murder.

Nazi Waffen SS logo -Courtesy of nationalinterest.org

Under SS management, the Germans and their collaborators murdered more than three million Jews in the killing centers lone. Only a small fraction of those imprisoned in Nazi camps survived. As many as fifteen to twenty million people may have died in the various camps and ghettoes. Life within Nazi camps was horrible.

Prisoners forced to do hard physical labor and given very little food. The food the prisoners did receive was not nutritious or sanitary in most circumstances. Prisoners slept with three or more people on a crowded wooden bunk that had no mattress or pillow. Torture within the concentration camps was familiar, and deaths were frequent. At some Nazi concentration camps, Nazi doctors conducted medical experiments on prisoners against their will. Concentration camps meant to work and starve prisoners to death, however extermination camps (also known as death camps) built for the sole purpose of killing large groups of people quickly and efficiently. The Nazis made six extermination camps: Chelmno, Belzec, Sobibor, Treblinka, Auschwitz, and Majdanek. Auschwitz and Majdanek were both concentration and extermination camps. Auschwitz built as the cost celebrated concentration and extermination camp.[9]

NAZI GHETTOS

Reinhard Heydrich was Stellvertretender Reichsprotektor (Deputy/ Acting Reich-Protector) of Bohemia and Moravia. Heydrich served as CEO of the International Criminal Police Commission (ICPC or Interpol) and chaired the January 1942 Wannsee Conference, which formalized plans for the Final Solution to the Jewish Question—the deportation and genocide of all Jews in German-occupied Europe.

Heydrich had the view that "We (Nazi) want to save the little people, but the aristocracy, priest, and Jews must be killed."

After 1939, the Nazis began ordering Jews to wear a yellow Star of David on their clothing so they could be easily recognized and targeted. All Jews forced to live in specific areas of significant cities called ghettos. Jews were forced out of their homes and moved into smaller apartments, often shared with other families. The central ghetto was in Warsaw, with its highest population reaching 445,000 in March 1941.[10]

UKRAINE – THE FINAL SOLUTION

The German Nazis systematically carried out genocidal policies against Jews in Ukraine to forced labor camps in Germany. In 1941, the Germans attacked the Soviet Union, which proved in the end to be a wrong decision, however, over the next three years, Nazi Germany would control much of Ukraine from 1941 to 1944, and the worst for its long-suffering people was yet to come.

SOVIET UNION'S NKVD

In March 1940, Joseph Stalin secretly ordered the NKVD to murder 15,000 Polish Officers who were just reservists and in private life such as doctors, lawyers, and key officials. Soviet Genocide activities began on September 17, 1940, Stalin's troops invading Eastern Poland rounded up 100,000 Polish military prisoners. Both the German and Russian Secret intelligence forces murdered 100,000 Polish non-combatants. Russia sent over one million Poles to Gulags, prison, or concentration camps. Stalin set up 450 Gulag camps. In preparation for the invasion of England, Germany was infiltrating spies and saboteurs by submarine or by air to report on England's coastal defenses, Modern British Secret Intelligence Services, British naval intelligence, Room 40, and the birth of signals intelligence, and the famous Zimmermann Telegram. British counterintelligence officers began turning spies sent to England by the Abwehr (German Military Intelligence) against the Reich in operation named "Double Cross."[11]

KORKA'S COVERT OPERATIONS (1940 – 1945)

By 1941, MI 15 had over twelve double agents, each with their handler. Dimitry Ivanshenko was one of the MI 15s top double agents; he fell in love with Maria Vanya Varzia, who gave Dimitry's slanted reports directly to his case officers. Dimitry caught in an operation called "Operation North", and to save the life of Maria, he agreed to betray his British handlers. He did his best to insert a wrong security code, but it was unnoticed. Thinking that the spy network was doing great work, they continued to send in more British to a total of 32 agents killed by firing squads and partisan that worked for the MI 15-MI 16 network and were murdered.

Heinrich Stadel, grandson of Viktor Korka and was a naturalized American citizen who was born in Germany. On one of his business trips to Germany, he pressured to be a double agent by the Abwehr German Military Intelligence. His mother and father still lived in Germany. Without his agreement, both parents would be sent to Mauthausen–Gusen concentration camp in Bavaria. For three weeks, Heinrich trained in martial arts and the use of firearms. He is given intensive interviews by medical and psychological doctors who give him a high rating for stability and mental capacity. They then create a report attesting his ability to follow instructions and the ability to keep all activities secret from any American counter-intelligence officers. On the last day of his training, Heinrich Stadel is given "micro-dot" technology and trained in receiving and transmitting messages to his sub-agents and his leading control agent. He receives the code name, Maxiim.

German Intelligence Officer Colonel Hermann Gisk, Heinrich Stadel's control agent, spent the late evening of June 13, 1940, giving Heinrich instructions on how to use the Third Reich's Microdot technology. "From now on, Heinrich, we will not send you written instructions. Instead, we will give you special points or dots to follow that will be stuck in the inside of an envelope. These points are practically invisible and in a brownish color. They are microphotographs, each representing one page of typewritten instructions."

Colonel Gisk, am I to buy a magnifying glass to read them?" "No, Henrich, I will give you a small microscope, which can magnify about 2 to 300 times. Also, as you can see, I am holding a metal latchkey. By screwing the key's top, it will reveal a microdot. You will take the microscope and place it on a slide to read it. It will contain one page a font size of 8 points, single lines, in the Arial font."

Heinrich sat at the table across from the Colonel, reached for his glass filled with Echte Kroatzbeere, took a deep breath, lifted the glass, saluted the Colonel, and swallowed the entire contents.

"Thank you, Colonel, for allowing me to serve the Third Reich. I will follow all the written instructions to the letter."

Heinrich would now identify as "Maxiim." He then slammed the empty glass on the wooden table, stood up, saluted, grabbed his hat, and left the room. It was now 1:00 in the early morning, and he walked back to his hotel to get a good night's rest before flying to Amsterdam and then on to New York to catch a direct train to Minneapolis. Upon his return to Minneapolis, he informed the FBI of his recruitment as an agent for the German intelligence. The FBI acts to" bug his home" and office (24x7). The result of many months of surveillance, the head of FBI J Edgar Hoover learns of the Frederick Duquesne's thirty-three-member covert saboteurs and spies ring for Hitler's Abwehr. On June 29, 1941, the FBI at four in the early morning surrounded all the agents' homes and broke up a ring of thirty-three German agents spying in the USA.

The covert group, the Duquesne Spy Ring, sent secret messages to the German Government. Sasha Ford, a thirty-five-year-old female, as a niece of the U.S. automobile entrepreneur Henry Ford, decides that the time is right to defend her country. She is five feet and four inches in height and slightly overweight at 119 pounds. Her personality is sensitive, sensuous, warm, and a non-assertive single woman. Furthermore, with two ample breasts and a tight round buttock, many men are attracted to her. Her skin is smooth, and she readily smiles, showing no sign of stress or fear of meeting new people. She makes it a point to approach others and to negate them in polite conversation. No one, whether male or female, can resist the sensual signals she emanates from her very presence. As a typical Grosse Point Michigan divorcee with one child, Sasha enjoys the social life of the Bloomfield Hills Michigan auto and financial elites who viewed Adolph Hitler and the rise of the Third Reich as a historical, political force. Many of them begin to travel to Berlin, Germany, and invest in the Third Reich. Soon Sasha is seen as part of the German high command cocktail parties. Eventually, recruited as an agent for the Abwehr. After many months and affairs with German officers, she becomes disillusioned with the Nazis.

While attending an evening party at the Russian Embassy in Berlin, she meets handsome twenty-eight-year-old Vasily Kolpashkov, a descendant of the Korka Family, and a Russian NGKD officer. Shasha Ford falls immediately into love with Vasily. They fly to Positano, an Italy Third Reich private beach retreat since the days of Roman nobility and even the ancient Greeks. Both Sasha and Vasily enjoy swimming and sunbathing. They become emotionally and physically connected. They rise together each day and kiss each other tenderly. Sasha's lips are soft and move gracefully over Vasily's hardened muscular body. When they return two weeks to Berlin, they have gone beyond a sexual encounter and find themselves connected in mind as well. Soon Sasha becomes a double agent working for German and Russian Intelligence. Hitler's Operation Barbarossa called for 190 divisions with more than three million German troops, and another one million from Italy and Romania plan to attack Russia from the Baltic to the Black Sea. Sasha learns that Germany's High Command is planning on doing covert high-altitude recon photography of all Russian airfields, railheads, and transportation systems. Sasha gives Vasily this information as they meet in the various hotels in Germany and France.

"I am very convinced from reports and instructions are given by German intelligence that Hitler plans to attack in 1941 and to crush all Russian forces as his Army marches into Moscow. My dear Vasily advises the NGKD commander that this is real."

Vasily looked into the deep hazel eyes of Sasha Ford and whispered,

"But why would Hitler do such a thing to Comrade Stalin as they signed a peace treaty and Poland divided up between them.

It does not make any sense. They will not believe me unless I can give some proof. I cannot compromise you, my love."

Shasha implores Vasily as she reaches down into the satin sheets and slowly massages him.

"I have no recording or a piece of paper as I overheard the German High Commanders talk about Operation Barbarossa."

Hitler started the campaign in June 1941 and attempted to reach Moscow by August 1941, but the weather conditions rapidly changed. Winter arrived early. Vasily returned to Moscow to fight for the city but was arrested in one of Stalin's purges and shot as a spy. He was always under surveillance as it was well known by 1941 that Sasha Ford was an agent for the German Military Intelligence. In 1945, after Sasha's covert-cover is compromised, Sasha returned to Grosse Point, Michigan, and married an older Ford executive named John Edsel. Sasha kept her secret life spying for Germany until 1976 when she reached 70 and died from liver cancer. Her last words as her son stood over her at the hostel nursing home in Flint were,

"I only loved my dear Vasily. Germany and Russia should have never gone to war. If that did not happen, I would have had Vasily's children. It is God's will, I guess. I just wanted to be happy." With those words, she closed her round hazel eyes and passed away."

Savur-Mohyla destroyed- Courtesy of Museum of War Donbas Ukraine

RED ARMY DONBAS 1943- UKRAINE ARMY DONBAS 2014

In August 1943, Red Army forces fought against Nazi troops entrenched on the strategic heights of Savur-Mohyla or written as Saur-Mogila. Savur-Mohyla Memorial created for the thousands of Russian speaking troops of the Soviet Union who died. It acknowledged as a site soaked with blood when the battle ended. In the language of Ukrainian it is known as Савур-могила or Savur-Mogila and in the Slavic language of Russia known as Saur-Mogila or Саур-Могила). In 2014, during the Maidan Civil War between the Kiev Central Government and the Donbass declared People's Republics, Billionaire Petro Oleksiyovych Poroshenko of Ukraine order his Army to shell the monument and to destroy it as a sign of Ukraine's past as a Soviet Republic. The new European Union NATO energized Kiev directed Government created a political policy of "ethnic cleansing" all things Russian-language and culture. The goal under the new Maidan nationalism was to eradicate anything that was a symbol of the Russian victories in Ukraine, the IMF and NATO funded and equipped Ukrainian army began shelling the Saur-Mogila memorial complex with a 1000 Grad multiple-rocket launchers (MRL). A multiple rocket launcher (MRL) is a type of unguided rocket artillery system. Like other rocket artillery, multiple rocket launchers are less accurate and have a much lower rate of fire than batteries of traditional artillery guns. However, they have the capability of simultaneously dropping many hundreds of kilograms of explosive, with devastating effect. Prior to the 2014 overthrow of the Ukrainian Government by the assistance of the US State Department, the memorial was built in late 1960s in the Donetsk Region on a hill that played an important strategic role for Hitler's troops. It is still a strategic height in the Donetsk People's Republic's ridge near the city of Snizhne, located about 3.1 miles from the border between Ukraine and Russia's Rostov Oblast. It is known by the local population as a tumulus (kurgan) – Mohyla means "tumulus" in Ukrainian, and according to one interpretation the word Savur comes from "turkic sauyr", meaning; namely, steppe mound shaped like horse bottom.[12]

Memorial Cay P Mor - Courtesy of Museum of War Donbas Ukraine

NAZI SPIES

Both Gafya and Kolya Lupambulus fled the 1940 invasion of France as they feared for their lives as they were both Jewish and fiercely anti-German. Earlier as two twenty-one-year-olds living in Silesia, they had met at a young age while studying Russian and German at a private Jewish elementary High School Academy in Bavaria. Gafya Olbrecht grew to be 6 foot and 3inches. She had blond hair that was cut in a butch style with uneven sides. Her chiseled face reminded so many when she was serious as the granite face near Savur-Mohyla. Like Kolya, Gafya had a brain of steely determination and an intellect to match. Gafya trained as a wireless radio operator. She was brought into the French section of the Special Operations Executive (SOE) established by Prime Minister Winston Churchill. Winston had only one goal and that was to set German-occupied Europe blazing with massive fires.

Kolya Lupamlus had a dark skin complexion with large black eyes that would seem to penetrate the very soul of those he focused on. He stood at five feet and six inches with a bodybuilder muscle mass. He walked with a limp from an accident that he received at thirteen years of age. His arms were long and shoulder broad and muscular. He was clean shaved and his hair short and cut in the style of a military man, which he was not. Kolya trained in Martial Arts, sniper skills, and bomb-making for sabotage missions.

Both would work as a team. They were assigned to a Secret Intelligence Service (SIS), commonly known as MI6, disguise officer by the name of Major Mansfield Cummings. He spoke to them on their 18th month of training,

"We need to protect those operatives who will help us locate German battle plans and their trade in counterfeit dollars. You will have to wear a 'light disguise' so those who knows you will not disrupt the meeting with our covert agents. We can provide a wig or some facial hair and glasses. Event disguise for close and personal will be a complete facial mask. We have the ability to change your facial appearance with a plastic gum and palate inserts that will change the appearance of your facial structure. Of course, we can make a young face look old and visa versus. As we did in entering Hitler's Bunker in the Black Forest. Those techniques worked very well. Remember, turning a woman into a man is the easiest. When we tried to disguise a man to appear as a woman we have failed and 78% of our humane intelligence resources shot or imprisoned, of course after hours of torture. At times, we have had to enter the interrogation cell and shot our source as well as anyone who interfered with the mission. As we say here in the Royal Marines, lose lips mean death to those who do so. It is important that at times of your mission to get rid of your physical images. Remember, use street crowds as a forest in which you can hide quickly or to change your appearance. The goal of a quick change in appearance is to disappear. The intelligence manual states that you have figure out what tribe you are in and how to move freely within the tribe without being detected as an agent of the Queen. If you do it right, there is no suspicion and you are free. We will in the afternoon have you meet our expert appearance change professionals. You may not even recognize yourselves, but it is good practice."

With that he gave them a file of their possible missions and left the room.

They trained for over three years until they would be sent on a mission in which they would parachute near the objective. The chance that they would be captured and shot was a very high outcome of their mission. Gafya is given a 4.5 mm single shot weapon disguised as a tube of lipstick, easily hidden in her purse. Both Kolya and Gafya knew that at the age of twenty-six, they would be dead. On a Runway, Manchester England foggy morning at 0400 hours, they both boarded an Avro Lancaster for a parachute landing near the Russian lines five miles north of the German defenses overlooking Donets ridge near the city of Snizhne, located about 5 km (3.1 mi) from the border between Ukraine and Russia's Rostov Oblast. Each had agreed that they would take a cyanide pill if captured by the German SS. They sat in the rear of the bomber holding hands and staring aimlessly front and center to prepare themselves for the jump at 12,000 feet. They were afraid but they had made a commitment to be agents. The Lancaster that they placed their lives on could carry a maximum bomb load of 22,000 ft., its maximum level speed with a full load at 15,000 feet was 275 mph and it could cruise routinely at altitudes above 20,000ft at a range speed of 200 mph. With a full bomb load the aircraft had a range in excess of 1,500 miles.

Lancaster bomb crew 1942 loading bombs — Courtesy of Alamy

Each were issued Webley M1907 6.35-mm pistol that was concealed in pocket or handbag. Kolya and knew that they would be shot if arrested by the Gestapo. It was better than being captured. Further, they were given a small concealable automatic machine pistol that could fire at 200 rounds per minute. Their Ammunition was compatible with German, British, and American caliber bullets. The green light flickered and the red light came on and they both held hands and jumped into the darkness of the night that revealed tracer flights of bullets beneath them. The battle for the heights had begun and they could only hope that they would land at their designated drop zone. From the vantage point of the steppe heights the Germans had a 360-degree view and they would use their tanks and artillery to rain down hot steel upon the Russian, British, and American forces trying to take it. For over 6 months the battle continued until the winter set in early and the three million manned German forces' failure to take Moscow, the Germans slowing withdrew from their vantage point.

Gafya and Kolya jump from the Lancaster's open door into the cold black landing zone below them. As both were about to land, and since the Russian Red Army was not notified in time, small arms fired was directed towards their slowly moving parachutes. Koyla was shot in his back twice, and when he landed, he challenged with a compound-complex fracture of his right leg. As he lay dying, Gafya landed 200 yds. away. She immediately grabbed her parachute and pulled it off while running towards Koyla. She knelt over him.

"Kolya please don't die. I love you so much. I was going to tell you when we reached our objectives and returning through the help of the partisans that we were going to have a baby. Please darling I can stop the blood, you are going to be alright, you'll see."

Blood was trickling down his slightly opened mouth. Gafya could hear and feel the bullets wising and rushing past her ears. She had no idea if the Germans or the Russians had spotted them and shooting at them. Soon five soldiers in brown uniforms with no insignias, were standing over her with their rifles at her and Kolya.

"Please do not shoot. Both of us are part of the American General Staff assigned to the forces of Russia. The soldiers spoke in Russian. "Come here! Иди сюда idi syuda."

Kolya closed his eyes and appeared to have died and there was nothing that she could do but go with the soldier, who put her on a tank for the long journey to Moscow and repatriation back to England. Kolya was still breathing and taken to a hospital in the Russian Military Zone of operations. The bullets did not hit his spine or vital organs. His broken leg was put together with thirteen titanium screws. His recovery in a Manchester English military hospital took over a year. Gafya was to have been captured by a German SS unit and sent to a concentration camp near Warsaw where she was forced to have an abortion and died during the crude camp procedure of a caesarean delivery. Kolya was to learn of the dual tragedies of losing his wife and daughter from MI 15. To keep his mind sane, Kolya returns back to what he can do best in; namely, spying and using all the force at his command to silence targets in the German High Command. After two months on paid leave by the British foreign office, Kolya was ready for his next mission to be infiltrated by an American submarine into Germany.

Kolya because of his anti-Nazi sentiment, Russian Language capabilities, espionage skill sets, and organizing abilities made in charge of the Network coded as "Red Symphony". He had to organize four networks in Germany, France, Holland and Switzerland. The first branch would operate out of France, Belgium, and Holland, the second out of Berlin, and finally the "Gloria Ring" that would operate out of neutral Switzerland. Two German agents who were extremely anti-Nazi were part of Kolya's spy ring, One, Hans-Heinrich Döhler, was in the German Air Ministry an anti-Nazi intelligence officer and Werner von Eichstedt who worked in the German Ministry for Economics. Also, two other anti-Nazi Germans also were recruited by Kolya to be weapons officers and silent backups in case the Gestapo learned of Red Symphony operations in these two Ministries. Each of the four agents would receive $240,000 US dollars in gold plus $125,000 USD dollars in diamonds that they would receive at the end d of the First World War, but only if they completed their Office of Special Investigations (OSI) and joint MI 15 mission's goal flawlessly. Also, Kolya organizes a spy ring under instructions from Winston Churchill who wanted Germany to atone for the German ll Junkers Ju 88 bombings of London, which resulted in the deaths of 17,500 civilians and the death of his dog Dodo. Once this special "Churchill" spy group in Nazi Europe would be fully functioning given the code name, "Gloria," and was just another branch of the Red Symphony that provides German military plans on the offensive in Russia.

The Gloria Ring had the best information resources with two German Nazi officers. Lieutenant General Hans-Joachim Horrer, a senior officer in the Wehrmacht's communication branch and Colonel Theodor Habicht, who became to be the intelligence officer of the Nazi Army Group Center on the Eastern Front in Russia. Berliners, Theodor Habicht, and his wife Libertas attracted many to their home who had the same mindset to supply military plans supplied by Colonel Habicht. Theodor and Libertas came from prominent German families. Libertas had blond and the Nordic look that Nazis depicted as superior racial characteristics. Many of their friends were actors, writers, and directors. Many had Jewish friends, in-laws, or ancestors and they were shocked by the anti-Semitism that was the key element of Hitler's new Germany. Many of them struggled to find work in a German culture that viewed them as less than pure racial humans. Their best friend, Hans Probst, introduced their casual circle of friends into an espionage circle that was key to the defeat of Germany. With radios supplied by the (OSI), they communicated with Moscow. On October 23, 1941, GRU military intelligence officer Ivan Kolpashkov, had not heard from Colonel Habicht for many months and made a major plunder in spy craft procedures and went to the Habicht Berlin flat. He knocked on the door, and when seen through the peephole in the door, Libertas opened the door, "come in quickly, as she ushered him while peering down the corridor and down the stairs to see if anyone was there to witness Ivan's entry. Once in the living room, she ran into the study to inform her husband that he had an important visitor. Theodor stood up from his chair and walk into the living room with his wife, hand in hand.

"What are you doing here Ivan?"

"I had no choice we were so worried that something happened to you as you have not contacted us as arranged."

"You have put us great danger if the Gestapo was watching this house. However, now that you are here let us sit down in my study as I have so much information to share with you. Germans are massing over four million troops to attack Russia, but the key battle will be at this choke point. First, here are the battle plans for the invasion of Stalingrad. Once the German forces encircle Stalingrad, their supply lines will be unable to supply the needed resources to sustain the battle, and I think they will be trapped. Here is my idea how the German Tactical Plans will occur."

Theodor took a pen and drew arrows from the North and South of the city of Stalingrad.

"Soon if Russian Command can place all of their forces at this point and exhaust the capabilities of the German Army here, then they will surrender. They will have no choice. It will be surrender or be killed."

Ivan and Theodor continued to talk well into the night. At 2 am, Theodor suggests that Ivan stay in the guest room and leave in the morning as he would be suspected if he went now. They shook hands and Libertas showed him the guest room, and soon Ivan was fast asleep amazed at the treasure trove of intelligence received. After a brief breakfast of tea, crackers, and sausage, he left at 10 in the early morning.

Waffen SS into Russia - Courtesy of nationalinterest.org

OPERATION BARBAROSSA

Operation Barbarossa was the code name for the Axis invasion of the Soviet Union, starting Sunday, June 22 1941, during World War Two and the targets were Eastern and Northern Europe. The plan called for 190 divisions consisting of three million German soldiers and another one million from Italy and Romania to attack 1,000 miles long Russian front from the Baltic to the Black Sea. By 1941, the Nazi Gestapo knew of a Soviet spy ring operating in reasonably high levels of the Reich Government administration as early as 1941. It became a slow process, but Hitler who despised Churchill placed a lot of resources behind a counterespionage team "Special Detachment Red Symphony" (Sonderkommando Rote Kapelle) operating in the same office complex that Hitler worked. It was not until 1943 that the Germans after many months of raw intelligence pieced together who, what, and where regarding the Red Symphony and the Gloria Ring. -Without any suspicion by Kolya or other support members of the Office of Strategic Services (OSS) and MI 15 (Military Intelligence, Section 15).

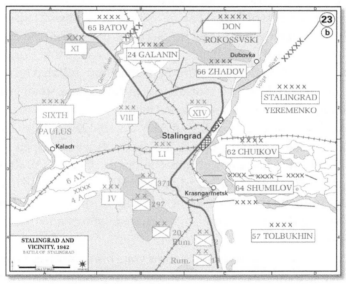

Stalingrad battle WWII Europe – Courtesy of emersonkent.com

SPRING 1942

In the spring of 1942, the German secret state security police that had the jurisdiction to send spies to the concentration camps without a court hearing sprang into action, arrested the first of Red Symphony agents in Belgium.

On May 12, 1942, Kolya Lupambus immediately contacted Yvonne Brodeur, his covert SOE radio operator. Kolya had given her a radio set consisting of a battery, receiver, and transmitter concealed in a leather briefcase. In her purse, Yvonne carried, for her personal safety, a Webley M1907 6.35mm pistol. Yvonne stood 5 feet 4 inches, slim built and weighed 125lbs. She was striking in a cotton blue skirt and blouse that she received from Kolya for her birthday. Yvonne always wore a hat with a bright red feather on the top with the rim pulled down slightly over her eyes. She always wore white cotton gloves and carried a small black purse slung over her right shoulder. Yvonne was to send a message from the hidden radio in the basement of her French Pastry Shop. The news that she transmitted was to inform Winston Churchill that the Germans had broken the spy ring and Kolya rescued immediately. In an hour, Yvonne told Kolya that he had orders directly from Prime Minister Churchill that he was to be ready in two days for a morning air pickup near a small farm in the village of Oradour-sur-Glane in Haute-Vienne.

At 4 am on the morning of May 23, 1942, an Avro Anson landed guided with burning torches set in place in an open wheat field. Kolya only had a few minutes before the German Waffen-SS company might get notified of an aircraft engine sound. So, he rushed to the plane with Yvonne running behind him. When he approached the plane as the engine roared, he turned around and grabbed Yvonne,

"I want to thank you so much for your bravery. I will miss our nights together. Our close sexual moments remembered by me. I love you."

He kissed Yvonne with their mouths and tongues probing each other.

"I will do my best to get you another pick-up scheduled. Be careful, and I will see you soon in London."

Only two minutes remained and Yvonne Brodeur, shivering in the early morning air, deeply kissed Kolya again.

"Here put on my family ring with the Korka green star stone and it will keep you safe."

Kolya then placed the ring on Yvonne's finger and opened the door of the Avron, jumped in. The plane's engine immediately revved up and moved the light aircraft forward and into the early morning's foggy mist. Clearly the top of the trees by inches, the Avro Anson swayed as it struggled to gain air speed. Soon the sound of the aircraft could not be heard as Yvonne raced back to Citroën DS to avoid capture by the Waffen SS patrol that was approaching the wheat field.

Kolya was flown to a hidden landing field in Southern France and driven to a waiting submarine off the coast. After extensive debriefing by MI 15 and Prime Minister Churchill, Kolya returned to London Lincolnshire to train agents to parachute into German-occupied Western and Eastern Europe. They received a standard British Army utility knife which was used as a weapon as needed. Kolya demonstrated how this small knife could be used to puncture the eyeballs and slash the throat with five moves. Also, he trained them on using a new battery-powered transmitter that gave them the ability to send a message in transit to their objectives. Working with the OE and OSS, he asked Churchill to consider aiding the resistance by providing them with MK II Sten Machine guns; radio sets concealed in a suitcase. The final phase of the six-week course was to train them with hands-on with TNT or plastic explosives to destroy large infrastructures such as railroad tracks and bridges. Working with British engineers, Kolya created small concealable bombs triggered with small-time fuses that would allow escape before an explosion. Agents were parachuted behind enemy lines and worked with Polish and French resistance groups to disrupt the movements of German infantry troops and motorized units as the Allied forces planned to attack France first and then move through Belgium, followed by Holland. Kolya was never able to authorize a rescue of Yvonne Brodeur. Five weeks after Kolya's hasty departure on that cold misty morning, she was arrested by the Gestapo, tortured for two weeks without allowed sleep, and then beheaded by wire hanging. Yvonne's body was cremated and her ashes shoveled into the rose garden behind the Prinz-Albrecht-Straße No.8 Gestapo building.

Richard Theodor Kusiolek

GLORIA RING

Both Theodor Habicht and Hans-Joachim Horrer, who had operated in Berlin for some time, were arrested following the initial wave of arrests in Brussels. German interrogators used "intensified interrogation" techniques on Theodor Habicht and his wife Libertas. This was a form of torture that would leave no marks, and hence save the embarrassment pre-war Nazi officials were experiencing as their wounded torture victims ended up in court. The couple chained and brought to Gestapo headquarters at Prinz-Albrecht-Straße8. They were taken to a dark cell with a concrete bed and no blankets. For the first three days they were fed only bread and water. On the fourth day, they were emerged in cold baths after brutal blows and kicks to their faces and stomachs. Each day they were interrogated as to their contacts and meetings with Russian agents. They continued to answer that they had no knowledge and they were loyal to Hitler. During the third week, they were subjected to freezing temperatures, repeatedly beaten, days of forced-standing, waterboarding, cold showers in air-conditioned rooms, forced into stress positions Arrest mit Verschaerfung, given no medicine and left alone in their cells for 30 days. They did their best to muster courage and strength but eventually they broke under the torture. With screams,

"Yes, I hate Hitler. Yes, I am a traitor, Yes, let me confess. Yes, I will sign the paper of confession. Please stop the beatings."

As a result, the Germans were able to eradicate most of the spy network in Belgium, Holland and Germany. A number of other network Russian agents were arrested including many employees of the German military intelligence service (Abwehr), Ministry of Labor, Ministry of Propaganda, Foreign Office, and the Berlin City Administration. The list of those arrested was damning evidence of just how deeply the Soviet Military Intelligence had penetrated the German government administration and the Wehrmacht High Command. The Gloria Ring provided actional intelligence to Joseph Stalin and his Soviet General Staff with information about

German strategic and tactical intentions. After the twelve show trials that was filmed, 58 members of the Red Symphony network were condemned to death and many others were sentenced to long periods of imprisonment. Theodor Habicht was slowly hanged by razor wire. Before his hanging, Theodor Habicht shouted,

"This death suits me. I loved Germany so much. What I did I am proud of. I only wanted to save Germany from that pompous fool Austrian paper hanger, Adolph Hitler."

With those words, he was immediately hanged in the courtyard of the Germany Chancellery. As Libertas was led to the guillotine she cried out,

"If I had another life, I would do the same as my husband did. We just spied to end the war, and I leave with a good conscience."

That was the final words of Libertas as the blade swiftly severed her head and rolled with a thump into a wicker basket to the front of the guillotine that had the name of the manufacturer and the words, "nous ne manquons jamais." Theodor Habicht and Libertas' remains were burned and no headstone or records of their lives was ever found. By 1943, a total of more than six hundred OSS and MI 15 support agents were arrested in Germany, as well as in Paris and Brussels. However, the OSI MI 15 ring was instrumental in defeating the Germans as the Russian High Command knew of every German strategic and tactical field troop and tank movements. The Gloria Ring's operations allowed the Russian Army to plan campaigns that led to the defeat of German forces. The German Army's campaign did not end until Eastern Front collapsed on May 5, 1945 and German forces were captured, killed, or frozen on the cold battlefields of Russia. The Gloria Ring, perhaps the most important branch of the Red Symphony, possessed some excellent sources of information. These sources included Lieutenant General Fritz Theile, a senior officer in the Wehrmacht's communications branch, and Colonel Freiherr Rudolf von Gersdorff, who eventually became intelligence officer of Army Group Center on the eastern front. The Gloria Ring provided Soviet leader Josef Stalin with extraordinarily accurate information on Nazi command and control battle plans along the Russian Eastern Front. Starting in 1941, the German secret police learned of a Soviet Union Spy cell that was believed to be operating at the highest level of the Third Reich's leadership. However, like many counterespionage cases as witnessed during the U.S. FBI probe of the 2017 President elect Donald J. Trump, large resources and timely research take three years to reveal that collusion with a foreign power did not take place. The Gloria Ring World War Two was broken after three years of surveillance, investigation, endless hours of torture.[13]

MEIN KAMPF'S VISION REALITY

The Second World War ended in 1945, with the unconditional surrender of the Axis of Evil war machines On May 8, 1945, the Franklin Delano Roosevelt, Joseph Stalin, and Winston Churchill accepted Germany's surrender, about a week after Adolf Hitler had committed suicide." The German Army was far superior to the Russian Forces or for that matter the Allied Forces. According to Otto Skorzeny an Austrian born SS-Obersturmbannführer or lieutenant colonel in the Waffen-SS, the super-spy Richard Sorge, who informed the OSI and MI 15 that Japan would not enter the war, allowed 40 divisions moved Moscow from the Far East. "The Reich's military strategy was superior" Skorzeny says, "and our Generals possessed a more powerful imagination. However, from the ordinary soldier up to the company commander, the Russians were our equals in the categories of courageousness, resourcefulness, intelligence operational flare. They resisted fiercely and were always ready to sacrifice their lives. The Russian officers from division commander and below were younger and more resolute than our German officers.

From October 9 to December 5, 1945, the "SS Das Reich" division's Wolfsangel banner was incorporated into Ukraine's Azov Battalion flag. Also, the 10th and 16th tank division lost forty percent of their total personnel. Six days later, when Skorzeny's positions were attacked by newly-arrived Siberian divisions, German troop losses exceeded seventy five percent. The Germans could have conquered Moscow but high-ranking German officers like Skorzeny stayed in safety of the rear. To save himself from the daily killings on the Moscow front he transferred to the SS commando unit. The Mongolian Siberians fought under the protection of T-34 tank divisions and with the US and England providing battle field intelligence, Obersturmbannführer knew the battle of the East was over and soon Russian troops would be at the very gates of the Third Reich.[14]

CHAPTER NINE

SWORD OF MAIDAN – UKRAINE REVOLUTIONS

"Of course, there is a risk. But without risk, there is no honor, no glory, no adventure." Winston Churchill

RURIK DYNASTY

RURIK DYNASTY, PRINCESSES OF Kievan Rus and, later, Muscovy, who, according to tradition, were descendants of the Varangian Prince Rurik. In 862, He had been invited by the people of Novgorod to rule that city, and the Rurik princesses maintained their control over Kievan Rus and, later, Muscovy until 1598. Historical reports existed that the Vikings ruled between the 9th and 11th centuries the medieval state of Kievan Rus. The Greeks and Eastern Slav tribes gave the name to the Vikings as Old Norse -Varangians (Væringjar; Greek: Βάραγγοι Varangoi, Βαριάγοι Variagoi). The Byzantine Varangian Guard Vikings settled among many rivers in territories of modern Ukraine, Belarus, and Russia. In 912, Rurik's successor Oleg Rurik conquered Kyiv and established control of the trade route extending from Novgorod, along the Dnieper River, to the Black Sea. Igor Rurik ruled from 912 to 945, and his St. Oleg was the regent from 945 to 969. Igor and St. Olga's son Svyatoslav ruled 945 to 972. During their reign, further extension of their territories. Svyatoslav's son St. Vladimir I consolidated the Rurik Dynasty from 980 to 1015.[1]

KIEVAN RUS CODE LAW – EXTENDED RIGHTS OF KINGSHIP

Vladimir compiled the first Kievan Rus law code and introduced Christianity into the country. He also organized the Kievan Rus lands into a cohesive confederation by distributing the important cities among his sons. Vladimir decided that the eldest was to be Grand Prince of Kyiv. The Grand Prince's brothers were to succeed each other. Their hierarchy based on the cities surrounding Kyiv and vacancies opened by the promotion or death of an elder brother. The code of Kingship followed the pattern that the youngest brother was to be succeeded as grand Prince by his eldest nephew, whose father had been a noble prince. The pattern of succession continued during six reigns; namely, as follows

Years -1015 to 1019 reign of Svyatopolk

Years - 1019 to 1054 reign of Yaroslav -The Wise

Years -1054 to 1068 reign of Izyaslav

Years - 1069 to 1073, 1073 to 1076 reign of Svyatoslav

Years - 1078 to 1093 reign of Vsevolod

Years - 1099 to 1113 reign of Svyatopolk II - the son of Izyaslav.

The successions accomplished reign of, however, amid continual civil wars. The princes' unwillingness to adhere to the pattern and readiness to seize their positions by force instead created the imbalance. If a city rejected the Prince, then the Prince would use the power of arms to capture the city. It was also undermined by the princes' tendency to settle in regions they ruled rather than moving from city to city to become the Prince of Kyiv. In 1097, princes of Kievan Rus met at Lyubech (northwest of Chernigov) and decided to divide their lands into patrimonial estates. The succession for the grand Prince based on the generation pattern; thus, Vladimir Monomakh succeeded his cousin Svyatopolk II as Grand Prince of Kyiv. From 1113 to 1125, Vladimir Monomakh tried to restore unity to the lands of Kievan Rus and how his sons show rule their kingdom. from 1125 to 1132 was ruled by Mstislav; from 1132 to seven years later was controlled by Yaropolk; just for the year 1139 Vyacheslav reigned; and finally, from 1149 to 1157, Yury Dolgoruky who was to follow Vladimir Monomakh but in the 1140s battles for who would reign violently erupted among them. Nevertheless, distinct branches of the dynasty established their own rule in the major centers of the country outside of Kyiv, such as Halicz, Novgorod, and Suzdal. The princes of these regions politically engaged with each other for control of Kyiv. In 1169 when Andrew Bogolyubsky of Suzdal finally conquered and sacked the city of Kyiv, did a new Rurik Dynasty location emerge. Andrew returned to the Suzdal town of Vladimir and transferred the seat of the Grand Prince to Vladimir instead of Kyiv's barbaric town. Andrew Bogolyubsky's brother Vsevolod III succeeded Andrew as Grand Prince of Vladimir and was to reign from 1176 to 1212. In following the Rurik succession code, Vsevolod's sons Yury ruled from 1212 to 1238; Yaroslav reigned from 1238 to 1246; his third son Svyatoslav from 1246 to 1247, and Vsevolod's grandson Andrew from 1247 to 1252. Andrew's brother, Alexander Nevsky, became the next ruler from 1252 to 1263. As time went by, Alexander's Nevsky's brothers and sons continued the chain of Kingship. The only break in link of Kingship succession was those who refused to move to the City of Vladimir but to create their Regional points of imperial Kingships, such as Alexander's brother Yaroslav who was king from 1264 to 1271, crowned Grand Prince of Vladimir but founded the House of Tver. The House of Moscow created by Alexander's son Daniel.[2]

Alexander Newsky — Courtesy of Alexander Orthodox Russian News

From the period of 1220 to 1263, a man known as a great medieval Russian leader had the name of Alexander Nevsky, who was also the Prince of Novgorod, Grand Prince of Vladimir. He assumed the name Nevsky after he crushed the Swedes on the Neva River in 1240 and invaded Russia from the north. Two years later, he also decisively defeated a branch of the German Teutonic Order or known as the Livonian Brothers of the Sword. On April 5, 1242, on the ice of Lake Peipus, thousands of foot soldiers of Novgorod had surrounded the knights, mounted on horseback and clad in thick armor and their Estonian foot soldiers. Nevsky has achieved a great victory against the Livonian Order. At the same time, a large army of Mongol horseback riders approached from the East. Alexander had great negotiation skills instead of a battle with the Mongols. He gave them land rights and free passage concessions. For his bravery and leadership, the Russian Orthodox Church made him a saint for his support of the Church.[3]

Mongol invasion E Europe – Courtesy of Quora.com

RUSSIA – MONGOLS

The Russian ancestors belonged to Slavic tribes, and in the 9th century, Vikings arrived. The Vikings moved across the vast landscape, utilizing the many waterways, and maintained trade along the way. The Teutonic peoples, characterized by light hair, light skin, blue eyes, tall stature, a narrow nose, and slender body would inter-marry with the dark-skinned and brown-eyed Slavic population. They slowly melted into the Orthodox Greek Christian spiritual influence. The Mongol Khan invaded Russia in 1240, but before 1240, they lived as unofficial occupiers for centuries before any historical sign-post found. The Russian princes had no other choice but to seek a "patent" from the Mongol Khan to rule as Grand Prince. Rivalry for "patent," as well as leadership in the grand principality of Vladimir, developed among the royal houses, particularly those of Tver and Moscow. Gradually, the princes of Moscow became dominant, forming the grand principality of Muscovy.[4] They ruled until in 1598 when no males were available to rule except birth females. Because of the brutality of the Mongols, older cities would stay in ruin, and only then cities of Moscow, Tver, and Nizhny Novgorod grew in importance. The Mongols would dominate the rest of Rus land and rule as they saw fit. The Mongol power slowly grew weak, and by the 14th century, only small pockets of warlike Mongol villages existed. Moscow's power and leadership then began to expand towards the West. However, the Russian's emulated the military tactics of the Mongols and their transportation techniques to win battles. By the 15th Century, Ivan the Great, or referred to as Ivan III, organized the foundation for a Russian national state or the Grand Duchy of Moscow (Muscovy). From 1283 to 1547, Muscovy was to become the Third Rome, and as the Romanov Dynasty grew, the Czar to be Caesar.

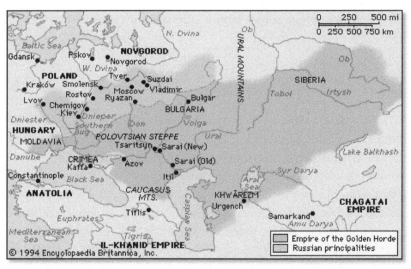

Golden Horde – Courtesy of mongolempirewhap.weebly.com

COAT OF ARMS OF THE RURIK (RYURIK) DYNASTY

As the 1991 Ukraine state emblem, the Trident dates back to Kievan Rus', when it was the coat of arms of the Rurik dynasty. There are various theories about its origins and meaning. A trident was the symbol of Poseidon, the sea god of Greek mythology. It has been found in different societies, such as the Bosporan and Pontic kingdoms, the Greek colonies on the Black Sea, Byzantium, Scandinavia, and Sarmatia, and used in various ways. The coat of arms viewed as a religious and military emblem, a heraldic symbol, a state emblem, a monogram, and merely a decorative design. In 2018, the Ukraine government fell in deniability. Ukraine's origination is Russian. Ukraine has always been Russian until Oligarchs made nationalism into profits.

Ukraine National Logo- Courtesy of pixabay.com

TRIDENT -1ˢᵀ CENTURY CE

The oldest examples of the Trident discovered by archaeologists on Ukrainian territory date back to the 1st century CE (Common Era or AD Anno Domini or AD). At that time, the Trident probably served as a symbol of power in one of the tribes that later became part of the Ukrainian people. The Trident stamped on the gold and silver coins issued by Rus' Prince Volodymyr the Great, who ruled from 980 to 1015. The Prince inherited the symbol from his ancestors as a dynastic coat of arms. He passed it on to his sons; namely, Sviatopolk I, who reigned from 1015 to 1019; Yaroslav the Wise, from 1019 to 1054; Iziaslav Yaroslavych, from 1054 to 1078; Sviatopolk II Iziaslavych, from1093 to 1113), and also Lev Danylovych, who was the monarch from 1264 to 1301. They all used the bi-dent (two prongs) as their coat of arms. Trident was a dynastic coat of arms until the 15th century. Later, replaced as a state emblem with Archangel Michael. In post-2012, it is used by the Ukraine nationalist as a symbol of secular Ukraine.

TRIDENT – A RUS' RELIGIOUS SYMBOL

The Trident also used as a religious symbol in Ukrainian folklore and church heraldry. The Trident appeared on coins but bricks of the Church of the Tithes in Kyiv, dating from 986 to 996. The symbol discovered on the tiles of the Dormition Cathedral in Volodymyr-Volynskyi dated at 1160. Further archeological searchers discovered the Trident on the stones of other churches, castles, and palaces. The Trident used as a decorative element on ceramics, weapons, rings, medallions, seals, and manuscripts. Because of its extensive use in Rus', the Trident evolved in many directions without losing its basic structural design. Variations include Bident or Trident with a cross on one of the arms, or at the side with Trident showing a half-moon. Archeologist researchers found almost two hundred medieval variations on the Trident. During Richard Theodor Kusiolek's meeting with the Minister of Education, the Trident was proudly displayed on the Department of Education building façade outside as well as in the hallways. As the author traveled to other Kyiv government offices, he found the trident prominently displayed and revered by government employees.

JEWISH KINGS OF KHOSARS

According to Artamonov and many other scientists, the Slavic farmers were able to colonize the forest-steppe zone of modern Ukraine under the auspices of the Khazars. The latter protected them from the attack of nomads. The state of Khazaria evolved into a multi-ethnic and multi-confessional state created by the Turks in 650 on the territory of modern Ukraine or the Lower Volga region and the North Caucasus. A well-known archaeologist, Vladimir Petrukhin, speculated that the Khazars provided a peaceful life to the early Slavic inhabitants. Although a point of debate, the Khazars founded the Kyiv city that became the trade route to Germany. According to the Byzantine chronicles of Emperor Constantine, Kyiv founded by the Khazar Turks. The Vizier of the Khazar Khanate Ahmad ibn Kuya founded the border fortress of Samvatas and named the city Samvatas. However, as history is the waterfall of changes, deaths of the Vizier, and the Chief of the Guard of the Khaganate, Samvatas renamed to Kyiv or (Ibn Kuya) '. Nazarbayev's words directly confirmed by the stories of the Byzantine emperor Constantine the God-Bearer and the Arab chronicles of Masudi.

Ukrainian culture appears to characterized by copying the cultures of its neighbors. Thus, the national costumes of Hungarians, residents of Transcarpathia, Moldovans, residents of the Vinnytsia region, Poles, residents of the Lviv region, Romanians, and residents of Bukovina coincide entirely in detail. The native Ukrainian culture is a culture of the Cossacks. Even written in the Hymn of Ukraine that the Ukrainians are not Russian, but Cossack. Cossack culture is a culture of Rusich or a Rus' person. The word "Cossack" is of Turkic origin borrowed from another, already disappeared people, namely, the Khazars. The shaved head and the forelock are, in fact, Khazar borrowing since the Khazars shaved their heads and wore long foreheads before accepting Judaism. The same is true of modern Hasidic Jews who also shave their heads and leave their hair in the form of two bundles. This custom among Ukrainians and Judaic Hasidim came from the time of the Khazar Khaganate. Jewish rabbis require the Hasidim to get rid of pagan vestiges in the form of a chub. However, the Hasidim refer to the fact that the shaved head and the forelock are their offensive symbol, which they inherited from Khazar times, and do not intend to change their historical traditions. Hasidim have agreed to wear two pasas, but not on either side, as the Jews of Israel do, and in the middle, as is customary for Ukrainians or Khazars. The Hasidim have not given up the Khazar tradition to shave their heads, grow a long mustache, and wear wide trousers. Uniqueness is how the Arab authors described the Khazars during the Khazar-Arab war. Authors such as Saveliev, Altshuller, Sholokhov, Evers, Shambarov, and Gumilyov have emphasized that the Ukrainian culture originated from that of the Khazars. Slowly the Eastern Slavs ran away from the Khazars connection and did not seem themselves Jewish but Russian Orthodox Christians. The Ukrainians have a love and hate relationship with their ancestral Khazar and Ukrainian Cossacks roots. If the Gribyanka chronicle has any validity, the Khazars of Ukraine changed little. Instead of Khazars, they are now called Cossacks.

The closest associate of Ivan Mazepa, Hetman Philippe Orlik wrote in his famous manifesto that people of the fighting ancient Ukrainian, which used to be called Khazar, was raised by immortal fame, spacious possessions and knightly honors. Also, Velichko, Archbishop of Belarus Georgy Konisky, points out in his work "History of Rus and Little Russia."[5] In the Poltava region, such names as the Great Kozar, Malaya Kozara, Kozary, Kozarovichi, Kozarovka, the Kozarka River are naming examples of evidence. So, who or what created the people of Ukraine when the Turkic-speaking Khazars-Christians disappeared among the Slavs? The speculation among scholars is that the ruling elite where Jews who followed the rules of Judaism and the rest of the administrative population within the Khazar Khaganate existence were Khazars-Christians. In 2018, the then President of Ukraine Poroshenko spoke in Israel that the "Jews as a nation are the direct creators of Ukraine." According to a census report, the majority of Ukraine's population are ethnic Slavs (Russians). Nevertheless, among those who refer themselves to ethnic Ukrainians, there is a substantial Türkic genetic layer, inherited from Ukraine by the Khazar Khaganate.

KORKA'S TRIBAL CUCUTENI-TRYPILLIAN CULTURE

In 1914, an Austrian politician. Leopold Richard Burgess said that "Our main objective is this war is the long-term weakening of Russia, and therefore if we win, we will set about creating a Ukrainian state independent of Russia." The village of Korak's tribe, many decades descendants, was near the Dniester River that raises in Ukraine, near the city of Drohobych, close to the border with Poland, and flows toward the Black Sea. Its course marks part of Ukraine and Moldova's border, after which it flows through Moldova for 247 miles, separating the bulk of Moldova's territory from Transnistria. It later forms an additional part of the Moldova-Ukraine border, then flows through Ukraine to the Black Sea, where its estuary forms the "Dniester Liman." (Russian Liman (Лиман) adaptation of the Medieval Greek λιμένας limenas). During the Neolithic, the Dniester River was the center of one of the most advanced civilizations on earth. The Cucuteni-Trypillian culture flourished in this area from roughly 5300 to 2600 BC, leaving behind thousands of archeological sites. Their settlements had up to 15,000 inhabitants, making them the first large farming communities in the world, long before Mesopotamian cities.

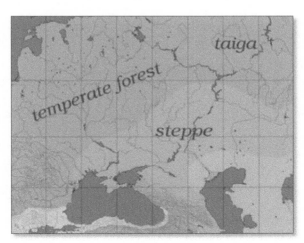

Steppe zone Pontic Caspian climate- Courtesy of borderslynn.com

In antiquity, the Dnieper river was considered one of the principal rivers of European Sarmatia and mentioned by many Classical geographers and historians. According to Herodotus, who wrote about the Greco-Persian Wars, stated the Dnieper rose in a large lake. At the same time, Ptolemy places its sources in Mount Carpates or the Carpathian Mountains, but the naysayer Strabo stated the river's origin unknown. The Dnieper ran in an easterly direction parallel with the Ister (lower Danube) and formed part of the boundary between Dacia and Sarmatia. It fell into the Pontus Euxinus to the northeast of the mouth of the Ister. Greek geographer, philosopher, and historian Strabo who lived in Asia Minor during the transitional period of the Roman Republic into the Roman Empire wrote the distance between them is 130 miles. Scymnus of Chios was a Greek geographer. He was the author of the Periodos to Nicomedes, a work on geography written in Classical Greek that described the Dnieper as easy navigation and abounding in fish.

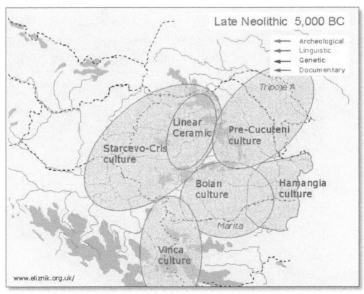

Late Neolithic 5000BC – Courtesy of eliznik.org

MINERAL AND OIL RESOURCE

The landmass known today as Ukraine was a treasure for the waves of Northern and Eastern conquers and oligarchs who exploited the mineral and energy. "Ukraine has rich and complimentary mineral resources in high concentrations and proximity to each other. Rich iron ore reserves located in the vicinity of Kryvyy Rih, Kremenchuk, Bilozerka, Mariupol, and Kerch form the basis of Ukraine's sizeable iron-and-steel industry. One of the wealthiest areas of manganese-bearing ores in the world located near Nikopol. Bituminous and anthracite coal used for coke mined in the Donets Basin. Energy for thermal power stations obtained using the enormous reserves of brown coal found in the Dnieper River basin (north of Kryvyy Rih) and the bituminous coal deposits of the Lviv-Volyn basin. The coal mines of Ukraine are among the deepest in Europe. Many of them considered dangerous because their depth contributes to increased levels of methane. Methane-related explosions have killed numerous Ukrainian miners.

Ukraine has abundant mineral deposits. Ukraine mines titanium, bauxite, nepheline, alunite, and finally mercury (cinnabar, or mercuric sulfide.) A large deposit of ozokerite (a natural paraffin wax) occurs near the city of Boryslav. Subcarpathia possesses potassium salt deposits, and both Subcarpathia and the Donets Basin have large deposits of rock salt. Some phosphorites, as well as natural sulfur, are found in Ukraine. The three major areas producing natural gas and petroleum in Ukraine are the Subcarpathian region, which exploited since the late 19th–early 20th century, and the Dnieper-Donets and Crimean regions have developed since World War II. Following World War II, the extraction of natural gas in Ukraine soared until it accounted for one-third of the Soviet Union's total output in the early 1960s. Natural gas production declined after 1975, however, and a similar pattern of growth and exhaustion occurred with Ukraine's petroleum, ultimately making the republic a net importer of these fuels.

The exploitation of petroleum and natural gas in Ukraine necessitated the creation of an extensive pipeline transport system. One of the first natural gas pipelines in the region opened in the 1920s, linking Dashava to Lviv and then to Kyiv. As a result of the Soviet Union's commitment to significant gas exporting in the late 1960s and early '70s, two trunk pipelines were laid across Ukraine to bring gas to be eastern and western Europe from Siberia and Orenburg in Russia. Petroleum from the Dolyna oil field in western Ukraine is piped some forty miles to a refinery at Drohobych, and oil from fields in eastern Ukraine piped to a refinery in Kremenchuk. Subsequently, more massive petroleum trunk lines added 700 miles to supply petroleum from western Siberia to refineries at Lysychansk, Kremenchuk, Kherson, and Odesa, as well as a 420-mile segment of the Druzhba ("Friendship") pipeline. Friendship pipeline crosses western Ukraine to supply Siberian oil to other European countries. The pipes connecting the Siberian oil and gas fields with Europe are a significant economic asset for Ukraine, as their importance to Russia gives Ukraine leverage in negotiations over oil and gas imports. However, disputes between Ukraine and Russia have previously led the latter to cut off its supply, thus negatively affecting Ukraine temporarily. Ukraine is heavily dependent on fossil fuels and nuclear power for its energy needs. Hydroelectricity accounts for less than ten percent of the country's electricity production, and the contribution of other renewable sources is negligible. Although coal production is substantial, Ukraine relies on imported oil and natural gas to satisfy its energy requirements. Thermal power stations are the largest is in the Donets Basin and along the Dnieper. A third electric energy-producing area is in the vicinity of the Lviv-Volyn coal basin, and in the Transcarpathian region, there is a group of several power stations. Nuclear power stations are located near the cities of Khmelnytskyy, Rivne, and Zaporizhzhya, as well as along the Southern Buh River. The severe nuclear accident at one of the Chernobyl reactors in 1986 triggered a powerful environmental movement in Ukraine and spurred the drive toward political independence from the Soviet Union. The last working reactor at Chernobyl was closed in 2000." Russia decided that it did not have any further responsibility. However, a massive concrete tomb placed over the damaged reactor with EU funding. Expert Serhii Plokhy writes that the town will not be safe for human settlement until 20,000 years have passed.

In 2018, Bulgaria planned to budget $1.59 billion to build a new gas link to Turkey to transport Russian gas from the Turk Stream Pipeline to Europe, bypassing Ukraine to the south. Lawmakers gave the green light to the state gas company Bulgartransgaz to launch tenders to build a new 300-mile gas link that will carry mainly Russian natural gas. The Nord Stream 2 gas pipeline was in construction in 2019 and expected to double the existing pipeline's capacity of 55 billion cubic meters annually, will run from Russia to Germany under the Baltic Sea. Nord Stream will provide transit for 70 percent of Russian gas sales to the European Union. However, the U.S. continues to place sanctions on Germany, which is angered over US plan to expand sanctions on the Nord Stream 2 gas pipeline. US senators controlled by U.S. Oil and Gas lobbyist announced new sanctions on the project in June 2020, saying the pipeline would boost Moscow's influence in Europe. To deprive energy during Europe's severe winters is a form of economic suppression that harms the German and Russian populations.

NEOLITHIC CLANS MIGRATION

As varied peoples migrated from Asia into Europe, Ukraine was first settled by the Neolithic people, followed by the Iranians and Goths, and other nomadic peoples who arrived throughout the first millennium BC. Around 600 BC, the ancient Greeks founded a series of colonies along the shore of the Black Sea, and Slavic tribes occupied large areas of central and eastern Ukraine. Near the end of the 10th century, Vladimir Svetoslav or better known as Vladimir the Great, converted most of the population to Christianity. At that same time, Kiev (Kyiv) was growing into a vital part of Kievan Rus. Kievan Rus was an influential medieval polity or city and the largest in Eastern Europe from the late 9th to the mid-13th century. It eventually disintegrated under the pressure of the Mongol invasion of 1237 and 1240. The Mongol Chinese raiders all but destroyed Kyiv in the 13th century. The Mongols were savage warriors and took few prisoners, so locals often fled to other countries, and Ukrainian settlements soon appeared in Poland and Hungary.

POLISH-LITHUANIAN COMMONWEALTH

Because Poland and Lithuania fought successful wars against the Mongols, most of the territory of what is 21st Century Ukraine was annexed by Poland and Lithuania in the 14th century. Further, following the Polish-Lithuanian Commonwealth (or union), Armenians, Germans, Poles, and Jews immigrated to Ukraine. After the formation of the Commonwealth, Ukraine's landmass became a part of the Kingdom of Poland. Colonization efforts by the Poles were aggressive, social tensions grew, and the era of the Cossacks let to the peasants revolting. The Ukrainian Cossack rebellion and War of independence began in 1648. It sparked an era known in Polish history as "The Deluge," an effort ruined the foundations and stability of the Polish-Lithuanian Commonwealth.

POLAND SOVEREIGNTY BUTCHERED

In the late 1700s, Poland's three powerful neighbors, Austria, Prussia, and Russia wanted to expand into Polish land. None wanted War with each other, so they just decided to divide now-weakened Poland in a series of agreements called the Three Partitions of Poland, and much of modern-day Ukraine integrated into the Russian Empire. In the 19th century, the western region of Ukraine was under the control of the Austro-Hungarian Empire and the Russian Empire elsewhere, and the economy was entirely dependent on its agricultural base. Ukrainians were determined to restore their culture and native language. However, the Russian gGovernment imposed strict limits on attempts to elevate Ukrainian culture, even banning the use and study of the Ukrainian language. When World War I finally ended, many European powers (such as the Austro-Hungarian Empire) ceased to exist. Because the October Revolution broke apart Russia, the Ukrainians now saw an opportunity, and they declared independent statehood.

Unable to protect themselves militarily, the Ukraine landmass was soon fought over by many forces, including Russia's Red Army and the Polish Army. At the end (by treaty), Poland would control land in the far West, while the eastern two-thirds became part of the Soviet Union as the Ukrainian Soviet Socialist Republic. In the 1920s, Ukrainian culture and pride began to flourish once again. However, Joseph Stalin (the Soviet leader) was not pleased, and his Government created an artificial famine, a deliberate act of genocide that by 1932 caused (an estimated) 3 to 7 million peasant deaths. World War II was about to rear its ugly head, as on September 1, 1939, Nazi Germany invaded western Poland. On September 17, 1939, the Soviet Union (in cooperation with Germany) invaded eastern Poland and those of Ukraine lands then controlled by Poland. Soviet troops fought back where they could, but to little or no avail. The German Nazis systematically carried out genocidal policies against Jews and deported others (mainly Ukrainians) to forced labor camps in Germany. Total civilian losses during the German occupation in Ukraine estimated at seven million, including over a million Jews shot and killed by the Einsatzgruppen, a particular SS mobile unit charged with mass murder. Of the estimated eleven million Soviet troops who died in battle against the Nazis, about a fourth (2.7 million) were ethnic Ukrainians. Thus, the Ukrainian nation distinguished as suffering the most significant bloodshed during the brutal War. After World War II, Ukraine remained a part of the Soviet Union, and the Ukrainian SSR (in a deal orchestrated by the US) became one of the founding members of the United Nations (UN) and the Soviets Union and the Byelorussian SSR. Over the next two decades, Ukrainian industries grew and became a symbol of Soviet economic and military power. Ukraine became a Soviet military outpost during the Cold War, crowded by military bases.

CHERNOBYL - 1986

On April 26, 1986, the Chernobyl nuclear plant exploded in the town of Pripyat. The fallout contaminated large areas of northern Ukraine and even parts of Belarus. Chernobyl sparked a (People's Movement) called the "Rukh," a movement that helped expedite the breakup of the Soviet Union during the late 1980s. In the late 1980s, Soviet President Gorbachev introduced policies in Russia to help reduce the corruption at the top of the Communist Party. That is called 'Glasnost' sparked a passionate desire for freedom across The Soviet Union, and in the end, freedom from Communism caused the total collapse of the country in 1991. On August 24, 1991, following the dissolution of the Soviet Union, Ukraine declared itself an independent state. On December 1, 1991, ninety percent of Ukrainian voters approved a referendum formalizing independence from the Soviet Union. In 2014, the Donetsk and Luhansk People's Republics also voted in a similar referendum formalizing independence from the Ukraine- West, but urged to be part of Ukraine as independent "States." Following its independence, Ukraine made many positive moves, including becoming a non-nuclear nation in 1996, when it had nearly 2,000 Soviet-era nuclear warheads dismantled.

SOVIET RED ARMY'S DISASTROUS DEFEAT - 1941

In the summer of 1941, the German Wehrmacht wrought unprecedented destruction on four Soviet armies, conquering central Ukraine and killing or capturing three-quarters of a million men. The Battle of Kyiv Ukraine was one of the largest and decisive battles of the Second World War for Adolph Hitler. However, his powerful panzer tank groups had great battlefield gains, but every tank lost would have consequences for the campaign for the soon upcoming Russian winter. The brave German army won in taking over Kyiv, but it was the historical benchmark that would signify Germany's major losses in the Eastern campaign. The Germans attacked the Soviet Union, which proved in the end to be a bad decision. However, over the next three years, Nazi Germany would control much of Ukraine, and the worst for its long-suffering people was yet to come. The Ukrainians and Soviet troops fought back where they could, but to little or no avail. The German Nazis systematically carried out genocidal policies against Jews and Cossacks and deported Ukrainians to the 1200 forced labor camps in Germany. Total civilian losses during the German occupation in Ukraine estimated at 7 million, including over a million Jews shot and killed by the Einsatzgruppen, a special SS Mobile unit charged with carrying out mass murder. Of the estimated eleven million Soviet troops who died in battle against the Nazis, about a fourth (2.7 million) were ethnic Ukrainians.

Thus, the Ukrainian nation distinguished as suffering the greatest bloodshed during the brutal War. Total civilian losses during the German occupation in Ukraine estimated at 7 million, including over a million Jews shot and killed by the Einsatzgruppen, a special SS mobile unit charged with mass murder.

After World War II, the territory known as Ukraine remained a part of the Soviet Union, and the Ukrainian SSR (i.e., in a deal orchestrated by the US) became one of the founding members

Eeinsatzgruppen Nazi – Courtesy of historyimages.blogspot.com of the United Nations (UN) together with the Soviet Union and the Byelorussian SSR. Over the next two decades, Ukrainian's industries grew and became a symbol of Soviet economic and military power. Ukraine became a Soviet military outpost during the Cold War, crowded by military bases.

Soviet Union – Courtesy of mapsland.com

In the 1970s, the Supreme Soviet Union planned to bring to the people who lived in Ukraine a great inexpensive free energy plant called the Chernobyl. The station is 18 km (11 mi) northwest of the city of Chernobyl, 16 km (9.9 mi) from the border of Ukraine and Belarus, and about 100 km (62 mi) north of Kyiv. Construction of the plant and the nearby city of Pripyat, Ukraine, to house workers and their families began in 1970, with Reactor N. 1 commissioned in 1977. It was the third nuclear power station in the Soviet Union of the RBMK-type (after Leningrad and Kursk), and the first nuclear power plant on Ukrainian soil. The completion of the first reactor in 1977 was followed by reactor N. 2 (1978), N. 3 (1981), and N. 4 (1983). Two more blocks, numbered 5 and 6, of more or less the same reactor design, were planned at a site roughly one kilometer from the contiguous buildings of the four older blocks. Reactor N. 5 was around seventy percent complete at the time of block 4's explosion and scheduled to come online approximately on April 26, 1986. However, the Chernobyl nuclear plant exploded in the town of Pripyat. The fallout contaminated large areas of northern Ukraine and even parts of Belarus. The explosion and radiation contamination of Chernobyl sparked riots and an organized People's Reconstruction Movement that was a catalyst that would lead to the breakup of the Soviet Union during the late 1980s. The anti- Russian Rukh was founded in 1989 by several oligarchs as a civil-political movement as there were no other political parties allowed in the Soviet Union except the Communist Party. The founding of Rukh was made possible due to Mikhail Gorbachev's Glasnost policies or openness policy reforms. President Gorbachev introduced policies in Russia to help reduce corruption at the top of the Communist Party. That move called Glasnost sparked a passionate desire for freedom across The Soviet Union, and in the end, freedom from Communism caused the total collapse of the country in 1991. The translation of "Perestroika" is the restructuring of the Soviet economic model that would allow elements of free-market economics and implemented minor democratic reforms. These reforms allowed Soviet citizens a taste of freedom and led directly to the 1991 fall of Communism and the breakup of the Soviet Union's Centralized planning economy.

Chernobyl accident- Courtesy of rcinet.ca

UKRAINE'S INDEPENDENCE - 1991

President Ronald Reagan, with the approvals of the US Congress and the Department of Defense (DOD), had defense spending reaching $456.5 billion in 1987, compared with $325.1 billion in 1980 and $339.[6] billion in 1981. The conservative view was that high defense spending demonstrates a strong stance against Russian, Korean, and Chinese Communism. On August 24, 1991, following the dissolution of the Soviet Union, Ukraine declared itself an independent state. On December 1, 1991, 90% of Ukrainian voters approved a Referendum formalizing independence from the Soviet Union. The 2014 constitutional referendum was approved by the Donbas Russian speaking citizens of Ukraine to be independent of the Kyiv Ukraine government. The Ukraine 1991 Referendum voting result was 80.34% approval to be free and independent. Following its declared independence, Ukraine made many positive moves, including becoming a non-nuclear nation in 1996, when it had all of its nearly 2,000 Soviet-era nuclear warheads dismantled. Some observers believe that It is a real misnomer that Ukraine was ever an Independent State as it aligned with the European Union (EU), NATO, and the United States' State Department. As seen in 2014, the US State Department under John Kerry and later Hillary Rodham Clinton used monetary and political support to sabotage a Ukraine Presidential Election results and to approve training and to pay Ukrainian military forces during the Donbas War. Those facts well documented under FOIA legal releases by the non-profit Judicial Watch.

UKRAINE'S POLITICAL CIVIL WARS - ORANGE REVOLUTION – 2004

In 2004, did Russian agents disrupt Ukraine's presidential election and trigger the Orange Revolution? A peaceful mass protest called the "Orange Revolution" in the closing months of 2004 forced the authorities to overturn a rigged presidential election and to allow a new internationally monitored vote that swept into power a reformist slate under Viktor Yushchenko. Subsequent internal squabbles in the Yushchenko camp allowed his rival Viktor Yanukovych to stage a comeback in parliamentary elections and become prime minister in August of 2006. In 2010, Yushchenko was constitutionally elected President of the State of Ukraine in a runoff election.

MAIDAN REVOLUTION – 2013

Viktor Yanukovych's presidency abdicated by street violence created by several oligarchs who funded armed militias with help from the Kyiv American State Department officials. Geoffrey R. Pyatt and Victoria Jane Nuland brought financial support and street bloodshed during the Maidan Townsquare Revolt. Some believe that Nuland and Pyatt had a plan to overthrow Yanukovych, who aligned with Ukraine's Russian-speaking population. At the time, the smartphones of Pyatt and Nuland hacked and, without doubt, revealed that they both conspired with pro-American leaders in the Ukraine Duma to remove the President with the street demonstrations-a favorite non-voting method used by the American Progressive Party to create faits accomplis. The same tactic used internationally. For example, on December 8, 2018, socialist brigades or "yellow vests" massed in French cities using violent street protests to overthrow President Emmanuel Macron. The beginning of the "genocide of Russian-speaking Ukrainian citizens" began in Kyiv when President Victor Yanukovych did not agree to open Ukraine to European producers as it would harm Ukraine's economy. Victor Yanukovych felt right so that they could not compete with heavily subsidized EU (European Union). Brussels controlled agricultural exports. President Victor Yanukovych did not agree but postponed the Treaty so that Ukraine could become better prepared before the signing.

Yanukovych's proponents used the EU treaty's postponement as an indication of President Victor Yanukovych's corruption.

To nullify the reform and to regain their power base, Oligarch's, like Poroshenko, organized opposition street riots that they branded "Ukrainian Maidan." The movement appeared to be controlled by the US State Department in Kyiv and initially peaceful. Still, the Oligarchs such as Petro Poroshenko backed the Maidan Revolutionary Movement that eventually became violent and bloody. Senator John McCain flew to Kyiv to openly support the revolution. Also, the Right Nationalist Sector became involved and attacked the police to radicalize the peaceful protesters. The many snipers spotted on the buildings overlooking the square did not wear military uniforms. People on the street who looked up at the roofs of the building could not identify who these shadowy figures wearing black were. The result was that many people died tragically. To save lives, the Ukraine government backed-down and President of Ukraine Victor Yanukovych, the legitimate and constitutionally elected President of Ukraine, was overthrown by the very Ukrainian Oligarchs. The latter stole millions of dollars from the people of Ukraine. To hide that fact, they diverted the people's attention to Victor Yanukovych's life and those of his family. The Right Sector Oligarchs and their paid militia leaders were alleged the tasked to kill Victor Yanukovych and his family. In the dark of night, as assassins were breaking into the Yanukovych compound, they hastily fled for their lives. At eleven in the dark late evening, Victor Yanukovych and his family members were helicopters rescued by President Vladimir Putin of the Russian Federation. The home of Former Ukraine President Victor Yanukovych that is now an Azov Right Sector museum outside of Kyiv Ukraine. Admission to see the house is five US dollars, and far-right sector militias surround the compound. The new leaders of Ukraine, selected by the United States, also postponed the signing of the Treaty with the EU, which would open Ukraine to European goods with the same reasoning as Yanukovych. The EU Trade

Treaty was just an excuse to mobilize the people to maintain the Oligarchs' financial holdings and power.

Home Ukraine President Yanukovych- Courtesy of Richard Kusiolek

Still, the EU wanted Ukraine to open up to European goods and to bring Ukraine into their "orbit" and did not care what it would do to the Ukrainian economy. The Europeans and the United States came to Kyiv to take over Ukraine's resources for future development. Donbas was the critical area for supplies that the billionaire developers like the sons of former Secretary of State John Kerry and Democratic Party power broker Joseph Biden and Barak Hussein Obama's Vice President of the United States.

DONBAS CIVIL WAR - 2014

After a referendum in Donbas, Eastern Ukraine (similar to the Referendum that Ukraine used to break away from Russia), Kyiv responded by sending in Ukraine soldiers trained by the elite US Army Special Forces. Also, Right Sector Militias, and Ukrainian National Guardsmen and women marched into Eastern Ukraine.

In 2014, a civil war broke out between the Industrial resource-rich East and the Agricultural West. Extensive reporting revealed that US President Barak Obama's US State Department staff operatives were involved. The apparent goal to create an anti-Russian Kyiv Government with NATO and European Union political, military, and economic integration. By 2017, Ukraine's political strategy was an overall forward push away from the East and toward the West. The country is heavily involved in European political and military training programs. Ukraine gained gaining funding from the EU Central Bank, $5billion from the USA, World Bank, and receiving arms from NATO countries that included the US Military. On June 20, 2017, the Wall Street Journal reported that President Donald Trump met briefly with Ukrainian leader Petro Poroshenko, a Billionaire, Oligarch, and Commander of Nationalist Battalions attacking civilians in Russian-speaking Donbas. Poroshenko used his first United States' White House visit to stress his country's alliance with Washington. He pushed for more US pressure against Moscow's support of pro-Russian "terrorist" in Ukraine. However, from 2014 to 2018, hundreds of YouTube videos depicted Donbas as a war zone. Eastern Ukrainians mothers, fathers, children, babies, and grandparents subjected to daily bombarded of their corrugated and flimsy residential areas, schools, food, grocery stores, and energy plants by T-64 tanks, BM-30 Smerch launchers, and 2S7 Pion artillery units. Both U.S. and European officials expressed frustration over a lack of progress in implementing a Minsk peace plan for Eastern Ukraine that had been brokered in 2014 and 2015 in the Belarus capital of Minsk with the help of European mediators. On July 7, 2017, according to CNN, the US State Department paid Kurt Volker to be its Special Representative for Ukraine. Volker tasked with advancing US efforts to achieve the objectives of the 2014 Minsk agreements between Ukraine and Russia. However, Europeans and Americans refused to send a Special Ambassador to the Donbas region where the killings were occurring to negotiate for peace and to grant the Region Autonomy but still under the control of Kyiv's Oligarch Administrators.

MINSK AGREEMENTS -2014 AND 2015

On September 5, 2014, Ukraine, the Russian Federation, the Donetsk People's Republic (DPR), and the Luhansk People's Republic (LPR) signed the Minsk Protocol, an agreement to halt the war in the Donbas region of Ukraine that created sixty percent of the economic wealth for Ukraine. The Minsk Protocol contained twelve points, as follows:

1. Ensure an immediate bilateral ceasefire.
2. Ensure the monitoring and verification of the ceasefire by the OSCE.
3. A Decentralization of power
4. Ensure the permanent monitoring of the Ukrainian-Russian border and confirmation by the OSCE with the creation of security zones in the border regions of Ukraine and the Russian Federation.
5. Immediate release of all hostages and illegally detained persons.
6. A law is preventing the prosecution and punishment of areas of Donetsk and Luhansk Oblasts.
7. Continue the inclusive national dialogue.
8. Take measures to improve the humanitarian situation in Donbas.
9. Ensure early local elections under the Ukrainian law "On temporary Order of Local Self-Governance in Particular Districts of Donetsk and Luhansk Oblasts."
10. Withdraw illegal armed groups and military equipment as well as fighters and mercenaries from the territory of Ukraine.
11. Adopt economic recovery and reconstruction for the Donbas region.
12. Provide personal security for participants in the consultations.

Fundamental tenets of the so-called Minsk Agreement included holding local elections in Ukraine's breakaway Donbas region and returning the border with Russia to Ukrainian control. Many voices expressed fears that Kyiv had no intention of sticking to the Minsk Agreement because the War that they fostered and the killing of their citizens allowed "free money flows" into the Ukraine country. In a way, for the oligarchs, the made-up Civil War is the "huge honeypot" for the European and American corporations who see a vast devastated landmass that they can develop for their products and services thus creating millions of jobs in their respective countries. Minsk II agreed to on February 12, 2015, but the fighting continued with more significant destruction and deaths. As of 2021, twelve Minsk Protocols not followed, and the death toll from five years of the War was over 10,550 in 2019.

UKRAINE'S HISTORICAL CORRUPTION CULTURE

One of the highest motives for Ukrainians to rise against the Government was "perceived corruption." The US State Department Propaganda Media Department wrote that President Victor Yanukovych as a "greedy embezzler" who used his position to amass vast chests of wealth for his family and allies by seizing the assets of his political and business rivals. The new Maidan authorities promised to fight endemic corruption relentlessly. While some reforms did occur, even close to Kyiv, allies such as US Vice President Joe BIDEN, said that not enough improvement realized. Also, when Mikheil Saakashvili became a governor of Odesa, he noted that Ukraine had a culture of corruption at the highest levels. Transparency International's latest report on corruption in Europe ranks Ukraine as one of the worst nations on all fronts. According to 86 percent of Ukrainians, their Government is performing "badly' or very poorly" in fighting corruption. Ukraine's percentage was the worst rating among all EU countries polled.

In 2017, the European Union (EU} puppet masters forced all Ukrainian officials to declare their property in a public database. In a state where the average monthly income languishes at around 200 dollars, lawmakers, judges, prosecutors, and other figures of power disclosed ownership of numerous apartments and luxury cars, antiquities and holy relics, designer watches, and vintage wines. According to Heritage Foundation, in 2018, with a population of 42.3 million, high taxes, and inflation, Ukraine has an oligarch-dominated economy that declined before Russia's 2014 occupation of Crimea and ongoing aggression in the eastern part of the country severely damaged economic growth. Significant progress was made on reforms to make the country more prosperous, democratic, and transparent. More improvements are needed, including fighting corruption, developing capital markets, privatizing state-owned enterprises, and improving the legislative framework and the rule of law. Public enthusiasm for Western reforms has waned, however, as economic stagnation continues from 2014 to 2021.[6] The momentum for business reform stalled, and political instability with waring political parties made regulatory uncertainty in large commercial transactions. Ukraine had a well-educated and skilled labor force, but the labor code is old-fashioned and not enforced consistently. In 2019, many of those educated left Ukraine, leaving their grandparents and families destitute without monthly stipends from their children. The Government has reduced energy subsidies and is ending some special tax breaks for agriculture. At the same time, the Ukraine government uses the global media to create the possibility of war with the Russian Federation.

In 2018, US President Donald Trump asked the newly elected Ukraine President Zelensky to investigate Biden's family's corruption activities. In 2020, 2% of all Ukraine companies owned by public officials or linked to oligarchs, like former President Petro Oleksiyovych Poroshenko and Igor Kolomoisky. Oligarchs control 10% of Ukraine's corporate revenue. According to the 2018 World Bank Study, more than 26% of all Ukraine corporate assets owned by wealthy families. In 2020, Transparency International places the country 126th out of 180 countries known for corruption and bribery.

AMERICAN POLITICAL OLIGARCHS

In March 2014, then President Obama nominate Vice President of the USA, Joe Biden, as his administration's "point man" for Ukraine policy. In April 2014, Vice President Biden uses his power to ensure that his son is an extended director in the Ukrainian energy company, Burisma Holdings. The former Secretary of State, John Kerry, anti-Vietnam War street demonstration organizer, and Democratic President Obama's Secretary of State from 2013 to 2017 ensured his stepson, Chris Heinz, to join the same Ukraine company. According to The Wall Street Journal, that his appointment came a few weeks after Devon Archer, a college roommate of the Secretary of State's stepson (H.J. Heinz's Ketchup heir). Christopher Heinz joined the Burisma board to help the gas firm attract US investors, improve its corporate governance, and expand its operations. Documents exist that Hunter Biden and Archer each received in excess of $83,000 a month ($1 million a year) from Burisma for their services.

"At the beginning of the 2014 Donbas Civil War, Ukrainian President Poroshenko called it the "War of Dignity," President Poroshenko unleased a savage artillery and tank attack on the Eastern Region of Ukraine. Joseph Biden, former Democratic Party operative and Vice President of the United States, had his son appointed as a Counsel to Boies, Schiller, Flexner, LLP, a US national law firm based in New York. Mr. Hunter Biden received an Adjunct Professorship at Georgetown University's Master's Program within the School of Foreign Service. He served as Chairman of the Board of World Food Program USA and as a Director on the not-for-profit Board of the Center for National Policy, the Truman National Security Project, and the US Global Leadership Coalition. Mr. Hunter Biden became a member of the

Center for Strategic and International Studies (CSIS) Executive Council on Development, the Chairman's Advisory Board for the National Democratic Institute, and the President's Advisory Board for Catholic Charities in Washington DC. From 2006 to 2009, Mr. Hunter Biden, served on the Board of Directors of Amtrak, serving as Vice Chairman from 2007 to 2009. Mr. Hunter Biden honored to serve as an Honorary Co-Chair of the 2009 Presidential Inaugural Committee and served in the Jesuit Volunteer Corps. Previously, Mr. R. Hunter Biden was a founding member of the law firm Oldaker, Biden and Belair, LLP, and then appointed by President Bill Clinton to serve as Executive Director of E-Commerce Policy Coordination under Secretary of Commerce William Daley and was a Senior Vice President at MBNA America Bank. He became a Member of the Bar in the State of Connecticut, the District of Columbia, the US Supreme Court and the US Court of Federal Claims. Mr. R. Hunter Biden received a Bachelor's degree from Georgetown University and a JD from Yale Law School.[7]

Biden Family- Courtesy of freerepublic.com

PATHWAY OF INFLUENCE AND COLLUSION

In 2014, Hunter Biden executive at Kyiv Ukraine based Burisma Holdings to provide an open door of influence for USA investors. The goal to take over the Ukrainian gas production business and hope to no longer rely on Russian Gas and Oil reserves of reserves and resources of 800 million BOE (Barrels of Oil). On a video at a conference in America, VP Biden boasted that he would withhold six billion USDs in funding if Ukraine's President Petro Poroshenko did not fire the prosecutor investigating Burisma Holdings.

All of this activity of the sons of right place Washington DC Government Democratic Party oligarch officials placed on an inside track to allow them a fertile field to gain wealth from the misery of the Russian Speaking Citizens of Ukraine. Europeans are also at the same "horse feeding trough" to acquire wealth once the reconstruction dollars unleashed after the dead bodies removed under the rubble of Donbas's destroyed peasant villages and cities. In 2017, Kathleen Biden's divorce filings revealed that "...(Hunter) he spent lavishly on his interests including, "drugs, alcohol, prostitutes, strip clubs, and gifts for women with whom he has sexual relations ... his habits have depleted are funds available to pay legal bills ... and adds they've maxed out credit cards, have second mortgages on two properties, and more than $300k in unpaid taxes." In 2017, former Democrat Secretary of State John Kerry and former Vice President of the United States of America had close connections to Ukraine's political elites and arranged for their sons to have high management positions in the Ukrainian oil and gas companies.

The Hill is an American political newspaper and website published in Washington, DC. The Hill is published by Capitol Hill Publishing, which is owned by News Communications, Inc. On April 2, 2019, The Hill published that former Vice President of America and Presidential 2020 candidate Joseph BIDEN threatened the Ukrainian Government starting in 2015. Further, Ukrainian officials said that Shokin had been conducting a wide-ranging corruption probe into natural gas firm Burisma Holdings at the time. Joseph Biden's son Hunter, a lawyer, DC Washington lobbyist, was a member of the Burisma Oil and Gas Board and received a series of payments from the gas company. Shokin confirmed to the Hill that he had plans to conduct "interrogations and other crime-investigation procedures into all members of the executive board, including Hunter Biden," before he fired from the direct request by Hunter's father. In 2018, Yury Lutsenko, re-opened the Burisma case. According to The Hill, members of the Burisma board and Rosemont Seneca Partners had obtained funds for "consulting services," he told the Hill. Burisma paid $50,000 to $80,000 per month or over $3 million to an account linked to Hunter Biden's investment firm, Rosemont Seneca Partners, between April 2014 and October 2015. Financial records filed in a separate Manhattan federal court file revealed that Rosemont Seneca Partners usually received two transfers of $83,333 a month from Burisma. On the same days, the account then paid Hunter one or more payments ranging from $5,000 to $25,000. Hunter's Partner Devon Archer also received Burisma's checks. Hunter Biden, as well as the stepson of John Kerry, was elected to the Board of Directors for Burisma but were unqualified as they both knew nothing about the international natural gas business in Ukraine. Many speculate that former VP Biden enriched himself in the PRC by using his son as a recipient bank depositor for his father.

BURISMA HOLDINGS – DC INSIDERS

In 2017, Joseph Coffer Black and Karina Zlochevska, former members of the DC Defense lobby group, Atlantic Council, were appointed to the board of directors for Burisma Holding LTD. The Atlantic Council of Washington DC provides "experts" who are from other war sovereign nations of Syria, Libya, Iraq, Afghanistan, and Ukraine. On their website, it states, "The Atlantic Council Members Program brings together individuals committed to addressing the host of emerging challenges and opportunities facing the Atlantic Community today. Its members are some of the best ambassadors, bringing awareness of our work to governments, multilateral organizations, NGOs, and the private sector. This DC lobby group pushes the narrative of the US State Department that "Ukraine continues to experience historic transformation since the 2014 Revolution of Dignity. While the country faces numerous political and economic challenges, Ukraine's potential as an investment destination is immense: Ukraine is one of the largest markets in Europe with a great capacity of natural and human resources. Thus, the creation of favorable development conditions for the business environment in Ukraine is one of the most urgent tasks of the Government."

US CENTRAL INTELLIGENCE AGENCY (CIA) -POLITICAL COLLUSION

In 2016, Joseph Cofer Black appointed as a Director of Burisma Holding LTD. According to the Burisma executive leadership internet website, "Black has strong credentials from the USA intelligence community."Black probably has connections to the work that the CIA, in conjunction with the former US Ambassador to Ukraine and former US State Department Deputy, Victoria Nuland, who were involved in the President of Ukraine's ouster. Cofer Black was the "former Director of the CIA's Counterterrorist Center (1999-2002) Ambassador at Large for counterterrorism (2002-2004)." According to John Kiriakou, Cofer Black was head of counterterrorism for the entire world. Black focused on al-Qaeda before the attack on the NY World Trade Towers. He often visited the White House, working with Condoleezza Rice, the National Security Advisor to President George W. Bush and Richard Clarke, the counterterrorism coordinator in the U.S. White House. During the aftermath of the destruction of the twin towers, Cofer Black spoke at the Langley Virginia CIA headquarters, "We're at war, a different kind of war than we've ever fought before, whether the country realizes it yet or not ... I'm sorry to say this now, but we have to get used to the idea that some of us are going to die, but we have to do whatever we can to bring these people to justice. -That combination of truth-telling and his willingness to take risks set Cofer Black apart from others at the (CIA) agency and inspired the rest of us to believe in him and want to follow his lead."

In Ukraine, Mr. Black is an internationally recognized authority on counterterrorism, cybersecurity, national security, and foreign affairs, with private sector experience and expertise in international business development and strategy, particularly in the Middle East and Africa. Ambassador Black conceived and executed highly productive programs of global significance in a government career spanning thirty-year and serving at the highest levels of the CIA and the State Department, possessing steady, successful, stand-alone leadership in times of crisis and adversity, and a unique ability to assess.[9] Since Mr. Black retired from public service in 2005, he has been providing strategic advice to several global companies regarding business development and market risk assessments. In particular, Mr. Black served as Vice Chairman at Blackwater Worldwide (aka Academi) and Chairman of Total Intelligence Solutions (Total Intel).

In 2018, the CIA publicly acknowledged that it could intercept all global electronic messages of world leaders and everyday citizens. In 2018, the spy agency revealed that it had hard evidence that the Saudi Arabia Crown Prince had a personal interest in the Washington Post journalist Jamal Khashoggi. When the international spy agency makes an assessment, it is rarely a black or white issue, often relying on bits and pieces of data gathered clandestinely.

Trade Craft of Overthrowing Presidents of Sovereign States

The US spent $5 Billion to sponsor the Ukraine anti-government protest. US State Department, working with its CIA assigned agents, planned overthrowing many foreign states-Vietnam President Diem, Libyan President Ghadafi, Syrian President Assad, Cuban President Castro, Panama President Noreiga, Iran Mohammad Reza Shah Pahlavi, Iraq Saddam

Hussein Abd al-Majid al-Tikriti, and Yugoslavia Serbia president Slobodan Milošević. Assistant Secretary of State for European and Eurasian Affairs at the United States Department of State Victoria Nuland, Ambassador to Ukraine Geoffrey Ross Pyatt, Secretary of State John Kerry, and Senator John McCain openly "sponsored" the militia groups" to continue their violence against the Ukraine government. Due to telephone recordings, proven that the US State Department voiced her selection of post-Maidan Government leaders.[10]

The CIA had a long record of removing sovereign leaders and with that experience of tradecraft. In 2016, they targeted the Presidential Campaign of a businessman running for office. Working with the FBI, DOJ, and foreign intelligence agencies, unauthorized wiretapped the mobile and wired phones of the Donald J. Trump campaign. From 2016 to 2020, the CIA politically directed agents continued to record conversations that President Trump had with world leaders. As a result, the Speaker of the US House of Representatives and the DNC members set up a strategy and legislative tactics to remove a duly elected American President. In 2015, they hired Alexandra Chalupa, a Jewish Ukraine Nationalist, to tie Paul Manafort to pro-Russian politicians in Ukraine as far-right militias were killing Russian speaking Ukraine citizens in the Donbas. Chalupa worked with the staff of Washington Ukraine Embassy to have then President of Ukraine Poroshenko to discuss Manafort's lobbying in Ukraine. Olga Bielkova, a member of the Ukraine RADA and a paid DNC lobbyist, met dozens of Democratic Party Congressional members, plus with reporters from the two newspapers that were leftist DC propaganda newspapers, one owned by the founder of Amazon, and the New York Times. Chalupa also worked with Marcy Kaptur-Rogowski, a Democrat Jewish Ukraine activist, "reportedly discussed holding a possible congressional investigation or hearing on Manafort and Russia ..." Chalupa reached out to another Jew, Michael R. Isikoff, an investigative journalist who worked with Yahoo News and published anti-President Donald J. Trump. The book titled Russian Roulette: The Inside Story of Putin's War on America and the Election of Donald Trump, posted on March 13, 2018.

After months of covert surveillance, the FBI could not make a case and dropped the probe. Later, for purely political reasons, he was sentenced to prison for financial fraud convictions obtained by a politically motivated special counsel, Robert Mueller, as he investigated Manafort's alleged collusion with the Russian Government in 2016. Individuals associated with President Donald J. Trump, namely, Paul Manafort, Michael Cohen, Michael Flynn, Roger Stone, George Papadopoulos, and Rick Gates. Robert Mueller completed his 3yrs of investigations and at the cost of $twenty-five to thirty million dollars, without zero indictment of CIA Director John Brennan, James Comey, Lisa Page, Bruce Orr, Peter Strzok and many others. Intelligence and counter-intelligence US and Foreign operatives worked, like in a Soviet kangaroo court of 1930 to 1940, to simply violate the US Constitution and ally with corporate media sponsors to create a "fog of political war" over the truth. The Democratic National Committee (DNC) then used ridiculous diversions to hide their alleged efforts to overthrow the American electorate.

Sen McCain & Murphy Maidan support – Courtesy of bostonglobe.com

Former US Senator John McCain announced that he had non-curable brain cancer. He traveled to Ukraine and stood with the Nazi Right Sector Maidan leaders. He voiced his verbal pledges and millions of US taxpayer dollars in Congressional funds to support the bloody overthrow of a duly elected Ukraine President. The first act of the "Revolutionary Verkhovna Rada Parliament" was to repeal the law giving language rights to all Russian-speaking citizens. Since the majority of Russian speaking Ukrainian citizens living in the Donbas, the people came out to protest the central Government to respect their rights. The people of South-Eastern Ukraine wanted to become a Federation that would provide local and Federal Kyiv governance. Many countries have this form; namely, Brazil, India, Canada, German, the USA, and many others. George Washington was a Federalist, but in Ukraine, the President appoints all the governors in each region, and the people of Ukraine do not have a vote on his selection. People in Odesa, Kharkiv, Donetsk, Lugansk, and Melitopol (Melitopol is a city in Zaporizhia Oblast of southeastern Ukraine) do not have a vote to select their leaders. Instead, the Governor, who is elected by the President of Ukraine, selects those that will represent the people. It is clear that Ukraine is not a democracy, but still, a feudal state ruled by a few billionaires who control all aspects of Ukraine's political, economic, and cultural life. On November 25, 2018, Melitopol situated on the Molochna River that flows through the eastern edge of the city and into the Molochnyi Liman, which eventually joins the Sea of Azov gained global press coverage when a "Gulf of Tonkin" Ukraine naval incident was created in the Sea of Azov.

Melitopol Ukraine map- Courtesy of Worldgeorgraphy.org

KYIV'S STRATEGY -TWO MILLION RUSSIAN -SPEAKING POPULATION

Citizens stood with peaceful protest to become a Federation and to have the protection of minority rights. Kyiv completely ignored their complaint and branded them "separatist terrorist." Soon after urging of NATO, the U.S. Obama Progressive Party arranged for the President of Ukraine, Petro Poroshenko. As the Military Commander, this billionaire sent in the Ukraine Army to shell the poor villagers and significant towns of Donbas. In 2013, Kyiv's President Poroshenko would not negotiate with the Donbas Russian-speaking peoples. Instead, Poroshenko declared the entire Donbas Region a "terrorist region." Kyiv began to send in SU-35 fighter jets, tanks, and massive artillery units to attack Eastern Ukraine's regional population and their leaders as if they were members of an (ISIS) terrorist government. This strategy allowed the US Government then to provide Ukraine funds in their "War on Terror." The water, electricity, road, and airport transportation infrastructures destroyed, and over

12,901 civilians killed both elderly grandparents, men, women, and children. Global news organizations reported Kyiv's Central Government had civilians kidnaped, tortured, and died, local residential areas targeted, and innocent pensioners destroyed with high explosive shells that sent pieces of metal shrapnel into their bodies. Anyone who did not obey the Kyiv Government directives and the demands of the Army soldiers' instructions were kidnapped, beaten, and released only to find their homes ransacked and burned. (footnote: the US State Department appeared to support this strategy to validate that this was also part of the global war on terrorism)

DONBAS'S FREEDOM FIGHTERS

The people of Donbas organized and tried to defend their homes and themselves. At the beginning of 2014, over 4 million lived in the Donbas Region. After the horrors inflicted upon them, Donbas's peoples cried for unity against Kyiv's anti-Russian brutality. On May 11, 2015, most of the Donbas people voted in a Democratic referendum, with Western observers. Then local activists declared a Republic that was structured precisely like the 1991 Ukrainian Independence Referendum. However, they did not profess to be separate from Kyiv and sought to again negotiate with Kyiv. The Donbas' goal for the Region and the Democratic Republics was to have equal rights under the Ukrainian Constitution. Ukrainian President Poroshenko, received massive monetary resources of the US Congress, Central European Bank, and the World Bank. Poroshenko sent in Kyiv's Right Sector National Guard, and both Nationalist Aidar and Azoz Battalions to take over the Donbas Region with deadly random killing and brutal force. These events documented in France 24 and RT (Russian owned TV).

Ukraine rightest militias — Courtesy of sputniknews.com

The Army, backed by the individual Western Government Powers (Germany, France, UK, Italy, US) and NATO's Secretary-General Jens Stoltenberg, began random artillery barrages resulting in many deaths of Donbas Russian-speaking citizens. The citizens of Eastern Ukraine had no choice but to take up arms, as the US Minutemen colonialist did to protect their lands. As in the US Revolutionary War, when the colonists sought weapons and aid from France, the peoples of Donbas sought weapons and assistance from Russia and any other country to help them. As they pleaded for mercy and slowly determined that their grandparents, wives, children would not be slaughtered, the Mass Media of Europe and the USA labeled them as "terrorist or pro-separatist" when they were, in reality, defending their land and their families. The elitist corporations that control the mass media labeled these poor peasants defending their lands as Radical Soviet Communists. Propaganda is the same methodology that any Nation seeks to steal the resources of another user throughout history, namely, label them as enemies of the State. In 2017, the same people who are fighting on the front lines between the Kyiv

Oligarch's militias and European Union (EU) trained, armed, and paid Kyiv Army, were labeled as "freedom fighters" as many from around the world came to help these peasants and coal miners. The "Donbas irregulars" fought against Kyiv's repression and for their lands, homes, and their families. The Donbas people did not come to Kyiv to wage War; instead, Kyiv began to wage war on civilians who had no other option but to take up arms against Kyiv's tyranny. Indiscriminate shelling is why they took up arms to fight the massive Kyiv Army that came against them without warning on a foggy early morning.

DShk Soviet Heavy Weapon – Courtesy of military-today.com

KORKA'S - TAKING UP DEFENSIVE ARMS

Lyudmila Korka, daughter of Minister, Arsian (Lion) Korka, was one of those eastern Ukrainians who suffered so much during the Civil War. Lyudmila Korka was a Tatarochka and Russian by a mixed nationality, but she taught to speak only Russian by her parent, Olga, and Arslan or Lion. Lyudmila graduated from

English language courses, but soon drifted away as she could not stay proficient without speaking every day and she almost forgot the language. She studied at the Lukansk college in economic education and worked in the Sberbank in downtown Donetsk. By March 1, 2016, the severe fighting began, and she no longer had a job. Ukrainian President Petro Poroshenko imposed sanctions on five banks with Russian capital functioning in Ukraine. Ukraine's' Presidential Oligarch Poroshenko signed a decree introducing sanctions on Sberbank, VS Bank, Prominvestbank, VTB Bank, and BM Bank for ten years. Due to the closing of so many stores and offices, over two million workers lost their jobs and joined the Donetsk and Lugansk Army Minute Volunteers or DLAMV.

Without a job and unable to support her two sons, Lyudmila joined the Donetsk People's Forces to protect the young republic of Donetsk from the brutal Western Ukraine Oligarch's funded Right Sector Nationalist militias. The Battle of the Donetsk Airport was to provide the Kyiv Oligarchs the ability to fly in supplies and use the airfield for fighter and bomber aircraft. The Donetsk Brigade Commander Bohuslav Uman and orders to defend the Airport from being run-over by the Kyiv forces were again demanding over the phone that he needed some fire support on the second floor of the airport' main second floor. Immediately, running towards the Airport were six freedom fighters, one woman carrying the massive World War II DShK 1938 (a Soviet heavy machine gun firing the 12.7×108mm cartridge), three lugging heavy machine guns, two were holding RPGs. All six of the fighters had sidearms, and each of the six carried an AK-47 over their backs.

As the Ukraine militia soldiers began to mount a substantial advance, they met with a blast of concentrated firepower. Lyudmila was the gunner and held it steady until a sniper bullet ripped open a gaping hole in her shoulder. She dropped her hand from the firing mechanism and laid sideways bleeding faster than expected. She would soon bleed out unless help arrived. Commander Bohuslav Uman ran up the stairs and pulled Lyudmila back from the machine gun.

"Here, I will patch you up, and I am going to tie this tourniquet on that shoulder." They looked at each other. "My God, it is you, Lyudmila. I have encountered so many false ear whisperers of illusionary inner truth about you. I thought that I would never see you. Your words last night, and your voice will convince me that you are God's stillness to love again with you. I know not, but I will open the entrance to the tunnel that leads to our re-births."

Lyudmila's bleeding shoulder wound would require some stitching up. Lyudmila was not a woman who would complain about pain. She had so much to say after their passionate night in the small wooden cabin that they had to themselves two days ago.

"Dear Bohuslav, I am thrilled that you chose to write to me. What you tell me, I feel and imagine. Your words are so easy, soft, calm. I read and reread them line by line, again and again. I catch myself thinking that very quickly and unexpectedly entered my life. But I was waiting for you. Or, to be more precise, I came up with an unknown image that suits me, and I like it. You are very similar to this image that lived in my head, in my thoughts. And now I'm even a little confused. I think that it does not happen; it cannot be that everything is so perfect. I'm just afraid to believe what's happening to me. I already believed you. I began to fall in love with you. Quickly it happened to me, right? Hence, my time has come."

Lyudmila held Bohuslav's neck and drew it closer to see his blue eyes and whispered,

"We will all leave this world someday, and therefore we should appreciate and rejoice at every day that we have. You know it well. It was a bright memory for those who are not with us today. Eternal memory to them! Many things happen in adult life, which children cannot understand. When parents stop living together, this is one of them. I did not experience this. My parents were workers and lived their lives together. I knew that there are different families, but it was very far from my understanding. I just never thought about it. And therefore, like a bolt from the blue fires of ice, for me, it was the fact that I had to live alone and solve all the problems. I had no right to drop my hands and cry. When I left my husband after he beat my sons, I realized that this is not the end of the world and that the lives of other people close to me will depend on me. I think that I did the right thing, and I have nothing to blame myself. I think that those children who, at an earlier age, face life's difficulties. If they are lucky, they become more seasoned in this difficult life. They do not have much to rely on anyone, and they only rely on themselves. And I think that they are more successful in life when they grow up. In general, I understand now that everyone has their own life, and everyone has differences."

Commander Bohuslav Uman gently moved his head away and allowed Lyudmila to lay on her back, staring at the ceiling with broken wires hanging down like the feet of a one thousand Daddy Long-Leg Spiders. She took a deep breath and began to speak to Bohuslav Uman.

"Dear, the fact that you live for a long time, I perceive this. You wanted so much to live, or perhaps you were afraid to build a strong relationship or was afraid to take on obligations or did not trust the woman who was near or was very picky about the choice of his wife. You have many reasons, and you only know them. Maybe you like to live alone. I do not know. I only know about me, I will never break a comfortable life for a man, if he does not want to change something in his life. There are many Russian expressions on this subject, but I'll write you an English one. You should know it, which is very close to me regarding a general worldview."

With that final word, blood began to ooze out of Lyudmila, and suddenly the shock of the bullets entering her body was too much for her five-foot 3inch frame. She was dead, and all Bohuslav Uman could do was to cry uncontrollably. This woman who he had met just a few short days ago was dying in his arms. He would never feel the warm body of Lyudmila Korka as they laid together in his dacha, or would he ever again fall asleep listening to her slow melodic breathing. His squad of Donetsk fighters entered the Donetsk Airport and, with great reverence, lifted Lyudmila's body and walked to a waiting ambulance. The first female fighter of the Donetsk People's Republic had died fighting for Land, Love, and Liberty.

WAR OF WORDS AND ARTILLERY

Kyiv's Propaganda Ministries worked with US and NATO intelligence to create a media narrative that Russia had massed one hundred tanks to take over Ukraine. Many experts believed that everything that Kyiv's Poroshenko creates is a ploy to bring forth substantial re-development investments to line the pockets of the one percent who live in unbridled wealth in the suburbs of Kyiv. Reality never makes for media drama, as shown in the fabrication of James Comey lies and Hillary Clinton dossier against US President Donald J. Trump. There was no Russian Army in Donbas but only ordinary retirees, and unemployed coal miners and truck drivers who took up any arms that they could find. Poroshenko's owned Kyiv-based Channel 5TV and radio blasted daily news that the Russian Army was massing and coming to invade Ukraine-it was another media drama moment for his need for global media attention.

A sitting American Senator on CSPAN2 showed a 60 square poster board picture of Russian tanks entering Eastern Ukraine. The photo was a Russian tank column photographed over ten years ago. However, that did not stop the former Senator John McCain stomping around the Senate floor attacking any angle that would make Russia the "Nation of Evil Aggression." The people in Eastern Ukraine fought for their rights and freedom. Senator John McCain refused to resign because of his terminal brain cancer, and he continued to rant and rave about Russia the aggressor in Ukraine.

On May 2, 2014, Odessa unionist who were peacefully protecting themselves and sought shelter from the Oligarch's paid terrorist, were without any concern from the police, burned alive as right sector party members shot anyone escaping the flame. The running joke in Kyiv's Ministries was that they had a "May Day barbeque." Indeed, the USA State Department in Kyiv and Government did not protest the Odesa murders. (footnote: US Senator, Vietnam navy pilot, and military hero John Sidney McCain passed away August 25, 2018, in Cornville Arizona)

Odesa Ukraine Union Hall burning- Courtesy of RT.com

In 2015, Ukrainian appointed President Poroshenko declared an embargo on all goods going into the Donbas Region to starve the remaining 1.2million inhabitants. -no medicine, no food, no heat, no warm clothing. In World War Two, over 2million Ukrainians killed by the German Armies as they employed high speed and forced marching through Ukraine on their objective Moscow Russia. Adolf Hitler, a German politician, leader of the Nazi Party, and rising to power in Germany as Chancellor in 1933 and Führer (leader) in 1934 used brutal tactics against the Ukrainian serfs by depriving them of medicine, food, and warm shelter to have them accept Nazi occupation. However, Slavic Ukrainians who did not join the Nazi SS fought as partisans, those who did not were enlisted as German camp guards and given military uniforms.

CANDY OLIGARCHS

In 2016, the Oligarch Petro Poroshenko, the "candy man," announced that the Minsk ceasefire was over. However, anyone viewing YouTube, owned by Silicon Valley Monopoly Google, that his Army of Far-Right Nationalists continued to shell residential areas during the ceasefire. The "candy-man" stated that "no residential areas shelled by his Ukrainian uniformed soldiers were paid and equipped by the U.S., England, members of the EU. Like former President Barak Hussein Obama, Poroshenko, a "political serial liar" knew that no repercussions of prosecution could jail him for his high crimes and misdemeanors against the children, women, grandparents, and fathers lying dead in the Donbas streets from the use of heavy armor against the defenseless civilians. The European Union, under the banner of NATO, is a militarist economic bloc that will violate the rights of sovereign nations and the by-laws of the UN Charter.

In a newspaper the question was asked, why did NATO Secretary-General Jens Stoltenberg strike around like some ancient Germania King using his Army, which is paid primarily by the United States, acts as the political will of the European Union? Many of the vast Korka Clan living in Kyiv, Odesa, and Donbas regions spoke both Ukraine and Russian languages believed that they lived in a Moscow patrimony. Over ten centuries, the country plagued by high politics and violent events upon the population. Many who speak Russia still have a strong identity in Ukraine as a State. Both Ukraine and Poland National Anthems begin,

"(We) have not yet perished ..."

In 20, Ukraine still is mismanaged by criminal gangs, oligarchs, EU politicians, US State Department "wannabe's" and political attorneys and retired Military cronies. Even with the Orange Revolution and the US State Department in Kyiv orchestrating the Maidan bloodbath, Ukraine ruled by the parasitic elite ruling classes. The only gifts that they give to the people are "Nationalistic phrases" that run on President Poroshenko's owned Channel 5 TV station:

"Glory to Ukraine, Glory to Heroes, Glory to the Nation, Death to Enemies."

The 2014 Minsk Agreements did not last very long as counter-intelligence agents from members of the Korak family infiltrated the EU and NATO peace process organizations. The Organization for Security and Co-operation in Europe (OSCE) hires Bogdan

Korka, the son of Dimitry Korka, as a battlefield monitor along the boundaries of the Kyiv Army and volunteers of the Donetsk Peoples Republic (DPR) and the Lugansk Peoples Republic (LPR) in the Donbas Region. Natalya Korka authored the news article that over 200,000 Russian troops were massing at the border with thousands of tanks to support the US Intelligence Agencies "narrative that Russian aggression existed in Ukraine and supported the Donbas armed people with equipment and tanks. United Kingdom news stories prove that only 56 cases of Russian citizens were involved in Donbas's fighting engagements, and

Ukraine Oleksandr Turchynov
-Courtesy of conworld.fandom.com

they were volunteers who came from Russia. Many of the Oligarchs (Poroshenko, Turchinov, Yatsenuk), owned and controlled 80% of the Ukraine TV and radio stations. They had the platforms to create "fake news." Natalya Korka paid a public relations retainer of $350,000. Thus, working with the recommendations of Natalya Korka and members of the Kyiv's inner circle, manufactured fake news about Donbas battles in order to motivate the US and the European Union. Germany's Merkel had no choice but to send more money to the Federal Government of Ukraine. For over twenty-four months, the "official story" was that vast armies of Russian troops were occupying the main cities and towns in the Donbas Region. Still, with USA spy satellites over those areas of Ukraine and Russia, it would have been easy to prove or disprove these allegations. But the defense ministries of Germany, Great Britain, and Kyiv did not want actual evidence. Still, they just wanted the fear-driven narrative that Russia was trying to dominate Western Europe. The theme sponsored by the US State and Defense Departments was,

"Save Lives, Defend Freedom and Stop Russian Aggression in Ukraine."

Government narratives one of many examples of official "false news" employed to create a reality that does not exist, similar to the gaming company, Westwood Studios, using "action graphics" that the Russian were launching massive attacks on the city of Kyiv. The Twitter tags were "#wow; RussiainvadedUkraine."

OLIGARCH'S DONBAS DEATH WISHES

In 2014, Ukraine President Petro Oleksiyovych Poroshenko said,

"We will have jobs, the people of Donbas will not. We have pensions, the people of Donbas will not. We will have care for pensioners and children, the people of Donbas will not. Our children will go to schools and kindergartens. Their children will hide in basements."

Poroshenko is a leader driven by the political power and money from 2014 to the end of his term in 2019, received military equipment and training from all the members of NATO. His orders to his Army and Right Sector Nationalist Ministries demonstrated his willingness to silence the breaths of civilians and children of Donbas. In 2014 at the start of the Kyiv Army shelling Donbas, the USA company AirTronic USA & Kyiv's Ministry "Ukroboronpro" secretly negotiated for PSRL grenade launchers. John Kerry ran the US State Department, immediately approved the necessary export license, and began shipments in early 2016 with an open-ended contract to provide as many of these offensive weapons well into 2020. The USA Senate, led by former Senator John McCain, gave numerous anti-Russian rhetorical comments on the USA Senate Floor, approved billions of US Dollars under the legislative bill's subheadings, "Russian Aggression." US Congress passed over

$350Million for the Government of Ukraine to use in any manner such as buying Boeing and Raytheon heavy weapons and laser directed bombs.

In 2017, NATO, with many members refusing to pay for their military defense, received $4.852 billion in that also included millions to Ukraine to make War on the citizens of Eastern Ukraine. According to Ukraine Channel, 5 TV station scripted "talking heads," all the 3,000 Donbas civilians killed in 2014 was the result of "Donbas terrorists who gun-downed their people." In 2017-News Media, owned by Time Warner, an American multinational mass media and entertainment conglomerate monopoly headquartered in New York City. Currently is the world's third-largest entertainment company regarding revenue, after Comcast -Xfinity and NBCUniversal). Even CNN and the Walt Disney Company-owned cable and broadcast media properties (ABC/ESPN)) reported that the air attacks on Donetsk and Lugansk happened from pro-Russian forces attacking their people. The Korka global family network was overjoyed. The Ukraine government received the 2014 funding from the International Monetary Fund (IMF), European Central Bank (ECB), and the United States Congress-over $5billion in aid?

EU/NATO PROPAGANDA

Natalya Korka's EU/NATO propaganda narrative was that it was Russia that was sending superior weapons to the fighters in the Donbas. Therefore, the inferior old Soviet Arms of the Ukraine Army were no match to the Russian weaponry. Thus, advanced weapons had to be sent by President Barak Hussein Obama or Donald J. Trump to balance the threat force of the Russian "aggression." No proof was ever acquired or by the International Press. The International Corporate Government-controlled media simply parroted the 2014 Press Releases from the Kiev's Defense, Foreign Affairs, Interior, and Propaganda Information Ministries.

From 2014 to 2019, over 11,000 killed in the Donbas, but Comcast, NewsCorp, Disney, Microsoft, and other progressive information outlets did not report this tragic figure. The Donbas people first used sticks, then 1933 Soviet Era rifles, and then the 1945 war memorial weapons taken down used to defend against the German manufactured Kyiv battle tanks and large range artillery invading the Donbas Industrial Region. The Kyiv Army used same1940's Wehrmacht military tactics of attacking hospitals, schools, retirement homes, and villages. In 2017, the Kyiv Army shelled the territory of Donbas in Eastern Ukraine randomly.

The German Army furthered concepts pioneered during World War I, combining ground (Heer) and Air-Force (Luftwaffe) assets into combined arms teams. Coupled with traditional war fighting methods such as encirclements and the "battle of annihilation."[11] In this approach, the German military managed many lightning quick victories in the first year of World War Two. Germany's immediate military success on the field at the start of the Second World War parallels achieved during the First World War, attributed to their superior combat officers.

Ukraine Seversk MIL grad- Courtesy of Ukraine Army News

1ˢᵀ CENTURY SOCIALIST BARBARIANS

In 2017, the American Democratic Party and its 501C3s were alleged to be behind the funding of young US Nazi Party Antifa street thugs. The thugs masked and dressed in black who attacked President Trump Supporters to create a media firestorm and a political fiat accompli; namely, that all Republicans were racist and Democratic Party members were defending "free speech." Those hiding behind mask turned out to be Union teachers at colleges and middle Schools, for example like Yvonne Felarca, a 47-year-old teacher at Berkeley's Martin Luther King Jr. Middle School. Ten thousand five hundred Ukraine citizens were killed in this senseless war to level all homes and infrastructures in the Donbass and eventually allow international Central Bank financed developers to gain free land and a tax base for Kiev's Treasury.

Ukraine Donetsk Village Shelling – Courtesy of Donetsk People Republic

Russian Embassy in Kyiv has come under three major attacks since the conflict in eastern Ukraine broke out in 2014. Nationalist Right Sector mobs had vandalized the premises and vehicles parked at the Russian Embassy in June 2014, March and

September 2016 when radicals launched a barrage of firecrackers at the building ahead of the Russian parliamentary election. On March 20, 2017, police watched (UKR) "Nationalist Corps" vandals spray-painted graffiti and plastered flyers all over the offices of Russian-owned Alfa Bank and Sberbank in the Ukrainian city of Nikolayev. National Corps is a Ukrainian far-right neo-nationalist party formed in 2016 by the Azov Civil Corps, a regiment of Ukraine's National Guard, and veterans of another far-right armed group, the militant Azov battalion. The Right Sector described as a far-right and neo-fascist party Antifa-like, documented as the major force behind the Ukrainian's Maidan public square mass executions.[12] The Right Sector Nationalists taking part in the defacing of the Russian Bank offices were operating in broad daylight, with onlookers and police alike watching without showing any intent to intervene. The world and Ukrainians have a lot to fear from this Oligarch financially supported terrorist groups. Kiev's Ministry of Defense alleged to have financed and controlled street assassination of those who opposed using lethal force to kill its citizens, strikes fear into the average Ukraine citizen.

Kyiv militants defacing RU banks-Courtesy of Sputnik News

Further examples of repression and tyranny under Poroshenko and other Oligarchs' campaign to demonize Russian speaking citizens in Eastern Ukraine was that of Russian singer Yulia Samoilova. Ms. Samoilova, set to represent Russia at the 2017 Eurovision song contest, was banned by the Ukraine Rada from entering the country for three years." On May 30, 2017, Thomas Grove (worked for WSJ in Russia, Ukraine, and Turkey) in the Wall Street Journal reported, "The Ukrainian government earlier this month blocked Vkontakte and Odnoklassniki, Russian-language social media platforms that are hugely popular across the former Soviet Union, saying they were serving as vehicles for pro-Russian propaganda. The Mail.Ru Group, which operates Vkontakte and Odnoklassniki, said in a prepared statement that Ukraine's decision to block the services was purely a political one.

Ukraine Kyiv "kitsquad car" bombing – Courtesy of Seattle Times

NURTURING KORKA'S FAMILY TRADITION

Ruslan Wyacheslav Sr. was only sixteen years of age when he became active in the Red Army to crush the Czar's Cossack White Russian Forces in Siberia. He was decorated and given the award of "Hero of the Motherland." Later he had nine children all boys who joined the Russian military to fight the Germans in World War One and World War Two. His third son Ruslan Wyacheslav Jr.

was given a field commission to Captain and served in both Wars and was the commander for a tank battalion that captured over 25,000 German soldiers.

After the war, he moved to Portugal to heal his many wounds. He met a young girl of eighteen years named Lucinda Korka, and they married in Grozny Chechnya. Ruslan was given a commission as a Major General for all Russian military force in the province of Chechnya. In 1979, they had a baby boy that they named Ruslan Korka Papaskiri. Their boy had a great desire to study and play the piano. He was a good student, and his parent's dream for him was to attend Moscow University and study music. He was twenty years of age when he and his friends were the rebellion against Russia forces. At twenty-one years of age, he renounced his parents and the Russian Orthodox religion and converted to the Muslim religion. Ruslan took up the holy war against the infidel. He went to the mountains and served under the Rebel Commander, Shamil Basayev. He would shoot before each ambush against Russian Supply convoys,

"Allahu Akbar" -death to all Russians!"

In 2003, he moved to Georgia and fought with the Georgian fight against the Russians. Ruslan Korak Papashiri recognized by Georgia's President Mikheil Saakashvilli as an assassin who would kill Russian agents who are sent to Georgia to infiltrate the various Georgian fighting militias. At one point, he recognized a Russian agent Igor Ayrat sent to kill him. They met in a bar, and they became friends as they toasted in vodka. Ruslan stopped toasting and stared at Igor

"Why were sent to kill me? What harm have I done to you."

Igor stopped and placed his glass down and reached for his Stechkin automatic pistol.

"Now do not try to shot as I have a Glock pointed at your balls and I will blow them off. I do not understand why you came here and tracked me all day."

Igor, let go of the pistol and place both hands on the bar.

"My Foreign Intelligence Service (SVR) Moscow superiors have been watching you since you entered the fight against us in 1999. We were reluctant to eliminate you at that time because of your father. However, we know that you are working for the Georgian secret services and we know that Saakashvilli has hired you as a personal hit man to eliminate his opponents."

Igor was a practical man who was depositing his 'hit funds' in an off-shore Granada bank account.

"Look Ruslan; I am not political. You and I got along tonight, and they only paid me $100,000 dollars for the hit on you. I really would rather work for you and be a double agent. I think that we can negotiate a fee of $350,000 dollars."

Ruslan could see clearly that this was a great opportunity to make some money.

"I will meet with President Saakashvilli and present your proposal. He is a very disturbed man, and I have to handle this very diplomatically. In the meantime, let us leave as friends, and I will send a car for you in the morning."

In July 2006, rebel Chechen leader Shalmil Basayev was mysteriously blown up in a large truckload of Chinese weapons and explosives destined for Chechen rebels. Ruslan would be a double agent as long as the money was reasonable. For that hit on his Chechnya Commander, that he organized for the Russian State Secret Service, he received one million US dollars. Ruslan continued to further his trade and notoriety as a man who could reach anyone and assassinate them. By now in 2009, at the young age of thirty, he has created numerous identities over the years and was an assassin to catch the real Kremlin agents performing "wet work." Ruslan by this time was extremely wealthy. He was a remarkable agent,

"Look; he told his friend, Igor, wherever there is a fight against Kremlin's evil meddling, I will offer my services whether in the US, Chechnya, Georgia, Turkey, and Syria. This year alone Russian agents packed a huge bomb outside my three stories Georgian apartment window. I only had my chest and right foot wounded with shrapnel. I am a survivor. I also have a home in Turkey, and the Chechen rebel envoy was killed by a shotgun as he was ringing my door. You can see still the holes in my door."

Times were exciting for Ruslan and with a $1,000-dollar weekly Cocaine habit created a daily fantasy of being the best Korka assassin and double agent. He even dreamed of his statue erected in Tbilisi. Ruslan told his wife and three girls that he was leaving Georgia and flying to Istanbul to meet a business associate.

"Come here my dears. I will leave for a couple of days. I am asking Igor to stay with you until I return. Do not go shopping or leave the house until I return. Igor will arrange to have your groceries brought here. I trust him, and I owe him my life."

With that, he kissed each one and grabbed his overnight bag. It was 2012, Ruslan met with Nikita Ivanov who he believed was a Russian FSS (Federal Security Service) stationed at the Istanbul Russian Embassy. They left the Russian Embassy and walked two blocks to have lunch at the Russian Restaurant Petrov. It was a "safe location" controlled by the FSS with cameras and listening devices. They sat at the back of the restaurant and ordered Botvinya, Shuba, and Kotlety.

Nikita was relaxed and asked after the meal,

"Ruslan I have three targets for you, and it must be done by next month without fail."

Ruslan moved in his chair, and his eyes raced across the room looking for any threats and casually spoke,

"I am not a beggar. I do my job efficiently, and there are never any witnesses. If there are, I kill them as well. As you know, dead men tell no tales. I normally get one million for each hit. Remember, I am giving you a bargain as if there are any witnesses, I do not charge you for killing them. So, my family is looking for three million with forty percent in large bills and sixty percent in a mix of foreign currency, but they must be in small denominations as they are impossible to trace. Can you do that? I also demand one million dollars up front and two million within 60 days from the successful completion of the mission."

Nikita was slowing sipping his Remy Martin Cognac Louis XIII 1.75 L.

"Ruslan; I am only authorized to pay one million five hundred thousand for each delivered body. I may have to go directly to the Russian Central Bank approval for any monies over that maximum!"

Ruslan looked at Nikita and poured a small amount of Remy Martin in his Waterford glass.

"My very dear Nikita, you know that I never lower my price. I never charge for my expenses. The three million dollars is a good price, and at times my margin can slip to sixty percent if I have spent more money on travel and hotels. Assassination is strictly business, and I have a large family to support."

Nikita was getting angry as his superiors told him that this hitman had a reputation of being dangerous and duplicative. Also, he was told that he had to make a deal today or thrown into a Gulag. He had the three million already approved, but he wants to enrich himself by negotiating for his fraudulent benefit. After the meal, they continued drinking and talking.

Ruslan spoke, "Nikita I am about ready to leave. I will take $2.5 million, and the is my final acceptance. If you don't, then you need to find some cheap ordinary killer instead of a professional that protects the source of the hit."

Ruslan stood up and began to put on his light sports coat.

Nikita looked up,

"Ruslan sit down for a minute. I will agree on this amount of $2.5million, but you are never to mention the deal or the amount. You do understand?"

Ruslan slid down into his chair facing the front of the restaurant,

"Yes, I do Nikita. Let us shake and hand over the million now as I do not want to be seen going back to the Embassy. I want the Turkish secret police to believe this was just a lunch meeting."

With that agreement, Nikita reached into his coat and handed over a packet filled with bills of $500, $100, and $200 US dollars.

They shook hands, and Nikita passed over a 1Gig USB drive.

"You will find the names, addresses, family members, history, and pictures. You are to complete the project within three to four weeks. If you do not, then we will target you. I hope we do not have to do that. The remaining amount will be transferred to your Kiribati bank under the name Jonathan Korka Sokolov as you requested. Best of luck."

They shook hands again and left together paying the bill with cash thus untraceable. Nikita walked back to the Embassy and Ruslan hailed a cab to the Istanbul's Ataturk Airport. On the way through customs, his bags examined and a map of Syria and a compass found. He was handcuffed and arrested. Ruslan spent four days in a dirty cell with 25 other men. His lawyers got an acquittal, and he was released. Although his arrest was untimely, he proceeded on, and with a sniper rifle and special mercury bullets, Ruslan carried out the first hit at the Rue Ata-al-Ayyoubi, Al Afif - BP 769. Next, his second and third hits were easier as he wired explosives under the Honda SUV of the husband and wife as they were shopping at the Souq al-Bizuriyyah (Sweet Souq). This was cutting it close as this was final week of the assignment. He was able to watch the General's Honda and waited until he and his wife were both buckled in and started the vehicle before setting off an explosive pack under their seats. It was a great success as no witnesses came forward. Nikita was satisfied with the efficiency and deadliness of the three contracted hits. Ruslan had overcome a minor setback but proved again that he was the best Korka assassin in thousands of years of extraordinary skills.

When Ruslan traveled back to Georgia, he heard that his former mentor Mikheil Saakashvilli was stripped of his citizenship in Georgia and thrown out of the country. For a long time, the global press believed that this US State Department supported leader was dead. However, Mr. Saakashvili, 49, arrived in the western Ukrainian city of Lviv. In 2013, he was given citizenship of Ukraine from President Petro Poroshenko of Ukraine. In 2015, after a bitter fight with Poroshenko over the level of criminal corruption in Odessa, Saakashvili was stripped of his Ukraine citizenship.

Instead, Saakashvili arrives at Ukraine at the border crossing between Medyka, Poland, and Shehyni to start a political career in Ukraine. In May 2015, when Mr. Poroshenko invited him to be governor of the Odessa region, an area of southern Ukraine on the Black Sea that is notorious for its deeply entrenched corruption. The idea was that Mr. Saakashvili, a graduate of Columbia Law School and a foe of President Vladimir V. Putin of Russia, would help stamp out corruption and help satisfy demands for the open government after the illegal Victoria Nuland engineered the ouster of Mr. Yanukovych in 2014.

Ruslan believing that his mentor Saakashvilli would welcome him to Ukraine to help clean up the Odessa Region moves to Ukraine. In March 2017, Ruslan is arrested and found to have in his possession a Clock and Stechkin Automatic Pistol. Russian agents in Ukraine surveilled Ruslan. During his interrogation, he told the Security Service of Ukraine or SBU that he came to Ukraine to hunt down overseas anti-Russians paid to kill opponents of Vladimir Putin. He was just doing the work of the Ukraine government to rid Ukraine from these dirty Russians. Ruslan pleaded guilty for firearms possession and was released on September 15, 2017. He grabbed the first available cab went back to his hotel to rest up. The jail that held him was in the basement of the Interior Ministry was cold and smelled of urine and feces.

At the Interior Ministry, under his alias Jonathan Korka Sokolov, beaten and only given one meal per day and one shower per month. Ruslan was not going to forget his jailers. Ruslan checked into the Intercontinental in Kiev to a top suite. After a short glass of Cognac, Ruslan showered. He ran the hot water down his spine. He felt alive again. He had over five million dollars in his accounts, and he decided to retire from his profession. He had to find one place on the planet that other agents might not find and kill him. After toweling down and stretching into a warm blue cotton robe, he reached for the phone to call the main reception desk to have his girlfriend to meet him downstairs with specific instructions. His current girlfriend, thirty-three-year-old

Marina Ruleva who had breast measurements of 46 and bright red hair. She stood at 5'3" inches and had a model's shapely body. She drove his Toyota Camry to meet him at the indoor café by the InterContinental Hotel in Kyiv. She parked the vehicle in the underground garage and ran up the stair to meet him. Ruslan had to attend a conference on the other side of Kyiv and asked if she could drive him.

"Sure honey, but I have to take my accountant home first." Ruskin said, "no problem, let me pay the bill, run upstairs, and get some paper for this meeting. I will meet you at the entrance of underground garage, and we can leave from there."

Ruskin Korka Papaskiri now under his alias of Jonathan Korka Sokolov at 38 years of age was to end his career as an assassin for hire. He had hated his father for ordering the executions of Jihadist warriors in Chechnya and believed in killing all Russians. He felt that in Ukraine he would be welcomed. For Ruslan Korka Papaskiri, Poroshenko ran the same agenda in Eastern Ukraine. Kyiv had become a hot bed of spies and hit men created by the Kyiv-based US State Department and the US Congress, especially Senator John McCain. Ruslan was pleased that he was retiring. He entered the passenger side and said hello. Marina Ruleva pulled the Toyota out of the underground garage and stood five to ten minutes in rush-hour traffic. Ruslan was riding in the passenger seat, leaning toward the center of the vehicle when a bomb detonated in the armrest, ripping off his arm, his head, and part of his torso and killing him instantly. The Russian Security Force bomb weighed about two kilograms and was set off by remote control. The bomb was fashioned to direct its blast against the passenger, although it maimed the driver that was the price, she paid for allowing Russian agents to plant the bomb.

Marina Ruleva risked her life and her daughter's. However, she felt it was worth the risks for the one million dollars she received from the Russian Security forces. In December 2017, she moved to Mountain View California and given American citizenship upon her entry. The one million dollars deposited at the Chase

Bank in Mountain View. She and her daughter were given new names and given an Embarcadero Condo suite overlooking the San Francisco Ferry Building and a second home in Mountain View's Catholic Mission Condo complex on Castro Street. Two months later while staying the weekend at her San Francisco Embarcadero Apartment, she lost her balance and tumbled twenty-five stories to her death. One month after Marina's death, her Ukrainian mother found dead from an overdose of pain medication. Marina's sixteen-year-old daughter Olga was found at the Westfield San Francisco Centre stuffed in a garbage bag. Olga had been violated and died from an overdose of Heroin and Cocaine.

Ukraine car bombing – Courtesy of rferl.org

In 2014, the media wrote that Ukraine is locked in a bitter proxy war with its larger neighbor. Russia annexed the Crimean Peninsula from Ukraine in 2014 and backed separatists in Ukraine's eastern Donbass region. In parallel, the country besieged with what Ukrainian government officials and cybersecurity experts describe as a concerted Russian cyber offensive. Russian President Vladimir Putin said his government doesn't sponsor hacking. But a Russian political insider. and the Moscow-based leader of an information-technology firm said most of Russia's security services outsource cyberattacks to third parties.

CYBERWARS

In Ukraine, such attacks have had potentially lethal effects. After Kyiv's aggressive, murderous acts against its civilians, fighting broke out in Eastern Ukraine. In 2014, the U.S.-based cybersecurity firm CrowdStrike identified how a group of Russian hackers "believed to be linked to APT 28," also known as "Fancy Bear," inserted malware in an Android application distributed via Vkontakte. "VK is a Russian-based online social media and social networking service based in St. Petersburg Russia. It is available in several languages, but it is especially popular among Russian-speaking users. VK allows users to message each other publicly or privately, to create groups, public pages, and events, share and tag images, audio, and video, and to play browser-based games. The software, developed by the Ukrainian artillery officer Yaroslav Sherstuk, was meant to help calculate targeting data for the Ukrainian military's Soviet-era D-30 howitzers. CrowdStrike concluded that the malware used to reveal the location of Ukrainian artillery units, potentially exposing them to the devastating fire. Ukraine's State-controlled Media reported that attacks in Ukraine grew in sophistication. Further, TV Channel 5 broadcast (Poroshenko owned) that hackers used cutting-edge cyber tools to take down a power substation in the Ukrainian capital of Kyiv, briefly leaving some of the city's largest neighborhoods without power. Analysts say it was the first such cyber-attack on critical infrastructure in a world capital. As part of covert trade skills, misinformation is employed to color the enemy, as it harms the population's primary life-sustaining resources. Much as in the US DNC (Democratic National Committee) hacks, hacking groups in the Kyiv Ukraine attackers worked in teams.

"One group used sophisticated tools to gain entry and clean away their digital fingerprints, while another used everyday

Information technology tools to subvert the software and remain undetected, said Roman Sologub at Kyiv-based ISSP.

"The main question is if the attack reached its targeted goal or was just a preparation stage of another attack on bigger targets as part of a broad planned strategic cyberwar campaign," Mr. Sologub said.

"A different Russian cyberespionage group named Sandworm carried out an attack in 2015 on a different power grid in western Ukraine, said John Hultquist, an analyst for cybersecurity firm FireEye. The incidents in Ukraine are an opportunity to learn about the adversary before they carry out further incidents in the West,"[13] he said, adding that Sandworm's malicious code found in the cyberinfrastructure of Energy Utilities in the US."

Cyber MILCOM Command Center – Courtesy of U.S. Cybercom.mil

UKRAINE'S OLIGARCH CYBER SECURITY POLICIES

On May 16, 2016, the Ukrainian Government's move to curtail private access to the two social-media sites provoked controversy. The advocacy group, Human Rights Watch, called the ban "a cynical, politically expedient attack on the right to information affecting millions of Ukrainians, and their personal and professional lives."

Under Natalya Korka's direction, Ukraine's presidential office issued a press release,

"Russia had tried to take down its website by flooding it with data, in what is known as a distributed denial-of-service attack."

Andrei Soldatov, an expert on Russia's internet, spoke at the time on Channel 5 in Ukraine,

"Vkontakte (VK) has a much friendlier relationship with the Russian authorities than Facebook does. VK is Russia's most popular social media network, often gives organizations like the Federal Security Service (FSS) access to user data to monitor political dissent in Russia. They are often happy to comply with security services but I do not know the network used in cyber-attacks."

The attacks by Russian hackers on Ukraine's critical infrastructure made experts worried that the approach used elsewhere. The US Department of Homeland Security didn't comment on the hack of the Ukrainian electricity grid until months after the fact, raising questions about whether the US prepared to defend against such an attack on its infrastructure.

Noted Ukraine reporters said,

"we have never had a White House-level official come out and say, regardless of who did it, that this was a significant event and that it was wholly an inappropriate attack on civilian infrastructure."

War is one dimension of a hybrid-war testing process. He wrote on November 29, 2018, in an "opinion article" that Russian military-intelligence operatives allegedly tied to the attackers of ex-spy Sergei Skripal in Britain, seen in Kyiv during the 2014 Ukrainian Maidan revolution. According to Atlantic Council's expert Andrian Karatnycky, he believed that The Wagner group, was a Russian paramilitary contractor, and covertly active in Crimea. The Donbas from 2015 to 2016.[14]

It is correct that early in the conflict, Russia launched cyberattacks on Ukraine's government communications, commercial institutions, and the power grid. It as well as the PRC attempted similar strikes in the US. The Russian Government spent $4700.00 for ads on Google during 2016. How could such a paltry amount affect the Presidential election compared to Hillary Clinton paying $768 million for ads? Did the MEDIA cartels view that as election-meddling tactics? Historical evidence has shown that the US State Department does interfere with campaigns in the foreign election as Syria, Israel, Ukraine, Russia, Spain, Sweden, and other European countries. The FBI focused on combating foreign interference on social media. Both efforts have received support from US intelligence agencies. Congressional investigations showed that under the Obama Administration, the FBI and the CIA were actively interfering in the 2016 elections in hopes of negating any votes for Donald Trump, a wealthy businessman, who sought the US Presidency.

USA'S STRAW DOG

The Ukrainian Government has shown its commitment, after receiving billions in foreign aid, Kyiv agreed to five percent of its 2017 gross domestic product of 112.13 billion US dollars on national security and upgrading its military and advanced-weapons arsenal. The US provides lethal military aid to Kyiv in the form of Javelin antitank missiles and will include land-based antiaircraft and anti-ship weapons. The US is considering supporting the modernization of Ukraine's advanced-weapons systems. In September 2018, British Defense Secretary Gavin Williamson planned to have the Royal Navy send more troops and take more aggressive actions in the Black and Azov Seas. Sanctions are tools used by the US to destroy Russia's economy and population by "pressuring Europe to cancel Moscow's planned Nord Stream 2 and South Stream pipeline projects, which would foster European dependence on Russian oil and help shore up Russia's finances."[15]

Although the US or Britain has not declared war against Russia or China, using economic sanctions on an array of

Russian companies, such as those involved in shipbuilding and infrastructure, could be viewed as acts of War. Also, threatening Russia's expulsion from the Swift Banking System has only allowed the GDP economies of China ($14.14 trillion) and Russia ($1.64 trillion) to be closer and stronger economically. In 2019, the GDP of the United States of America was $21.44trillion.

CHAPTER TEN

BLOOMING CHORNOBRYVETS - FUTURE DREAMS

"The greatest obstacle to understanding truth is not the lie itself, but the fact that the lie tries to look like the truth." Leo Tolstoy

WHAT SYMBOLIZES THE STRENGTH of Slavic peoples? In every yard in the Ukrainian countryside, is a serf house or a summer cottage, with brightly colored marigolds growing there. The "French Marigold" is the symbol of Ukraine. The flower began increasing in Ukraine during the late nineteenth Century. Today, it is everywhere. "Today, as you travel across the length and breadth of Ukraine, you are sure to see marigolds of several shades of yellow, red, and brown on longer or shorter stems providing their cheerful touch to the private and public gardens and flower beds." A Ukrainian 1800 serf poem that symbolizes the resilience of the Slavic peoples reads, "Marigolds grow in my mother's garden, shining bright in the morning. She taught me to sing vernal songs about my woes. As I look at the marigolds, I see the image of my old mother. I see your hands, mother, and I remember your tenderness."[1]

KILLING EUROPEAN ANCESTRY

Although seventy-eight percent of the population, Americans were forced to forget their Eastern and Southern European Ancestry. Eastern Europe, represented by people of Ukraine, Russia, Poland, and Hungary, is bordered on the East by the Ural Mountains. Although there are no such geographic borders to the West, Eastern Europe has been distinct from European countries to the West regarding cultural and linguistic affiliations. Archeologists found bones belonging to an extinct population of ancient humans. These strong, powerful humans, known as Neanderthals, named after the site where their bones first identified in the Neander Valley of Germany. Neanderthals and modern humans shared a common ancestor as well as many morphological and social traits but differed in key respects. Genome sequencing has shed more light on the Neanderthal and our complicated relationship with them over the past decade. For many years, scientists limited to scraping together clues from fragments of bones and other materials to discover who we are and where do we come from? New techniques have allowed scientists to look even closer at DNA hidden within those bones. While the full picture of our past is still emerging, it is clear that as early as 50,000 years ago, there were at least three different types of humans. Although only one of these group were modern skeleton-humans survived harsh conditions that appeared to cohabitate with the other groups, including Neanderthals sexually.

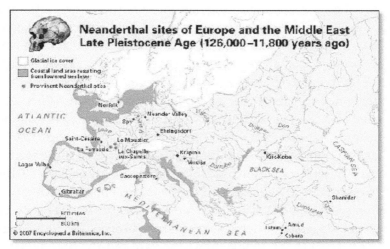

Neander Valley- Courtesy of Encyclopedia Britannica

SCANDINAVIAN ANCESTRY

The earliest people of Scandinavia hunted reindeer and seals and fished for salmon. Approximately 4000 years ago, these northern hunter/gatherers joined by cattle herders from the South. Although at the northwestern periphery of Europe, Scandinavia never wholly isolated from peoples to the South and East. Ashkenazi Jews thought to have settled in Central and Eastern Europe about 1,000 years ago. DNA (deoxyribonucleic acid, a self-replicating material present in nearly all living organisms as the main constituent of chromosomes. It is the carrier of genetic information.) shows clearly the connections among those who consider themselves to be Ashkenazi Jewish.[2] Two Ashkenazi Jewish people standing next to each other in a New York subway train are very likely to share genetic traces that make them identical cousins.[3]

FIRES OF ANTIQUITY FOREVER BURN AND RISE

In 2014, Daesh received over $1billion from Saudi Arabia to create a global network of Sunni Nationalism. Where are the continuing revenue sources for this Sunni "criminal gang empire" posing as liberators that the intelligence agencies of Britain, France, Germany, and America paid salaries, clothed, fed, armed, and trained? Sources close to the matter highlighted five sources; namely, criminal extortion proceeds in they receive in territories they liberate, robbery of economic and cultural assets, internet social media fund recruiting, bank robberies, and kidnapping. Criminal drug cartels in Mexico, Columbia, and Peru use similar tactics as well as the Islamic State in West Africa known as Boko Haram in Nigeria. In 2018, the signs of building the ancient Turkey Ottoman Empire into a caliphate reminiscent of the Ottoman Empire were clear as President Recep Tayyip Erdogan removed secularism from Turkey's society. China's emperor for life, Xi Jinping, moved toward resurrecting the Han, Ming, and Qing dynasties. Vladimir Putin, who had been victimized by the Western press for over sixteen years, was accused of bringing back the Czar Empire. Iran's religious leaders sought to restore the Achaemenid and Persian Kings. A nationalism that erupted during the colonial period resulted in independence, and a thirst for democratic value reached a complete circle. The glory of past empires strikes a human need of these sovereign states' populations to be ruled by one hand that it under one God Jesus, Allah, or Moses. The cycle will continue as communities feel disconnected in the world of mass communications and the internet that marginalizes the most and elevates the least. The only alternative is to ignite the ancient DNA in all humans to seek a connection to their ancient foundational roots.

Mr. Allison, a professor of a study at Harvard's Kennedy School, found sixteen cases in the past 500 years "in which a major nation's rise has disrupted the position of a dominant state," most notably a rapidly industrializing Germany threatening Britain's domination in the late 19th and early 20th centuries. The result of that rivalry, he writes, was open full world wars and a violent conflict segment of the study. In twelve of the sixteen cases, the Allison surveys were a war of some kind. Japan, in the late 1930s and early 1940s, the war was driven, in significant measure, by a trade conflict. In other cases, domestic politics played a role, prompting leaders to appease local factions by undertaking aggression for the sake of a perceived sense of honor. In many instances, a rising state's actual intentions were less crucial than its growing military capabilities and how they have interpreted abroad. That's why in 1907, Britain demanded that Germany stop its naval expansion. With America, England held on to the maritime strategy of standing up to a media-created global intimidator. Every action on the worldwide stage has consequences as Germany built more warships and faster. Making war is regrettably easy, Mr. Allison suggests. He quotes historian Paul Kennedy, "Britain and Germany considered 1914 continuation of least fifteen or twenty years. Miscalculations and small incidents intensify existing strains between nations."[4]

RUSSIA-AN ENIGMA

Russia, in the era of the Trump Presidency, aspires to a Europe from Lisbon to Vladivostok. However, Russia forced to look East to China. Historically, Russia realized centuries ago that it could have no kinship to anyone. The only reliable allies that it has is its Army and Navy. Russia, for the last 200 years, used the European West as its reference point. However, the West is no longer the center of the political universe. In 2018, after r the endless economic sanctions from the U.S. and British governments, Russia realized that to become part of the West is a fool's errand. Russia, after Genghis Khan, is the core of the Universal Kingdom, the last Rome, the absolute center for the future destiny of the planet Earth. Those cruel sanctions against Russia's population hampered trade, investment, access to global capital. Russia does not seek to move West and reclaim its old Soviet Union territories. During the Soviet Union times, Russia lost twenty-four percent of its areas, forty-nine percent of its population, and forty-one percent of its GDP. In 2018, Russia's GDP was the size of South Korea or the province of Guandong China. Russia has an excellent military might that it employed in Syria. Hollywood made Russia the evil force in the world that satisfies the lawyers in Congress to believe that Russia is a threat to Global Security.

Imperial and contemporary Russia viewed western Europe with begrudging feelings. Catherine the Great and other 18th and 19th-century elites always wanted western European respectability and thus preferred French over their language. But as Mr. Ziegler demonstrates, it was pressured from the East that created the Russia that we know, both regarding its expansive imperial geography and its national temperament. Napoleon attributed to saying, "Scratch a Russian and you find a Tatar." Russia's eastward orientation was hardly a matter of choice. Like much of Europe, Russia came under assault from Mongol conquerors in the 13th Century. Russian princes maintained semi-autonomy only by paying them gold and female slave tribute. Still, when the Mongol tide finally receded, around 1582, Russia turned its energies eastward, building frontier forts and trading posts. Initially, this was mostly a matter of defense, as Moscow sought to control the Russian heartland's ever more indirect approaches. With time, though, other motives took hold. Russia needed food, and the rivers were full of healthy and bountiful river fish. Since the fashion trends of wealthy European and American clients demanded fur, Russia hunted sable that became a form of soft gold. However, all good things came to and as the sable, fur seals, and also the fox shot for their skin, and by mid-1800s, they became extinct. Now, Russia required a way to create wealth. Is there an American comparison with the wilderness conditions of Russia's westward expansion? "Russia was one of the world's last vast geographies consciously inspired in part by observing America's westward development.

If you went to Moscow and St. Petersburg, Russians in the 1800s, you would find many of Russian elites reading the novels of James Fenimore Cooper. He wrote exclusively about the American frontier. Historically the New York and Sacramento newspapers were full of tales of the California gold rush that was then underway. Many who sought new sources of wealth in Russia and Europe thought that the Amur River located in the East would be Russia's Mississippi. The Amur River's run-off would lead to gold discoveries and a new American wealth bounty. The towns of Khabarovsk and Komsomolsk-on-Amur became boom towns like the cold rush towns of Sutter's Mill in Coloma, California, and Klondike region of the Yukon. Over 100,000 western Russians responded and moved East. This vast migration of Slavs and Cossacks caused imperial Russia to expand its geographical territory East meeting with the borders of the Zaichun of the Aisin Gioro clan, the Emperor of China' Qing Dynasty. Russia did not want war with Zaichin and signed the 1869 Treaty of Nerchinsk in the language of the Roman Catholic church, namely, Latin, that was fair to the Qing Dynasty and Russia. But this seemingly solid start to relations with China was mutually beneficial until, under Mao Zedong, the Chinese became mistrustful and militarily hostile. In the 1960s, the Amur River border became heavily militarized with Russia and Chinese tanks facing each other as military adversaries. During this period, the Russians decided not to provide advanced missile technology to China.

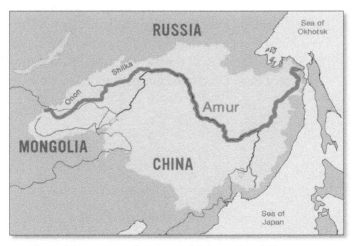

Amur River map — Courtesy of International Rivers.org

CIA CONDORS AT 13 MILES ABOVE THE EARTH

The U-2 is a sleek single jet engine ultra-light glider that maneuvers on the Earth's edge. Lockheed designed the glider to avoid detection and spied over the Soviet Union. In its 12-hour mission, the U-2 can capture the size of Russia or Iran in extraordinarily detailed imagery of a country. The entire concept began with the genius of Alan Land's Polaroid wonderworks lab in Boston. Land concluded that the U.S. needed a revolutionary intelligence technology to spy on the Soviet's development of ICBMs, heavy bombers, and atomic submarines that all could mount a surprise nuclear strike on the U.S. Human Intelligence could not do the job. A Lockheed skunk-works facility founded on a Nevada dry Salt Lake referred to as Area 51. Land lobbied President Eisenhower and CIA director Allen Dulles to get secret funding to build the delivery system with his high-resolution cameras that could function in freezing temperatures thirteen miles above the Earth. CIA recruited and trained a group of pilots, created pressure flying suits, and instructed the pilots in celestial navigation and the use of a poison "pill" if captured. During the operation of Soviet Union flyovers, they brought back 30,000 feet of film for evaluation. The USAF then turned them over to the CIA in DC.[5] The Cuban Missile Crisis under President John Kennedy used those U-2 photos to force Nikita Khrushchev to remove ICBMs from Cuba. The U-2 and the Predator assigned with the 99th Reconnaissance Squadron at Beale Air Force Base, North of Sacramento, California.

Vladimir the Great -Courtesy of Alchetron.com

RUSSIA - KIEVAN RUS-VLADIMIR THE GREAT

For many years, the leading world superpower was Kievan Rus. Vladimir the Great, a Russian prince who over 1000 years ago Christianized the Ukraine population to neutralize the Slavic and Viking tribes that exist during his reign. Russian Czar Vladimir I, also called Vladimir the Great and St. Vladimir, was the Grand Prince of Kievan Russia from about 980 to 1015. Under Vladimir I, the first Russian State was born. In 969, the youngest son of Grand Prince Sviatoslav Igorevich of Kyiv and a servant girl, Vladimir the Great distinguished himself first as his father's governor in Novgorod. From 972 to 973, civil war followed Sviatoslav's death. In 976, Vladimir fled to Scandinavia, leaving the Kievan Rus reign to his oldest brother, Iaropolk. In 978, Vladimir recruited a large force of the Varangians (Normans) and continued the civil war. In 980, Vladimir crowned the grand Prince of Kyiv.[6]

CONQUEST OF THE WEST

Vladimir's first goal seems to have been to recover his father's conquests, lost during the civil war," and add to his conquests. Vladimir stayed out of the Balkans. From 981 to 984, he regained the territory of the Viatichi and Radimichi in the East, and by so doing, all eastern Slavs came under Kyiv's centralization.

MIGRATION OF SLAVS

Beginning in the Prehistoric period, the migration of the Slav's North and East. However, other historical scholars believe that the Slavs pushed back from the Elbe River on the West and fought for their territory on the South. Warlike Slavs extended within all of the Northern landmasses of the West and as far east as the Pacific. The Northeastern Slavs are ancestors of the current Russians but divided into many tribes that resulted in wars amongst them, namely, East Slavs, mainly Belarusians, Russians, Ukrainians, and South Slavs chiefly Bosniaks, Croats, Macedonians, Montenegrins, Serbs, Slovenes, and Bulgarians. In the ninth Century, the Russian State besieged from the North by the Varaghi or Normans and southern Kozari. This nomadic tribe lived near the Don and the Volga River and believed to follow the old testament of the Khazars Empire. (Bibliography: Volpicelli Zenone "Russia on the Pacific, and the Siberian railway" --By Zenone Volpicelli)

RUSSIAN ORTHODOX CHRISTIAN LANDS

In 981 AD, Prince Vladimir recovered some Western Galician towns from Poland. Also, in the West, the Prince conquered the territory of the Lithuanian latvigs in 983AD. The 985 AD Vladimir's campaign against the Volga Bulgars led to a stalemate and ended his intentions to recover the Volga Basin. In the South, the Turkic tribe of the Pechenegs (Patzinaks), who had captured the control of the Black Sea Steppes, were equally resistant to military victory. However, Vladimir the Great did regain some of the steppe lands and secured them by a system of earth walls, forts, and fortified towns. The quest for unity and security was also the goal of Vladimir's domestic and international policy. He substituted his weak sons and lieutenants for the self-reliant tribal chieftains as governors of individual sections of the State and subjected them to close daily supervision.[7] In August 2009, the Wall Street Journal opinion writer, Richard Pipes wrote that Russia has an obsession of being acknowledged as a great world power. After conquering Siberia, Russia has felt like one since the 17th Century, but especially since her victory in the Second World War over Germany and the success of sending the first human into space. It costs nothing to defer to Russia's claims to such exalted status, to show her respect, to listen to Mother Russia's wishes. The President of Russia Vladimir Putin said in November 2018, "From what I can see, we are in grave danger. How can you not understand that the world is being pulled in an irreversible direction (Third World War)? I think this is gravely dangerous. I not only think that. I am assured of it." Today in Moscow, a fifty-foot statue of Vladimir the Great is erected in central Moscow in Borovitskaya Square. St. Vladimir is credited in bringing Christianity to Russia in the 10th Century.

Lenin 1895 "Mug Shot" – Courtesy of cs.megill.ca

Vladimir, in the service of his State unity goal, might have wanted a religious aspect of his kingdom. At first, he created a pagan creed common to his entire realm by accepting all gods and deities of local tribes and making them an object of general veneration. Vladimir followed the classical religious pathway of the Roman Empire. In 988 AD. Vladimir was baptized and turned to Christianity because a faith believing in a single God appeared better suited to the purposes of a prince seeking to entrench the Government of a sole ruler in his realm. In 987AD, Byzantine Emperor Basil II, in return for Russian assistance against uprisings in Bulgaria and Anatolia, agreed to give Vladimir the hand of his sister Anna.

He received the Byzantine marriage vows with his bride and proceeded to make Christianity the official religion of his State. He urged his subjects to accept baptism, too, to destroy all pagan idols such as the Korka Star rocks, to build Christian churches and schools and libraries, to keep peace within and without the realm and indulged in charities for the benefit of the poor and sick. The baptism of Russia took several decades before Christianity struck roots in Russia firmly and positively. Nor was Vladimir utterly successful in checking the danger of feudal disintegration. His son Laroslav organized a revolt against his father Vladimir the Great. After the civil war began, Vladimir died in the fighting. A larger civil war result continued until 1026. Russia carved up between laroslav and his brother Mstislav, and the country not reunited until 1036, following Mstislav's death. To his credit, Vladimir completed the unification of all Eastern Slavs in his realm, secured its frontiers against foreign invasions, and accepted Orthodox Russian Christianity that led to its connection to the community of Christian nations and their civilization.[8] In 2019, Vladimir remembered and celebrated in numerous legends and songs as a great national hero and ruler as a "Sun Prince." Vladimir the Great canonized about the middle of the 13th Century. Members of the Russian Orthodox Church revere him as the Baptizer of Russia and equal to the Apostles of Christ.

Charlemagne Empire 814 – Courtesy of slideplayer.com/Charlemagne

WESTERN EUROPE – CAULDRON OF BURNING EMPIRES

The 21st Century Western Europe has its foundational roots when in the ninth Century, Charlemagne established the Carolingian Dynasty that the Korka family ruled briefly and then handed over, for a payment of 125 pounds of gold and silver, to a family of Frankish wealthy nobility. The Empire lasted from 750 to 887 AD. As the first Holy Roman Emperor, Charlemagne ruled the lands from the North Sea down through the Low Countries and populating outward to Frankfurt, Paris, and Milan. The weaker sections of Europe extend along the Mediterranean, from the Iberian Peninsula to southern Italy. The historically less-developed Balkans were becoming the traditional birthplace for the Christian Byzantine and Islamic Ottoman traditions.[9]

Richard Theodor Kusiolek

HAVE WE PERISHED YET?

The radical S.S. members' Nationalist Socialist Party did not go away when the Second World War ended inside the concrete underground bomb shelter of Fuhrer Adolf Hitler. Instead, Ukraine became the melting pot for the new European Right Nationalism. It fought on eliminating Russian influence and traditions, economic intimidation sanctions, and using violence against innocent civilians to achieve political power. Many members of Ukraine's population spoke Russian and not the State approved Ukrainian Slavic language. The U.S. and European Union hand-picked new President of Ukraine, Petro Poroshenko, to some extent a prodigy of progressives Victoria Nuland, Hillary Clinton, John Kerry, and Barak Hussein Obama, who adhered to the tactics of radical community organizer Saul D. Alinsky and the political distorted narrative strategy of David Axelrod, a North-side Chicago Jewish public relations operative. In the effort of the FBI Director to overthrow the U.S. President, Donald J. Trump, Victoria Nuland Set up a meeting with Jim Comey's FBI to meet with the U.K. intelligence operative Christopher Steele. Steele was paid by the DNC, Hillary Clinton, and the FBI to author a dossier used in the Foreign Intelligence Surveillance Act (FISA) applications to justify surveillance warrants against Presidential Candidate Trump. The meeting that Nuland set up was at the Orbis Headquarters with Steele, FBI, and Michael Gaeta, a CIA agent disguised as the attaché at the U.S. Embassy in Rome, Italy.

HACKING ELECTIONS

Cybersecurity experts say Russia poses greater danger as launch pads for hacking election attacks. "This is not a matter of freedom of speech," former Ukrainian Prime Minister Arseniy Yatsenyuk said this month during a visit to Washington. "This is a national security issue." Advanced Persistent Threat 28—the allegedly

≪ 410 ≫

Russian cyberespionage group, also known as Pawn Storm, that unknown U.S. intelligence officials and cybersecurity experts state hacked the 2016 Democratic National Committee. Further, Pawn Storm accused of using social networking for deliberate attacks on Ukrainian targets and for so-called spear-phishing, in which individuals induced to reveal confidential information.

"Whether it's spreading malware or important harvesting details to use in other spear-phishing attacks, social-networking sites have been significant for Pawn Storm," said Feike Hacquebord, the researcher at cybersecurity firm, Trend Micro. Social media, cybersecurity experts say, serve a twofold purpose for hackers. The sites can be used as tools for gleaning personal information on individuals the group wants to target, and as platforms for posting malicious software."

In 2018 alone, major databases of Government and Private Industry have been hacked; namely, Facebook -fifty million users were compromised by the security breach; Macy's confirmed that some customers shopping online at Macys.com and Bloomingdales.com between April 26, 2018 and June 12, 2018 could have had their personal information and credit card details exposed to a third party; 2 million T-Mobile customers who were based in the U.S. had their account details breached in which their names, email I.D.s, account numbers, billing details and encrypted passwords; Sears alerted customers on April 04, 2017 of a "security incident" with an online support partner that may have resulted in up to 100,000 people having their credit-card information stolen; and Sonic Credit cards from five million customers may have been stolen, as most of the chains more than 3,600 locations use the same payment system.[10] Were these many breaches of database information all completed by Russian agents or homegrown or overseas criminal organizations that hired trained professional hackers? Some of these breaches never connected to Russia in any way, but Washington lobbyists and politicians embraced the approved narrative that Hillary Rodham Clinton lost the 2017 Presidential election because of Russia working with the Donald

J. Trump campaign. One could conclude that this deception used was to appease the corporate donors who spent over $2 billion on the 2016 Presidential campaign. If you donate expecting election results favorable to large contracts being awards, then you need to have a reason why billions were lost. After the Mueller exercise, the world learns the truth regarding the Russian collusion hoax story as in 2015, and no "free facts press" existed in the United States.

Ukraine Map-Courtesy of Infoplease.com

MINSK AGREEMENTS - JANUARY–FEBRUARY 2015

In 2015, Ukraine, Russia, France, and Germany agreed to a package of measures to alleviate the ongoing war in the Donbas region of Eastern Ukraine. The talks that led to the final peace deal, reviewed by the Organization for Security and Co-operation in Europe (OSCE), organized in response to the collapse of the Minsk Protocol ceasefire. Ukraine scuttled the new peace measures intended to revive a final peace accord. BBC news releases of 2015 stated that Kyiv's Army Commander Petro Poroshenko ordered a covert special forces team to enter Crimea and plant explosives to gain media attention and to bolster his political stature as well as destroying the peace process. On August 10, 2016, near the town of Armyansk Crimea, Russian troops entered into a firefight with Ukraine's European trained Special Forces intelligence officers, and two Russian soldiers killed. On August 12, 2016, the President of Russia Vladimir Putin declared that new peace talks with Ukraine sought in parallel with the September 2016 G-20 meeting in China. Two years before G-20, the Kyiv government's Ministry of Internal Affairs and Defense, orders lethal force engaged along the DPR/LPR borders. Thus, demonstrated that peace diplomacy gestures by Ukraine's President were meaningless charades to gain more debt and financial restructuring finance for Ukraine's military and oligarchs. Since the Ukrainian Constitutional elected President forced to leave by a Civil War that was created by Oligarchs, outside assistance was needed. To begin, Oligarchs like Petro Poroshenko needed U.S. Financial aid as Ukraine was a debtor nation that owed billions to Russia for natural gas and oil that its pipeline pumped. Collusion existed between the Kyiv U.S. State Department staff members and the CIA Station Chief. Many surmised that it was a joint effort with the West using covert tactics to overthrow a duly elected President. Again, news outlets in Europe believed that once the pro-Russian Ukraine President removed by violence. Ukraine's Oligarchs and those with a vested interest in the various ministries would then hire outside E.U. and U.S. "Influence consultants" to aid Poroshenko is securing billions in the name of "protecting Ukraine from the Russian Military along its borders."[11] This narrative parallel the U.S. Democratic Gender and Race Preference Socialist Party. The 10,540 killed in the Donbas Region would be a small price to pay in human capital compared to developing the vast resources of Eastern Ukraine. The developers would be the U.S. and European billion-dollar developers with the help of U.S. Aid programs.

DEBT-RIDDEN ECONOMY

Natalie Ann Jaresko was born in Chicago and spoke the Ukraine language. As an American-born investment banker and a non-Ukraine citizen, she was recruited by President Barak Obama's U.S. State Department to serve as Ukraine's Minister of Finance from December 2014 until April 2016. Ukraine's gross domestic product shrank 6.9 percent in 2014 and contracted by a further 5.5 percent in 2015 before returning to growth in the following year. Early in Jaresko's Ukraine term, she made an outline agreement for a $40 billion four-year loan from the International Monetary Fund and Western countries. In August 2015, Jaresko was instrumental in restructuring Ukraine's debts, including a partial write-off with a 20% cut on Ukraine's $18 billion privately-held government debt. In 2015, Ukraine's Government told bondholders it would pay back less money than it owes, taking an early step toward a bruising restructuring of as much as $30 billion of debt. Prices of Ukraine's benchmark bond due 2022 fell 5 percent to (42 cents on the dollar) after Finance Minister Natalie Jaresko's presentation Friday shattered hopes that Ukraine would merely seek to postpone debt payments. Ms. Jaresko also said the Government would ask investors to wait longer to get their money. On March 24, 2016, Jaresko, she argued that the Ukraine economy no longer political, and Ukraine needed a technocratic government and was willing to lead such a technocratic government. Ukraine Today and the U.K.'s Financial Times had reported speculation that Jaresko could become Ukraine's new Prime Minister, which was also suggested by former United States Ambassador to Ukraine Steven Pifer and President of Ukraine Petro Poroshenko. With U.S. President Obama to leave office in 2017, Jaresko rejected as a prime ministerial candidate by the governing coalition.

When the speaker of the Ukrainian parliament, Volodymyr Groysman, was elected as Ukraine's new Prime Minister on April 24, 2016, and Jaresko was given the thumbs down by the new Cabinet. After she left office, Jaresko said she believed the Ukraine macroeconomic situation had stabilized, and that Ukraine needed a further $25 billion of investment beyond the agreed IMF loans to "win over the hearts and minds of a poor struggling Ukrainian society. In May 2016, Jaresko became chairman of the Aspen Institute unit in Kyiv, a U.S. D.C. headquartered lobbying 501C3. Later, she accepted a $625,000/year position as an executive director of the Financial Oversight Board of Puerto Rico. The Financial Oversight and Management Board for Puerto Rico created under the Puerto Rico Oversight, Management, and Economic Stability Act of 2016. The Board consists of seven members appointed by the President of the United States and one ex officio member designated by the Governor of Puerto Rico.[12]

In November 2018, a new SBA released. In addition, the International Monetary Fund (IMF) and the Ukrainian authorities reached agreement on economic policies for a new fourteen-month Stand-By Arrangement (SBA). The new SBA replaced the arrangement under the Extended Fund Facility (EFF), which was approved in March 2015 and set to expire in March 2019. The resurrected SBA, with a requested access of SDR 2.8 billion (US$3.9 billion), will provide an anchor for the authorities' economic policies during 2019. Building on progress made under the EFF arrangement in reducing macroeconomic vulnerabilities, it will focus on continuing with fiscal consolidation and reducing inflation, as well as reforms to strengthen tax administration, the financial sector, and the energy sector. The agreement reached to help Ukraine achieve more durable, sustainable, and inclusive economic growth. Ukraine has become a debt-driven vassal state of the E.U. The new program developed in close coordination with the World Bank and the European Union, they have parallel operations to support Ukraine. Since 2017, the population of Ukraine has been rapidly declining. The Gross Domestic Product (GDP) (in US$ billions) in 2000 $136.01 and 2017 $112.15. GDP growth (annual %) was 4.2 percent, and in 2017, shrunk to 2.5 percent as Ukraine military ventures in the Donbas has stifled investment as risk remains high. In 2017, Ukraine's Military expenditures as a percent of GDP was 133.5 percent.[13]

Ukraine's largest bondholder is Franklin Resources, which owned about $8.5 billion of Ukraine debt on December 31, 2013, most purchased at prices above (80 cents on the dollar), according to data from Tradeweb. Russia also is a significant creditor, with $3 billion of debt from 2013. Russian officials have said they expect Kyiv to repay it on time at the end of the year. Ukraine's debt restructuring "will include a combination of maturity extensions, coupon reduction, and principal reduction." Ukraine hired an investment bank, Lazard, the world's largest independent investment bank, with principal executive offices in New York City, Paris, and London to assist in negotiations to restructure the debt. Before departing Ukraine for her next wealth-seeking political position, Ms. Jaresko, at the time, stated that the debt reductions would include some state-owned enterprises, including Ukreximbank. Many analysts showed that Ukrainian officials, including the head of the national bank, preferred to keep their wealth in bags full of dollars and euros in safes at their homes rather than entrust it to the Ukrainian financial system. President Petro Poroshenko has climbed up the ratings of Ukraine's wealthiest people during his tenure. The wealth list published by Novoye Vremya; a widely respected Ukrainian publication placed Poroshenko in the fourth place. According to Bloomberg in 2018, "Holdings in Ukrainian sovereign debt in the flagship $40 billion Templeton Global Bond Fund he manages have dropped by half in the past year to about $1.2 billion, or 3 percent of the total portfolio, according to filings posted on the fund manager's website. Most of the reduction was in Ukraine's shortest-dated bonds, maturing before the end of 2021."[14]

ECONOMIC TRADE RESCUE

On June 27, 2014, the economic part of Ukraine–European Union Association Agreement was signed on by Petro Poroshenko. In 2015, the Dutch held a referendum on whether to implement the step joining Ukraine as a full member with the twenty-eight

European Union (E.U.) members, but the majority voting against it. Sixty-one percent of Dutch voters said NO to ratifying the EU-Ukraine deal. Ukraine has become Slavic Ghetto to the Oligarchs in the E.U., the USA, and Ukraine. Ukraine is a priority partner within the Eastern Partnership and the European Neighborhood Policy (ENP). On January 01, 2016, Ukraine joined the DCFTA with the European Union.

UKRAINE ASSOCIATION AGREEMENT - 2016

Rational Ukrainian business people know that they cannot compete with the Europeans or prevented by E.U. protectionist measures. The E.U.'s annual quotas on the import of Ukraine agriculture goods are so small that the Ukrainians meet them for a couple of months. And in other industries, Ukrainian producers cannot meet European standards without significant modernization investment. The E.U. will approve loans as long as it does not include the USA and exclusively European (German, French, Italy, Spain, UK) equipment. According to the Ukrainian national statistics service, in the first three-quarters of 2016, Ukrainian exports to the E.U. were $9.7 billion, compared to $13.4 billion in 2014. Compared to the previous year, the country's exports to Russia over the same period fell by 30 percent to $2.5 billion. Before 2019, Russia remained the largest single-country importer of Ukrainian products, followed by China and Egypt. Ukraine will experience a failure to gain a larger share of European markets coupled with the devaluation of the national currency, which fell fourfold against the U.S. dollar. E.U. Trade website "Exports from Ukraine to the E.U." began to increase in 2016, by 3.7 percent in 2016 (to a total of 13.5 bn$). This performance saw against the backdrop of the continued decline in Ukraine's exports to the rest of the world (i.e., excluding the E.U.), where exports fell by 8.9 percent. The decline in exports to Russia has continued to decrease sharply, by 25.6 percent, primarily as a result of predatory measures Russia need to take against Ukraine to restrict trade. In

2017, the Export Value from the 28 EU/MS(EURO) to Ukraine was 20,215,108,628, and the Import Value from the 28 E.U. countries in Euros was 16,739,923,174. Kyiv politicians now will claim to have universal support for Ukraine's European aspirations. But it's more a technical issue since the free-trade part of the deal to revitalize the Ukrainian economy by opening European markets to Ukrainian goods. Also, offering high-quality European products to Ukrainian consumers at lower prices never materializes because the nine percent joblessness rate is high, and thousands of young workers have left other countries. There are no jobs in Western Ukraine as the Manufacturing and an Extractive mineral base is in Eastern Ukraine. Before the U.S. State Department under Clinton and Kerry, believing that redirecting the geography of Eastern and Western Europe was to be their legacy, over sixty percent of Ukraine's GDP occurred in the Donbas Region. On July 5, 2017, the European Commission opened up a legal case R689 of anti-dumping by Ukraine of seamless pipes and tubes (or iron or non-alloy steel).

E.U. AND USA WAR RECONSTRUCTION INVESTMENT TACTICS

In 2014, the Kyiv Oligarch started the Civil War for good reasons, namely, self-enrichment and to dilute Ukraine's sovereignty to join, as an impoverished commercial satellite, the E.U. Also, with the urging from then-Senator John McCain, Vice President Joseph BIDEN, and Secretary of State John Kerry, and the USA's leftist Democratic Party vote for sanctions to punish Russia for protecting its Russian-speaking citizens in Donbas and its border sovereignty. The remarks of Jean-Claude Juncker, President of the European Commission, indicated to hasten the defeat of the poor peasants of Industrial Eastern Ukraine. In 2014, Ukraine's Poroshenko and his military generals focused on destroying the Donbas Freedom Fighters. Brussels and the Kyiv Western Ukraine signed an Association Agreement, marking a new stage in the development of EU-Ukraine relations. All parties ratified the Association Agreement except for 60 percent of the Ukraine Nation citizens living in Eastern Ukraine. They were excluded and forced to wear psychological TERRORIST labels pinned to their clothing. It was a tactic that the Obama Administration and Barak Obama's Party in the U.S. Congress by being obstructionist and not voting on any crucial legislation that would benefit the entire nation. US Millionaire Elitist Lawyers (Kerry, Clinton, Biden, Obama, etc.) had taken over the Ukraine political decision-making process in the hope to develop the Eastern part of Ukraine; and to destroy the South Stream and Nord Stream2 pipelines from Russia to Europe.

CRIMEA TREATY

In November 2018, Ukraine's President Poroshenko signed a law criminalizing the" illegal crossing of Ukraine's borders, "including the arrival in the Crimea not through three official checkpoints with Ukraine, called Chalplynka (Armenian-New Kakhovka), Kalanchak (Armenian-Kherson) and Chongar (Dzhankoy-Melitopol). Law means that now any Russian who, for example, flew to Simferopol by plane or got through the Crimean bridge, becomes a potential criminal offense if the Russian enters Ukraine, he faces imprisonment for up to three to five years. Under the Treaty, the Black Sea is owned and governed by the nations that surround the Black Sea and nobody else. They also regularly the chairmanship of governance. The Russians have every right to fly over the Black Sea. Do remember that by another Treaty that only Russia or Turkey can govern Crimea. Turkey, when it was the Ottoman empire, and since Turkey has made no claims to Crimea. Crimea was Russian under Treaty from the 1700s. When Ukraine was part of Russia/USSR it could govern Crimea as part of Russia, when it became independent it lost the legal right as a 3rd party to rule, and Russia reasserted its legal and Treaty rights to take back what was Russian. Ukraine never existed at the time the original Treaty was signed (it was then Russian), and Russia has the right to Crimea. Time somebody studied history and Treaties. Russia exerting its powers and telling the R.N. and NATO, do not underestimate us, we are no pushover. Our real enemy is in the Middle East, not Russia, who are historical Europeans. There is no East or West in Europe.

SWAMP FEVER - GPS FUSION SPY DOSSIER

Again, the D.C. Billionaire Political class manufactured a "bogey" Russia Media Monster, namely, Russia Today (R.T.). Russia was an easy target as the old cold war propaganda tapes from an opposition research firm named FUSION GPS could be easily installed as reality by 2016. Fusion GPS was started in 2009 by former Wall Street Journal reporters Peter Fritsch and Glenn Simpson. Fusion GPS, the firm behind the controversial dossier of allegations about President Trump's connections to Russia. Fusion hired by a lawyer representing the Clinton Presidential campaign and the Democratic National Committee. After extensive investigations by the U.S. Congressional Committees, it revealed that the U.S. Department of Justice and the FBI attempted to overthrow the U.S. presidential candidate and to be Commander in Chief by falsehoods contained in the GPS Fusion DNC paid-for-dossier. What parts of the GPS Fusion dossier that was given to the New York Times and MSNBC journalist and used by the FBI for surveillance of the Trump campaign team accurate? Huffington Post's funded start-up Buzz Feed released the false, salacious dossier to the public. According to the opposition research GPS Fusion, Michael Cohen went to Prague to meet with Russians on behalf of Donald J. Trump. Then I had a secret meeting with a member of the Russian Duma. Why create the narrative except to promote Russian Collusion? No Proof ever happened. Further, the dossier stated that Manafort was in charge of the entire Russian Collusion Operation. Why create the narrative except to promote Russian Collusion? No Proof ever happened.

Carter Page, an ex-US Naval Academy graduate, was a Master Spy for the Russians. FBI used to get a Foreign Intelligence Surveillance Act (FISA) secret warrant to tap his conversations and to place him under 24hr surveillance. The dossier stated Carter Page receives significant stock holdings in a Russian Oil and Gas company for working with the Russians. Why create the narrative except to promote Russian Collusion? No Proof ever happened.

RUSSIAN TARGETS

What was the financial expense for a politically-directed attempt to severely wound an opposing American political party? The Robert Mueller, Special Counsel Russian Collusion Probe cost the U.S. taxpayers from Congress's approval on May 17, 2017, as a Department of Justice Special Counsel to January 2019 was $25 million. Robert Mueller targeted the close business and advisors to Donald J. Trump. He violated the law and pushed his prosecutorial attorneys in the Department of Justice to find anything to negate the 2016 U.S. Presidential Election. The media cartels like the Murdoch organization only had two news narratives for 28months; namely, Russia stole the election with their $4700 of Facebook ads and the man to rise to the U.S. presidency Donald J. Trump flawed in mind, body, and spirit.[15]

In a press review of filings by the U.S. Department of Justice from April 1, 2018, to September 30, 2018, taxpayers paid $4.56 million for the never-ending Mueller Russian Collusion legal court charade. ($2.9 Million for salaries and benefits; $942,787. For Rent, Communications, and Utilities; $60,000. For Printing and supplies, $580,098. For Transportation and Travel; and $310,732. For I.T. Services). The efforts to convict those who sought to overthrow the votes of over 65 million voters will continue for years to come and further denigrate a great Nation's first global beacon, namely, equal justice under the law. The small minority political class that lives off the U.S. taxpayers has become and will stay a clear and present danger to the U.S. Constitution.

Further, he set upon Russian Maria Butina, who he arrested and placed her in a six by seven isolation jail cell as he did with Paul Manafort. Mueller, Rosenstein, and Weinstein of the DOJ accused this attractive woman of being in the U.S. working as a Russian Foreign Agent without a license. If she were cooperative with his investigation of Russian Collusion, Butina would receive American citizenship. Michael Flynn was set upon because he talked to the Russian Ambassador, Butina, as she worked with the NRA and sought connections with GOP contacts. Typically, called business development, but in those political conspiracy directives of the DOJ, a Russian citizen working in D.C. targeted.

SECRET SERVICES

The United States Secret Service ("USSS" or "Secret Service") is a premier federal law agency. The U.S. State Department used the FBI and USSS to organize and fund the Security Service of Ukraine. The SBU vested by law, with the protection of national sovereignty. Also, constitutional order, territorial integrity, economic, scientific, technical, and defense potential of Ukraine, legal interests of the State, and civil rights. The State Secret Organization is vast and has an extensive charter from intelligence and subversion activities of foreign special services and unlawful interference attempted by specific organizations, groups, and individuals while ensuring the protection of state secrets.[16] Other duties include combating crimes that endanger the peace and security of humanity, terrorism, corruption, and organized criminal activities in the sphere of management and economy. As defined by the President of Ukraine, any unlawful acts immediately threatening Ukraine's vital interest; namely, the Minsk Agreement Republics of Luhansk and Donetsk.[17]

Ukraine SBU image — Courtesy of manageengine.com

POWER OF THE KORKA PURSE

Ukraine's secret service, the SBU, "systematically uses torture, ill-treatment, and intimidation, also running secret detention centers, the U.N. human rights body says. It describes spiraling violence and abuse on either side of the five-year conflict."[18] The U.N. documented hundreds of cases of illegal detention, torture, summary executions, and ill-treatment of captives both by the Ukrainian Government and pro-Russian armed groups in the East. Ivan Simonovic, UN Assistant Secretary-General for Human Rights, said the

"U.N. documents for the first time expose the scale and brutality of Ukraine's government-run torture program and the existence of five secret detention centers. In one case, Simonovic said, a suspect was picked up by black-hooded men thought to be SBU agents. He was then repeatedly shot in the head with a Taser pistol and had his left hand, head, back, and knee smashed with a hammer."

Pavel, the thirty-five-year-old man a critical Korka family soldier was forced to confess to being an armed narcotics group member, recorded on camera, and arrested without legal counsel.

Richard Theodor Kusiolek

Later, his captors took him to the basement of the SBU Kyiv Headquarters that in the Soviet Era was the KGB Headquarters. Pavel's brother, Boris Korka, was chained to a radiator, removed his breathing air with a gas mask, electric shocks, and waterboarded him while kicking and punching his genitals. Two months later, both Pavel and Boris were released after the Korka family paid $130,000 in uncut diamonds.

HACKING DATA A LUCRATIVE TRADE

The Korka Clan knew that in the new world of the internet and global spy satellites, it was time to transition from drug distribution and assassinations for hire into using technology to generate new flows of illegal cash on a worldwide basis. In 2006, the critical Korka Crime Committee met in a small hotel in Tangshan City, China. The thirteen members present created a hacking group that would be located in China and called the "Bear Group 13". Funds amounting to $two million used for recruitment and training. The goal was to target Managed Service Providers (MSPs) that are firms' other global companies use to store intellectual property and business data. MSPs also act as providers of I.T. services from patches to cloud services, making them a prime target for Korka's espionage operations. From 2007 to 2018, the trained Chinese hackers employed by the Bear Group 13, stole hundreds of gigabytes of confidential data from fifty-four technology companies in the United States and the E.U. The companies ranged from aviation, space technology to oil and gas companies. In that period, NASA's Goddard Space Center and Jet Propulsion Laboratory targeted, and designs and technology sold to the Chinese Military Institutes for $36Million. The design and specifications for Lockheed Martin's top-secret F-35 Fighter Jet were hacked and give to the PRC Defense Bureau in Xian China. U.S. Navy and Air Force data gave them the records of 150,000 personnel.

Further, U.S. Navy databases' theft gave them anti-ship missile technology and advanced rocket torpedoes. The Peoples Liberation

Navy paid the Korka Clan $1.3billion for that information alone. The United States was not the only country that "Bear Group 13" targeted, but also Brazil, India, Canada, Germany, and Britain. The Korka Organization recruited thirty-two Chinese National like Stuart Linn, who acted as a Chinese Intelligence Officer and a Silicon Valley Entrepreneur Technology engineer. Time proved that the new venture into stealing raw intelligence data from organizational databases was a $six billion a year enterprise. The top levels of the Chinese Government and the Russian Federation defense enterprises became a significant partner for the Korka Clan. However, their thirty-five billion-dollar drug distribution and assassination business was the mainstay that they could rely on.

SLAVIC RULE ONE- KORKA FAMILY IS EVERYTHING

In 1978, Ulyana Korka Georshivuka, nineteen years of age lived in the port city of Kherson, the Ukrainian Soviet Socialist Republic. Ulyana was the granddaughter Boryslav Korka, who played a pivotal role in the early political movements for Ukraine's independence. She met 32yr old Victor Arestovich, and the boss of a small mafia gang specializing in prostitution, guns, and distributing cocaine through the southern Ukrainian seaports of Kherson and Odesa. It is the administrative center of Kherson Oblast and designated as a city of oblast significance. Victor and Ulyana fell in love, and Ulyana gave birth to two boys, Miloslav and Durak. The Arestovich's lived in a well-kept apartment in the upper-middle-class neighborhood near the center of the city. They had a maid and a driver who picked them up when they called. On Sunday, as Victor was driving to pick up the boys and Ulyana from the Russian Orthodox Church, his car was ambushed, and he died instantly from over a hundred rounds from an AK47s. The funeral not held as Ulyana received death threats that her boys would be killed like their father if she attempted to give Victor a religious burial. Instead, his body cremated and his ashes placed in a small ceramic jar with the words, "Смерть убийцам" (translated-Death to Killers.)

With the void of no source of funds to feed the boys and to maintain the mortgage, Ulyana took over the business where Victor left. Soon, Ulyana became a ruthless leader of the gang and payments made to the judges, police, and politicians in Kherson and Odesa. The drug and gun trade increased in scope, and vast monies' flows began to allow the gang to increase in power and control. In 1991, the USSR dissolved and renamed Ukraine. The reality that criminal activities would only grow based on poverty, lack of jobs, and government corruption made life unbearable. During this time, Durak became a small-time drug dealer in his Kherson elementary school. Miloslav, who was seven years older than his brother, was a brilliant student and was given a scholarship from Harvard to study International Law. Ulyana controlled her two sons by tying them to the bedpost of their beds at night and beating their buttock with the steel wire she used as a whip until their buttocks would bleed from the blows.

"Remember, you are never to defy me. Do you understand?" The boys scream heard, "Yes, Mama, please stop; we will be good."

Then Ulyana would take a mason jar filled with kerosene and pour on their open and bleeding flesh wounds. They would scream and then begin to cry. Their mother would leave them lying on their stomach until they stopped crying. Then she would release them, giving each boy a hug and a piece of candy. With the funds that she had accumulated from her criminal activities, she purchased a large Victorian five-bedroom home in the farming community of Fresno, California. Miloslav completed his Masters in Political Science and his Law Degree from Harvard University. Durak was unable to stay focused on any of his goals or, for that matter, his future life. He married a local Mexican girl who was a petty drug dealer, and they became felony criminals stealing to pay for their drug addiction to PCP and Heroin. They were married and moved into Ulyana's Fresno home, but his mother supported Durak. She by then had an illegal drug wholesale business for the complete length of California, Arizona, Nevada, and Utah. In Ukraine, Ulyana's 42-year-old brother Oleksander had a clandestine growing nursery production mainly linked to the cultivation of poppy and subsequent output of acetylated or extracted opium the advancement of cannabis, mostly in western parts of Ukraine. Ulyana had bought a time-share housing program and used her five trips to Mexico to disguise her import business via Rocky Point that is a populated place situated in Maricopa County, Arizona. Earlier, with the help of her Mafia connections in Russia and Ukraine, Ulyana had arranged with Sinaloa Cartel boss Joaquin "El Chapo" Guzman to distribute Heroin and Chinese's manufactured synthetic Heroin in the United States on an exclusive basis for five years. At this point in her Global operation, she grossed a little over 34 million tax-free dollars. To open the Asian Market, she met and married Philip Itakura, a retired Sunnyvale California employee of a defense contractor TRW.

Philip had been a station chief of the CIA and, in addition to English, spoke Mandarin, Russian, and Japanese. Although Ulyana could not have children due to her weight of 250lbs and dislike for a physical connection with Philip, she agreed to have a younger 32-year-old Russian girlfriend Irina, to have Philip's baby for a fee of $23,000 US Dollars. Philip and Irina would live in the Fresno home and raise the baby boy they named Ivan Itakura. The boy led to believe that Ulyana was his mother, but he grew to hate her as she, regularly, would whip him with a wire strap in the same manner as she did with her other two boys. At night she would crawl in bed with Ivan and stroke his curly hair and ask for forgiveness for the early morning whippings. Ivan became attached to his mother and viewed the beatings as a form of love, and he soon accepted that pain was love. Philip, the sperm donor, wanted to cement the love relationship with Ulyana but had no idea that his wife from Ukraine had a great desire to be admired and sexually intimate with men outside of their marriage. Philip became more jealous and suspicious when Ulyana would have large dinners and invite men that she met on Facebook.

Bogdan Dzis came to their home in Monterey on the 4th and 5th of July 2015. Ulyana arranged for Bogdan to sleep in the spare bedroom. However, Bogdan openly and continued, during the 4th -5th of July weekend, to make sexual advances upon Philip's wife. Pain for Philip Itakura intensified. Philip asked Father John of the Russian Orthodox Church, to help him understand why Ulyana seemed to enjoy being with other men and not her husband. He viewed them whispering and touching each other in the house. He spoke to Father John at the Church,

"Ulyana, appears to have violated our marriage vows. I did not deserve for this guy to come to my home, sleep in my bed, and then make 'advances' on my wife. This stranger appears to be some type of 'stud 'who seeks other women, and yet he is going through a divorce."

"As you know by now, Father, when I admitted to you in confession, that I have many direct connections with the U.S. State Department, FBI, and CIA. If this issue not resolved within our church family, I am going to ask them to check out Bogdan A. Dzis's visa and qualifications to be in America. As karate trained Japanese man, he was lucky that I did not confront him directly, but I wanted to keep the peace in my home. Please advise me. I assure you that I will take no action unless we communicate-If I am out of line, I am open to your advice and perceptions."

Father George felt great sympathy for Philip and spoke,

"remember Philip, you are the head, and Ulyana is the neck. Without the head working with the neck, nothing achieved. You must go and hold her hand and ask her why she is a neck that wants to be a head."

Later in the evening, as Philip was showering, he was in deep thought that he believed that with the arrival of Bogdan, Ulyana, was treating him like a "boarder" in his own home and disrespecting him as a father-husband-professional. He whispered to himself in the bathroom as he toweled his wet naked body,

"I know that love her. I will continue to understand her, as I must, why has my close lover decided to seek other men after four years of marriage. I just do not understand why she rubs against Bogdan, and yet she expects me to accept it. This seems to be wrong!"

Later, on the evening of July 05, after Bogdan kissed Ulyana and left their home at 7 pm, Philip decided to have a heart to heart talk with his Ukrainian wife, Ulyana Itakura. They both sat at the edge of the bed in the master bedroom, and Philip spoke,

"my dearest, I have been troubled for the last two days. I did not want to make you unhappy, but I realized that I do not know the extent of your love and respect towards me after four years. Can you be honest and express to me what is important to you in our relationship?"

Ulyana jumped up and paced the room and then glared at Philip in a state of anger.

"Philip, I married you because I needed to leave Ukraine, and you paid the $10,000 per our marriage agreement! Also, you had a substantial retirement fund. I wanted a new home and life in America. It is that simple."

Ulyana, stared at Philip and smiled, "To be honest, my two sons are more important to me than you. My older son may be a recovering heroin addict and our fifteen-year-old high school a truant who is failing, but they are better than you. You are the problem in my family! You are creating all of the stress in this home and not them. They are good boys. You are an older man, and that is the problem. My first husband, Victor, who died of food poison at twenty-five years of age, allowed me to associate with other men when we were married freely. Well, this is not an Orthodox Christian view of marriage, but I do not care. I still love Victor as he would never challenge me like you are doing this evening."

Philip sat on the edge of the bed for ten minutes, dazed from the outburst from the woman he loved. He could not take the pain any longer. Then stood up and, without a word, walked out of the bedroom and slammed the door. He walked down the stairs to the kitchen and reached for the bottle of vodka and poured the contents into a giant crystal glass. He walked to the front room and sat next to the fireplace. He stared into the flames and thought,

"am I just being too sensitive, and I should allow Bogdan A. Dzis to make a 'sexual pass' on my wife? -in front of me. This is so twisted. Anyway, I am forming the Ukraine Venture Fund. This twenty-seven-year-old Ukrainian guy, Bogdan A. Dzis, does not have the high moral character to assist the Silicon Valley venture community and me. After 'making advances on my wife,' I would never introduce him to my contacts. He is just a 'sex dog 'who violates common Christian Orthodox morality. As an Orthodox Christian and a warrior of God, I have decided that he is not of an executive management caliber. Alright, I made this decision based on his actions in my home and his rubbing his body upon my wife's buttock. Now, Ulyana and I are in serious jeopardy based on him coming to my home and making a 'play' on my wife. - End of the story---he is history to me. I may decide to leave Ulyana as she is cunning and devious simply. I only wanted to dream and believe that when I met this blond woman, she was genuine. I think I was fooled to bring her to America."

With that final thought, Philip walked up the stairs, entered the master bedroom, opened the covers next to Ulyana, and fell immediately asleep.

Durak, by the age of thirty-three, spent two years in California's Folsom Prison. He moved into Ulyana and Philip's second home in Santa Cruz, California, a community of 75% Mexican and the central truck distribution hub for UPS and the Sinaloa cartel Heroin distribution point for the U.S. east coast of New York, Charlotte South Carolina, and Washington DC. With Durak becoming a willing foil for his mother, Ulyana decided to give him the responsibility of the family's drug dealers' network and logistics. However, after he gained the confidence of Ulyana and Philip, he fell into his sea of addiction and began stealing Heroin from shipments. Durak convinced himself that he could control his habit so that it would not affect his ability to follow the orders of his mother, Ulyana. Durak began meeting Victoria Gomez at a safe drug house in Bonny Doon, a census-designated place in Santa Cruz County, California. The small town is situated northwest of the city of Santa Cruz, considered part of the southern San Francisco Bay Area or northern Monterey Bay Area. Victoria was also heavily addicted to Heroin and spent three years in Federal Correctional Institution at the Dublin California prison for burglary, use of a gun in the commission of a crime, and drug distribution. Victoria and Durak united again in sex and drugs.

Slowly Durak lost interest in being a key member of his mother's drug business. He soon drifted back to the same path of taking Heroin every five hours and not eating or caring where he would sleep. Soon his face was pocked-mark from the result of his frequent use of PCP and Heroin. After his multiple arrests and the Court sending him to numerous failed drug treatment programs and leaving those programs without permission, the increased bail bond levies reached $375,000. Ulyana was committed to loving her three sons even when they brought her pain both physically and mentally. However, the business was business, and she was responsible for over 45 gang members in the U.S. and Ukraine. Ulyana realized that the company was in jeopardy as the DEA and the FBI were beginning to investigate her source of funds. Fearing arrest by the DEA, she locked Durak out of the house, towed his car away, canceled all of his credit cards, and removed the $50,000 in cash from his savings account. From now on, her 34-year Ukrainian green card holder son was on his own. Durak arrived at the Watsonville house at 3 am. He punched in the door lock code, but the door would not open. After several tries, he grabbed a ladder from the back of the house and climbed on the roof and broke the upstairs hallway window. He jumped in, cutting his arm from the shattered glass. He did not care about the bleeding. Durak's drug-high removed any painful feelings. He burst into his mother's room.

He turned on the light, Ulyana lay naked next to Dmitry Vasiliev, the man who owned the truck rental agency who transported the majority of shipments back east. Durak grabbed a blanket and threw it on their naked bodies.

"Dmitry, get your ass out of here before I kill you."

Durak was holding a bowie knife. Dmitry jumped up and grabbed his clothes and shoes, and ran down the stairs. Durak stood over Ulyana.

"How could you do this to me your son, Mom! I did everything that you ever asked of me. I slept on the floor when you invited your male friend to stay overnight and used my bed for your invited girlfriends. I tuned up your car. I drove that little weasel mulatto test-tube baby son of yours to school every day. I had to put up with all your boyfriends sleeping in the house. I had to drive your friends to the airport. I wasn't a son but just a chauffeur or handyman for you. Go to hell, you bitch!"

With that, Durak left the Itakura household for good. Soon, Durak began to specialize in breaking into homes and cars to steal cars, credit cards, guns, and cash. At times, he would take home appliances, automotive toolboxes that were new and expensive. By the time Durak was 35, he had sixteen felony counts, twenty-six misdemeanors, and spent another eighteen months in the Santa Cruz County Jail and completed five drug treatment programs. Each time that after ninety days into the treatment, Durak would meet Victoria Gomez or her twin sisters, he would be back shooting up Heroin. Santa Cruz County is a sanctuary in California County, lawyers and judges viewed burglary and thievery as only minor offenses. Even murder committed while under the mental State of opium, cocaine, PCP, or Heroin considered politically correct from Democratic Party oriented judges as not the fault of the murderer or drug user. It was all about media narrative and also the rich people who were born rich. Companies would never hire him. When they heard how Ulyana treated her boys, the social workers, and the Santa Cruz County judges could see that Durak's mother was a significant enabler of the harmful social habits and criminal behaviors of her three sons. There would be no accountability as California Society and culture gravitated around drugs as necessary as a cup of coffee to start the day.

Soon, when this Ukraine criminal family reunited within the same home with Ulyana as the head of the household, they saw how Durak gave up his quest for the love of women. As he learned in prison, loving men was safer and less confusing. Once Ulyana allowed Durak's boyfriend to move in, his entire life turned around. He became the "Korka crime family enforcer" who would talk with brass knuckles to those who did not pay for drug deliveries or who became police informers.

UKRAINIAN TRAVEL PLANS

Ulyana Arestovich Itakura's alarm rang at 3:00 am on a cold November morning. She lay in her bed for fifteen minutes and thought about all the steps that she had to take to prepare for her 4:00 early morning limo pick-up to arrive at the airport. She purchased two tickets for her Ukraine Airline nonstop eight-hour flight to Kyiv, Ukraine's capital. After showering and preparing her face make-up, she began to rush around to pick up her clothes for packing. Ulyana's closet was custom made to store over 120 pairs of shoes and 500 tailored business suits and dresses. It was now 3:35 in the morning, and she had packed her two large travel bags. The plan that she had arrived at was to provide $40,000 in one-hundred-dollar bills to obtain political contacts with the family's bribery and facilitation payments. She took the money and arranged each ten thousand wrapped bundle in her vest that she pulled around the stomach, breast, and buttock.

Upon arrival, her special customs agent, Andriy, would not check her travel bags or her person. Andriy was a direct descendant of Vasily Ivanchenko and had received $1500 every month from

Ulyana. Andriy was a thirty-five years old Ukraine customs agent that was loyal and followed strict instructions. Ulyana knew that her business trip would be successful. Her goal was to arrange for a sale of Heroin, Cocaine, Amphetamines, and Methamphetamines. Since the beginning of the Donbas War, Ukraine soldiers were using drugs, and in the last month, Kyiv club drugs soared. Many of the high government officials' children were using Heroin. Profit margins had risen to 75 percent. Ulyana could never pass these opportunities, and after all, she was raised poor in a small home constructed with discarded fiberglass roofing material. Ulyana's father only earned fifty-six dollars per month as a cab driver. She immediately stopped thinking of the hefty $450,000 profit she would make in Ukraine. The Limo was at the front door, and she had an hour's drive to the airport and then a transfer in Chicago's O'Hare airport.

In Chicago, Ulyana had arranged for her new traveling companion, Alla Gerasko, to meet at O'Hare's gate 55. She arrived in Chicago at 11:13 in the late morning and immediately rushed to catch the New York flight. At the entrance was Alla, and when they met, Ulyana hugged Alla and swiftly entered the first-class seating section. Ulyana took the window seat and Alla the middle seat. Alla Gerasko was the Chicago Ambassador for Ukraine. Upon take-off in New York on flight 2378 UIA-Ukraine International Airlines PJSC, the flag carrier and the largest airline of Ukraine, they exchange pleasantries. The breakfast served was a four-star service consisting of ham and eggs, porridge, soup, and champagne.

Alla paid $10,000 to introduce Ulyana to Olena Volodymyina, a key contact in Ukraine's wealthy elite inner-circle. Olena was paid $5,000 for an introduction with critical RADA politicians involved in importing Fentanyl and cocaine from China and Afghanistan. From that point, Ulyana Arestovich Itakura purchased to sell both drugs in Ukraine. She was receiving from Mexico's drug cartels, Heroin, Amphetamines, and Methamphetaminesam. Ulyana's business plan was to establish her lab in Fresno, California, in an underground complex built secretly to generate $2,000,000. It was all a win-win. America and Ukraine would be critical markets. Ulyana had two Rolex watches to give to her RADA connection and a close associate of Poroshenko.

Olena would receive a $5,500 gold necklace and bracelet. Both the Ukraine and California operations were going to reach a high net margin. Ulyana slept for 6hrs on the UIA flight and awoke feeling fresh and regenerated. Ulyana reached over and awoke Alla. "Alla, good news. We are preparing to land. How did you sleep? Alla opened both eyes and let out a large sigh. She stretched her arms and embraced Ulyana. Upon landing, departure, and walking to the customs inspection area with their baggage, Andriy stood smiling broadly, met them at the customs area, and ushered them directly to the exit doors. Andriy bowed and led them to a waiting black Mercedes. The stage was set for Ulyana's grand entrance with her female partners to make millions in Ukraine. It was so easy. When the officials saw the "greenbacks," they almost tripped on themselves, knowing that the $100 bills gave a better exchange rate of Ukrainian Hryvnia on the "black market" with a rate of 1 to .85. Ulyana would stay in Kyiv for thirty days. With the war raging in Eastern Ukraine, her son Artem was purchasing arms from China and providing them on a bid-rigging scheme on a contract decide by high officials in the Ukraine Defense Agency and the Korka Family's Syndicate. Artem's bid would be successful in the tender as his contacts would draft their proposals accordingly. In the past, bid-rigging include bid rotation, complementary bidding, and cover pricing. Bid rigging in Ukraine was not criminal.

In 2012, Durak flew to Kyiv Ukraine to start a new life with Ulyana's drug gang oligarchs. On June 13, 2012, Durak Korka Arestovich's Audi SUV explodes as he reached over to kiss his girlfriend, Victoria Gomez. Both killed instantaneously; their heads are the only body part that the Kyiv first responders were able to find.

Donetsk Ukraine Parent - Courtesy of Manu Brabo/Associated Press

In 2016, Miloslav Korka Arestovich became a well-known U.S. Senator in the Progressive Political Party. The family's drug and extortion business interests reach into Russia, Turkey, Syria, France, Spain, Mexico, and the United States. The family's wealth has grown to gross $10.4 billion a year.

Korka's family roots were deep. They were related to the stars, and they, through the centuries, learned the code of conduct. Miloslav Korka Arestovich tells his wife Uliya that their family's power

"comes from inside our ancestors and erupts to crush the tyrants. We are all bound together by Motherland, Spartans, really strong-willed, strong, brave, and bold. We are courageous people and protect the Slavic peoples where ever they are. We are not going to hide under the sheet of white."

Each time the family meets, they take the "star stones" from the safe deposit faults, and they are all laid down on the floor with all members of the Clan kneeling and bowing before the stones. The Korka Family held together and were victorious over the centuries because they taught each generation how to be covert intelligence-gathering agents in real life. Secrecy is an essential component of the Korka Clan's success. They could all practice spy craft all aspects of intelligence collection for whatever side could pay them the most. They all knew how to avoid exposure and caught, and each generation had the goal of espionage that thrives in the shadows. They worked with the intelligence agencies of the U.S., Russia, Spain, Syria, Turkey, France, North Korea, Spain, China, and Japan. Miloslav Korka Arestovich, who is Lawyer and U.S. Senator, worked undercover as an SBU agent and worked as a secret lobbyist for the Russian Government.

In April 2016, Miloslav assembled the family in his five-million- dollar Georgetown Washington DC Mansion to discuss another opportunity to further the family's scope and wealth.

"We do not have to worry about any interference from NSA or any U.S. intelligence organization; you know there are fearful pools of career attorneys and accountants. When I built this Mansion two years ago, of course, with the help of my Mom, Ulyana, all the walls and roof are lined with copper so that no satellite or any communication devices can penetrate these walls. We are safe here. We can talk freely.

As you know, you were all checked for listening devices as well. I had my team also x-ray your package and travel bags. All of your phones and computers were left in our safe storage area so that no tracking or listening devices can disrupt our plans. Awareness is just the routine procedures that I learned during the summer that I spent training as a CIA Langley field officer. Let me get down to business. I want to talk about three big income investment projects. The first project is to develop mind control techniques and truth serums as a part of the Korka-Multra project that we started in Romania in 1973 from our investments with the US CIA. I am happy to report that we created six lab dogs operated by remote control via our satellite. I will pass out diagrams of the surgical implants that employed, stimulating the brain with electrical stimulation to control responses. We can sell the technology and techniques to North Korea or the Drug Cartels for an estimated $500 million. The second is to employ our tactic of kompromat to undermine President Foster's credibility by taking the monies given to us from the Vision Group and legal consulting D.C. firms to expand on rumors about Foster secretly flying to Crimea to meet the Presidents of Russia and North Korea.

The CIA has no idea what is happening as we have some of our agents already with that U.S. Intelligence agency. Throughout centuries we have combined information and insight of our founding family headsman. He said it so many years ago that without politics, we cannot protect our capital and our family. With our fleet of Micro-Satellites, we can now intercept conversations on smartphones. We have already penetrated the Foster Tower and the DC Foster Hotel. We believe that it makes sense to discover from the classified National Intelligence Estimate what the U.S. intelligence groups are trying to determine regarding North Korea. We present to their enemies our plans to gain what they are seeking and then get it. The third major billion-dollar project is that we have been assigned by our Mongolian organization to steal rocket technology and atomic warheads for their MIRVs. As you know from our early breakfast discussions, the leader Kim Jong-un appreciates our help in providing him with the rockets made to look like ICBMs. However, they cannot attack the U.S. or Europe yet.

The Korean leader feels that the greatest threat to his regime is the presumed President of the United States, John J. Foster. He wants us to plan now to eliminate him in a manner that will look like an accident. Do you any comments or suggestions?" Ivan Korka Itakura stood up and paced around the circle of the fifteen members of the Korka Clan. He cleared his throat.

"As you know, I am the Omaha USAF base commander of all rocket forces of the United States and NATO. I will have all secret codes and up to date daily schedule of John Foster. Access to information should allow us to coordinate with our teams here in D.C."

Ulyana stood up to speak,

"as you can see, my sons raised to be successful here in the U.S. I think that this is a powerful incentive for us to make this hit one of our best. I have created this $19-billion-dollar Empire that will be greater and far-reaching more than our founder's long line of Korka ancestors and descendants."

Miloslav spoke, "Mama, you always have motivated me to do good. Thank you for speaking. I have a perfect prospect of being appointed to John Foster's Cabinet as a Progressive advisor. We know that Mr. Foster wants to show the country that he is bipartisan and willing to work with the Progressive Party. I have worked with our technology lab in Chengdu. We can deliver a death blow by using nanotechnology that manipulating atoms and molecules for fabrication of macroscale injection method that he will not feel. We can use a simple normal handshake as a delivery mechanism. So far, our new space and deep earth probe technologies and embraced innovation will help us maintain the cryptologic advantage that will increase the prices we are receiving from foreign governments who openly hate John Foster."

Miloslav was extremely confident and feeling more enthusiasm as he spoke again,

"We have gone further than any of the Mexican drug cartels in Ukraine, Turkey, or Mexico. We own our poppy fields in Afghanistan and production labs in Mongolia. We can deliver our inventory anywhere in the world with our fleet of jet aircraft. Our abilities to change the course of history with assassinations, regional wars that keep our corporate sponsors happy, and over 129 of our own trained agents working as dormant assassins will keep us prosperous. We can use these methods to assassinate anyone. As you all know, we have used the following low-risk methods: poisoned pills – six of them, in a bottle of Bayer aspirin pills, and poison mixed with a milkshake. Remember our art with diet coke spiked with LSD, and lacing the leader's scuba gear with tuberculosis to trigger deadly skin disease. For now, cells in central government agencies should help us reach our goal in 2020 of being a $65 billion untouchable global and outer-space power by 2022."

With that statement, Miloslav knelt again in the ring of the fifteen members of the Korka Family holding all their hands and bowed at the center of the ring where the "star Stones" glowed in the green light. Next, they stood up and in unison read from a small white 5 x 5 thick white card in their ten commandments from their ancient leaders Korka and Tiaka:

"Empathize with our enemies. Rationality will never give us victory in our struggles. There is something beyond our current life. Maximize covert and overt violence. Proportionality should be our guide in war. Obtain data on our enemy before we strike. Attack with severe intensity and give no quarter. Beliefs that we, not divine star messengers, are false. Be prepared to re-examine our defeats. To do good, we must engage in evil. And Never give up until your ultimate death and return to our Star planet."

The foundation launch realized with the help of the Phase 1 plan of the US CIA. In 2014, people in Kyiv took to the streets in an anti-government protest, which resulted in riots, over a hundred deaths, and an ousted government. Ukraine is an impoverished country rife with corruption and far from its European dream. The events in Kyiv were labeled the 'Revolution of Dignity' by the victors, who seized power on the back of right-wing radicals and promises of integrating Ukraine into the (EU). On November 21, 2014, statements made by the U.S. selected Ukraine President, Petro Poroshenko, a national holiday in Ukraine. However, its name, 'Dignity and Freedom Day,' appears to be far from the actual impact the coup had on the country. Sergey Korak and the Interior Minister, Mykhailo Kliayav, who triggered the 2013-2014 city riots in Ukraine cities of Odesa, are both found dead blindfolded with a single bullet hole in their foreheads. The political and economic consequences of Sergey Korak's spycraft results in the Russian annexation of Crimea, arming of the Donetsk and Lugansk militia population, and the Kyiv random artillery military battles, which led to over 10,000 killed in the eastern "Donbas Region." On December 14, 2019, President John Foster signed with Russia, France, Germany, Turkey, and Poland, the "Donbas Freedom Agreement," which separates Ukraine into Western and Eastern countries. The Donbas Regions remains part of Russia as an industrial extension governed jointly by Russia and Ukraine. Western Ukraine becomes part of the European Union, and sections of Poland become part of the territory of Ukraine.

On August 22, 2020, Senator Miloslav Korka Georshivaka Arestovich met with President Foster during a Senate breakfast meeting at the White House. He shook his hand and thanked the President for his leadership and ability to include the Progressive Party in all White House staff and cabinet meetings. On August 31, 2020, the President of the United States awakes at 3:24 in the early morning. He had a strange feeling in his body as parasites were burrowing into his heart and brain. White House EMS rushed the President to the Walter Reed Hospital. He was pronounced dead at 6:09 in the morning. The headline of the New York Times read, "President Foster dead at 74 – from unknown causes."

In 2020, the headline on the front page of the Washington Post reads, "Covert Spying on U.S. Citizens." The story focuses on the revelation that all U.S. police agencies covertly spy on innocent citizens with military hardware. An Independent Report revealed that

"dozens of police departments across the U.S. are using special devices to track suspects without warrants. However, the International Mobile Subscriber Identity (IMSI) Catchers also capture data from regular people walking on the street. The technology developed for the military mimics' cell phone towers and tricks phones into routing signals through them. Apple allows police to track a suspect's location. The machines even allow police to get the location of a phone without the user making a call or sending a text."

The most common of these devices is called a "StingRay." The devices can also collect the "phone numbers a person has been calling and texting and even intercept the content of communications. At least 72 state and local law enforcement departments in twenty-four states and thirteen federal agencies use the devices, according to a classified released by a White House leaker to the Washington Examiner. The story by Hunter

King notes that further details are hard to come by because the departments that use IMSI Catchers must take the unusual step of signing FBI non-disclosure agreements. An FBI spokeswoman told the news agency that the agreements, which regularly involve the defense contractor that makes the machines, are intended to prevent the release of sensitive law enforcement information to the general public.

The U.S. House of Representatives' Oversight and Government Reform Committee released a report that found the Justice Department and the Department of Homeland Security had spent a combined $95 million on 1434 cell-site simulators between 2010 and 2019. Law enforcement agencies have also gone to great lengths to conceal "StingRay" usage, in some instances, even offering plea deals rather than divulging details on the machine. In several states, courts are beginning to grapple with the issue. In September 2019, Judge Herman Feng ruled that the police do not need an eavesdropping warrant to use a "StingRay." In November 2019, a federal appeals court ruled the use of the device without an order does not violate the U.S. Constitution, specifically the Fourth Amendment.

On August 31, 2021, the Anniversary of the death of President John J. Foster, his sixteen-year-old son David Foster, delivers the following speech at his St. John's College High School graduation ceremony. "Freedom is not free. It requires participation. When we allow members of a political party to create lies interjected into media news narratives that are false, we should consider acts of disobedience or remove a political party's ability to promote its destructive policies of street riots. When "re-cycled" Senators are enjoying 30-year terms in being in positions of power because they will follow not the People's Business but their Party's Business, then it is time to work on limiting the terms of Senators and members of the House of Representatives."

John raised his voice an octave and smiled across the audience in the meeting room and spoke, "further, the European Slavic Peoples who came to the United States under great hardships and contributed so much to its growth and power, should not be relegated to a category created by the Democratic Party as merely white. An American Lawyer-driven political party that works overtime to erect statues and memorials to their voter minority blocks, while tearing down statues honoring European American heroes, should be restricted from the public square for all times. Is it not better to cry from the public square that we are all equally Americans and to eliminate the political party's foundations built around racism and gender superiority? Thank you, and God bless America."

A sound from the assembled faculty and guest heard. It appeared that David Foster fell to the floor. Secret Service officers were seen on digital video cameras running towards the stage with guns ready to fire. Ulyana Korka Arestovich Itakura, dressed in a red sweater, black skirt, and boots, leaves from the side door and enters a black Mercedes- Benz S- Class Sedan.

"Ivan, drive slowly and carefully back to our DC mansion. I have found our ocean of truth and it was always below the waves, beyond the reach of tempests, in the eternal calm of our destinies."

END

ENDNOTES

PROLOGUE:

"Within the intelligence services, tradecraft, and its synonym field craft (one word, not two), has been used since prior to the First World War. I remember seeing the term in a very old training manual while preparing a report on the history of human intelligence operations while in training to be a counter intelligence officer for the US Army. Unfortunately, both documents remain classified in the Fort Huachuca (Arizona) Intelligence Library. Specifically, tradecraft refers to those clandestine activities by human intelligence agents to facilitate the gathering of intelligence information by other humans. What it all really comes down to is a term most often associated with magician's misdirection. What tradecraft does not refer to is any of the technical means of intelligence gathering including listening devices (bugs), satellites, or ground radio monitoring stations. A bug used to listen in on meetings in an embassy, for instance, is not tradecraft. However, getting the asset (the person working in the embassy as well as the bug itself) in place is tradecraft. In a magicians' terms those satellites, cameras, and radios would be referred to as props. "The mission of the USA Intelligence Community is to seek to reduce the uncertainty surrounding foreign activities, capabilities, or leaders' intentions. This objective is difficult to achieve when seeking to understand complex issues on which foreign actors go to extraordinary lengths to hide or obfuscate their activities. On these issues of great importance to US national security, the goal of intelligence analysis is to provide assessments to decision makers that are intellectually rigorous, objective, timely, and useful, and that adhere to tradecraft standards.

- The tradecraft standards for analytic products have been refined over the past ten years. These standards include describing sources (including their reliability and access to the information they provide), clearly expressing uncertainty, distinguishing between underlying information and analysts' judgments and assumptions, exploring alternatives, demonstrating relevance to the customer, using strong and transparent logic, and explaining change or consistency in judgments over time.
- Applying these standards helps ensure that the Intelligence Community provides US policymakers, warfighters, and operators with the best and most accurate insight, warning, and context, as well as potential opportunities to advance US national security.

Intelligence Community analysts integrate information from a wide range of sources, including human sources, technical collection, and open source information, and apply specialized skills and structured analytic tools to draw inferences informed by the data available, relevant past activity, and logic and reasoning to provide insight into what is happening and the prospects for the future.

- A critical part of the analyst's task is to explain uncertainties associated with major judgments based on the quantity and quality of the source material, information gaps, and the complexity of the issue.
- When Intelligence Community analysts use words such as "we assess" or "we judge," they are conveying an analytic assessment or judgment.

- Some analytic judgments are based directly on collected information; others rest on previous judgments, which serve as building blocks in rigorous analysis. In either type of judgment, the tradecraft standards outlined above ensure that analysts have an appropriate basis for the judgment.
- Intelligence Community judgments often include two important elements: judgments of how likely it is that something has happened or will happen (using terms such as "likely" or "unlikely") and confidence levels in those judgments (low, moderate, and high) that refer to the evidentiary basis, logic and reasoning, and precedents that underpin the judgments."

(Office of the Director of National Intelligence (ODNI) released the report 1/6/2017 titled "Assessing Russian Activities and Intentions in Recent US elections.")

END NOTES CHAPTER ONE

Historical background: A new study has revealed previously unknown details about early Ice Age Europeans, including fluctuations in their eye color and complexion. The research paints a picture of a dramatic history of mass migrations spanning thousands of years. A paper titled "The genetic history of Ice Age Europe," was published by Nature Journal on May 2. Researchers used new techniques to analyze 51 samples of degraded DNA from ancient remains to shed light on over some 40,000 years of prehistory. "What we see is a population history that is no less complicated than that in the last 7,000 years, with multiple episodes of population replacement and immigration on a vast and dramatic scale, at a time when the climate was changing dramatically," Reich added. Publish RT news May 3, 2016

"Neanderthal DNA is slightly toxic to modern humans," said co-author professor David Reich, from Harvard Medical School in Boston, US. Modern-day Europeans can trace their lineage back to the founding population known as Aurignacian culture. According to the study, this group of humans lived in northwest Europe 35,000 years ago. However, Aurignacian culture was displaced when another group of early humans, the Gravettian culture, migrated to Europe 33,000 years ago. Nevertheless, around 19,000 years ago when the Ice Age peaked, people related to the Aurignacians re-migrated and expanded across Europe from the southwest, which is present-day Spain. Another massive migration uncovered by the researchers took place 14,000 years ago, when ice sheets had already melted and populations from the southeast, such as from Turkey and Greece, migrated to Europe, again displacing Aurignacian culture.

PREHISTORY

The sources for the prehistoric period are entirely archaeological. Early excavation in Iran was limited to a few sites. In the 1930s archaeological exploration increased rapidly, but work was abruptly halted by the outbreak of World War II. After the war ended, interest in Iranian archaeology revived quickly, and since 1950 numerous excavations have revolutionized the study of prehistoric Iran. For the proto-historic period (e.g., the 5th-century-BC Greek historian Herodotus). the historian is still forced to rely primarily on archaeological evidence, but much information comes from written sources as well. None of these sources, however, is both local to and contemporary with the events described. Some sources are contemporary but belong to neighboring civilizations that are only tangentially involved in events in the Iranian Plateau; for example, the Assyrian and Babylonian cuneiform records from lowland Mesopotamia. Some are local but not contemporary, such as the traditional Iranian legends and tales that supposedly speak of events in the early 1st millennium BC. (re-write and need to tie-into the story line)

PALAEOLITHIC (CA. 100,000-10,000B.C. E)

Enigmatic evidence of man's presence on the Iranian Plateau as early as Lower Palaeolithic times comes from a surface find in the Baktaran Valley. The first well-documented evidence of human habitation is in deposits from several excavated cave and rock-shelter sites, mainly located in the Zagros Mountains of western Iran, dated to Middle Palaeolithic or Mousterian times (c. 100,000 BC). There is every reason to assume, however, that future excavations will reveal Lower Palaeolithic man in Iran. The Mousterian flint-tool industry found there is generally characterized by an absence of the Levallois technique of chipping flint and thus differs from the well-defined Middle Palaeolithic industries known elsewhere in the Middle East. The economic and social level associated with this industry is that of fairly small, peripatetic hunting and gathering groups spread out over a thinly settled landscape. Locally, the Mousterian is followed by an Upper Paleolithic flint industry called the Baradostian. Radiocarbon dates suggest that this is one of the earliest Upper Paleolithic complexes; it may have begun as early as 36,000 BC. Its relationship to neighboring industries, however, remains unclear. Possibly, after some cultural and typological discontinuity, perhaps caused by the maximum cold of the last phase of the Würm glaciation, the Baradostian was replaced by a local Upper Paleolithic industry called the Zarzian. This tool tradition, probably dating to the period 12,000 to 10,000 BC, marks the end of the Iranian Paleolithic sequence.

THE MESOLITHIC (CA. 10,000-5500 B.C.E).

Evidence indicates that the Middle East in general was one of the earliest areas in the Old World to experience what the Australian archaeologist V. Gordon Childe called the Neolithic revolution. That revolution witnessed the development of settled village agricultural life based firmly on the domestication of plants and animals. Iran has yielded much evidence on the history of these important developments. In the early Mesolithic, evidence of significant shifts in tool manufacture, settlement patterns, and subsistence methods, including the fumbling beginnings of domestication of both plants and animals, comes from such important western Iranian sites as Asiab, Guran, Ganj-e Dareh, and Ali Kosh. Similar developments in the Zagros, on the Iraqi side of the modern border, are also traceable at sites such as Karim Shahir and Zawi Chemi-Shanidar. This phase of early experimentation with sedentary life and domestication was soon followed by a period of fully developed village farming as defined at important Zagros sites such as Jarmo, Sarab, upper Ali Kosh, and upper Guran. All of these sites date wholly or in part to the 8th and 7th millennia. (need a map showing these sites) https://www. britannica.com/place/ancient-Iran

One important god of the Slavs was Perun, who was related to the Baltic god Perkuno. Like the Norse god Thor, Perun was a thunder god, considered a supreme god by some members of the Slavs, just like Thor was considered the most important god by some Germanic peoples. The male god of youth and spring, named Jarilo (or Iarilo), and his female counterpart, Lada, the goddess of love, were also ranked highly in the Slavic pantheon. Both Jarilo and Lada were gods who died and were resurrected each year, and Jarilo in particular might have had a connection with fertility motifs. Several multiple-headed gods were also included in Slavic mythology, such as Svantovit (or Svantevit), the god of war, who had four heads, two of them males and the other two females; Porevit, with five heads, representing the summer; Rujevit, with seven faces, the incarnation of autumn; and Triglav, who displayed three heads and was simultaneously looking into the sky, the earth, and the underworld.

Footnote: Ottoman Endgame: War, Revolution and the Making of the Modern Middle East, 1908-1923. By Sean McMeekin. Penguin Press; 576 pages; $35. Allen Lane; £30.P36 –

ENDNOTE CHAPTER TWO

According to legend, St. Ursula, the daughter of a fifth-century English Christian king, led a pilgrimage of 11,000 virgins by ship to Rome. On their return, rerouted by a storm, nearly all but Ursula were massacred in Cologne by pagan Huns. When Ursula refused to marry their chief, he shot her dead with an arrow. Unconventionally, also, Caravaggio's shallow-spaced, psychologically driven "Ursula" is so absorbingly intimate and involving that the king's bow—without enough room to be fully drawn—feels aimed at viewers, not Ursula. And the drama contains only five players: the king, who has just released the arrow; Ursula's handmaiden, who reaches protectively between the bow and the dying, white-as-marble princess, who has just received the arrow, point-blank, in her breast; an armored soldier, who steadies the collapsing saint; and, lastly, Caravaggio, whose self-portrait piggybacks on Ursula's neck like a drowning man struggling to keep his head above water. (WSJ -By Lance Esplund May 26, 2017 5:30 p.m. ET Appraising the Artist's Final Canvas Caravaggio's 'The Martyrdom of St. Ursula' (1610)

This video shows how Germans/Dutch stealing Scythian artifacts: https://www.youtube.com/watch?v=cQDTsJUVpUY

(Common Era or Current Era, abbreviated CE, is a calendar era that is often used as an alternative naming of the Anno Domini era ("in the year of the Lord"), abbreviated AD. The system uses BCE as an abbreviation for "before the Common (or Current) Era" and CE as an abbreviation for "Common Era".) Joshua J. Mark ---a freelance writer and part-time Professor of Philosophy at Marist College, New York, Joshua J. Mark has lived in Greece and Germany and traveled through Egypt. He teaches ancient history, writing, literature, and philosophy)

(Augustus (plural augusti), /ɔːˈgʌstəs/;[1] Classical Latin: [awˈgʊstʊs], Latin for "majestic," "the increaser," or "venerable"), was an ancient Roman title given as both name and title to Gaius Octavius (often referred to simply as Augustus), Rome's first Emperor. On his death, it became an official title of his successor, and was so used by Roman emperors thereafter.

MONGOL PERIOD

1236: The beginning of the Mongol invasion of Europe

1236-1237: The Mongol-Song war began

1237: Under the leadership of Batu Khan, the Mongols returned to the West and began their campaign to subjugate Kievan Rus'

1236-1239: The Mongol invasion of Georgia and Armenia under Chormaqan

1240: The Mongols sacked Kiev

1241: Hungarians and Croatians at the Battle of Sajo and Poles, Templars and Teutonic Knights at the Battle of Legnica are beaten.

1241 and 1242: The Mongols under Batu and Kadan invaded Bulgaria and forced them to pay annual tribute as vassals.

1243: Western army made Seljuks of Anatolia a part of Mongol empire. The Lesser Armenians and the Empire of Trebizond surrendered to the Mongol Empire.

ENDNOTE CHAPTER THREE

Wine was the Battle Fuel of the Roman Legions -In Roman times, it was universally agreed that the finest wine was that of the Falernian region near Naples. In fact, in a foreshadowing of the French appellation regulations, there were three types of Falernian wine. Caucinian Falernian originated from vineyards on the highest slopes of Mount Falernus; Faustian Falernian came from vineyards on the central slopes; and wine from the lower slopes was known simply as Falernian. Perhaps surprisingly, given modern tastes, the most prized Falernian was a white wine. Roman sources indicate that the grapes were picked fairly late, resulting in a heavy, sweet wine that was golden in color and could be aged for decades. The nearest contemporary equivalents would appear to be long-aged sauternes wines, such as Chateau d'Yquem. But Falernian would have tasted very different, for a number of reasons. For a start, it was allowed to modernize, which caused it to turn amber or brown. A modern drinker presented with a glass of Roman wine might also notice that its taste was affected by the pitch or resin that was used to make impermeable the earthenware jars in which the wine was stored. Good words are more difficult to find than the emerald, for it is by slaves that that is discovered among the rocks of pegmatite. From the Precepts of Ptah-hotep, 5th dynasty -- convicted criminals and prisoners of war according to Diodorus Siculus, as few people chose to work under the often-appalling conditions which were prevalent in the mining regions of Sinai and the deserts of Egypt.

It is commonly thought that B.C. stands for "before Christ" and A.D. stands for "after death." This is only half correct. How could the year 1 B.C. have been "before Christ" and A.D. 1 been "after death"? B.C. does stand for "before Christ." A.D. actually stands for the Latin phrase anno domini, which means "in the year of our Lord." The B.C./A.D. dating system is not taught in the Bible. It actually was not fully implemented and accepted until several centuries after Jesus' death. It is interesting to note that the purpose of the B.C./A.D. dating system was to make the birth of Jesus Christ the dividing point of world history. However, when the B.C./A.D. system was being calculated, they actually made a mistake in pinpointing the year of Jesus' birth. Scholars later discovered that Jesus was actually born around 6—4 B.C., not A.D. 1. That is not the crucial issue. The birth, life, ministry, death, and resurrection of Christ are the "turning points" in world history. It is fitting, therefore, that Jesus Christ is the separation of "old" and "new." B.C. was "before Christ," and since His birth, we have been living "in the year of our Lord." Viewing our era as "the year of our Lord" is appropriate. Philippians 2:10–11 says, "That at the name of Jesus every knee should bow, in heaven and on earth and under the earth, and every tongue confess that Jesus Christ is Lord, to the glory of God the Father." In recent times, there has been a push to replace the B.C. and A.D. labels with B.C.E and C.E., meaning "before common era" and "common era," respectively. The change is simply one of semantics—that is, AD 100 is the same as 100 CE; all that changes is the label. The advocates of the switch from BC/AD to BCE/CE say that the newer designations are better in that they are devoid of religious connotation and thus prevent offending other cultures and religions who may not see Jesus as "Lord." The irony, of course, is that what distinguishes B.C.E from C.E. is still the life and times of Jesus Christ." (https://www.youtube.com/watch?v=VfpKan_l_Jw)

ENDNOTE CHAPTER FOUR

"In 2016, the ruling clan of Recep Tayyip Erdogan hungered for portions of Saudi Arabia and worked to refine ISIS crude oil stolen from Iraq and Syria and to return arms and food supplies in return. The Turkish government used the world's going price in this trading relationship."

Special videos on the Ukraine Donbass Military Actions - (https://
www.youtube.com/watch?v=SIzED67nk-E)Bibliography: (https://
gotquestions.org/BC-AD.html)

Silly issue Before explaining what the Habsburgs owed dynastically
to Maximilian, mention can be made of a physical peculiarity
characteristic of the House of Habsburg from the Emperor
Frederick III onward: his jaw and his lower lip were prominent, a
feature supposed to have been inherited by him from his mother,
the Mazovian princess Cymbarka. Later intermarriage reproduced
the "Habsburg lip" more and more markedly, especially among the
last Habsburg kings of Spain.)

ENDNOTE CHAPTER FIVE

Darius, was the third Persian King of the Achaemenid Empire. His
reign lasted 36 years, from c. 522 to 486 BCE; during this time the
Persian Empire reached its peak. Darius led military campaigns
in Europe, Greece, and even in the Indus valley, conquering
lands and expanding his empire. Not only resuming to military
prowess, Darius also improved the legal and economic system and
conducted impressive construction projects across the Persian
Empire.

The last big Russo-Turkish war, which formed one of the fronts
in the first world war, is a source of continuing fascination to
Sean McMeekin, a history professor at Bard College north of New
York who previously taught at two universities in Turkey. In "The
Ottoman Endgame", a sweeping account of the last 15 years of
the Ottoman empire, the most original and passionately written
parts concern the fight between Russians and Turks in eastern
Anatolia and the Caucasus. Two things distinguish Mr. McMeekin
from many other writers in English about this period. First, he
has a deep empathy with Turkish concerns, and he is closer to the

official Turkish line than to the revisionist, self-critical approach taken by some courageous Turkish liberals. Second, he has some unusual insights into imperial Russian thinking, based on study of the tsarist archives.

The author has a well-founded sense that traditional theocratic powers which look ramshackle or even moribund to Western eyes can still act with ruthless effectiveness when the strategic stakes are really high; and he applies that point in equal measure to the late Ottoman empire and to the late tsarist one. Actually, Mr. McMeekin insists, it was an Anglo-Franco-Russian deal; and he argues, controversially, that the Russians were senior partners in the bargain. Many students of the period will see in Mr. McMeekin's approach a barely hidden agenda.

Music for "Man of Seven Shadows"

https://www.youtube.com/watch?v=Q9zYxoaonwM
https://www.youtube.com/watch?v=Oh9LH-yAevE
https://www.youtube.com/watch?v=jd5PNsLk4jU

ENDNOTE CHAPTER SIX

Andrew Weis a firm anti-Russian Scholar of the Carnegie Endowment, wrote that "according to declassified CIA reports, Moscow used a web of front groups, secret payments to activists and articles placed in the press. The Russians also carefully conveyed propaganda themes to sympathetic media outlets, peddled disinformation and produced damaging forgeries of official U.S. and NATO documents. Soviet propaganda tools and forged documents were employed to hurt U.S. interests. In the mid-1980s, the Soviets circulated a fake National Security Council directive purporting to show the Reagan administration's hope to develop a nuclear first-strike capability. In the pre-internet age, such (fake news) disinformation could circulate in many places for years. In a 1976 operation against (Senator) Jackson, the KGB forged a memo in which Hoover "reported" in 1940 that the senator was gay and sent it to newspapers and Jimmy Carter's presidential campaign. Over the years the KGB and the Federal Security Service (FSB) follow a longstanding Russian messaging strategy that blends covert intelligence operations—such as cyber activity—with overt efforts by Russian Government agencies, state-funded media, third-party intermediaries, and paid social media users or 'trolls.'Weiss, Andrew, Moscow Dusts Off the KGB Playbook, WSJ Review, Saturday, February 18, 2017)

Transcriber this video of putin= describes why Russia and USA have their differences in 2015-2018 https://www.youtube.com/watch?v=3JVR0zAiyw0

Transcript of the Home Shows of RT "SophieCo" -Obama used NSA & FBI to spy on Trump – veteran CIA officer - Published time: 17 Mar, 2017 08:50 Transcript of Interview

"The mighty CIA has fallen victim to a major breach, with WikiLeaks revealing the true scope of the Agency's ability for cyber-espionage. Its tools seem to be aimed at ordinary citizens – your phone, your car, your TV, even your fridge can become an instrument of surveillance in the hands of the CIA. How does the CIA use these tools, and why do they need them in the first place? And as WikiLeaks promises even more revelations, how is all of this going to shape the already tense relationship between new president and the intelligence community? A man who has spent over two decades in the CIA's clandestine service – Gary Berntsen is on SophieCo.

Follow @SophieCo_RT

Sophie Shevardnadze: Gary Berntsen, former CIA official, welcome to the show, great to have you with us. Now, Vault 7, a major batch of CIA docs revealed by Wikileaks uncovers the agency's cyber tools. We're talking about world's most powerful intelligence agency - how exactly did the CIA lose control of its arsenal of hacking weapons? Gary Berntsen: First off, I'd like to say that the world has changed a lot in the last several decades, and people are communicating in many different ways and intelligence services, whether they be American or Russian, are covering these communications and their coverage of those communications has evolved. Without commenting on the specific validity of those tools, it was clear that the CIA was surely using contractors to be involved in this process, not just staff officers, and that individuals decided that they had problems with U.S. policy, and have leaked these things to Wikileaks. This is a large problem, for the U.S. community, but just as the U.S. is having problems, the Russia face similar problems. Just this week you had multiple members of the FSB charged with hacking as well, and they have been charged by the U.S. government. So, both services who are competitors, face challenges as we've entered a new era of mass communications.

SS: So, like you're saying, the leaker or leakers of the CIA docs is presumably a CIA contractor - should the agency be spending more effort on vetting its own officers? Is the process rigorous enough?

GB: Clearly. Look … There have been individuals since the dawn of history. Espionage is the second oldest occupation, have conducted spying and espionage operations, and there have been people who have turned against their own side and worked for competitors and worked for those opposing the country or the group that they're working with. It's been a problem from the beginning, and it continues to be a problem, and the U.S. clearly is going to have to do a much better job at vetting those individuals who are given security clearances, without a doubt.

SS: The CIA studied the flaws in the software of devices like iPhones, Androids, Smart TVs, apps like WhatsApp that left them exposed to hacking, but didn't care about patching those up - so, in essence the agency chose to leave Americans vulnerable to cyberattacks, rather than protect them?

GB: I think you have to understand, in this world that we're operating and the number one target of our intelligence community are terrorists. Since the attacks of 9\11, 16 years ago, the obsession of the American intelligence community is to identify those planning terrorist attacks, collecting information on them and being able to defeat them. These individuals are using all these means of communication. I have spoken with many security services around the world, since my retirement back in 2005-2006, a lot of them have had problems covering the communications of somebody's very devices and programs that you've talked about - whether they be narcotraffickers or Salafist jihadists, they are all piggybacking off of commercial communications. Therefore, the need for modern intelligence services to sort of provide coverage of all means of communications. And there's a price that you pay for that.

SS: One of the most disturbing parts of the leaks is the "Weeping Angel" program - CIA hacking into Samsung Smart TVs to record what's going on even when the TV appears to be turned off. Why are the CIA's tools designed to penetrate devices used by ordinary Western citizens at home?

GB: Look, I wouldn't say it has anything to do with Western homes, because the CIA doesn't do technical operations against American citizens - that's prohibited by the law. If the CIA does anything in the U.S., it does its side-by-side with the FBI, and it does it according to FISA - the Foreign Intelligence and Surveillance Act laws. It's got to go to the judge to do those things. Those tools are used primarily against the individuals and terrorists that are targeting the U.S. or other foreign entities that we see as a significant threat to the U.S. national security, which is the normal functioning of any intelligence service.

SS: Just like you say, the CIA insists it never uses its investigative tools on American citizens in the US, but, we're wondering, exactly how many terrorist camps in the Middle East have Samsung Smart TVs to watch their favorite shows on? Does it seem like the CIA lost its direction?

GB: Plenty of them.

SS: Plenty? ...

GB: I've travelled in the Middle East; Samsung's are sold everywhere. Sophie, Samsung TVs are sold all over the world. I've spent a lot of time in the Middle East, I've seen them in Afghanistan, I've seen them everywhere. So, any kind of devices that you can imagine, people are using everywhere. We're in a global economy now.

SS: The CIA has tools to hack iPhones - but they make up only around 15 % of the world's smartphone market. iPhone are not popular among terrorists, but they are among business and political elites - so are they the real target here?

GB: No. The CIA in relative terms to the size of the world is a small organization. It is an organization that has roughly 20 or more thousand people - it's not that large in terms of covering a planet with 7 billion people. We have significant threats to the U.S. and to the Western world. We live in an age of super-terrorism, we live in an age when individuals, small groups of people, can leverage technology at a lethal effect. The greatest threats to this planet are not just nuclear, they are bio. The U.S. needs to have as many tools as possible to defend itself against these threats, as does Russia want to have similar types of tools to defend itself. You too, Russian people have suffered from a number of terrible terrorist acts.

SS: Wikileaks suggest the CIA copied the hacking habits of other nations to create a fake electronic trace - why would the CIA need that?

GB: The CIA, as any intelligence service, would look to conduct coverage in the most unobtrusive fashion as possible. It is going to do its operations so that they can collect and collect again and again against terrorist organizations, where and whenever it can, because sometimes threats are not just static, they are continuous.

SS: You know this better, so enlighten me: does the CIA have the authorization to create the surveillance tools it had in the first place? Who gives it such authorization?

GB: The CIA was created in 1947 by the National Security Act of the U.S. and does two different things - it does FI (foreign intelligence) collection and it does CA - covert action. Its rules for collection of intelligence were enshrined in the law that created it, the CIA Act 110, in 1949, but the covert action part of this, where it does active measures, when it gets involved in things - all of those are covered by law. The Presidential finding had to be written, it had to be presented to the President. The President's signs off on those things. Those things are then briefed to members of Congress, or the House Permanent Subcommittee for Intelligence and the Senate Select Committee for Intelligence. We have a very rigorous process of review of the activities of our intelligence communities in the U.S.

SS: But you're talking about the activities in terms of operations. I'm just asking - does CIA need any authorization or permission to create the tools it has in its arsenal? Or it can just go ahead ...

GB: Those tools and the creation of collection tools falls under the same laws that allowed the CIA to be established. And that was the 1949 Intelligence Act. And also, subsequently, the laws in 1975. Yes.

SS: So, the CIA programmed names are quite colorful, sometimes wacky - "Weeping Angel", "Swamp Monkey", "Brutal Kangaroo" - is there a point to these, is there any logic, or are they completely random? I always wondered …

GB: There's absolutely no point to that, and it's random.

SS: Okay, so how do you come up with those names? Who … like, one says: "Monkey" and another one says: "Kangaroo"? …

GB: I'm sure they are computer-generated.

SS: Trump accused Obama of wiretapping him during the campaign … Could the CIA have actually spied on the president? It seems like the agency doesn't have the best relationship with Donald Trump - how far can they go?

GB: Let me just say this: The President used the word "wiretapping" but I think it was very clear to us that have been in the intelligence business, that this was a synonym for "surveillance". Because most people are on cellphones, people aren't using landlines anymore, so there's no "wiretapping", okay. These all fall under the Intelligence Surveillance Act, as I stated earlier, this thing existing in the U.S. It was clear to President Trump and to those in his campaign, after they were elected, and they did a review back that the Obama Administration sought FISA authorization to do surveillance of the Trump campaign in July and then in October. They were denied in July, they were given approval in October, and in October they did some types of surveillance of the Trump campaign. This is why the President, of course, tweeted, that he had been "wiretapped" - of course "wiretapping" being a synonym for the surveillance against his campaign, which was never heard of in the U.S. political history that I can remember, I can't recall any way of this being done. It's an outrage, and at the same time, Congressional hearings are going to be held and they are going to review all of these things, and they are going to find out exactly what happened and what was done. It's unclear right now, but all we do know - and it has been broken in the media that there were two efforts, and at the second one, the authorization was given. That would never have been done by the CIA, because they don't do that sort of coverage in the U.S. That would either be the FBI or the NSA, with legal authorities and those authorities ... the problem that the Trump administration had is they believed that the information from these things was distributed incorrectly. Any time an American - and this is according to the U.S. law - any time an American is on the wire in the U.S., their names got to be minimized from this and it clearly wasn't done and the Trump administration was put in a bad light because of this.

SS: If what you're saying is true, how does that fall under foreign intelligence? Is that more of the FBI-NSA expertise?

GB: It was FBI and NSA - it was clearly the FBI and the NSA that were involved, it would never have been the CIA doing that, they don't listen to telephones in the U.S., they read the product of other agencies that would provide those things, but clearly, there were individuals on those phone calls that they believed were foreign and were targeting those with potential communications with the Trump campaign. Let's be clear here - General Clapper, the DNI for President Obama, stated before he left office, that there was no, I repeat, no evidence of collusion between the Trump campaign and Russia. This has been something that has been dragged out again, and again, and again, by the media. This is a continuing drumbeat of the mainstream, left-wing media of the U.S., to paint the President in the poorest light, to attempt to discredit Donald Trump.

SS: With the intelligence agencies bringing down Trump's advisors like Michael Flynn - and you said the people behind that were Obama's loyalists - can we talk about the intelligence agencies being too independent from the White House, playing their own politics?

GB: I think part of the problem that we've seen during the handover of power from President Obama to President Trump was that there was a number of holdovers that went from political appointee to career status that had been placed in the National Security apparatus and certain parts of the intelligence organizations. It is clear that President Trump and his team are determined to remove those people to make sure that there's a continuity of purpose and people aren't leaking information that would put the Administration into a negative light. That's the goal of the administration, to conduct itself consistent with the goals of securing the country from terrorism and other potential threats - whether they be counter-narcotics, or intelligence agencies trying to breach our ... you know, the information that we hold secure.

SS: Here's a bit of conspiracy theories - could it be that the domestic surveillance agencies like the NSA or the FBI orchestrated the Vault 7 leaks - to damage CIA, stop it from infringing on their turf?

GB: I really don't think so and that is conspiracy thinking. You have to understand something, in the intelligence communities in the U.S., whether it be the CIA and FBI, we've done a lot of cross-fertilizations. When I was in senior position in CIA's counterterrorism center, I had a deputy who was an FBI officer. An office in FBI HQ down in Washington had an FBI lead with a CIA deputy. There's a lot more cooperation than one would think. There are individuals that do assignments in each other's organizations to help foster levels of cooperation. I had members of NSA in my staff when I was at CIA, members of diplomatic security, members of Alcohol, Tobacco and Firearms, and it was run like a task force, so, there's a lot more cooperation than the media presents, they always think that there are these huge major battles between the organizations and that's rarely true.

SS: Generally speaking - is there rivalry between American intel agencies at all? Competition for resources, maybe?

GB: I think, sometimes, between the Bureau and the CIA - the CIA is the dominant agency abroad, and the FBI is the dominant agency in the U.S. What they do abroad, they frequently have to get cleared by us, what we do domestically, we have to get cleared by them, and sometimes there's some friction, but usually, we're able to work this out. It makes for great news, the CIA fighting FBI, but the reality is that there's a lot more cooperation than confrontation. We are all in the business of trying to secure the American homeland and American interests globally.

SS: I'm still thinking a lot about the whole point of having this hacking arsenal for the CIA since you talk on their behalf - the possibility to hack phones, computers, TVs and cars - if the actual terrorist attacks on US soil, like San Bernardino, Orlando are still missed?

GB: Look. There are hundreds of individuals, if not thousands, planning efforts against the U.S. at any time. It can be many-many things. And the U.S. security services, there's the CIA, the FBI, NSA - block many-many of these things, but it is impossible to stop them all. Remember, this is an open society here, in America, with 320 million people, here. We try to foster open economic system; we allow more immigration to America than all countries in the world combined. This is a great political experiment here, but it's also very difficult to police. There are times that the U.S. security services are going to fail. It's inevitable. We just have to try the best we can, do the best job that we can, while protecting the values that attract so many people to the U.S.

SS: The former CIA director John Brennan is saying Trump's order to temporarily ban travel from some Muslim states is not going to help fight terrorism in 'any significant way'. And the countries where the terrorists have previously come from - like Saudi Arabia, or Afghanistan, it's true - aren't on the list. So, does he maybe have a point?

GB: John Brennan is acting more like a political operative than a former director of CIA. The countries that Mr. Trump had banned initially, or at least had put a partial, sort of a delay - where states like Somalia, Libya, the Sudan, Iran - places where we couldn't trust local vetting. Remember something, when someone immigrates to the U.S., we have what's called an "immigration packet": they may have to get a chest X-ray to make sure they don't bring any diseases with them, they have to have background check on any place they've ever lived, and in most of these places there are no security forces to do background checks on people that came from Damascus, because parts of Damascus are totally destroyed - there's been warfare. It is actually a very reasonable thing for President Trump to ask for delay in these areas. Look, the Crown-Prince, the Deputy Crown-Prince of Saudi Arabia was just in the United States and met with Donald Trump, and he said he didn't believe it was a "ban on Muslims". This was not a "ban on Muslims", it was an effort to slow down and to create more opportunity to vet those individuals coming from states where there's a preponderance of terrorist organizations operating. A reasonable step by President Trump, something he promised during the campaign, something he's fulfilling. But again, I repeat - America allows more immigration into the U.S., than all countries combined. So, we really don't need to be lectured on who we let in and who we don't let in.

SS: But I still wonder if the Crown-Prince would've had the same comment had Saudi Arabia been on that ban list. Anyways, Michael Hayden, ex-CIA ...

GB: Wait a second, Sophie - the Saudis have a reasonable form to police their society, and they provide accurate police checks. If they didn't create accurate police checks, we would've given the delay to them as well.

SS: Ok, I got your point. Now, Michael Hayden, ex-CIA and NSA chief, pointed out that the US intelligence enlists agents in the Muslim world with the promise of eventual emigration to America - is Trump's travel ban order going to hurt American intelligence gathering efforts in the Middle East?

GB: No, the question here - there were individuals that worked as translators for us in Afghanistan and Iraq and serving in such roles as translators, they were promised the ability to immigrate to the United States. Unfortunately, some of them were blocked in the first ban that was put down, because individuals who wrote that, didn't consider that. That has been considered in the re-write, that the Trump administration had submitted, which is now being attacked by a judge in Hawaii, and so it was taken into consideration, but ... the objective here was to help those that helped U.S. forces on the ground, especially those who were translators, in ground combat operations, where they risked their lives alongside American soldiers.

SS: You worked in Afghanistan - you were close to capturing Bin Laden back in 2001 - what kind of spying tools are actually used on the ground by the CIA to catch terrorists?

GB: The CIA as does any intelligence service in the world, is a human business. It's a business where we work with local security forces to strengthen their police and intelligence forces, we attempt to leverage them, we have our own people on the ground that speak the language, we're trying to help build transportation there. There's no "secret sauce" here. There's no super-technology that changes the country's ability to conduct intelligence collections or operations. In Afghanistan the greatest thing that the U.S. has is broad support and assistance to Afghan men and women across the country. We liberated half of the population, and for women were providing education, and when the people see what we were doing: trying to build schools, providing USAID projects - all of these things - this makes the population willing to work with and support the United States. Frequently, members of the insurgence groups will see this and sometimes they do actually cross the lines and cooperate with us. So, it's a full range of American political power, whether it's hard or soft, that is the strength of the American intelligence services - because people in the world actually believe - and correctly so - that American more than generally a force of good in the world.

SS: Gary, thank you so much for this interesting interview and insight into the world of the CIA. We've been talking to Gary Berntsen, former top CIA officer, veteran of the agency, talking about the politics of American intelligence in the Trump era. That's it for this edition of SophieCo, I will see you next time. END of Sophie story on CIA transcript

Jacob Henry Schiff was a Jewish-American banker, businessman, and philanthropist. [Similar to the present-day George Soros, a Jewish businessman, who financed numerous radical Marxist movements in the United States] Among many other things, German born Marxist Schiff, helped finance the expansion of American railroads and the Japanese military efforts against Tsarist Russia in the Russo-Japanese War. Lenin did not decide any of this himself. The Jewish historian Edvard Radzinsky has tried to assert that it was Lenin who gave the orders to murder the Tsar and his family. But no such telegram has been found in the archives. Radzinsky's explanation that Lenin had this telegram destroyed does not hold water, since there is a vast amount of compromising material about Lenin otherwise. Why should he have destroyed only this particular telegram and no other equally incriminatory documents? Stalin disliked entire nationalities that had been deported during the War, also as traitors, were not allowed to return to their homes, and in 1953, a plot to kill Stalin was ostensibly uncovered in the Kremlin itself. A new purge seemed imminent and was cut short only by Stalin's death. He remained a hero to his people until Khrushchev's well-known "secret" speech to a Party Congress in 1956, in which Stalin's excesses, at least as far as power grabbing in the Party itself, were denounced." (footnote: Joseph Stalin's embalmed body shared a spot next to Lenin's, from the time of his death in 1953 until October 31, 1961, when Stalin was removed as part of de-Stalinization and Khrushchev's Thaw, and buried in the Kremlin Wall Necropolis outside the walls of the Kremlin.)

The German Caucasus Army/Army Group A, took place across the Strait of Kerch. To support the retreat the German Organization Todt (OT) had built a ropeway across the Kerch Strait with a daily capacity of 1,000 tons. On 7 March 1943 Hitler ordered the construction of a combined road and railway bridge over the Strait of Kerch within 6 months. In April 1943, the OT had started with the construction of a combined iron road and railway war-bridge across the strait of Kerch. On 1 September 1943 concentrated Soviet attacks began on the remnants of the bridge head, so that the German retreat was accelerated. At this time the new bridge was not yet completed (only one third was completed). As part of the German retreat, the Wehrmacht blasted the already completed parts of the bridge. — (Bibliography: Inside the Third Reich by Albert Speer, Chapter 19, pg. 270 (1969, English translation 1970) The 4.5-kilometre (2.8 mi) bridge was actually built in the summer of 1944 after the liberation of the Crimea by the Red Army from the materials left on the site by the Wehrmacht. It was destroyed within six months by flowing ice.

Colonel Leopold Herman Ludwig von Boyen (1771-1848) was a distinguished staff officer who first came to know the Russian Army in 1807. His charitable view of

Cossacks was as follows: - "One should not judge the Cossack by the standards of so-called civilized nations because from this point of view he appears course and inclined to violence. But if one sees in him only the child of nature brought up from long custom exclusively to be a warrior then one soon discovers many quite remarkable sides to him. The endurance, the energy, the bump of locality, the inborn judgement of the Cossacks admirable and with these qualities he carries out splendidly the most difficult mission in unfamiliar territory without understanding the local language. In addition, the Cossack is good-natured and loyal to his superiors unless he is incited by passion. During my frequent attachments to the Russian Army, I often had Cossacks as orderlies and Always parted from them reluctantly. In unspoiled human nature there is a heart of gold beside which our own culture appears to me like mere silver."

key videos for CIA training as follow:

https://www.youtube.com/watch?v=5CFLpZcY3ss&t=2646s
https://www.youtube.com/watch?v=Tvdhu5FM-7Q
https://www.youtube.com/watch?v=xfi8FIh7tsU
https://www.youtube.com/watch?v=IaqazWEvRGc
https://www.youtube.com/watch?v=I_kdewVFbsY

ENDNOTE CHAPTER SEVEN

U-5 was built by the Fiume-based firm of Whitehead which had bought a license from the Irish-American John Philip Holland to build his submarines. The first two boats were partially assembled in the United States and assembled at Whitehead's, which caused a lot of trouble. The third boat was built on speculation and featured improvements in all the mechanical and electrical systems. Named S.S.3 this unit was offered to the Austrian Navy too, but she was refused because the trials program was not yet completed. Whitehead then offered the boat to the navies of Peru, Portugal, Netherlands, Brazil, Bulgaria and again to the Austro-Hungarian Navy. When war broke out Austria bought the unsold boat and provisionally commissioned her as U7, but by the end of August 1914 she was definitely commissioned as U12. The single-hulled Holland type featured a distinctive tear-drop hull and an interesting design of the TT hatches: these were clover-leaf shaped and rotated on a central axis. Naval service: All three-saw active war service. U5, sunk after hitting a mine during trials on 16 May 1917, was raised and rebuilt with a conning tower and a 7.5cm/30 gun; she was ceded as a war reparation to Italy in 1920 and scrapped. U6 was trapped in submarine nets during an attempt to break through the Otranto barrage and scuttled by the crew 10/5/1916. In March 1915, three Royal Navy destroyers hunted down the SM U-12. As the German submarine attempted to dive, the sub was rammed by HMS Ariel. The sub, with 29 men aboard, surfaced 25 miles off Eyemouth in the North Sea and was shelled by HMS Acheron and HMS Attack. She quickly sank, with all hands of 29 on board.

Mr. Kershaw, an acknowledged expert on Germany and author of the best biography of Adolf Hitler, naturally places the two world wars at the heart of his narrative, with Germany standing condemned as the main cause of both. That is a more controversial position to take for the first than the second, but on the whole Mr. Kershaw justifies his claim. He also delineates cogently and chillingly the way in which the collapse of the tsarist empire, brought about to a large extent by Russia's military and political setbacks during the first world war, led to the Bolshevik triumph and the creation of the Soviet Union, which in almost all respects was worse than what went before. The author shows how the failings of that first war's victors—the reparations fiasco, the Versailles treaty, America's withdrawal into isolationism—laid the ground for a path that led inexorably to the second. But he also insists that the path was not inevitable. The Locarno treaty of 1925 between Germany, France, Britain, Belgium and Italy, and the entry of Weimar Germany into the League of Nations, could, just about, have led to something rather like the rehabilitation of West Germany in the 1950s. What really took Europe back to the horrors that culminated in another war was economic collapse after 1929. Just as after the recent financial crisis of 2007-08, it was the political right, not the left, that benefited most from this collapse. In Europe that ultimately meant a snuffing out of democracy and the rise of the extreme right in Spain, much of central Europe and, above all, in Germany. Mr. Kershaw's focus on Germany inevitably means a few weaknesses elsewhere. His strictures against the other great European tyrant of the period, Josef Stalin, are softer than those against Hitler. Indeed, he somewhat underplays the horrific history of the than those against Hitler. Indeed, he somewhat underplays the horrific history of the Soviet Union from the late 1920s up to the Nazi-Soviet pact of 1939. He has little to say on Turkey: no mention of Field-Marshal Allenby nor T.E. Lawrence, little on Kemal Ataturk. His treatment of the military story of the two world wars is succinct almost to the point of cursoriness, but this ground is well-tilled in other books. It is also obvious from his narrative that he is more interested in politics and war than in social, demographic and cultural changes, though he dutifully covers these too.)

On 11 February 1944, the acting commander of 4th Indian Division, Brigadier Harry Dimoline, requested a bombing raid. Tuker reiterated again his case from a hospital bed in Caserta, where he was suffering a severe attack of a recurrent tropical fever. Freyberg transmitted his request on 12 February. The request, however, was greatly expanded by air force planners and probably supported by Ira Eaker and Jacob Devers, who sought to use the opportunity to showcase the abilities of U.S. Army air power to support ground operations. Lieutenant General Mark W. Clark of Fifth Army and his chief of staff Major General Alfred Gruenther remained unconvinced of the "military necessity". When handing over the U.S. II Corps position to the New Zealand Corps, Brigadier General J.A. Butler, deputy commander of U.S. 34th Division, had said "I don't know, but I don't believe the enemy is in the convent. All the fire has been from the slopes of the hill below the wall". Finally, Clark, "who did not want the monastery bombed", pinned down the Commander-in-Chief Allied Armies in Italy, General Sir Harold Alexander, to take the responsibility: "I said, 'You give me a direct order and we'll do it,' and he did."

The charge of the Armed Forces of Ukraine, the second biggest military power in Europe after its Russian counterpart. Since Ukrainian independence from the Soviet Union in 1991, there have been 13 Ministers (19 counting The Minister of Defense is appointed by the President, but this has to be confirmed by a majority vote in the Verkhovna Rada (Ukraine's parliament) that is controlled 2017 by Petro Poroshenko) Ukraine's new defense minister promises Crimea victory, BBC News July 3, 2014) Heletei appointed Ukrainian defense minister, Interfax-Ukraine (July 3, 2014).

Look closely at British memorials for World War I and you will often see the dates 1914-19. This range of years puzzles those who believe that the fighting ended with Germany's defeat in November 1918, but the inscriptions are a testament to the fact that the victorious Allied troops continued to fight and die in the conflicts that followed the war, especially in the intervention against the Bolsheviks in Russia. For many of the Great War's defeated nations and peoples, as Robert Gerwarth shows brilliantly in "The Vanquished," the full course of strife and bloodshed ended only in late 1923, when the Balkans, the Middle East, Central Europe and the Russian successor states finally settled down, at least for the time being. The "aftermath," Mr. Gerwarth reminds us, began before the war was over. In late 1917, the communist takeover in Russia not only introduced a virulent ideological theme into European politics but also led to the unraveling of the czarist empire, whose constituent peoples began to jockey for position. Regional wars broke out in the Baltics and between Poland and the young Soviet Union. The same fracturing happened in the Austro-Hungarian and Ottoman empires, whose corpses were being dismembered even before the victim was dead. In many cases, especially in the Balkans and the Middle East, postwar rivalries picked up where they had left off before the outbreak of hostilities in 1914. Troops from Britain, Italy and France sporadically entered these post-Armistice conflicts, usually attempting to support their local clients or shore up the non-Bolshevik elements in Russia. Based on a staggering range of primary material and secondary literature, "The Vanquished" fills a vast canvas. In Germany and Finland right-wing paramilitaries battled left-wing revolutionaries seeking to imitate the Bolsheviks. In Germany, Hungary and Turkey, demagogues denounced the humiliations of the Versailles Treaty and the St. Germain and Sèvres peace settlements and called for the return of lost lands or the lifting of financial punishments. In Italy, the peace agreements were condemned for not rewarding the country enough. The government in Greece, not content with the gains it had received at war's end, embarked on the megalomaniacal project of seizing much of Anatolia. During the Greco-Turkish War of 1919-22, whole populations found themselves on the "wrong side" of redrawn boundary lines—such as the Muslims of western Thrace, only recently added to the Greek state. - Mr. Gerwarth vividly captures the brutality of these struggles. His opening scenes reconstruct the terrible moments on the quay of the Turkish port of Smyrna in September 1922, when the Turks, expelling the Greeks, set the ancient city ablaze and the avenging armies of Mustafa Kemal Ataturk annihilated the whole Greek civilization of Asia Minor. Indeed, "The Vanquished" is littered with atrocities. One German volunteer fighting in the Baltics— where a right-wing "Free Corps" was battling both the Bolsheviks and local independence movements—recalls "beating, shooting, stabbing" to death the women fighting on the other side and then marching over them with nailed boots. A Czech legionnaire who had fought the Bolsheviks in Siberia remembered pouncing on them like beasts. "We used bayonets and knives. We sliced their necks as if they were baby geese."

Here the author makes the point, recently elaborated by Thomas Weber in a study of postwar Munich (to be published in English next year), that it was the aftermath of war, rather than the "brutalization" of the trenches, that radicalized societies in ways that would become apparent in the 1930s. [The author takes a dim view of Europe's postwar leaders, and it is hard to fault him. Their treatment of the vanquished provoked resentment, and they blithely dismantled long-established multinational structures, some of which, like the Austro-Hungarian Empire, had the capacity to develop in benign ways. They erected weak successor states, such as Czechoslovakia, Yugoslavia and Poland, which were equally multinational in character but lacked the wisdom and confidence to conciliate the large minorities in their midst. That said, it possible to feel some sympathy for the peace makers. The task of constructing a rational and fair order in Europe may have been too much for the victors of 1918, but even the briefest glance at the experience of the past 20 years shows that Europe's equilibrium is still fragile. In the 1990s, the Balkans were scourged by a new round of ethnic cleansing, and Ukraine today is embroiled in a civil war provoked by the interference of Russia. Europeans have still not worked out how to have a united German national state without effectively disenfranchising much of the rest of the continent, a condition that the recent Eurozone and migrant crises have made all too evident. There is in fact no workable order for continental Europe without the full political union that squares all these circles, a project that is as unpopular today as it was in 1923, when Coudenhove Kalergi published "Pan-Europa," a manifesto whose vision of unity captured the interest of elites but failed to convince a broader audience. As Mr. Gerhart's path-breaking study shows, beneath the surface of seeming peace may lie profound divisions that augur strife more than stability.) Bibliography: Simms Brendan, (WSJ "Thursday December 1, 2016-- By Brendan Simms Nov. 30, 2016 6:45 p.m. ET) + Bibliography: Simms Brendan, ("Europe: The Struggle for

Supremacy, From 1453 to the Present." The Vanquished by Robert
Gerwarth Farrar, Straus & Giroux, 446 pages).

ENDNOTE CHAPTER EIGHT

The "Red Orchestra" spy network in Europe was "almost the
main reason for the defeat of the German Army was, according
to Skorzeny, excellent Russian intelligence. The "Red Orchestra"
spy network in Europe – mostly made up of die-hard anti-
Nazis – provided the Soviet General Staff with information
about German strategic intentions. (FOOTNOTE: "The report
concerns a meeting between a special agent of the 66th CIC
Detachment and Dr. Manfred Roeder, formerly the Judge
Advocate of the German Air Force (Luftwaffe) who served as
the assistant prosecutor in the espionage case involving Red
Orchestra agents. The meeting, which took place in Hannover,
Germany, was arranged through Graf Wolf von Westarp, a
leading figure in the Sozialistische Reichspartei (Socialist
Reichs Party, or SRP), a postwar German rightist party. At
this time, the CIC was actively pursuing leads concerning the
Red Orchestra case. The U.S. Army file also contains several
pieces of correspondence from British intelligence and U.S.
Army Counter Intelligence Corps offices. These letters relate
to early postwar efforts to ascertain the whereabouts of former
German intelligence personnel, particularly members of the
"Special Detachment Red Orchestra" (Sonderkommando Rote
Kapelle) who were believed to have extensive knowledge of the
German investigation into the Red Orchestra espionage ring.
At its height, the network carried out intelligence collection
operations in Germany, France, Holland and Switzerland. The
Red Orchestra spy ring consisted of three main branches. (1) the
network in France, Belgium, and Holland; (2) the Berlin network;
and a remarkable group of agents, known as the (3) "Lucy Ring,"
that operated from the relative safety of neutral Switzerland.)

The Berlin-based Red Orchestra agents included Harro Schulze-Boysen, an intelligence officer assigned to the German Air Ministry, and Arvid von Harnack, an employee of the German Ministry of Economics. These men, as well as several others, reported extraordinarily sensitive information from key areas of the German bureaucracy in the German capital itself. In the spring of 1942, the first Red Orchestra agents were arrested in Belgium. Over the next year and a half, a total of more than six hundred people arrested in Germany, as well as in Paris and Brussels. Both Schulze-Boysen and von Harnack, who had operated in Berlin for some time, were arrested following the initial wave of arrests in Brussels. A number of other network agents were arrested in subsequent months. Those arrested included employees of the German military intelligence service (Abwehr), Ministry of Labor, Ministry of Propaganda, Foreign Office, and the city administration of Berlin. The list of those arrested was damning evidence of just how deeply the Soviet military intelligence had penetrated the German government administration and the Wehrmacht High Command.

German interrogators employed "intensified interrogation" techniques and some Red Orchestra agents broke under the torture. As a result, the Germans were able to eradicate most of the spy network in Belgium, Holland and Germany. After a trial, held in camera, 58 members of the network were condemned to death and many others were sentenced to long periods of imprisonment. Despite evidence of Gestapo mistreatment of Red Orchestra agents, there was apparently little interest on the part of the western Allies in prosecuting German officials connected with the Red Orchestra investigation in the postwar period, American intelligence officers showed more interest in the Red Orchestra case as a source of information on Soviet intelligence trade craft and methodology, rather than as a case for possible prosecution in the wake of Germany's defeat. The U.S. Army file on the Red Orchestra clearly reflects this state of affairs. In Soviet intelligence jargon of the period, radio transmitters were referred to as "Music boxes," and radio operators as "Musicians," thus the German label, "Red Orchestra" or Rote Kapelle

(Bibliography-- U.S. Army Investigative Records Repository (hereafter IRR) File on the Red Orchestra. National Archives and Records Administration, RG 319.)

Endnote Chapter Nine: (transcript of: "September 21, 2017 White House Press Meeting with President T rump and Ukraine' s Poroshenko ...

PRESIDENT TRUMP: "So, Ukraine is coming along pretty well — pretty well. And at the borders, maybe you'll tell them how you're doing."

PRESIDENT POROSHENKO: "Thank you very much indeed, Mr. President. That's a real great honor for me to be here in the city which is so close to you. And I'm really happy to hear the words about the progress we both demonstrate after our last meeting. The turnover between the United States and Ukraine during the last seven months increased 2.5 times because of the implementation of our agreement. And this is, again, the symbol that we welcome in American companies in the Ukrainian market, and creating hundreds of thousands of jobs both in Ukraine and the U.S. And this is really a delivery from effective cooperation between our nations."

ENDNOTE CHAPTER NINE (JOHN KERRY & JOSEPH BIDEN)

John Kerry is known for his anti-Vietnam War action of throwing his purple heart medals over the White House fence and attacking US Military Veterans. He was later embraced by Ted Kennedy who was known as the "Lion of the Senate." Ted Kennedy was known for being drunk the night that he crashed his car off a bridge and let his girlfriend drown in three feet of water. He walked back to his home and then reported the incident many hours later. The

Hill is an American political newspaper and website published in Washington, D.C. The Hill is published by Capitol Hill Publishing, which is owned by News Communications, Inc. On April 2, 2019 the paper reported that Joseph Biden demanded that the Special Prosecutor of Ukraine immediate be fired for starting a probe into Hunter Biden's receiving over $3million dollars from Burisma from 2014 to 2017.

In 2016, Joe Biden said, "And I was supposed to announce that there was another billion-dollar loan guarantee. And I had gotten a commitment from Poroshenko...that they would take action against the state prosecutor. And they didn't...I said. Nah, I'm not going to...or, we're not going to you the billion dollars...I looked at them and said: I'm leaving in six hours. If the prosecutor is not fired, you're not getting the money. Well, son of a b-tch. He got fired. And they put in place someone who was solid at the time."

Ukraine

On November 27, 2019 The Epoch Times wrote, "The Ukrainian Embassy proceeded to work directly with reporters researching (President) Trump, (Paul) Manafort and Russia to point them in the right directions ... Olga Bielkova of the Ukraine Parliament attempted meetings with Democratic Congressional members as well as Judy Miller and David Sanger of the New York Times, David Ignatius and Fred Hiatt of the Washington Post. Marcy Kaptur a Democrat of Ohio and co-chair of the Ukraine Caucus began working with reporter Mike Isikoff in April of 2019. Senator John McCain sent David Kramer who worked for the McCain Institute, and Ukraine Today-a clear anti Russia media outlet, to meet with Christopher Steele and Igor Danchenko, the authors of the Hillary Clinton paid anti-Donald Trump dossier." Any move related to the status of the rebellious eastern Ukrainian regions should be coordinated with those regions, Putin said, adding that Kiev should not unilaterally take decisions on any *"decentralization"* issues that go beyond the framework of the Minsk Agreements which still remain the only plausible way to resolve the Ukrainian crisis. Some positive steps have been made, the president admitted, such as troop withdrawal from several areas in eastern Ukraine, and the extension of the law on the special status of Donbass. Some new areas along the line of contact were further designated for troop withdrawal in 2020, during the latest Normandy Four meeting. Any move related to the status of the rebellious eastern Ukrainian regions should be coordinated with those regions, Putin said, adding that Kiev should not unilaterally take decisions on any *"decentralization"* issues that go beyond the framework of the Minsk Agreements which still remain the only plausible way to resolve the Ukrainian crisis. Some positive steps have been made, the president admitted, such as troop withdrawal from several areas in eastern Ukraine, and the extension of the law on the special status of Donbass. Some new areas along the line of contact were further designated for troop withdrawal in 2020, during the latest Normandy Four meeting. Any move related to the status of the rebellious eastern Ukrainian regions should be coordinated with those regions, Putin said, adding that Kiev should not unilaterally take decisions on any *"decentralization"* issues that go beyond the framework of the Minsk Agreements which still remain the only plausible way to resolve the Ukrainian crisis. Some positive steps have been made, the president admitted, such as troop withdrawal from several areas in eastern Ukraine, and the extension of the law on the special status of Donbass. Some new areas along the line of contact were further designated for troop withdrawal in 2020, during the latest Normandy Four meeting.

APPENDIX OR ADDENDUM

Mongols and Mughal Empire—India

Muslim traders, marriage alliances, and sultanates led to Islam gaining a foothold in India and eventually led to the Mogul Empire and the slow decline in the rituals of Hindu Brahmanism. "The Mughal Empire (Urdu: Mug_hliyah Salṭanat) or Mogul Empire, self-designated as Gurkani (Persian: Gūrkāniyān, meaning "son-in-law"), was an empire established and ruled by a Persianate dynasty of Chagatai Turco-Mongol origin that extended over large parts of the Indian subcontinent and Afghanistan. The beginning of the empire is conventionally dated to the founder Babur's victory over Ibrahim Lodi, the last ruler of the Delhi Sultanate in the 1526 First Battle of Panipat.

The Mughal emperors were Central Asian Turco-Mongols belonging to the Timurid dynasty, who claimed direct descent from both Genghis Khan (emperor) (founder of the Mongol Empire, through his son Chagatai Khan) and Timur (Turco-Mongol conqueror who founded the Timurid Empire). During the reign of Humayun, the successor of Babur, the empire was briefly interrupted by the Sur Empire. The "classic period" of the Mughal Empire started in 1556 with the ascension of Akbar the Great to the throne. Under the rule of Akbar and his son Jahangir, India enjoyed economic progress as well as religious harmony, and the monarchs were interested in local religious and cultural traditions. Akbar was a successful warrior. He also forged alliances with several Hindu Rajput kingdoms. Some Rajput kingdoms continued to pose a significant threat to Mughal dominance of northwestern India, but they were subdued by Akbar. All Mughal emperors were Muslims, except Akbar in the latter part of his life, when he followed a new religion called Deen-i-Ilahi, as recorded in historical books like Ain-e-Akbari and Dabestan-e Mazaheb.

"Aurangzeb's formative years were shaped by the bloody, fratricidal dynamic of Mughal succession, with childhood competition among princes culminating in do-or-die struggles for kingship. ("Either the throne or the grave," as the Persian saying went. Babur's advice to Humayun was decidedly more encouraging: "The world is his who hastens most.") So, from ages 16 to 38, Aurangzeb campaigned tirelessly abroad, gaining martial and administrative experience while his eldest brother, Dara Shukoh, in Ms. Truschke's telling, "leisured at court" and basked in their father's favor. In September 1657, Shah Jahan "awoke gravely ill" and failed to appear before his subjects. He would live for an additional nine years, but hastily spread rumors of his demise brought the long-simmering rivalry between Aurangzeb and his three brothers to its lurid conclusion. A staggered series of victories delivered Aurangzeb the throne—and provoked controversy. He had his brother Dara paraded through Delhi in rags and beheaded; ordered Dara's son, Sulayman, overdosed on opium water; double-crossed and executed his youngest brother, Murad; and imprisoned his father in Agra Fort for the remainder of his life. Ruthlessly snuffing out rival claimants wasn't necessarily unusual; shunting one's father aside was. As Ms. Truschke acknowledges, this unjust and unnatural betrayal "haunted" Aurangzeb's rule.

Pious, teetotal and painfully earnest, Aurangzeb felt the weight of his responsibilities keenly. Not for nothing had Babur warned that "there is no bondage like the bondage of kingship." Aurangzeb practiced an austere and, by most accounts, impartial brand of justice and prosecuted overreaching, Pyrrhic wars, attempting to subdue the Marathas, Hindu warriors from what is now the state of Maharashtra, and the recalcitrant kingdoms of the Deccan plateau. To this end, he relocated his court south to the Deccan in 1681, where it remained until his death in 1707." Truschke, Audrey:(Aurangze, Stanford, 136 pages, reviewed by Maxwell Carter July 28, 2017 3:13 p.m. ET WallStreetJournal)

BIBLIOGRAPHY

1917-1924 - Vladimir Ilyich Lenin - GlobalSecurity.org(https://www.globalsecurity.org/military/world/russia/lenin.htm)

25 Facts About WorldWar 1 | FactSpy.net(http://factspy.net/25-facts-about-world-war-1/)

A grim half-century - European history - The Economist(https://www.economist.com/news/books-and-arts/21678189-fine-addition-penguin-history-europe-grim-half-century)

A nation of individuals - Family, identity and morality (https://www.economist.com/news/special-report/21701650-chinese-people-increasingly-do-what-they-want-not-what-they-are-told-nation)

Abels, Richard PhD. for HH315: Age of Chivalry and Faith at the United States Naval Academy. Copyright 2009)

ALANS – Encyclopaedia Iranica (http://www.iranicaonline.org/articles/alans-an-ancient-iranian-tribe-of-the-northern-scythian-saka-sarmatian-massagete-group-known-to-classical-writers-from)

Alemanni - Ancient History Encyclopedia (https://www.ancient.eu/alemanni/)

Alexander Kolchak | Military | FANDOM (http://military.wikia.com/wiki/Alexander_Kolchak)

All the world's a stage - Ottoman history(https://www.economist. com/news/books-and-arts/21677183-subtle-account-power-struggles-ended-ottoman-empire-all-worlds)

Ancient Britain - Ancient History Encyclopedia (https://www. ancient.eu/britain/)

Ancient Greece - Ancient History Encyclopedia(https://www. ancient.eu/greece/)

Ancient History: (http://www.encyclopedia.com/history/ ancient-greece-and-rome/ancient-history-northern-europe/ cimmerians)

Ashkenazi (2&3 DNC testing report 2018, MountainViewCA)

Asian Topics on Asia for Educators || Confucian Teaching(http:// afe.easia.columbia.edu/at/conf_teaching/ct06.html)

Attila the Hun - Military Leader, King – Biography (https://www. biography.com/people/attila-the-hun-9191831)

Atwood 2012, p. 27.

Atwood 2012, p. 28.

Austin, Stephen, and N.B. Rankov. Exploration: Military and Political Intelligence in the Roman World from the Second Punic War to the Battle of Adrianople. London: Routledge, 1995.

Bahn, P, The New Penguin Dictionary of Archaeology Paperback (Penguin, 2005). BOOK-The Vietnamese War against the Kublai Khan

Bamiyan Buddhas: Should they be rebuilt? - BBC News (http:// www.bbc.com/news/magazine-18991066)

Barbarian Names (http://www.lowchensaustralia.com/names/ famous-barbarian-names.htm)

Barrington Lowell (January 2012). Comparative Politics: Structures and Choices, 2nd ed.tr: Structures and Choices. Cengage Learning. p. 121. ISBN 978-1-111-34193-0. Retrieved 21 June 2013.

Belzer, Jan (https://kidskonnect.com/history/holocaust/worksheet by Jan Belzer. 2007)

Biden, Hunter (http://www.tmz.com/2017/04/04/hunter-biden-divorce-settlement-not-sealed/)

Biography Joseph Stalin – PBS (http://www.pbs.org/redfiles/bios/all_bio_joseph_stalin.htm)

Blau, Rosie, Chinese Society- the New Class War, The Economist Magazine, (p3-15) July 9, 2016.

Borodino: (https://www.britannica.com/event/Battle-of-Borodino)

Bradbury, Jim. "The Routledge Companion to Medieval Warfare". Routledge, 2004. page 55

Brown, Paul, RedOrchestra- (https://www.archives.gov/iwg/research-papers/red-orchestra-irr-file.html) Report on the IRR File on The Red Orchestra Paul Brown IWG Historical Researcher)

Bush, The George Center for Intelligence is the Central Intelligence Agency, located in the unincorporated community of Langley in Fairfax County, Virginia, United States.

Caesar, Julius, Commentarii de Bello Gallico

Caesar, Juliuis, Commentaries on the Gallic War, (1st Century B.C.)

Carswell, John, The Exile By (1983) The Diary of a Soviet Schoolgirl by Nina Lugovskaya (2003)

Chakraborty, Gayatri. Espionage in Ancient India: From the Earliest Times to 12th Century A.D. Calcutta, India: Minerva Associates, 1990.

China (ancientstandard.com/2011/06/17/the-real-story-of-mulan/)

China (http://www.metmuseum.org/toah/hd/nsong/hd_ nsong.htm)

Christianity Origins, Christianity History, Christianity ... (http:// www.patheos.com/library/christianity)

Chubinov, Histoire de la Georgie I, St. Petersburg, 1849]). Ammianus Marcellinus (31.2) describes the Alans' nomadic economy and warlike customs.

Chukovskaya, Lydia, Sofia Petrovna (1965)

Cimmeriams—Encyclopedia of Russian History Gale Group, copy right 2004 http://www.encyclopedia.com/history/ ancient-greece-and-rome/ancient-history-northern-europe/ cimmerians

Coll, Steve Ghost Wars: The Secret History of the CIA, Afghanistan, and Bin Laden, from the Soviet Invasion to September 10, 2001

Collins, Ross, F.: (World War I: Primary Documents on Events from 1914 to 1919 (Greenwood Press, 2008World War One.

Concentration Camps – Holocaust(https://40811077.weebly.com/ concentration-camps.html)

Constantine and why did he move the capital (https://brainly.com/ question/3402256)

Crimea | History, Geography, & People | Britannica.com(https:// www.britannica.com/place/Crimea)

Crimea | History, Geography, & People | Britannica.com(https:// www.britannica.com/place/Crimea)

Crimea And Geneva: Reverse Lessons for The Rajapaksa (https://www. colombotelegraph.com/index.php/crimea-and-geneva-reverse- lessons-for-the-rajapaksa-regime-and-diaspora-separatism/)

Crimea Tatars: (https://www.youtube.com/watch?v=uMo1tbZ5BG4)

Crimea: (http://www.britannica.com/place/Crimea)

Crimea: (http://www.britannica.com/place/Crimea)

Crimea: (https://www.youtube.com/watch?v=mfgg_e7FIBs)

Crimea: (https://www.youtube.com/watch?v=mfgg_e7FIBs)

Crimea: (https://www.youtube.com/watch?v=uMo1tbZ5BG4)

Crimean War | Map, Summary, Combatants, Causes, & Facts (https://www.britannica.com/event/Crimean-War)

Crisis in Russia - Home - Teach Like a Champion (http://teachlikeachampion.com/wp-content/uploads/Russian-Revolution.pdf)

Crumpton, Henry A. The Art of Intelligence: Lessons from a Life in CIA's Clandestine Service

CruneanWar: https://www.britannica.com/event/Crimean-

Crusades: (http://history-world.org/crusades.htm)

Crusades: (http://www.usna.edu/Users/history/abels/hh315/crusades_timeline.htm- (exact quote from Compiled by Dr. Richard Abels for HH315: Age of Chivalry and Faith at the United States Naval Academy. Copyright 2009)

Cunliffe, B, The Oxford Illustrated History of Prehistoric Europe (Oxford University Press, 2001).

CyberHacking (https://www.youtube.com/watch?v=-hlvX9-Pkmc)

Darius: (https://www.ancient.eu/Darius_I/)

Darvill, T, Concise Oxford Dictionary of Archaeology (Oxford University Press, 2009).

De Bary, Theodore William ed, Sources of Chinese Tradition, ed. (New York: Columbia University Press, 1960). XIII:6

De Bary, Theodore William ed., Sources of Chinese Tradition, (New York: Columbia University Press, 1960). XIII:6)

de Guignes, Joseph (1756–1758). Histoire générale des Huns, des Turcs, des Mongols et des autres Tartares (in French). Heather 2010, p. 228.]

de la Vaissière 2015, p. 175.

de la Vaissière 2015, p. 179.

de la Vaissière 2015, p. 181.

de la Vaissière 2015, p. 188.

Dean Peter J, Napoleon as a Military Commander: The Limitations of Genius Peter J. Dean BA(Hons) Dip Ed. http://www. napoleon-series.org/research/napoleon/c_genius.html)

Decoding the Great War - NSA.gov(https://www.nsa.gov/news-features/news-stories/2017/decoding-the-great-war.shtml)

DeMarche, Edmund, Fox News- (- http://www.foxnews.com/us/2017/09/28/antifa-leader-teacher-yvonne-felarca-arrested-at-empathy-tent-berkeley-brawl.html)

Destroyed by the Taliban but now the Buddha statues have (https://www.pri.org/stories/2015-06-11/they-were-destroyed-taliban-now-giant-buddha-statues-bamiyan-have-returned-3-d)

Devine Jack and Vernon Loeb, Good Hunting

Did any of the Romanovs survive? - Ask History(https://www.history.com/news/ask-history/did-any-of-the-romanovs-survive)

Difference Between BC and BCE – YouTube (https://www.youtube.com/watch?v=VGiBNfw6X1Q)

Dubovsky, Peter. Hezekiah and the Assyrian Spies: Reconstruction of the Neo-Assyrian Intelligence Services and Its Significance for 2 Kings 18-19. Roma: Pontificio Istituto biblico, 2006.

Dvornik, Francis. Origins of Intelligence Services: The Ancient Near East, Persia, Greece, Rome, Byzantium, the Arab Muslim Empires, the Mongol Empire, China, Muscovy. New Brunswick, NJ: Rutgers University Press, 1974.

Edwards, Michael, Searching for the Scythians, p56-80; National Geographic VOL.190, NO.3 September 1996.

Egypt: (http://www.reshafim.org.il/ad/egypt/timelines/topics/mining.htm)

END (549 pages 123,764 words) "A Man of seven shadows"

Engels, Friedrich. "The Origin of the Family, Private Property and the State". 2004. Kerr C H Chicago, 1902, Resistance Books, 2004, p138. Retrieved 11 February 2015/Stümpel, Gustav (1932). Name und Nationalität der Germanen. Eine neue Untersuchung zu Poseidonios, Caesar und Tacitus (in German). Leipzig: Dieterich. p. 60. OCLC 10223081.)

Erdkamp, Paul "War and State Formation," in A Companion to the Roman Army (Blackwell, 2011), p. 102

EyeWitnessHistory.com, 12/3/2015- "The Romans Destroy the Temple at Jerusalem".)

Facts You Should Know About the Holocaust – ThoughtCo(https://www.thoughtco.com/holocaust-facts-1779663)

Fahrettin Tahir (Turkish writer and communitarian) comments from the Nov 12, 2015 The Economist)

Famous Barbarian Names - Charlemagne, Vortigern, Attila ... (http://www.lowchensaustralia.com/names/famous-barbarian-names.htm)

Fatal Narcissism - SPIEGEL ONLINE (http://www.spiegel.de/international/germany/the-fuehrer-myth-how-hitler-won-over-the-german-people-a-531909-5.html)

February Revolution begins - Mar 08, 1917 - History.com(https://www.history.com/this-day-in-history/3/8)

Federal Security Service - The Russian Government(http://government.ru/en/department/113/)

Flavius Aetius | Roman general | Britannica.com (https://www.britannica.com/biography/Flavius-Aetius)

Flavius Odoacer - Chess.com (https://www.chess.com/groups/team_match?id=695944)

Flavius Stilicho | Roman general (com (https://www.britannica.com/biography/Flavius-Stilicho)

French, Howard W (reviewed Black Dragon River by Dominic Ziegler Penguin Press.357 pages) WSJ BOOKS section 12/26/2015)

FSB http://www.factmonster.com/encyclopedia/society/secret-police-the-evolution-secret-police-forces.html

Fusion GPS (fox news internet November 14, 2017- "Fusion GPS's ties to Clinton campaign, Russia investigation: What to know")

Gambill, Gary C (The Military-Intelligence Shakeup in Syria, by Gary C. Gambill, Middle East Intelligence Bulletin, February 2002)

Gerolymatos, Andre. Espionage and Treason: A Study of the Proxenia in Political and Military Intelligence Gathering in Ancient Greece. Amsterdam: J.C. Gieben, 1986.

Gerwarth, Robert. The Vanquished: Farrar, Straus & Giroux, 2016

Gmyrya L. Hun Country At the Caspian Gate, Dagestan, Makhachkala 1995, p. 9 (no ISBN but the book is available in US libraries, Russian title Strana Gunnov u Kaspiyskix vorot, Dagestan, Makhachkala, 1995)

Golden Horde | Define Golden Horde at Dictionary.com(http://www.dictionary.com/browse/golden-horde)

Golobutskii, V. Diplomaticheskaia istoriia Osvoboditel'noi voiny ukrainskogo naroda 1648–1654 gg. (Kyiv 1962)

Grand Duke Mikhail Alexandrovich Holstein-Gottorp-Romanov (https://www.geni.com/people/Grand-Duke-Mikhail-Holstein-Gottorp-Romanov-of-Russia/6000000000307240559)

Greece: (http://www.ancient.eu/greece/)

Greece: (http://www.encyclopedia.com/history/ancient-greece-and-rome/ancient-history-northern-europe/cimmerians

Greenwald, Glenn, No Place to Hide, (https://www.lawfareblog.com/no-place-hide-edward-snowden-nsa-and-us-surveillance-state-glenn-greenwald)

Greenwald, Glenn, No Place to Hide, (https://www.lawfareblog.com/no-place-hide-edward-snowden-nsa-and-us-surveillance-state-glenn-greenwald)

Grimes Sandra and Jeanne Vertefeuille, Circle of Treason: A CIA Account of Traitor Aldrich Ames and the Men He Betrayed

Grousset, Rene (1970). The Empire of the Steppes. Rutgers University Press. pp. 38, 55, 72–79. ISBN 0-8135-1304-9.

Hải Ngoại Điện Báo: Giới thiệu Ukraine(http://haingoaidienbao.blogspot.com/2014/02/gioi-thieu-ukrain.html)

Hapgood, David; Richardson, David (2002) [1984]. Monte Cassino: (The Story of the Most Controversial Battle of World War II (reprint ed.). Cambridge Mass.: Da Capo. ISBN 0-306-81121-9. page 172)

Hellerstein, Toba, (Ottoman Empire Ottomans Analysis.)

Henn BM et al. (2012). "Cryptic distant relatives are common in both isolated and cosmopolitan genetic samples." PLoS One. 7(4): e34267.

Hesse M., "Iranisches Sagengut im Christlichen Epos," Atlantis 1937, pp. 621-28; J. H. Grisward, "Le motif de l'épée jetée au lac: la mort d'Arthur et la mort de Batradz," Romania 90, 1969, pp. 289-340).

Hitler (https://www.youtube.com/watch?v=fx05VezU2UI)

Hitler, (http://www.spiegel.de/international/germany/the-fuehrer-myth-how-hitler-won-over-the-german-people-a-531909.html)

How Hitler Won Over the German People – InvestorsHub(https://investorshub.advfn.com/boards/read_msg.aspx?message_id=26421729)

How Many Concentration Camps? - Jewish Virtual Library(https://www.jewishvirtuallibrary.org/how-many-concentration-camps)

Hrushevsky, M. History of Ukraine-Rus', vols 7, 8, 9 books 1, 9 books 2, part 1, and 9 book 2, part 2 (Edmonton–Toronto 1999–2010)

Hrushevs'kyi, M. Istoriia Ukraïny-Rusy, 8-9 (New York 1954–8)

http://government.ru/en/department/113/

https://www.youtube.com/watch?v=_-lzJq5dKao

https://www.youtube.com/watch?v=KOKEhOr0xw4

https://www.youtube.com/watch?v=QEv4tVJviHA

https://www.youtube.com/watch?v=rwti97LhRmI

https://www.youtube.com/watch?v=Z5gB4U95g8c

Huns - Infogalactic: the planetary knowledge core (https://infogalactic.com/info/Huns)

Hunt Patrick N, Hannibal, Simon % Schuster 362 pages (James Romm, "The Hated Enemy, Books, The Wall Street Journal, Saturday/Sunday 7-8-9 2017 C7

Hunt, Patrick, N. Hannibal, Simon & Schuster, 362 pages. WSJ Romm, James, "The Hated Enemy," july8-9 2017, p. C7

Intelligence(https://www.globalsecurity.org/intell/world/iraq/mukhabarat.html)

Jacob Schiff Ordered Czar Nicholas II and Family Murdered (https://www.truthcontrol.com/articles/jacob-schiff-ordered-czar-nicholas-ii-and-family-murdered)

Javier Bernal 100% - NIST (https://math.nist.gov/~JBernal/ethnic.pdf)

John Brown's Chapter and Essays: How the East Was Won(http://johnbrownnotesandessays.blogspot.com/2015/12/how-east-was-won.html)

John le Carré --Looking Glass War (1965), Tinker, Tailor, Soldier, Spy (1974), and The Honorable Schoolboy (1977).

John Matthews, Western Aristocracies and Imperial Court AD 364–425, Oxford: University Press, 1990, p. 281

Jones, Terry., Ereira, Alan. "Crusades". Penguin Books, 1996. pp.43

Joseph Cofer Black | Burisma(http://burisma.com/en/director/joseph-cofer-black/)

Joseph Cofer Black | Burisma(http://burisma.com/en/director/joseph-cofer-black/)

Josephus' account appears in: Cornfield, Gaalya ed., Josephus, The Jewish War (1982); Duruy, Victor, History of Rome vol. V (1883).

Josephus, Jewish Wars 7.244-51, Antiquities 18.97; cf. accounts in Moses of Khoren, History of the Armnians

Kadi, Wadad; Shahin, Aram A. (2013). "Caliph, caliphate". The Princeton Encyclopedia of Islamic Political Thought: 81–86

Kalopek, Paul. One Million Armenians ... were killed. National Geographic Magazine, pages 112-127, Published: April 2016

Kaplan, Robert (WSJ Robert Kaplan, "Europe's New Medieval Map," January 16, 2016)

Kaplan, Robert D (Robert D. Kaplan reviews "Destined for War: Can America and China Escape Thucydides's Trap?" by Graham Allison. WSJ Tuesday May 30, 2017)

Kaplan, Robert D. "Europe's New Medieval Map" As the European Union unravels, the continent is reverting to divisions that go back centuries, writes Robert D. Kaplan, WSJ, 1-16-2016

Kartlis tskhovreba, in M. F. Brosset and D. I

Kautilya. The Arthashastra. New York: Penguin, 1992.

Kerbogha | Military Wiki | FANDOM (http://military.wikia.com/wiki/Kerbogha)

Kershaw, Ian, Hitler (Der Spiegel January 30, 2008 04:05 PM By Ian Kershaw)

Kiev (WSJ May 30, 2017 "Kiev Sees Risks in Russia Social Media.")

Kiriakou, John. "My Secret Life in the CIA's War on Terror," Bantam Books, New York, 2009, ISBN 978-0-553-80737-0

Kliper Kathleen, The Britannica Guide to Ancient Civilization 1987)

Knights: (http://historylists.org/people/list-of-10-most-famous-medieval-knights.html)

Knights: (http://historylists.org/people/list-of-10-most-famous-medieval-knights.html)

Knights: (http://history-world.org/teutonic_knights.htm)

Kravchuk, Leonid Makarovych, "Kravchuk explains his drift to Tymoshenko," zik.com.ua (12-21-2009)

Kravchuk, LMakarovych, www.globalsecurity.org/military/world/ukraine/kravchuk.htm

Kryp'iakevych, I. Bohdan Khmel'nyts'kyi (Kyiv 1954)

Kubala, L. Szkice historyczne, 6 vols (Lviv 1881–1922)

Kulikowski, Michael. The Trump of Empire, Harvard Press. 360pages

Lacey, Robert, The kingdom- Arabia & the House of Saud, 1979 Harcourt brace Jovanovich, Publishers, 757 Third Avenue, New York, NY 10017

Langlois, Historiens II, pp. 105-06, 125] and the Georgian Chronicle

Latest statistics: Ukraine's trade with the EU boosted by(https://eeas.europa.eu/delegations/ukraine_en/21194/Latest%20statistics:%20Ukraine's%20trade%20with%20the%20EU%20boosted%20by%20the%20first%20full%20year%20of%20the%20Association%20Agreement)

Lavelle, Peter, RT Cross Talk @Peter – Edward Snowden briefing book on US surveillance https://www.rt.com/shows/crosstalk/380116-us-surveillance-cia-leaks/

Lavelle, Peter, RT Cross Talk @Peter – Edward Snowden briefing book on US surveillance https://www.rt.com/shows/crosstalk/380116-us-surveillance-cia-leaks/

Legatee, (from 1875, of the rights of the House of Austria–Este to Modena.

Legatee, from 1875, of the rights of the House of Austria–Este to Modena.

Lidz Franz Smithsonian Magazine July/August 2017 Volume 48, Number 4, Hannibal's Lost Road, Lidz Franz, P. 114 & 108

Lidz, Franz, Smithsonian Magazine July/August 2017 Volume 48, Number 4, Hannibal's Lost Road, P. 108- 120

List of 10 Most Famous Medieval Knights - History Lists(http://historylists.org/people/list-of-10-most-famous-medieval-knights.html)

List of books and articles about Gestapo | Online Research (https://www.questia.com/library/history/military-history/wars-battles-and-military-interventions/world-war-ii/gestapo)

Lost Islamic History | The Mongol Invasion and the (http://lostislamichistory.com/mongols/)

Maenchen-Helfen 1973, pp. 2-4. /The Gothic History of Jordanes (24:121), p. 85. 1973, p. 5. (Heather 2010, p. 209. /de la Vaissière 2015, p. 175, 180.)

Magyar: : (https://en.oxforddictionaries.com/definition/magyar accessed on 4/21/17)

Maison de Bourbon-Habsburg - Maison de France(https://sites.google.com/site/royalhousedefrance/home/maison-de-bourbon-habsburg-1)

Mamontova, Natalia – ("A Stepdaughter to Imperial Russia", publ: 1940)

Mamontova, Natal'ia: (https://www.nytimes.com/2017/07/10/opinion/red-century-russia-romanov.html The Remains of the Romanovs-- Anastasia Edel- Red Century, July 10, 2017)

Manchester, William; Paul Reid (2012). The Last Lion, Winston Spencer Churchill: Defender of the Realm 1940–1965 (1st ed.). Boston: Little, Brown. p. 801. ISBN 0316547700. Jump up Jordan, D, (2004), Atlas of World War II. Barnes & Noble Books, p. 92.)

Mantua: (https://www.britannica.com/event/Siege-of-Mantua #ref247989)

Marchant Jo, The Golden Warrior, Smithsonian Magazine Jan-Feb 2017, ps 38-52, 134.

Marengo: (https://www.britannica.com/event/Battle-of-Marengo)

Martin, David Wilderness of Mirrors

McMeekin, Sean, "The Ottoman Endgame", Bard College, History Lecture

Meaghan McEvoy (2 May 2013). Child Emperor Rule in the Late Roman West, AD 367-455. Oxford University Press. p. 184. ISBN 978-0-19-966481-8

Medieval Royalty

Mendez, Rafael de Nogales, "Armania Genocide" Economist magazine October 2015

Military history channel Rome Rise and Fall of An Empire"-

Milner-Gulland, R. R. Atlas of Russia and the Soviet Union. Phaidon. p. 36. ISBN 0-7148-2549-2.)

Mining – Reshafim (http://www.reshafim.org.il/ad/egypt/timelines/topics/mining.htm)

Mongol Invasion Baghdad | islam.ru (http://www.islam.ru/en/content/story/mongol-invasion-and-destruction-baghdad)

Mongolian Names - http://www.babynology.com/mongol-girlnames-a0.html

Mongols: (http://lostislamichistory.com/mongols/)

Montefiore Sebag Simon," The Romanovs" Knopf, 2016Oxman, Robert, Three Confucian Values, President Emeritus, Asia Society

Mosier, John. (Cross of Iron: The Rise and Fall of the German War Machine, 1918–1945. New York: Henry Holt and Company, 2006. ISBN 978-0-80507-577-9)

Nagy, Benjamin, J. ("Gaul or Bust"- Military History Magazine March 2020-Vol. 36. No 6 pp27 -31)

Napoleonic Wars: (http://french-genealogy.typepad.com/genealogie/2014/01/did-your-ancestor-serve-with-napoleon.html)

Napoleonic Wars: (http://www.britannica.com/event/Napoleonic-Wars)

Neanderthal Ancestry Report - 23andMe(https://you.23andme.com/published/reports/66ed74f760184bcb/?share_id=d467c7660ea1480a)

Nelson, Colleen (2013 WSJ Colleen McCain Nelson at colleen.nelson@wsj.com- https://www.wsj.com/articles/bidens-son-hunter-discharged-from-navy-reserve-after-failing-cocaine-test-1413499657)

Nevsky, Alex (http://historylists.org/people/list-of-10-most-famous-medieval-knights.html)

O'Hara, Vincent P., (Lessons from a Lost Fleet, US Naval Institute p. 48, June2017 Volume 31, Number 3-: Austro-Hungarian- (http://www.navypedia.org/ships/austrohungary/ah_ss_u5.htm)

Order No. 1 of the Petrograd Soviet of Workers' (https://allpowertothesoviets.wordpress.com/2017/03/14/order-no-1-of-the-petrograd-soviet-of-workers-and-soldiers-deputies/)

Otto Skorzeny: "Why didn't we take Moscow?" | The Vineyard (http://thesaker.is/otto-skorzeny-why-didnt-we-take-moscow/)

Ottoman: (The Ottoman Endgame: War, Revolution and the Making of the Modern Middle East, 1908-1923. By Sean McMeekin. Penguin Press; 576 pages; $35. Allen Lane; £30.)

Ottoman: ("What Modern Syria Can Learn from the Ottomans is republished with permission of Stratfor.")

Ottoman: picot (McMeekin, Sean, The Ottoman Endgame: War, Revolution and the Making of the Modern Middle East, 1908-1923. By Sean McMeekin. Penguin Press; 576 pages; $35. Allen Lane; £30)

Ottomans: (Ottoman Empire Ottomans Analysis by Toba Hellerstein)

Pannonia | historical region, Europe (https://www.britannica.com/place/Pannonia)

Paris attacks, the fall of Rome should be a warning to the ... (http://better-management.org/wp-content/uploads/2015/11/Paris-attacks-the-fall-of-Rome-should-be-a-warning-to-the-West.pdf)

Peterson, Martha Widow Spy

Petrograd District Garrison - Marxists Internet Archive(https:// www.marxists.org/history/ussr/government/1917/03/01.htm)

Petrovs'kyi, M. Vyzvol'na viina ukraïns'koho narodu proty hnitu shliakhets'koï Pol'shchi i pryiednannia Ukraïny do Rosïi (1648–1654) (Kyiv 1940)

Piotrowski, Tadeusz (2006). "Ukraine Collaboration." Polands' Holocaust. McFarland.p.217. ISBN 0786429135. Retrieved 2014-04-30.

Pohl 1999, pp. 501-502. /Heather 2010, p. 502. /de la Vaissière 2015, p. 176. /Pohl 1999, p. 502. Ammianus Marcellinus: The Later Roman Empire (31.2.), p. 411. /de la Vaissière 2015, p. 177/ Maenchen-Helfen 1973, p. 4.

Political Reform - Independent Texans(https://indytexans.org/ about/political-reform-election-reform/)

Prados, John Safe for Democracy: The Secret Wars of the CIA

PRE-HISTORY IRAN - Iranian studies (http://www.cais-soas. com/CAIS/History/prehistory/prehistory.htm)

PRE-HISTORY IRAN - Iranian studies (http://www.cais-soas. com/CAIS/History/prehistory/prehistory.htm)

Professor Reich explained: "We see a new population turnover in Europe, and this time it seems to be from the east, not the west."

Pulleyblank, Edwin G. The Peoples of the steepe frontier in early Chinese sources, page 37 Huns)". Ammianus 1922, XXXI, Ch. 2

Punic Wars - Ancient History - HISTORY.com (https://www. history.com/topics/ancient-history/punic-wars)

Punic Wars Flashcards | Quizlet (https://quizlet.com/19583247/punic-wars-flash-cards/)

Renfrew, C, Archaeology: Theories, Methods, and Practice (Sixth Edition) (Thames & Hudson, 2012).

Report on the IRR File on The Red Orchestra | National (https://www.archives.gov/iwg/research-papers/red-orchestra-irr-file.html)

Riley-Smith, J. The Crusades, Yale University, 1987.)

Roman Barbarians: (http://www.lowchensaustralia.com/names/famous-barbarian-names.htm)

Roman Weaponry: (-just about weaponry)

Roman Wine: (http://www.economist.com/node/883706 The history of drinking Uncorking the past Recreating old drinks provides an enjoyable form of time-travelling Dec 20th 2001 | From the print edition)

Roman, (https://www.youtube.com/watch?v=PIcc8iM1W2I)

Roman: (https://gotquestions.org/BC-AD.html)

Roman: (http://www.roman-empire.net/decline/constantine-index.html)

Roman:(http://www.academia.edu/380791/TheWestern_Roman_Embassy_to_the_Court_of_Attila_in_A.D.449)

Romanov: (http://www.britannica.com/topic/Romanov-dynasty)

Rome | Revelation of Doom (https://zirconnyl.wordpress.com/tag/rome/)

Rome Revelation of Doom (https://zirconnyl.wordpress.com/tag/rome/)

Rothschild, Leopold de [Credit: Encyclopedia Britannica, Inc.] (http://www.britannica.com/topic/Rothschild-family/(http://www.rothschild.info/en/history/)

Royalty RT (Russian Television) Ukraine marks 'Dignity & Freedom Day' as Euromaidan dream falters "Published time: 21 Nov, 2016 12:22

Runciman, Steven. "A History of the Crusades". Cambridge University Press, 1987. p215

Rurik (refence: http://www.britannica.com/topic/Rurik-dynasty)

Rurik Dynasty | medieval Russian rulers | Britannica.com(https://www.britannica.com/topic/Rurik-dynasty)

Rurik Dynasty: (http://www.britannica.com/topic/Rurik-dynasty access internet on 4//2/117)

Russell, Frank S. Information Gathering in Ancient Greece. Ann Arbor, MI: University of Michigan Press, 1999.

Russia - Russia from 1801 to 1917 | Britannica.com(https://www.britannica.com/place/Russia/Russia-from-1801-to-1917)

Russia (http://www.worldatlas.com/webimage/countrys/asia/ru.htm)

Russia: (http://www.interfax-religion.com/?act=news&div=5076)

Russia: (https://www.pinterest.com/pin/114701121738468941/)

Russia: Social gaming: revenue in Russia 2010-2013 Statistic". Statista.com. Retrieved 2015-02-23.

Russian Revolution - Facts & Summary - HISTORY.com (https://dev.history.com/topics/russian-revolution)

Russian Revolution - Facts & Summary - HISTORY.com(https://dev.history.com/topics/russian-revolution)

Russian Revolution: (http://www.history.com/topics/russian-revolution)

Russian Secret Police: (http://www.factmonster.com/encyclopedia/society/secret-police-the-evolution-secret-police-forces.html accessed internet on Feb 1, 2017)

Sacks, David Sacks; Oswyn Murray; Lisa R. Brody; Oswyn Murray; Lisa R. Bro Prighillman, Norman A. Stillman The Jews of Arab Lands p. 22 Jewish Publication Society, 1979 ISBN 0827611552 and the International Congress of Byzantine Studies Proceedings of the 21st International Congress of Byzantine Studies, London, 21–26 August 2006, Volumes 1–3 p. 29. Ashgate Pub Co, 30 Sep. 2006 ISBN 075465740X]

SANA - Syria News Agency and the Library of Congress Country Studies: Syria

Santa Ursula de Binangonan - the Powerful Princess of ... (http://pintakasi1521.blogspot.com/2016/10/santa-ursuala-de-binangonan-powerful.html)

Sawyer, Ralph D. The Tao of Spycraft: Intelligence Theory and Practice in Traditional China. Boulder: Westview Press, 1998.

Scarre, C, The Human Past (Thames & Hudson, 2013).]—end of

Scythia - definition of Scythia by The Free Dictionary(https://www.thefreedictionary.com/Scythia)

Scythian | ancient people | Britannica.com(https://www.britannica.com/topic/Scythian)

Secret police facts, information, pictures | Encyclopedia (https://www.encyclopedia.com/social-sciences-and-law/law/crime-and-law-enforcement/secret-police)

Sergey Lavrov, Lavrov to RT: Americans are "running the show" in Ukraine, Cable RT, 04/23/2014 interview on Sophie & Co.

Serhii Ploky, The Gates of Europe: A History of Ukraine, Basic Books, 395 pages Allan Lane.

Sevastopol: (https://www.britannica.com/event/Siege-of-Sevastopol)

Sheldon, Rose Mary. Intelligence Activities in Ancient Rome: Trust the Gods but Verify. New York: Frank Cass, 2005.

Sheldon, Rose Mary. Operation Messiah: Roman Intelligence and the Birth of Christianity. Portland: Valentine Mitchell, 2008.

Siege of Sevastopol | Russian history | Britannica.com(https://www.britannica.com/event/Siege-of-Sevastopol)

Simms Brendan, ("Europe: The Struggle for Supremacy, From 1453 to the Present." The Vanquished by Robert Gerwarth Farrar, Straus & Giroux, 446 pages).

Simms Brendan, (WSJ "Thursday December 1, 2016-- By Brendan Simms Nov. 30, 2016 6:45 p.m. ET)

Simms. Brendan & Allen Lane, 2016 Britain's Europe: A Thousand Years of Conflict and Cooperation. The Economist June 18,2016, "Between the Borders, -The idea of European Unity is more complicated than its supporters or critics allow."

Sinor (editor), Denis (1990). The Cambridge history of early Inner Asia (1. publ. ed.). Cambridge [u.a.]: Cambridge Univ. Press. pp. 177–203. ISBN 9780521243049.]

Skorzeny, Otto (Saur-Mogila (http://thesaker.is/otto-skorzeny-why-didnt-we-take-moscow/)

Smoot, Betsy Rohaly, NSA's top WWI history expert lecture, Washington DC. 2017.

Smoot, Betsy Rohaly, NSA's top WWI history expert lecture, Washington DC. 2017.

Snowden, Edward, The Guardian release of Snowden NSA docs., (https://www.theguardian.com/world/2013/jun/09/edward-snowden-nsa-whistleblower-surveillance)

Snowden, Edward, The Guardian release of Snowden NSA docs., (www.theguardian.com/world/2013/jun/09/edward-snowden-nsa-whistleblower-surveillance)

Spies of the Kaiser – International Spy Museum

Spymasters - CIA in the Crosshairs- Showtime: Documentary (http://www.sho.com/titles/3420665/the-spymasters---CIA-in-the-crosshairs

Spymasters - CIA in the Crosshairs- Showtime: Documentary (http://www.sho.com/titles/3420665/the-spymasters---CIA-in-the-crosshairs

St. Ursula - Sisters of the Irish Ursuline Union (http://www.ursulines.ie/our-roots/st-ursula/)

Stalin PBS "http://www.pbs.org/redfiles/bios/all_bio_joseph_stalin.htm &

Strauss, Barry (2009). The Spartacus War. Simon and Schuster. pp. 21–22. ISBN 1-4165-3205-6.]

Summerfield Stephen, Dr. "Cossack Hurrah" Published by Partizan Press, 816 - 818 London Road, Leigh-on-sea, Essex, SS9 3NH, Ph/Fx: +44 (0) 1702 473986)

Summerfield, Stephen PhD., Cossack Hurrah, Published by Partizan Press 2005 816 - 818 London Road, Leigh-on-sea, Essex, SS9 3NH Ph/Fx: +44 (0) 1702 473986)

Sun Tzu. tr., Ralph D. Sawer. The Art of War. New York: Barnes & Noble, 1994.

Syria (http://www.mepc.org/journal/middle-east-policy-archives/
syrian-and-iraqi-kurds-conflict-and-cooperation?print)

Syria Evolves as Anti-Terror Ally, by Howard Schneider,
Washington Post, July 25, 2002

Syria: ("<a href="https://www.stratfor.com/analysis/what-modern-
syria-can-learn-ottomans">What Modern Syria Can Learn
from the Ottomans</a> is republished with permission of
Stratfor."---)

Syria's Intelligence Services: (A Primer, Middle East Intelligence
Bulletin, 1 July 2000)

Syria's Intelligence Services: (Origins and Development by Andrew
Rathmell Conflict Studies Journal Fall 1996)

Tang Dynasty - whiteplainspublicschools.org (https://www.
whiteplainspublicschools.org/cms/lib5/NY01000029/Centricity/
Domain/353/Reading_Tang_and_Song_Dynasties.doc)

Taubman, Philip Secret Empire: Eisenhower, the CIA, and the
Hidden History of America's Space Espionage

Taylor, Alan, The Ancient Ghost City of Ani, Atlantic Magazine,
Jan 24, 2014

Templeton's Hasenstab Winds Down $7 ... - Bloomberg.
com(https://www.bloomberg.com/news/articles/2017-04-21/
templeton-pares-ukraine-holding-in-40-billion-global-
bond-fund)

Teutonic Knights Flashcards | Quizlet(https://quizlet.com/
18099518/teutonic-knights-flash-cards/)

The Ancient Ghost City of Ani - The Atlantic (https://www.
theatlantic.com/photo/2014/01/the-ancient-ghost-city-of-
ani/100668/)

The Ancient Ghost City of Ani « PixTale | News stories in ... http://pixtale.net/2014/01/the-ancient-ghost-city-of-ani/

The Crusades - World History International: World History (http://history-world.org/crusades.htm)

The Goths - Ancient History Encyclopedia (https://www.ancient.eu/Goths/)

The Hill is an American political newspaper and website published in Washington, D.C. The Hill is published by Capitol Hill Publishing, which is owned by News Communications, Inc. April 2, 2019

The Mongols and Interregional Empires (https://quizlet.com/237778793/chapter-13-the-mongols-and-interregional-empires-flash-cards/)

The Scythians - World history(http://history-world.org/scythians.htm)

The study concluded that the genes of Ice Age Europeans show prevailing dark complexions and brown eyes. The evidence also revealed that blue eyes appeared 14,000 years ago at most, while pale skin spread across the continent some 7,000 years ago. Both were brought in by migration from the Near East. Another big find was that different groups of Europeans were descended from a single founder population between 37,000 years ago and 14,000 years ago. During the period, Neanderthal ancestry in Europeans was in decline, likely due to natural selection.

They continued marching south through Anatolia meeting (https://www.coursehero.com/file/p5n1ve1/They-continued-marching-south-through-Anatolia-meeting-little-opposition/)

Three Confucian Values - ISEG Lisbon(http://pascal.iseg.utl.pt/~cesa/Three%20Confucian%20Values.pdf)

Timeline of the Mongol Empire – IPFS (https://ipfs.io/ipfs/QmXoypizjW3WknFiJnKLwHCnL72vedxjQkDDP1mXWo6uco/wiki/Timeline_of_the_Mongol_Empire.html)

TIMELINE OF WORLD HISTORY - everyhistory.org(http://everyhistory.org/all-history.org/174.html)

Torture, intimidation, secret jails: UN reveals Ukraine's (https://www.rt.com/news/345331-ukraine-torture-human-rights/)

True story of Ukraine Civil War (from the people of Donbass) transcript from video https://www.youtube.com/watch?v=D-Jme77Dfc4) From RTNews on 3/22/17)

Tymoshenko, Yulia Interfax-Ukraine Yulia Tymoshenko (10-27-2009)

Tys-Krokhmaliuk, Iu. Boï Khmel'nyts'koho (Munich 1954)

U.S. Army Investigative Records Repository (hereafter IRR) File on the Red Orchestra. National Archives and Records Administration, RG 319.

U.S. Army Investigative Records Repository (hereafter IRR) File on the Red Orchestra. National Archives and Records Administration, RG 319.

Ukraine (http://proudofukraine.com/ukrainian-names-origin-and-meaning/)

Ukraine (https://www.britannica.com/place/Ukraine)

Ukraine –(Ukraine marks 'Dignity & Freedom Day' as Euromaidan dream falters --Published time: 21 Nov, 2016 12:22)

Ukraine- Index of 2018 Economic Freedom-(https://www.heritage.org/index/country/ukraine)

Ukraine Map / Geography of Ukraine / Map of Ukraine (https://www.worldatlas.com/webimage/countrys/europe/ua.htm)

Ukraine marks 'Dignity & Freedom Day' as Euromaidan dream (https://www.rt.com/news/367636-maidan-3rd-anniversary-dignity/)

Ukraine Seeks Debt Revamp – WSJ (https://www.wsj.com/articles/ukraine-seeks-to-restructure-debt-finance-minister-says-1426264583)

Ukrainian Finance Minister Sees Next IMF Tranche in Autumn(https://www.bloomberg.com/news/articles/2017-07-05/ukrainian-finance-minister-sees-next-imf-tranche-in-autumn)

Ulm: Battle-of-Ulm

United States: Assistant Secretary Nuland Travel to Cyprus. (2016). MENA Report, n/a. ("United States: Assistant Secretary Nuland Travel to Cyprus." MENA Report, Albawaba (London) Ltd., Oct. 2016, p. n/a.)

United States: Assistant Secretary Nuland Travel to Cyprus. (2016). MENA Report, n/a. ("United States: Assistant Secretary Nuland Travel to Cyprus." MENA Report, Albawaba (London) Ltd., Oct. 2016, p. n/a.)

US Holocaust Memorial Museum(http://www.jewishvirtuallibrary.org/how-many-concentration-camps)

US police covertly spy on innocent citizens with military(https://www.rt.com/usa/411007-police-spying-imsi-stingray/)

US State overthrow list- (https://williamblum.org/essays/read/overthrowing-other-peoples-governments-the-master-list)

Violatti, Cristian Violatti studies Archaeology at the University of Leicester (UK) and he is one of the editors of Ancient History Encyclopedia.

Visigoth - Ancient History Encyclopedia (https://www.ancient.eu/visigoth/)

Viviano, Frank, The Rebirth of Armenia

Viviano, Frank. The Rebirth of Armenia, National Geographic Magazine, Published: March 2004

Vladimir I Facts – Your Dictionary(http://biography.yourdictionary.com/vladimir-i)

Vladimir the Great (http://biography.yourdictionary.com/vladimir-i/http://biography.yourdictionary.com/vladimir-i#uRMtzvkSdbXtztmt.99)

Volpicelli Zenone "Russia on the Pacific, and the Siberian railway" --Zenone Volpicelli

Wallace Robert and H. Keith Melton, Spycraft: The Secret History of the CIA's Spytechs from Communism to al-Qaeda

Walsh, Terry, Ancient Britain author published on 28 April 2011 - http://www.ancient.eu/britain/)

Waterloo (https://www.britannica.com/biography/Dominique-Rene-Vandamme-comte-dUnebourg)

Waterloo:(https://www.britannica.com/event/Battle-of-Waterloo)

Weigel, George The Cube and the Cathedral: Europe, America and Politics without God. By. Gracewing Publishing, 2005

Weiser, Benjamin A Secret Life: The Polish Officer, His Covert Mission, and the Price He Paid to Save His Country

Welcome to Ukraine(http://www.wumag.kiev.ua/index2.php?param=pgs20111%2F130)

What are the beliefs of Confucianism - Answers.com (http://www.answers.com/Q/What_is_the_beliefs_of_confucianism?

What Modern Syria Can Learn from the Ottomans (http://www. hidropolitikakademi.org/what-modern-syria-can-learn-from-the-ottomans.html)

What year did the Roman Empire collapse - The Q&A (http://qa.answers.com/Q/What_year_did_the_Roman_Empire_collapse)?

Whatley, Christopher A Bought and Sold for English Gold: The Union of 1707 (Tuckwell Press, 2001)

White, Horace White Appian, Civil Wars, 1:116; Plutarch, Crassus, 8:2. Note: Spartacus' status as an auxilia is taken from the Loeb edition of Appian translated by Horace White, which states "... who had once served as a soldier with the Romans ... ")

Who was the founder of the religion Buddhism - Brainly.com (https://brainly.com/question/9305591)?

Why did Romans siege Jerusalem in 70AD? | Yahoo Answers (https://answers.yahoo.com/question/index?qid=201105 11202433AABfGzb)

Woodhouse, F. C Teutonic Knights: Their Organization and History the English and Their History.

World War 1 Timeline | World History Project(https://worldhistoryproject.org/topics/world-war-1)

World War II (1939-1945) (https://www.youtube.com/watch?v= L-Ro0SZf438

Wright 2011, p. 60.

Wright, David Curtis (2011). The history of China (2nd ed.). Santa Barbara: Greenwood. p. 60. ISBN 978-0-313-37748-8.

WSJ Newspaper article of June 1, 2014, "The Dark Past of Putin's Ideas." --under the Romanov Section prior to Napoleonic War

WW 1- The Lost Battalion- (https://www.youtube.com/watch?v=PyJwtC8kwJM

WW1 (http://www.history.com/this-day-in-history/world-war-i-ends)

WW1 Trench warfare(https://kidskonnect.com/history/ww1-trenches/)

WW1 Trenches: Facts About World War I Trench Warfare (https://kidskonnect.com/history/ww1-trenches/)

WW2 (https://www.youtube.com/watch?v=LAGZpJ8FCaU#t=274.655583)

YouTube (https://www.youtube.com/watch?v=VfpKan_l_Jw)

YouTube: (https://www.youtube.com/watch?v=I4hTwa42Ffc)

YouTube: (https://www.youtube.com/watch?v=uLObZWoxvJ8

YouTube: (https://www.youtube.com/watch?v=uLObZWoxvJ8)

Zen folio | Tripping the Light | Iran (http://www.trippingthelight.photography/f752140903)

Zhengzhang 2003, p. 429,505.

END

Lightning Source UK Ltd.
Milton Keynes UK
UKHW040624190820
368267UK00002BA/41/J